Hidden Heirs:

Behind Palace Doors

CAITLIN CREWS

AMY RUTTAN

JESSICA GILMORE

MILLS & BOON

First Published in Great Britain 2023
by Mills & Boon, an imprint of HarperCollins*Publishers* Ltd,
1 London Bridge Street, London, SE1 9GF

www.harpercollins.co.uk

HarperCollins*Publishers*
Macken House, 39/40 Mayor Street Upper,
Dublin 1, D01 C9W8, Ireland

ISBN 978-0-263-31895-1

MIX
Paper | Supporting
responsible forestry
FSC™ C007454

About the Authors

USA Today bestselling, *RITA*®-nominated, and critically-acclaimed author **Caitlin Crews** has written more than 130 books and counting. She has a Master's and PhD in English Literature, thinks everyone should read more romance, and is always available to discuss her beloved alpha heroes. Just ask. She lives in the Pacific Northwest with her comic book artist husband, is always planning her next trip, and will never, ever, read all the books in her to-be-read pile. Thank goodness.

Born and raised just outside of Toronto, Ontario, **Amy Ruttan** fled the big city to settle down with the country boy of her dreams. After the birth of her second child, Amy was lucky enough to realise her lifelong dream of becoming a romance author. When she's not furiously typing away at her computer, she's a mum to three wonderful children who use her as a personal taxi and chef.

Jessica Gilmore is a charity-working, dog-walking, child-wrangling, dust-ignoring bookworm. She lives in the beautiful and historic city of York with one patient husband, one daughter, one very fluffy dog, two dog-loathing cats, and a goldfish called Bob. As day dreaming is her very favourite hobby, and she loves a good happy-ever-after, Jessica can't believe she's lucky enough to write romance for a living. Say hi on Twitter at @yrosered or visit sprigmuslin.blogspot.com

Hidden Heirs

THE PRINCE'S NINE-MONTH SCANDAL

CAITLIN CREWS

CHAPTER ONE

NATALIE MONETTE HAD never done a rash thing in her entire twenty-seven years, something she'd always viewed as a great personal strength. After a childhood spent flitting about with her free-spirited, impetuous mother, never belonging anywhere and without a shred of anything resembling permanence including an address, Natalie had made her entire adulthood—especially her career—a monument to all things *dependable* and *predictable*.

But she'd finally had enough.

Her employer—never an easy man at the best of times—wasn't likely to accept her notice after five long years with anything like grace. Natalie shook her head at the very notion of grace and her cranky billionaire boss. He preferred a bull-in-china-shop approach to most things, especially his executive assistant. And this latest time, as he'd dressed her down for an imagined mistake in front of an entire corporate office in London, a little voice inside her had whispered: *enough.*

Enough already. Or she thought she might die. Internally, anyway.

She had to quit her job. She had to figure out what her life was like when not at the beck and call of a tyrant—because there had to be better things out there. There

had to be. She had to do *something* before she just…
disappeared.

And she was thinking that a rash move—like quitting here and now and who cared if her boss threw a tantrum?—might just do the trick.

Natalie was washing her hands in the marbled sink in the fancy women's bathroom that was a part of the moneyed elegance evident everywhere in the high-class lounge area at her boss's preferred private airfield outside London. She was trying to slow her panicked breathing and get herself back under control. She prided herself on being unflappable under normal circumstances, but nothing about the messy things swirling around inside of her today felt *normal*. She hardly paid any attention when one of the heavy stall doors behind her opened and a woman stepped up to the sink beside hers. She had the vague impression of the sort of marked glamour that was usually on display in these places she only visited thanks to her job, but then went back to wondering how on earth she was going to walk out of this bathroom and announce that she was done with her job.

She couldn't imagine how her boss would react. Or she could, that was the trouble. But Natalie knew she had to do it. *She had to do it.* Now, while there was still this feverish thing inside her that kept pushing at her. Because if she waited, she knew she wouldn't. She'd settle back in and it would be another five years in an instant, and then what would she do?

"I beg your pardon, but you seem to look a great deal like someone I know."

The woman's voice was cultured. Elegant. And it made Natalie feel…funny. As if she'd heard it before when she knew that was impossible. Of course she hadn't. She never knew anyone in these ultra high-class places her job took her. Then she looked up and the world seemed to tilt off its axis. She was shocked she didn't crumple to the ground where she stood.

Because the woman standing beside her, staring back at her through the mirror, had her face. *The exact same face.* Her coppery hair was styled differently and she wasn't wearing Natalie's dark-rimmed glasses over her own green eyes, but there was no denying that every other aspect was *exactly the same*. The fine nose. The faintly pointed chin. The same raised eyebrows, the same high forehead.

The other woman was taller, Natalie realized in a rush of something more complicated than simple relief. But then she looked down to see that her impossible, improbable twin was wearing the sort of sky-high stilettos only women who didn't have to walk very often or very far enjoyed, easily making her a few inches taller than Natalie in the far more serviceable wedges she wore that allowed her to keep up with her irascible employer's long, impatient stride.

"Oh." The other woman breathed the syllable out, like a sigh, though her eyes gleamed. "I thought there was an amusing resemblance that we should discuss, but this…"

Natalie had the bizarre experience of watching her own mouth move on another woman's face. Then drop open slightly. It was unnerving. It was like the mirror coming alive right in front of her. It was *impossible*.

It was a great deal more than an "amusing resemblance."

"What is this?" she asked, her voice as shaky as she felt. "How…?"

"I have no idea," the other woman said quietly. "But it's fascinating, isn't it?" She turned to look at Natalie directly, letting her gaze move up and down her body as if measuring her. Cataloging her. Natalie could hardly blame her. If she wasn't so frozen, she'd do the same. "I'm Valentina."

"Natalie."

Why was her throat so dry? But she knew why. They said everyone on earth had a double, but that was usually a discussion about mannerisms and a vague resemblance. Not *this*. Because Natalie knew beyond the shadow of any possible doubt that there was no way this person standing in front of her, with the same eyes and the same mouth and even the same freckle centered on her left cheekbone wasn't related to her. No possible way. And that was a Pandora's box full of problems, wasn't it? Starting with her own childhood and the mother who had always rather sternly claimed she didn't know who Natalie's father was. She tried to shake all that off—but then Valentina's name penetrated her brain.

She remembered where she was. And the other party that had been expected at the same airfield today. She'd openly scoffed at the notification, because there wasn't much on this earth she found more useless than royalty. Her mother had gotten that ball rolling while Natalie was young. While other girls had dressed up like princesses and dreamed about Prince Charming, Natalie had been taught that both were lies.

There's no such thing as happily-ever-after, her mother had told her. *There's only telling a silly story about painful things to make yourself feel better. No daughter of mine is going to imagine herself anything but a realist, Natalie.*

And so Natalie hadn't. Ever.

Here in this bathroom, face-to-face with an impossibility, Natalie blinked. "Wait. You're that princess."

"I am indeed, for my sins." Valentina's mouth curved in a serene sort of half smile that Natalie would have said she, personally, could never pull off. Except if someone with an absolutely identical face could do it, that meant she could, too, didn't it? That realization was...unnerving. "But I suspect you might be, too."

Natalie couldn't process that. Her eyes were telling her a truth, but her mind couldn't accept it. She played devil's advocate instead. "We can't possibly be related. I'm a glorified secretary who never really had a home. You're a royal princess. Presumably your lineage—and the family home, for that matter, which I'm pretty sure is a giant castle because all princesses have a few of those by virtue of the title alone—dates back to the Roman Conquest."

"Give or take a few centuries." Valentina inclined her head, another supremely elegant and vaguely noble gesture that Natalie would have said could only look silly on her. Yet it didn't look anything like silly on Valentina. "Depending which branch of the family you mean, of course."

"I was under the impression that people with lineages that could lead to thrones and crown jewels tended to keep better track of their members."

"You'd think, wouldn't you?" The princess shifted back on her soaring heels and regarded Natalie more closely. "Conspiracy theorists claim my mother was killed and the death hushed up. Senior palace officials assured me that no, she merely left to preserve her mental health, and is rumored to be in residence in a hospital devoted to such things somewhere. All I know is that I haven't seen her since shortly after I was born. According to my father, she preferred anonymity to the joys of motherhood."

Natalie wanted to run out of this bathroom, lose herself in her work and her boss's demands the way she usually did, and pretend this mad situation had never happened. This encounter felt rash enough for her as it was. No need to blow her life up on top of it. So she had no idea why instead, she opened up her mouth and shared her deepest, secret shame with this woman.

"I've never met my father," she told this total stranger who looked like an upscale mirror image of herself. There was no reason she should feel as if she could trust a random woman she met in a bathroom, no matter whose face she wore. It was absurd to feel as if she'd known this other person all her life when of course she hadn't. And yet she kept talking. "My mother's always told me she has no idea who he was. That Prince Charming was a fantasy sold to impressionable young girls to make them silly, and the reality was that men are simply men and untrustworthy to the core. And she bounces from one affair to the next pretty quickly, so I came to terms with the fact it was possible she really, truly didn't know."

Valentina laughed. It was a low, smoky sound, and Natalie recognized it, because it was hers. A shock of recognition went through her. Though she didn't feel like laughing. At all.

"My father is many things," the princess said, laughter and something more serious beneath it. "Including His Royal Majesty, King Geoffrey of Murin. What he is not now, nor has ever been, I imagine, is forgettable."

Natalie shook her head. "You underestimate my mother's commitment to amnesia. She's made it a life choice instead of a malady. On some level I admire it."

Once again, she had no idea why she was telling this stranger things she hardly dared admit to herself.

"My mother was the noblewoman Frederica de Burgh,

from a very old Murinese family." Valentina watched Natalie closely as she spoke. "Promised to my father at birth, raised by nuns and kept deliberately sheltered, and then widely held to be unequal to the task of becoming queen. Mentally. But that's the story they would tell, isn't it, to explain why she disappeared? What's your mother's name?"

Her hands felt numb, so Natalie shifted her bag from her shoulder to the marble countertop beside her. "She calls herself Erica."

For a moment neither one of them spoke. Neither one of them mentioned that *Erica* sounded very much like a shortened form of *Frederica,* but then, there was no need. Natalie was aware of too many things. The far-off sounds of planes outside the building. The television in the lounge on the other side of the door, cued to a twenty-four-hour news channel. She was vaguely surprised her boss hadn't already texted her fifteen furious times, wondering where she'd gone off to when it was possible he might have need of her.

"I saw everyone's favorite billionaire, Achilles Casilieris, out there in the lounge," Valentina said after a moment, as if reading Natalie's mind. "He looks even more fearsome in person than advertised. You can almost *see* all that brash command and dizzying wealth ooze from his pores, can't you?"

"He's my boss." Natalie ran her tongue over her teeth, that reckless thing inside of her lurching to life all over again. "If he was really oozing anything, anywhere, it would be my job to provide first aid until actual medical personnel could come handle it. At which point he would bite my head off for wasting his precious time by not curing him instantly."

She had worked for Achilles Casilieris—and by extension the shockingly hardy, internationally envied and recession-proof Casilieris Company—for five very long years. That was the first marginally negative thing she'd said about her job, ever. Out loud, anyway. And she felt instantly disloyal, despite the fact she'd been psyching herself up to quit only moments ago. Much as she had when she'd opened her mouth about her mother.

How could a stranger who happened to look like her make Natalie question who *she* was?

But the princess was frowning at the slim leather clutch she'd tossed on the bathroom counter. Natalie heard the buzzing sound that indicated a call as Valentina flipped open the outer flap and slid her smartphone out, then rolled her eyes and shoved it back in.

"My fiancé," she said, meeting Natalie's gaze again, her own more guarded. Or maybe it was something else that made the green in her eyes darker. The phone buzzed a few more times, then stopped. "Or his chief of staff, to be more precise."

"Congratulations," Natalie said, though the expression on Valentina's face did not look as if she was precisely awash in joyous anticipation.

"Thank you, I'm very lucky." Valentina's mouth curved, though there was nothing like a smile in her eyes and her tone was arid. "Everyone says so. Prince Rodolfo is objectively attractive. Not all princes can make that claim, but the tabloids have exulted over his abs since he was a teenager. Just as they have salivated over his impressive dating history, which has involved a selection of models and actresses from at least four continents and did not cease in any noticeable way upon our engagement last fall."

"Your Prince Charming sounds…charming," Natalie murmured. It only confirmed her long-held suspicions about such men.

Valentina raised one shoulder, then dropped it. "His theory is that he remains free until our marriage, and then will be free once again following the necessary birth of his heir. More discreetly, I can only hope. Meanwhile, I am beside myself with joy that I must take my place at his side in two short months. Of course."

Natalie didn't know why she laughed at that, but she did. More out of commiseration than anything else, as if they really were the same person. And how strange that she almost felt as if they were. "It's going to be a terrific couple of months all around, then. Mr. Casilieris is in rare form. He's putting together a particularly dramatic deal and it's not going his way and he...isn't used to that. So that's me working twenty-two-hour days instead of my usual twenty for the foreseeable future, which is even more fun when he's cranky and snarling."

"It can't possibly be worse than having to smile politely while your future husband lectures you about the absurd expectation of fidelity in what is essentially an arranged marriage for hours on end. The absurdity is that *he* might be expected to curb his impulses for a year or so, in case you wondered. The expectations for *me* apparently involve quietly and chastely finding fulfillment in philanthropic works, like his sainted absentee mother who everyone knows manufactured a supposed health crisis so she could live out her days in peaceful seclusion. It's easy to be philanthropically fulfilled while living in isolation in Bavaria."

Natalie smiled. "Try biting your tongue while your famously short-tempered boss rages at you for no reason, for the hundredth time in an hour, because he pays you to stand there and take it without wilting or crying or selling whinging stories about him to the press."

Valentina's smile was a perfect match. "Or the hours

and hours of grim palace-vetted pre-wedding press interviews in the company of a pack of advisors who will censor everything I say and inevitably make me sound like a bit of animated treacle, as out of touch with reality as the average overly sweet dessert."

"Speaking of treats, I also have to deal with the board of directors Mr. Casilieris treats like irritating schoolchildren, his packs of furious ex-lovers each with her own vendetta, all his terrified employees who need to be coached through meetings with him and treated for PTSD after, and every last member of his staff in every one of his households, who like me to be the one to ask him the questions they know will set him off on one of his scorch-the-earth rages."

They'd moved a little bit closer then, leaning toward each other like friends. *Or sisters,* a little voice whispered. It should have concerned Natalie like everything else about this. And like everything else, it did and it didn't. Either way, she didn't step back. She didn't insist upon her personal space. She was almost tempted to imagine her body knew something about this mirror image version of her that her brain was still desperately trying to question.

Natalie thought of the way Mr. Casilieris had bitten her head off earlier, and her realization that if she didn't escape him now she never would. And how this stranger with her face seemed, oddly enough, to understand.

"I was thinking of quitting, to be honest," she whispered. Making it real. "Today."

"I can't quit, I'm afraid," the impossibly glamorous princess said then, her green eyes alight with something a little more frank than plain mischief. "But I have a better idea. Let's switch places. For a month, say. Six weeks at the most. Just for a little break."

"That's crazy," Natalie said.

"Insane," Valentina agreed. "But you might find royal protocol exciting! And I've always wanted to do the things everyone else in the world does. Like go to a real job."

"People can't *switch places*." Natalie was frowning. "And certainly not with a princess."

"You could think about whether or not you really want to quit," Valentina pointed out. "It would be a lovely holiday for you. Where will Achilles Casilieris be in six weeks' time?"

"He's never gone from London for too long," Natalie heard herself say, as if she was considering it.

Valentina smiled. "Then in six weeks we'll meet in London. We'll text in the meantime with all the necessary details about our lives, and on the appointed day we'll just meet up and switch back and no one will ever be the wiser. Doesn't that sound like *fun*?" Her gaze met Natalie's with something like compassion. "And I hope you won't mind my saying this, but you do look as if you could use a little fun."

"It would never work." Natalie realized after she spoke that she still hadn't said no. "No one will ever believe I'm you."

Valentina waved a hand between them. "How would anyone know the difference? I can barely tell myself."

"People will take one look at me and know I'm not you," Natalie insisted, as if that was the key issue here. "You look like a *princess*."

If Valentina noticed the derisive spin she put on that last word out of habit, she appeared to ignore it.

"You too can look like a princess. This princess, anyway. You already do."

"There's a lifetime to back it up. You're elegant. Poised.

You've had years of training, presumably. How to be a diplomat. How to be polite in every possible situation. Which fork to use at dinner, for God's sake."

"Achilles Casilieris is one of the wealthiest men alive. He dines with as many kings as I do. I suspect that as his personal assistant, Natalie, you have, too. And have likely learned how to navigate the cutlery."

"No one will believe it," Natalie whispered, but there was no heat in it.

Because maybe she was the one who couldn't believe it. And maybe, if she was entirely honest, there was a part of her that wanted this. The princess life and everything that went with it. The kind of ease she'd never known—and a castle besides. And only for a little while. Six short weeks. Scarcely more than a daydream.

Surely even Natalie deserved a daydream. Just this once.

Valentina's smile widened as if she could scent capitulation in the air. She tugged off the enormous, eye-gouging ring on her left hand and placed it down on the counter between them. It made an audible *clink* against the marble surface.

"Try it on. I dare you. It's an heirloom from Prince Rodolfo's extensive treasury of such items, dating back to the dawn of time, more or less." She inclined her head in that regal way of hers. "If it doesn't fit we'll never speak of switching places again."

And Natalie felt possessed by a force she didn't understand. She knew better. Of course she did. This was a ridiculous game and it could only make this bizarre situation worse, and she was certainly no Cinderella. She knew that much for sure.

But she slipped the ring onto her finger anyway, and it fit perfectly, gleaming on her finger like every dream she'd ever had as a little girl. Not that she could live a magical life, filled with talismans that shone the way this ring did, because that was the sort of *impracticality* her mother had abhorred. But that she could have a home the way everyone else did. That she could *belong* to a man, to a country, to the sweep of a long history, the way this ring hugged her finger. As if it was meant to be.

The ring had nothing to do with her. She knew that. But it felt like a promise, even so.

And it all seemed to snowball from there. They each kicked off their shoes and stood barefoot on the surprisingly plush carpet. Then Valentina shimmied out of her sleek, deceptively simple sheath dress with the unselfconsciousness of a woman used to being dressed by attendants. She lifted her brows with all the imperiousness of her station, and Natalie found herself retreating into the stall with the dress—since she was not, in fact, used to being tended to by packs of fawning courtiers and therefore all but naked with an audience. She climbed out of her own clothes, handing her pencil skirt, blouse and wrap sweater out to Valentina through the crack she left open in the door. Then she tugged the princess's dress on, expecting it to snag or pull against her obviously peasant body.

But like the ring, the dress fit as if it had been tailored to her body. As if it was hers.

She walked out slowly, blinking when she saw...herself waiting for her. The very same view she'd seen in the mirror this morning when she'd dressed in the room Mr. Casilieris kept for her in the basement of his London town house because her own small flat was too far away to be to-ing and fro-ing at odd hours, according to him, and it was easier to acquiesce than fight. Not that it had kept him from firing away at her. But she shoved that aside because Valentina was laughing at the sight of Natalie in obvious astonishment, as if she was having the same literal out-of-body experience.

Natalie walked back to the counter and climbed into the princess's absurd shoes, very carefully. Her knees protested beneath her as she tried to stand tall in them and she had to reach out to grip the marble counter.

"Put your weight on your heels," Valentina advised. She was already wearing Natalie's wedges, because apparently even their feet were the same, and of course she had no trouble standing in them as if she'd picked them out herself. "Everyone always wants to lean forward and tiptoe in heels like that, and nothing looks worse. Lean back and you own the shoe, not the other way around." She eyed Natalie. "Will your glasses give me a headache, do you suppose?"

Natalie pulled them from her face and handed them over. "They're clear glass. I was getting a little too much attention from some of the men Mr. Casilieris works with, and it annoyed him. I didn't want to lose my job, so I started wearing my hair up and these glasses. It worked like a charm."

"I refuse to believe men are so idiotic."

Natalie grinned as Valentina took the glasses and slid them onto her nose. "The men we're talking about weren't exactly paying me attention because they found me enthralling. It was a diversionary tactic during negotiations and yes, you'd be surprised how many men fail to see a woman who looks smart."

She tugged her hair tie from her ponytail and shook out her hair, then handed the elastic to Valentina. The princess swept her hair back and into the same ponytail Natalie had been sporting only seconds before.

And it was like magic.

Ordinary Natalie Monette, renowned for her fierce work ethic, attention to detail and her total lack of anything resembling a personal life—which was how she'd become the executive assistant to one of the world's most ferocious and feared billionaires straight out of college and now had absolutely no life to call her own—became Her Royal Highness, Princess Valentina of Murin in an instant. And vice versa. Just like that.

"This is crazy," Natalie whispered.

The real Princess Valentina only smiled, looking every inch the smooth, super competent right hand of a man as feared as he was respected. Looking the way Natalie had always *hoped* she looked, if she was honest. Serenely capable. Did this mean…she always had?

More than that, they looked like twins. They had to be twins. There was no possibility that they could be anything but.

Natalie didn't want to think about the number of lies her mother had to have told her if that was true. She didn't want to think about all the implications. She couldn't.

"We have to switch places now," Valentina said softly, though there was a catch in her voice. It was the catch that made Natalie focus on her rather than the mystery that was her mother. "I've always wanted to be…someone else. Someone normal. Just for a little while."

Their gazes caught at that, both the exact same shade of green, just as their hair was that unusual shade of copper many tried to replicate in the salon, yet couldn't. The only difference was that Valentina's was highlighted with streaks of blond that Natalia suspected came from long, lazy days on the decks of yachts or taking in the sunshine from the comfort of her very own island kingdom.

If you're really twins—if you're sisters—it's your is-

land, too, a little voice inside whispered. But Natalie couldn't handle that. Not here. Not now. Not while she was all dressed up in princess clothes.

"Is that what princesses dream of?" Natalie asked. She wanted to smile, but the moment felt too precarious. Ripe and swollen with emotions she couldn't have named, though she understood them as they moved through her. "Because I think most other little girls imagine they're you."

Not her, of course. Never her.

Something shone a little too brightly in Valentina's gaze then, and it made Natalie's chest ache.

But she would never know what her mirror image might have said next, because her name was called in a familiar growl from directly outside the door to the women's room. Natalie didn't think. She was dressed as someone else and she couldn't let anyone see that—so she threw herself back into the stall where she'd changed her clothes as the door was slapped open.

"Exactly what are you doing in here?" growled a voice that Natalie knew better than her own. She'd worked for Achilles Casilieris for five years. She knew him much, much better than she knew herself. She knew, for example, that the particular tone he was using right now meant his usual grouchy mood was being rapidly taken over by his typical impatience. He'd likely had to actually take a moment and look for her, rather than her magically being at his side before he finished his thought. He hated that. And he wasn't shy at all about expressing his feelings. "Can we leave for New York now, do you think, or do you need to fix your makeup for another hour?"

Natalie stood straighter out of habit, only to realize that her boss's typical scowl wasn't directed at her. She was hidden behind the cracked open door of the bathroom stall. Her boss was aiming that famous glare straight at Valentina, and he didn't appear to notice that she wasn't Natalie. That if she was Natalie, that would mean she'd lightened her hair in the past fifteen minutes. But she could tell that all her boss saw was his assistant. Nothing more, nothing less.

"I apologize," Valentina murmured.

"I don't need you to be sorry, I need you on the plane," Achilles retorted, then turned back around to head out.

Natalie's head spun. She had worked for this man, night and day, for *half a decade.* He was Achilles Casilieris, renowned for his keen insight and killer instincts in all things, and Natalie had absolutely no doubt that he had no idea that he hadn't been speaking to her.

Maybe that was why, when Valentina reached over and took Natalie's handbag instead of her own, Natalie didn't push back out of the stall to stop her. She said nothing. She stood where she was. She did absolutely nothing to keep the switch from happening.

"I'll call you," Valentina mouthed into the mirror as she hurried to the door, and the last Natalie saw of Her Royal Highness Valentina of Murin was the suppressed excitement in her bright green eyes as she followed Achilles Casilieris out the door.

Natalie stepped out of the stall again in the sudden silence. She looked at herself in the mirror, smoothed her hair down with palms that shook only the slightest little bit, blinked at the wild sparkle of the absurd ring on her finger as she did it.

And just like that, became a fairy princess—and stepped right into a daydream.

CHAPTER TWO

CROWN PRINCE RODOLFO of the ancient and deeply, deliberately reserved principality of Tissely, tucked away in the Pyrenees between France and Spain and gifted with wealth, peace and dramatic natural borders that had kept things that way for centuries untold, was bored.

This was not his preferred state of existence, though it was not exactly surprising here on the palace grounds of Murin Castle, where he was expected to entertain the royal bride his father had finally succeeded in forcing upon him.

Not that "entertainment" was ever really on offer with the undeniably pretty, yet almost aggressively placid and unexciting Princess Valentina. His future wife. The future mother of his children. His future queen, even. Assuming he didn't lapse into a coma before their upcoming nuptials, that was.

Rodolfo sighed and stretched out his long legs, aware he was far too big to be sitting so casually on a relic of a settee in this stuffily proper reception room that had been set aside for his use on one of his set monthly visits with his fiancée. He still felt a twinge in one thigh from the ill-advised diving trip he'd taken some months back with a group of his friends and rather too many sharks. Rodolfo rubbed at the scarred spot absently, grateful that while his father had inevitably caught wind of the feminine talent who'd graced the private yacht off the coast of Belize, the fact an overenthusiastic shark had grazed the Crown Prince of Tissely en route to a friend's recently caught fish had escaped both the King's spies' and the rabid tabloids' breathless reports.

It was these little moments of unexpected grace, he often thought with varying degrees of irony, that made his otherwise royally pointless life worth living.

"You embarrass yourself more with each passing year," his father had told him, stiff with fury, when Rodolfo had succumbed to the usual demands for a command appearance upon his return to Europe at the end of last summer, the salacious pictures of his "Belize Booze Cruise" still fresh in every tabloid reader's mind. And more to the point, in his father's.

"You possess the power to render me unembarrassing forevermore," Rodolfo had replied easily enough. He'd almost convinced himself his father no longer got beneath his skin. Almost. "Give me something to do, Father. You have an entire kingdom at your disposal. Surely you can find a single task for your only son."

But that was the crux of the matter they never spoke of directly, of course. Rodolfo was not the son his father had wanted as heir. He was not the son his father would have chosen to succeed him, not the son his father had planned for. He was his father's only *remaining* son, and not his father's choice.

He was not Felipe. He could never be Felipe. It was a toss-up as to which one of them hated him more for that.

"There is no place in my kingdom for a sybaritic fool whose life is little more than an extended advertisement for one of those appalling survival programs, complete with the sensationalism of the nearest gutter press," his father had boomed from across his vast, appropriately majestic office in the palace, because it was so much easier to attack Rodolfo than address what simmered beneath it all. Not that Rodolfo helped matters with his increasingly dangerous antics, he was aware. "You stain the principality with every astonishingly bad decision you make."

"It was a boat ride, sir." Rodolfo had kept his voice even because he knew it irritated his father to get no reaction to his litanies and insults. "Not precisely a scandal likely to topple the whole of the kingdom's government, as I think you are aware."

"What I am aware of, as ever, is how precious little you know about governing anything," his father had seethed, in all his state and consequence.

"You could change that with a wave of your hand," Rodolfo had reminded him, as gently as possible. Which was perhaps not all that gently. "Yet you refuse."

And around and around they went.

Rodolfo's father, the taciturn and disapproving sovereign of Tissely, Ferdinand IV, held all the duties of the monarchy in his tight fists and showed no signs of easing his grip anytime soon. Despite the promise he'd made his only remaining son and heir that he'd give him a more than merely ceremonial place in the principality's government following Rodolfo's graduate work at the London School of Economics. That had been ten years back, his father had only grown more bitter and possessive of his throne, and Rodolfo had...adapted.

Life in the principality was sedate, as befitted a nation that had avoided all the wars of the last few centuries by simple dint of being too far removed to take part in them in any real way. Rodolfo's life, by contrast, was...stimulating. Provocative by design. He liked his sport extreme and his sex excessive, and he didn't much care if the slavering hounds of the European press corps printed every moment of each, which they'd been more than happy to do for the past decade. If his father wished him to be more circumspect, to preserve and protect the life of the hereditary heir to Tissely's throne the way he should—the way he'd raced about trying to wrap Felipe in cotton wool, restricting him from everything only to lose him to something as ignoble and silly as an unremarkable cut in his finger and what they'd thought was the flu—he needed only to offer Rodolfo something else with which to fill his time. Such as, perhaps, something to *do* besides continue to exist, thus preserving the bloodline by dint of not dying.

In fairness, of course, Rodolfo had committed himself to pushing the boundaries of his continued existence as much as possible, with his group of similarly devil-may-care friends, to the dismay of most of their families.

"Congratulations," Ferdinand had clipped out one late September morning last fall in yet another part of his vast offices in the Tisselian palace complex. "You will be married next summer."

"I beg your pardon?"

In truth, Rodolfo had not been paying much attention to the usual lecture until that moment. He was no fan of being summoned from whatever corner of the world he happened to be inhabiting and having to race back to present himself before Ferdinand, because his lord and father preferred not to communicate with his only heir by any other means but face-to-face. But of course, Ferdinand had not solicited his opinion. Ferdinand never did.

When he'd focused on his father, sitting there behind the acres and acres of his desk, the old man had actually looked...smug.

That did not bode well.

"You've asked me for a role in the kingdom and here it is. The Crown Prince of Tissely has been unofficially betrothed to the Murin princess since her birth. It is high time you did your duty and ensured the line. This should not come as any great surprise. You are not exactly getting any younger, Rodolfo, as your increasingly more desperate public displays amply illustrate."

Rodolfo had let that deliberate slap roll off his back, because there was no point reacting. It was what his father wanted.

"I met the Murin princess exactly once when I was ten and she was in diapers." Felipe had been fourteen and a man of the world, to Rodolfo's recollection, and the then Crown Prince of Tissely had seemed about as unenthused about his destiny as Rodolfo felt now. "That seems a rather tenuous connection upon which to base a marriage, given I've never seen her since."

"Princess Valentina is renowned the world over for her commitment to her many responsibilities and her role as her father's emissary," his father had replied coolly. "I doubt your paths would have crossed in all these years, as she is not known to frequent the dens of iniquity you prefer."

"Yet you believe this paragon will wish to marry me."

"I am certain she will wish no such thing, but the princess is a dutiful creature who knows what she owes to her country. You claim that you are as well, and that your dearest wish is to serve the crown. Now is your chance to prove it."

And that was how Rodolfo had found himself both hoist by his own petard and more worrying, tied to his very proper, very dutiful, very, very boring bride-to-be with no hope of escape. Ever.

"Princess Valentina, Your Highness," the butler intoned from the doorway, and Rodolfo dutifully climbed to his feet, because his life might have been slipping out of his control by the second, but hell, he still had the manners that had been beaten into him since he was small.

The truth was, he'd imagined that he would do things differently than his father when he'd realized he would have to take Felipe's place as the heir to his kingdom. He'd been certain he would not marry a woman he hardly knew, foisted upon him by duty and immaculate bloodlines, with whom he could hardly carry on a single meaningful conversation. His own mother—no more enamored of King Ferdinand than Rodolfo was—had long since repaired to her preferred residence, her ancestral home in the manicured wilds of Bavaria, and had steadfastly maintained an enduring if vague health crisis that necessitated she remain in seclusion for the past twenty years.

Rodolfo had been so sure, as an angry young man still reeling from his brother's death, that he would do things better when he had his chance.

And instead he was standing attendance on a strange woman who, in the months of their engagement, had appeared to be made entirely of impenetrable glass. She was about that approachable.

But this time, when Valentina walked into the reception room the way she'd done many times before, so they could engage in a perfectly tedious hour of perfectly polite conversation on perfectly pointless topics as if it was the stifling sixteenth century, all to allow the waiting press corps to gush about their visits later as they caught Rodolfo leaving, everything…changed.

Rodolfo couldn't have said how. Much less why.

But he *felt* her entrance. He *felt it* when she paused in the doorway and looked around as if she'd never laid eyes on him or the paneled ceiling or any part of the run-of-the-mill room before. His body tightened. He felt a rush of heat pool in his—

Impossible.

What the hell was happening to him?

Rodolfo felt his gaze narrow as he studied his fiancée. She looked the way she always did, and yet she didn't. She wore one of her efficiently sophisticated and chicly demure ensembles, a deceptively simple sheath dress that showed nothing and yet obliquely drew attention to the sheer feminine perfection of her form. A form he'd seen many times before, always clothed beautifully, and yet had never found himself waxing rhapsodic about before. Yet today he couldn't look away. There was something about the way she stood, as if she was unsteady on those cheeky heels she wore, though that seemed unlikely. Her hair flowed around her shoulders and looked somehow wilder than it usually did, as if the copper of it was redder. Or perhaps brighter.

Or maybe he needed to get his head examined. Maybe he really had gotten a concussion when he'd gone on an impromptu skydiving trip last week, tumbling a little too much on his way down into the remotest peaks of the Swiss Alps.

The princess moistened her lips and then met his gaze, and Rodolfo felt it like her sultry little mouth all over the hardest part of him.

What the hell?

"Hello," she said, and even her voice was…different, somehow. He couldn't put his finger on it. "It's lovely to see you."

"Lovely to see me?" he echoed, astonished. And

something far more earthy, if he was entirely honest with himself. "Are you certain? I was under the impression you would prefer a rousing spot of dental surgery to another one of these meetings. I feel certain you almost admitted as much at our last one."

He didn't know what had come over him. He'd managed to maintain his civility throughout all these months despite his creeping boredom—what had changed today? He braced himself, expecting the perfect princess to collapse into an offended heap on the polished floor, which he'd have a hell of a time explaining to her father, the humorless King Geoffrey of Murin.

But Valentina only smiled and a gleam he'd never seen before kindled in her eyes, which he supposed must always have been that remarkable shade of green. How had he never noticed them before?

"Well, it really depends on the kind of dental surgery, don't you think?" she asked.

Rodolfo couldn't have been more surprised if the quietly officious creature had tossed off her clothes and started dancing on the table—well, there was no need to exaggerate. He'd have summoned the palace doctors if the princess had done anything of the kind. After appreciating the show for a moment or two, of course, because he was a man, not a statue. But the fact she appeared to be teasing him was astounding, nonetheless.

"A root canal, at the very least," he offered.

"With or without anesthesia?"

"If it was with anesthesia you'd sleep right through it," Rodolfo pointed out. "Hardly any suffering at all."

"Everyone knows there's no point doing one's duty unless one can brag forever about the amount of suffering required to survive the task," the princess said, moving farther into the room. She stopped and rested her hand on the high, brocaded back of a chair that had likely cradled the posteriors of kings dating back to the ninth century, and all Rodolfo could think was that he wanted her to keep going. To keep walking toward him. To put herself within reach so he could—

Calm down, he ordered himself. *Now.* So sternly he sounded like his father in his own head.

"You are describing martyrdom," he pointed out.

Valentina shot him a smile. "Is there a difference?"

Rodolfo stood still because he didn't quite know what he might do if he moved. He watched this woman he'd written off months ago as if he'd never seen her before. There was something in the way she walked this afternoon that tugged at him. There was a new roll to her hips, perhaps. Something he'd almost call a swagger, assuming a princess of her spotless background and perfect genes was capable of anything so basic and enticing. Still, he couldn't look away as she rounded the settee he'd abandoned and settled herself in its center with a certain delicacy that was at odds with the way she'd moved through the old, spectacularly royal room. Almost as if she was more uncertain than she looked...but that made as little sense as the rest.

"I was reading about you on the plane back from London today," she told him, surprising him all over again.

"And here I thought we were maintaining the polite fiction that you did not sully your royal eyes with the squalid tabloids."

"Ordinarily I would not, of course," she replied, and then her mouth curved. Rodolfo was captivated. And somewhat horrified at that fact. But still captivated, all the same. "It is beneath me, obviously."

He sketched a bow that would have made his grandfather proud. "Obviously."

"I am a princess, not a desperate shopgirl who wants nothing more than to escape her dreary life, and must imagine herself into fantastical stories and half-truths presented as gospel."

"Quite so."

"But I must ask you a question." And on that she smiled again, that same serene curve of her lips that had about put him to sleep before. That was not the effect it had on him today. By a long shot.

"You can ask me anything, princess," Rodolfo heard himself say.

In a lazy, smoky sort of tone he'd never used in her presence before. Because this was the princess he was going to marry, not one of the enterprising women who flung themselves at him everywhere he went, looking for a taste of Europe's favorite daredevil prince.

There was no denying it. Suddenly, out of nowhere, he wanted his future wife.

Desperately.

As if she could tell—as if she'd somehow become the sort of woman who could read a man's desire and use it against him, when he'd have sworn she was anything but—Valentina's smile deepened.

She tilted her head to one side. "It's about your shocking double standard," she said sweetly. "If you can cat your way through all of Europe, why can't I?"

Something black and wild and wholly unfamiliar surged in him then, making Rodolfo's hands curl into fists and his entire body go tense, taut.

Then he really shocked the hell out of himself.

"Because you can't," he all but snarled, and there was no pretending that wasn't exactly what he was doing. *Snarling.* No matter how unlikely. "Like it or not, princess, you are mine."

CHAPTER THREE

PRINCE RODOLFO WAS not what Natalie was expecting.

No picture—and there were thousands, at a conservative estimate, every week he continued to draw breath—could adequately capture the *size* of Europe's favorite royal adrenaline junkie. That was the first thing that struck her. Sure, she'd seen the detailed telephoto shots of his much-hallowed abs as he emerged from various sparkling Mediterranean waters that had dominated whole summers of international swooning. And there was that famous morning he'd spent on a Barcelona balcony one spring, stretching and taking in the sunlight in boxer briefs and nothing else, but somehow all of those revealing pictures had managed to obscure the sheer *size* of the man. He was well over six feet, with hard, strong shoulders that could block out a day or two. And more than that, there was a leashed, humming sort of *power* in the man that photographs of him concealed entirely.

Or, Natalie thought, *maybe he's the one who does the concealing.*

But she couldn't think about what this man might be hiding beneath the surface. Not when the surface itself was so mesmerizing. She still felt as dazed as she'd been when she'd walked in this room and seen him waiting for her, dwarfing the furniture with all that contained physicality as he stood before the grand old fireplace. He looked like an athlete masquerading as a prince, with thick dark hair that was not quite tamed and the sort of dark chocolate eyes that a woman could lose herself in for a lifetime or three. His lean and rangy hard male beauty was packed into black trousers and a soft-looking button-down shirt that strained to handle his biceps and his gloriously sculpted chest. His hands were large and aristocratic at once, his voice was an authoritative rumble that seemed to murmur deep within her and then sink into a bright flame between her legs, his gaze was shockingly direct—and Natalie was not at all prepared. For any of it. For *him*.

She'd expected this real-life Prince Charming to be as repellent as he'd always been in the stories her mother had told her as a child about men just like him. Dull and vapid. Obsessed with something obscure, like hound breeding. Vain and huffy and bland, all the way through. Not...*this*.

Valentina had said that her fiancé was attractive in an offhanded, uncomplimentary way. She'd failed to mention that he was, in fact, upsettingly—almost incomprehensibly—stunning. The millions of fawning, admiring pictures of Crown Prince Rodolfo did not do him any justice, it turned out, and the truth of him took all the air from the room. From Natalie's lungs, for that matter. Her stomach felt scraped hollow as it plummeted to her feet, and then stayed there. But after a moment in the doorway where she'd seen nothing but him and the world had seemed to smudge a little bit around its luxe, literally palatial edges, Natalie had rallied.

It was hard enough trying to walk in the ridiculous shoes she was wearing—with her weight back on her heels, as ordered—and not goggle in slack-jawed astonishment at the palace all around her. *The actual, real live palace*. Valentina had pointed out that Natalie had likely visited remarkable places before, thanks to her job, and that was certainly true. But it was one thing to be treated as a guest in a place like Murin Castle. Or more precisely, as the employee of a guest, however valued by the guest in question. It was something else entirely to be treated as if it was all…hers.

The staff had curtsied and bowed when Natalie had stepped onto the royal jet. The guards had stood at attention. A person who was clearly her personal aide had catered to her during the quick flight, quickly filling her in on the princess's schedule and plans and then leaving her to her own devices. Natalie had spent years doing the exact same thing, so she'd learned a few things about Valentina in the way her efficient staff operated around her look-alike. That she was well liked by those who worked for her, which made Natalie feel oddly warm inside, as if that was some kind of reflection on her instead of the princess. That Valentina was not overly fussy or precious, given the way the staff served her food and acted while they did it. And that she was addicted to romance novels, if the stacks of books with bright-colored covers laid out for her perusal was any indication.

Then, soon enough, the plane had landed on the tiny little jewel of an island nestled in the Mediterranean Sea. Natalie's impressions were scattered as they flew in. Hills stretched high toward the sun, then sloped into the sea, covered in olive groves, tidy red roofs and the soaring arches of bell towers and churches. Blue water gleamed everywhere she looked, and white sand beaches nestled up tight to colorful fishing villages and picturesque marinas. There were cheerful sails in the graceful bay and a great, iconic castle set high on a hill. A perfect postcard of an island.

A dream. Except Natalie was wide-awake, and this was really, truly happening.

"Prince Rodolfo awaits your pleasure, Your Highness," a man she assumed was some kind of high-level butler had informed her when she'd been escorted into the palace itself, with guards saluting her arrival. She'd been too busy trying to look as if the splendor pressing in on her from all sides was so terribly common that she hardly noticed it to do more than nod, in some approximation of the princess's elegant inclination of her head. Then she'd had to follow the same butler through the palace, trying to walk with ease and confidence in shoes she was certain were not meant to be walked in at all, much less down endless marble halls.

She'd expected Prince Rodolfo to be seedier in person than in his photos. Softer of jaw, meaner of eye. And up himself in every possible way. She had not expected to find herself so stunned at the sight of him that she'd had to reach out and hold on to the furniture to keep her knees from giving out beneath her, for the love of all that was holy.

And then he'd spoken, and Natalie had understood—with a certain, sinking feeling that only made that breathlessness worse—that she was in more than a little hot water. It had never crossed her mind that *she* might find this prince—or any prince—attractive. It had never even occurred to her that she might be affected in any way by a man who carried that sort of title or courted the sort of attention Prince Rodolfo did. Natalie had never liked *flashy*. It was always a deliberate distraction, never anything real. Working for one of the most powerful men in the world had made her more than a little jaded when it came to other male displays of supposed strength. She knew what real might look like, how it was maintained and more, how it was wielded. A petty little princeling who liked to fling himself out of airplanes could only be deeply unappealing in person, she'd imagined.

She'd never imagined...*this*.

It was possible her mouth had run away with her, as some kind of defense mechanism.

And then, far more surprising, Prince Rodolfo wasn't the royal dullard she'd been expecting—all party and no substance. The sculpted mouth of his...*did things* to her as he revealed himself to be something a bit more intriguing than the airhead she'd expected. Especially when that look in his dark eyes took a turn toward the feral.

Stop, she ordered herself sternly. *This is another woman's fiancé, no matter what she might think of him.*

Natalie had to order herself to pay attention to what was happening as the Prince's surprisingly possessive words rang through the large room that teemed with antiques and the sort of dour portraits that usually turned out to have been painted by ancient masters, were always worth unconscionable amounts of money and made everyone in them look shriveled and dour. Or more precisely, she had to focus on their conversation, and not the madness that was going on inside her body.

You are mine didn't sound like the kind of thing the man Valentina had described would say. Ever. It didn't sound at all like the man the tabloids drooled over, or all those ex-lovers moaned about in exclusive interviews, mostly to complain about how quickly each and every one of them was replaced with the next.

In fact, unless she was mistaken, His Royal Highness, Prince Rodolfo, he of so many paramours in so many places that there were many internet graphs and user forums dedicated to tracking them all, looked as surprised by that outburst as she was.

"That hardly seems fair, does it?" she asked mildly, hoping he couldn't tell how thrown she was by him. Hoping it would go away if she ignored it. "I don't see why I have to confine myself to only you when you don't feel compelled to limit yourself. In any way at all, according to my research."

"Is there someone you wish to add to your stable, princess?" Rodolfo asked, in a smooth sort of way that was at complete odds with that hard, near-gold gleam in his dark eyes that set off every alarm in her body. Whether she ignored it or not. "Name the lucky gentleman."

"A lady never shares such things," she demurred. Then smiled the way she always had at the officious secretaries of her boss's rivals, all of whom underestimated her. Once. "Unlike you, Your Highness."

"I cannot help it if the press follows me everywhere I go." She sensed more than heard the growl in his voice. He was still standing where he'd been when she arrived, arranged before the immense fireplace like some kind of royal offering, but if he'd thought it made him look idle and at his ease he'd miscalculated. All she could see when she looked at him was how *big* he was. Big and hard and beautiful from head to toe and, God help her, she couldn't seem to control her reaction to him. "Just as I cannot keep them from writing any fabrication they desire. They prefer a certain narrative, of course. It sells."

"How tragic. I had no idea you were a misunderstood monk."

"I am a man, princess." He didn't quite bare his teeth. There was no reason at all Natalie should feel the cut of them against her skin. "Were you in some doubt?"

Natalie reminded herself that she, personally, had no stake in this. No matter how many stories her mother had told her about men like him and the careless way they lived their lives. No matter that Prince Rodolfo proved that her mother was right every time he swam with sharks or leaped from planes or trekked for a month in remotest Patagonia with no access to the outside world or thought to his country should he never return. And no matter the way her heart was kicking at her and her breath seemed to tangle in her throat. This wasn't about *her* at all.

I'm going to sort out your fiancé as a little wedding gift to you, she'd texted Valentina when she'd recovered from her shell shock and had emerged from the fateful bathroom in London to watch Achilles Casilieris's plane launch itself into the air without her. The beauty of the other princess having taken her bag when she'd left—with Natalie's phone inside it—was that Natalie knew her own number and could reach the woman who was inhabiting her life. You're welcome.

Good luck with that, Valentina had responded. He's unsortable. Deliberately, I imagine.

As far as Natalie was concerned, that was permission to come on in, guns blazing. She had nothing to lose by saying the things Valentina wouldn't. And there was absolutely no reason she should feel that hot, intent look he was giving her low and tight in her belly. No reason at all.

She made a show of looking around the vast room the scrupulously correct butler who had ushered her here had called a *parlor* in ringing tones. She'd had to work hard not to seem cowed, by the butler or the scale of the private wing he'd led her through, all dizzying chandeliers and astoundingly beautiful rooms clogged with priceless antiques and jaw-dropping art.

"I don't see any press here," she said, instead of debating his masculinity. For God's sake.

"Obviously not." Was it her imagination or did Rodolfo sound a little less...civilized? "We are on palace grounds. Your father would have them whipped."

"If you wanted to avoid the press, you could," Natalie pointed out. With all the authority of a person who had spent five years keeping Achilles Casilieris out of the press's meaty claws. "You don't."

Was it possible this mighty, beautiful prince looked... ill at ease? If only for a moment?

"I never promised you that I would declaw myself, Valentina," he said, and it took Natalie a moment to remember why he was calling her Valentina. Because that's who he thought she was, of course. Princess Valentina, who had to marry him in two months. Not mouthy, distressingly common Natalie, who was unlikely to marry anyone since she spent her entire life embroiled in and catering to the needs of a man who likely wouldn't be able to pick her out of a lineup. "I told you I would consider it after the wedding. For a time."

Natalie shrugged, and told herself there was no call for her to feel slapped down by his response. He wasn't going to marry *her*. She certainly didn't need to feel wounded by the way he planned to run his relationship. Critical, certainly. But not *wounded*.

"As will I," she said mildly.

Rodolfo studied her for a long moment, and Natalie forced herself to hold that seething dark glare while he did it. She even smiled and settled back against the delicate little couch, as if she was utterly relaxed. When she was nothing even remotely like it.

"No," he said after a long, long time, his voice dark

and lazy and something else she felt more than heard. "I think not."

Natalie held back the little shiver that threatened her then, because she knew, somehow, that he would see it and leap to the worst possible conclusion.

"You mistake me," she said coolly. "I wasn't asking your permission. I was stating a fact."

"I would suggest that you think very carefully about acting on this little scheme of yours, princess," Rodolfo said in that same dark, stirring tone. "You will not care for my response, I am certain."

Natalie crossed her legs and forced herself to relax even more against the back of her little couch. Well. To look it, anyway. As if she had never been more at her ease, despite the drumming of her pulse.

She waved a hand the way Valentina had done in London, so nonchalantly. "Respond however you wish. You have my blessing."

He laughed, then. The sound was rougher than Natalie would have imagined a royal prince's laugh ought to have been, and silkier than she wanted to admit as it wrapped itself around her. And all of that was a far second to the way amusement danced over his sculpted, elegant face, making him look not only big and surprisingly powerful, but very nearly approachable. Magnetic, even.

Something a whole lot more than magnetic. It lodged itself inside of her, then glowed.

Good lord, Natalie thought in another sort of daze as she gazed back at him. *This is the most dangerous man I've ever met.*

"I take it this is an academic discussion," Rodolfo said when he was finished laughing like that and using up all the light in the world, so cavalierly. "I had no idea you felt so strongly about what I did or didn't do, much less with whom. I had no idea you cared what I did at all. In fact, princess, I wasn't certain you heard a single word I've uttered in your presence in all these months."

He moved from the grand fireplace then, and watching him in motion was not exactly an improvement. Or it was a significant improvement, depending on how she looked at it. He was sleek for such a big man, and moved far too smoothly toward the slightly more substantial chair at a diagonal to where Natalie sat. He tossed himself into the stunningly wrought antique with a carelessness that should have snapped it into kindling, but didn't.

It occurred to her that he was far more aware of himself and his power than he appeared. That he was something of an iceberg, showing only the slightest bit of himself and containing multitudes beneath the surface. She didn't want to believe it. She wanted him to be a vapid, repellant playboy who she could slap into place during her time as a make-believe princess. But there was that assessing gleam in his dark gaze that told her that whatever else this prince was, he wasn't the least bit vapid.

And was rather too genuinely *charming* for her peace of mind, come to that.

He settled in his chair and stretched out his long, muscled legs so that they *almost* brushed hers, then smiled.

Natalie kept her own legs where they were, because shifting away from him would show a weakness she refused to let him see. She refused, as if her life depended on that refusal, and she didn't much care for the hysterical notion that it really, truly did.

"I don't care at all what you do or don't do," she assured him. "But it certainly appears that you can't say the same, for some reason."

"I am not the one who started making proclamations about my sexual intentions. I think you'll find that was you. Here. Today." That curve of his mouth deepened. "Entirely unprovoked."

"My mistake. Because a man who has grown up manipulating the press in no way sends a distinct message when he spends the bulk of his very public engagement 'escorting' other women to various events."

His gaze grew warmer, and that sculpted mouth curved. "I am a popular man."

"What I am suggesting to you is that you are not the only popular person in this arrangement. I'm baffled at your Neanderthal-like response to a simple statement of fact, when you have otherwise been at such pains to present yourself as the very image of modernity in royal affairs."

"We are sitting in an ancient castle on an island with a history that rivals Athens itself, discussing our upcoming marriage, which is the cold-blooded intermingling of two revered family lines for wealth and power, exactly as it might have been were we conducting this conversation in the Parthenon." His dark brows rose. "What part of this did you find particularly modern?"

"The two of us, I thought, before I walked in this room." She smiled brightly and let her foot dangle a bit too close to his leg. As if she didn't care at all that he was encroaching into her personal space. As if the idea of even so innocuous a touch did nothing at all to her central nervous system. As if he were not the sort of man she'd hated all her life, on principle. *And as if he were not promised to another,* she snapped at herself in disgust, but still, she didn't retreat the way she should have. In case she was wondering what kind of person she was.

"Now I suspect the Social Media Prince is significantly more caveman-like than he wants his millions of adoring followers to realize."

"I am the very soul of a Renaissance man, I assure you. I am merely aware of what the public will and will not support and I hate to break it you, princess, but the tabloids are not as forgiving of royal indiscretions as you appear to be."

"You surprise me again, Your Highness. I felt certain that a man in your position could not possibly care what the tabloid hacks did or did not forgive, given how much material you give them to work with. Daily."

"The two of us can sit in this room and bask in our progressive values, I am sure," Rodolfo murmured, and the look in his dark eyes did not strike Natalie as particularly progressive. "But public sentiment, I think you will find, is distressingly traditional. People may enjoy any number of their own extramarital affairs. It doesn't make them tolerant when a supposed fairy-tale princess strays from her charmed life. If anything, it makes the stones they cast heavier and more pointed."

"So, to unpack that, you personally wish to carry on as if we are single and free, but are prevented from following your heart's desire because you suddenly fear public perception?" She eyed him balefully and made no attempt to hide it. "That's a bit hard to believe, coming from the man who told me not twenty minutes ago that he refused to be *declawed*."

"You are not this naive, princess." And the look he gave her then seemed to prickle along her skin, lighting fires Natalie was terribly afraid would never go out. "You know perfectly well that I can do as I like with only minimal repercussions. It is you who cannot. You have built an entire life on your spotless character. What would happen were you to be revealed as nothing more or less than a creature as human as the rest of us?"

CHAPTER FOUR

RODOLFO HAD LONG ceased recognizing himself. And yet he kept talking.

"It will be difficult to maintain the fiction that you are a saint if your lovers are paraded through the tabloids of Europe every week," he pointed out, as if he didn't care one way or the other.

Somehow, he had the sense that the confounding woman who sat close enough to tempt him near to madness knew better. He could see it in the way her green eyes gleamed as she watched him. She was lounging in the settee as if it was a makeshift throne and she was already queen. And now she waved a languid hand, calling attention to her fine bones and the elegant fingers Rodolfo wanted all over his body. Rather desperately.

"It is you who prefer to ignore discretion," she said lightly enough. "I assume you get something out of the spotlight you shine so determinedly into your bedroom. I must congratulate you, as it is not every man who would be able to consistently perform with such an audience, so many years past his prime."

"I beg your pardon. Did you just question my... performance?"

"No need to rile yourself, Your Highness. The entire world has seen more than enough of your prowess.

I'm sure you are marvelously endowed with the—ah—necessary tools."

It took Rodolfo a stunned moment to register that the sensation moving in him then was nothing short of sheer astonishment. Somewhere between temper and laughter and yet neither at once.

"Let me make sure I am following this extraordinary line of thought," he began, trying to keep himself under control somehow—something that he could not recall ever being much of an issue before. Not with Princess Valentina, certainly. Not with any other woman he'd ever met.

"Whether or not it is extraordinary is between you and your revolving selection of aspiring hyphenates, I would think." When he could only stare blankly at her, she carried on almost merrily. "Model slash actress slash waitress slash air hostess, whatever the case may be. You exchange one for another so quickly, it's hard to keep track."

"I feel as if I've toppled off the side of the planet into an alternate reality," Rodolfo said then, after a moment spent attempting to digest what she'd said. What she'd actually dared say directly to his face. "Wherein Princess Valentina of Murin is sitting in my presence issuing veiled insults about my sexual performance and, indeed, my manhood itself."

"In this reality, we do not use the word *manhood* when we mean penis," Princess Valentina said with the same serene smile she'd always worn, back when he'd imagined she was boring. He couldn't understand how he'd misread her so completely. "It's a bit missish, isn't it?"

"What I cannot figure out is what you hope to gain from poking at me, Valentina," he said softly. "I am not given to displays of temper, if that is what you hoped.

Perhaps you forgot that I subject myself to extreme stress often. For fun. It is very, very difficult to get under my skin."

She smiled with entirely too much satisfaction for his comfort. "Says the man who had a rather strong reaction to the idea that what he feels constitutes reasonable behavior for him might also be equally appropriate for his fiancée."

"I assume you already recognize that there is no stopping the train we're on," he continued in the same quiet way, because it was that or give in to the simmering thing that was rumbling around inside of him, making him feel more precarious than he had in a long, long time. "The only way to avoid this marriage is to willfully cause a crisis in two kingdoms, and to what end? To make a point about free will? That is a lovely sentiment, I am sure, but it is not for you or me. We are not free. We belong to our countries and the people we serve. I would expect a woman whose very name is synonymous with her duty to understand that."

"That is a curious statement indeed from the only heir to an ancient throne who spends the bulk of his leisure time courting his own death." She let that land, that curve to her lips but nothing like a smile in her direct green stare. And she wasn't done. "Very much as if he was under the impression he did, in fact, owe nothing to his country at all."

Rodolfo's jaw felt like granite. "I can only assume that you are a jealous little thing, desperate to hide what you really want behind all these halfhearted feints and childish games."

The princess laughed. It was a smoky sound that felt entirely too much like a caress. "Why am I not surprised that so conceited a man would achieve that conclusion so quickly? Alas, I am hiding nothing, Your Highness."

He felt his lips curl in something much too fierce to be polite. "If you want to know whether or not I am marvelously endowed, princess, you need only ask for a demonstration."

She rolled her eyes, and perhaps that was what did it. Rodolfo was not used to being dismissed by beautiful women. Quite the contrary, they trailed around after him, begging for the scraps of his attention. He'd become adept at handling them before he'd left his teens. The ones who pretended to dislike him to get his attention, the ones who propositioned him straight out, the ones who acted as if they were shy, the ones so overcome and starstruck they stammered or wept or could only stare in silence. He'd seen it all.

But he had no way to process what was happening here with this woman he'd dismissed as uninteresting and uninterested within moments of their meeting as adults last fall. He had no idea what to do with a woman who set him on fire from across a room, and then treated him like a somewhat sad and boring joke.

He could handle just about anything, he realized, save indifference.

Rodolfo simply reached over and picked the princess up from the settee, hauling her through the air and setting her across his lap.

It was not a smart move. At best it was a test of that indifference she was flinging around the palace so casually, but it still wasn't smart.

But Rodolfo found he didn't give a damn.

The princess's porcelain cheeks flushed red and hot. She was a soft, slight weight against him, but his entire body exulted in the feel of her. Her scent was something so prosaic it hit him as almost shockingly exotic—soap. That was all. Her hands came up to brace against his chest, her copper hair was a silky shower over his arm and she was breathing hard and fast, making her exactly as much of a liar as he'd imagined she was.

She was many things, his hidden gem of a princess bride, but she was not *indifferent* to him. It felt like a victory.

"Do you think I cannot read women?" he asked her, his face temptingly, deliciously close to hers.

Her gaze was defiant. "There has long been debate about whether or not you can read anything else."

"I know you want me, princess. I can see it. I can feel it. The pulse in your throat, the look in your eyes. The way you tremble against me."

"That is sheer amazement that you think you can manhandle me this way, nothing more."

He moved the arm that wasn't wrapped around her back, sliding his hand to the delectable bit of thigh that was bared beneath the hem of her dress and just held it there. Her skin was a revelation, warm and soft. And her perfect, aristocratic oval of a face was tipped back, his for the taking.

Maybe he was the Neanderthal she'd claimed he was, after all. For the first time in his life, he felt as if he was that and more. A beast in every possible way, inside and out.

"What would happen if I slid my hand up under your skirt?" he asked her, bending even closer, so his mouth was a mere breath from hers.

"I would summon the royal guard and have you cast into the dungeons, the more medieval the better."

He ignored that breathy, insubstantial threat, along with the oddity of the Princess of Murin talking of dungeons in a palace that had never had any in the whole of its storied history. He concentrated on her body instead.

"What would I find, princess? How wet are you? How much of a liar will your body prove you to be?"

"Unlike you," she whispered fiercely, "I don't feel the need to prove myself in a thousand different sexual arenas."

But she didn't pull away. He noted that she didn't even try.

"You don't need to concern yourself with any arena but this one," he said, gruff against her mouth and his palm still full of her soft flesh. "And you need not prove yourself to anyone but me."

Rodolfo had kissed her once before. It had been a bloodless, mechanical photo op on the steps of Murin Castle. They had held hands and beamed insincerely at the crowds, and then he had pressed a chaste, polite sort of closemouthed kiss against her mouth to seal the deal. No muss, no fuss. It hadn't been unpleasant in any way. But there hadn't been anything to it. No fire. No raw, aching need. Rodolfo had experienced more intense handshakes.

That was not the way he kissed her today. Because everything was different, somehow. Himself included.

He didn't bother with any polite, bloodless kiss. Rodolfo took her mouth as if he owned it. As if there was nothing *arranged* about the two of them and never had been. As if he'd spent the night inside her, making her his in every possible way, and couldn't contain himself another moment.

Her taste flooded his senses, making him glad on some distant level that he'd had the accidental foresight to remain seated, because otherwise he thought she might have knocked him off his feet. He opened his mouth over hers, angling his jaw to revel in the slick, hot fit.

She was a marvel. And she was his, whether she liked it or not. No matter what inflammatory thing she said to rile him up or insult him into an international incident that would shame them both, or whatever the hell she was doing. How had he thought otherwise for even a moment?

Rodolfo lost his mind.

And his lovely bride-to-be did not push him off or slap his face. She didn't lie there in icy indifference. Oh, no.

She surged against him, wrapping her arms around his neck to pull him closer, and she kissed him back. Again and again and again.

For a moment there was nothing but that fire that roared between them. Wild. Insane. Unchecked and unmanageable.

And then in the next moment, she was shoving away from him. She twisted to pull herself from his grasp and then clambered off his lap, and he let her. Of course he bloody let her, and no matter the state of him as she went. That it was a new state—one he'd never experienced before, having about as much experience with frustrated desire as he did with governing the country he would one day rule—was something he kept to himself. Mostly because he hardly knew what to make of it.

The princess looked distressed as she threw herself across the room and away from him. She was trembling as she caught herself against the carved edge of the stone fireplace, and then she took a deep, long breath. To settle herself, perhaps, if she felt even a fraction of the things he did. Or perhaps she merely needed to steady herself in those shoes.

"Valentina," he began, but her name seemed to hit

her like a slap. She stiffened, then held up a hand as if to silence him. Yet another new experience.

And he could still taste her in his mouth. His body was still clamoring for her touch. He wanted her, desperately, so he let her quiet him like an errant schoolboy instead of the heir to an ancient throne.

"That must never happen again," she said with soft, intense sincerity, her gaze fixed on the fireplace, where an exultant flower arrangement took the place of the fires that had crackled there in the colder months.

"Come now, princess." He didn't sound like himself. Gruff. Low. "I think you know full well it must. We will make heirs, you and I. It is the primary purpose of our union."

She stood taller, then turned to face him, and he was struck by what looked like *torment* on her face. As if this was hard for her, whatever the hell was happening here, which made no sense. This had always been her destiny. If not with Rodolfo, then with some other Crown-sanctioned suitor. The woman he'd thought he'd known all these months had always seemed, if not precisely thrilled by the prospect, resigned to it. He imagined the change in her would have been fascinating if he wasn't half-blind from *wanting* her so badly.

"No," she said, and he was struck again by how different her voice sounded. But how could that be? He shook that off and concentrated instead on what she'd said.

"You must be aware that there can be no negotiation on this point." He tamped down on the terrible need making his body over into a stranger's, and concentrated instead on reality.

She frowned at him. "What if we can't produce heirs? It's more common than you think."

"And covered at some length in the contracts we

signed," he agreed, trying to rein in his impatience. "But we must try, Valentina. It is part of our agreement." He shook his head when she started to speak. "If you plan to tell me that this is medieval, you are correct. It is. Literally. The same provisions have covered every such marriage between people like us since the dawn of time. You cannot have imagined that a royal wedding at our rank would allow for anything else, can you?"

Something he would have called fierce inhabited her face for a moment, and then was gone.

"You misunderstand me." She ran her hands down the front of her dress as if it needed smoothing, but all Rodolfo could think of was the feel of her in his arms and the soft skin of her thigh against his palm. "I have every intention of doing my duty, Your Highness. But I will only be as faithful to you as you are to me."

He shook his head. "I am not a man who backs down from a challenge, princess. You must know this."

"It's not a challenge." Her gaze was dark when it met his. "It's a fact. As long as you ignore your commitments, I'll do the same. What have I got to lose? I'll always know that our children are mine. Let's hope you can say the same."

And on that note—while he remained frozen in his chair, stunned that she would dare threaten him openly with such a thing—Rodolfo's suddenly fascinating princess pulled herself upright and then swept out of the room.

He let her go.

It was clear to him after today that not only did he need to get to know his fiancée a whole lot better than he had so far, he needed to up his game overall where she was concerned. And when it came to games, Rodolfo had the advantage, he knew.

Because he'd never, ever lost a single game he'd ever played.

His princess was not going to be the first.

It was difficult to make a dramatic exit when Natalie had no idea where she was going.

She was on her third wrong turn—and on the verge of frustrated tears—when she hailed a confused-looking maid who, after a stilted conversation in which Natalie tried not to sound as if she was lost in what should have been her home, led her off into a completely different part of the palace and into what were clearly Valentina's own private rooms. Though "rooms" was an understated way to put it. The series of vast, exquisitely furnished chambers were more like a lavish, sprawling penthouse contained in the palace and sporting among its many rooms a formal dining area, a fully equipped media center and a vast bedroom suite complete with a wide balcony that looked off toward the sea and a series of individual rooms that together formed the princess's wardrobe. The shoe room alone was larger than the flat Natalie kept on the outskirts of London, yet barely used, thanks to her job.

Staff bustled about in the outer areas of the large suite, presumably adhering to the princess's usual schedule, but the bedroom was blessedly empty. It was there that Natalie found a surprisingly comfortable chaise, curled herself up on it with a sigh of something not quite relief and finally gave herself leave to contemplate the sort of person she'd discovered she was today.

It left a bitter taste in her mouth.

She'd always harbored a secret fantasy that should she ever stumble over a Prince Charming type—and not be forced into studied courtesy because she represented her employer—she'd shred him to pieces. Because even if the man in question wasn't the one who'd taught her mother to be so bitter, it was a fair bet that he'd ruined someone else's life. That was what Prince Charmings *did*. Even in the fairy tale, the man had left a trail of mutilated feet and broken families behind him everywhere he went. Natalie had been certain she could slap an overconfident ass like that down without even trying very hard.

And instead, she'd kissed him.

Oh, she tried to pretend otherwise. She tried to muster up a little outrage at the way Rodolfo had put his hands on her and hauled her onto his lap—but what did any of that matter? He hadn't held her there against her will. She could have stood up at any time.

She hadn't. Quite the contrary.

And when his mouth had touched hers, she'd *imploded*.

Not only had Natalie kissed the kind of man she'd always hated on principle, but she'd kissed one promised to another woman. If that wasn't enough, she'd threatened to marry him and then present him with children that weren't his. As punishment? Just to be cruel? She had no idea. She only knew that her mouth had opened and out the threat had come.

The worst part was, she'd seen that stunned, furious look on the Prince's face when she'd issued that threat. Natalie had no doubt that he believed that she would do exactly that. Worse, that *Princess Valentina* was the sort of person who, apparently, thought nothing of that kind of behavior.

"Great," she muttered out loud, to the soft chaise beneath her and the soothing landscapes on the walls. "You've made everything worse."

It was one thing to try to make things better for Valentina, who Natalie imagined was having no fun at all contending with the uncertain temper of Mr. Casilieris. Natalie was used to fixing things. That was what she did with her life—she sorted things out to be easier, smoother, better for others. But Rodolfo hadn't been as easily managed as she'd expected him to be, and the truth was, she'd never quite recovered from that first, shocking sight of him.

There was a possibility, Natalie acknowledged as she remained curled up on a posh chaise in a princess's bedroom like the sort of soft creature she'd never been, that she still hadn't recovered. *And that you never will,* chimed in a voice from deep inside her, but she dismissed it as unnecessarily dire.

Her clutch—Valentina's clutch—had been delivered here while she'd been off falling for Prince Charming like a ninny, sitting on an engaged man's lap as if she had no spine or will of her own, and making horrible threats about potential royal heirs in line to a throne. Was that treason in a kingdom like Murin? In Tissely? She didn't even know.

"And maybe you should find out before you cause a war," she snapped at herself.

What she did know was that she didn't recognize herself, all dressed up in another woman's castle as if that life could ever fit her. And she didn't like it.

Natalie pushed up off the chaise and went to sweep up the clutch from where it had been left on the padded bench that claimed the real estate at the foot of the great four-poster bed. She'd examined the contents on the plane, fascinated. Princesses apparently carried very little, unlike personal assistants, who could live out of their shoulder bags for weeks in a pinch. There was no money or identification, likely because neither was necessary when you had access to an entire treasury filled with currency stamped with your own face. Valentina carried only her mobile, a tube of extremely high-end lip gloss and a small compact mirror.

Natalie sat on the bench with Valentina's mobile in her hand and looked around the quietly elegant bedroom, though she hardly saw it. The adrenaline of the initial switch had given way to sheer anxiety once she'd arrived in Murin. She'd expected to be called out at any moment and forced to explain how and why she was impersonating the princess. But no one had blinked, not even Prince Rodolfo.

Maybe she shouldn't be surprised that now that she was finally alone, she felt a little lost. Maybe that was the price anyone could expect to pay when swapping identities with a complete stranger. Especially one who happened to be a royal princess to boot.

It was times like this that Natalie wished she had the sort of relationship with her mother that other people seemed to have with theirs. She'd like nothing more than to call Erica up and ask for some advice, or maybe just so she could feel soothed, somehow, by the fact of her mother's existence. But that had never been the way her mother operated. Erica had liked Natalie best when she was a prop. The pretty little girl she could trot out when it suited her, to tug on a heartstring or to prove that she was maternal when, of course, she wasn't. Not really. Not beyond the telling of the odd fairy tale with a grim ending, which Natalie had learned pretty early on was less for her than for her mother.

No wonder Natalie had lost herself in school. It didn't matter where they moved. It didn't matter what was going on in whatever place Erica was calling home that month. Natalie could always count on her studies. Whether she was behind the class or ahead of it when she showed up as the new kid, who cared? School always gave her a project of one sort or another. She'd viewed getting into college—on a full academic scholarship, of course, because Erica had laughed when Natalie had asked if there would be any parental contributions to her education and then launched into another long story about the evils of rich, selfish men—as her escape. College had been four years of an actual place to call home, at last. Plus classes. Basically nirvana, as far as Natalie had been concerned.

But that kind of overachieving behavior, while perfect for her eventual career as the type A assistant to the most picky and overbearing man alive, had not exactly helped Natalie make any friends. She'd always been the new kid in whatever school she'd ended up in. Then, while she wasn't the new kid at college, she was so used to her usual routine of studying constantly that she hadn't known how to stop it. She and her freshman-year roommate had gotten along well enough and they'd even had lunch a few times over the next few years, all very pleasant, but it hadn't ever bloomed into the sort of friendships Natalie knew other women had. She'd had a boyfriend her junior year, which had been more exciting in theory than in fact. And then she'd started working for Mr. Casilieris after graduation and there hadn't been time for anything but him, ever again.

All of this had been perfectly fine with her yesterday. She'd been proud of her achievements and the fact no one had helped her in equal measure. Well. She'd wanted to quit her job, but surely that was a reasonable response to five years of Achilles Casilieris. And today, sitting on the cushioned bench at the foot of a princess's bed with a medieval castle looming all around her like an accusation, it was clear to Natalie that really, she could have used someone to call.

Anyone except the person she knew she had to call, that was.

But Natalie hadn't dealt with a terrifying man like Achilles Casilieris for years by being a coward, no matter how tempting it was to become one now. She blew out a breath, then dialed her own mobile number. She knew that the flight she should have been on right now, en route to New York City, hadn't landed yet. She even knew that all the calls she'd set up would likely have ended—but she wasn't surprised when Valentina didn't answer. Mr. Casilieris was likely tearing strips out of the princess's hide, because no matter how she'd handled the situation, it wouldn't have been to his satisfaction. She was a bit surprised that Valentina hadn't confessed all and that the Casilieris plane wasn't landing in Murin right now to discharge her—and so Achilles Casilieris could fire Natalie in person for deceiving him.

Really, it hadn't been nice of Natalie to let Valentina take her place. She'd known what the other woman was walking into. God help the poor princess if she failed to provide Mr. Casilieris with what he wanted three seconds before he knew he wanted it. When she'd started, Achilles Casilieris had been famous for cycling through assistants in a matter of hours, sometimes, depending on the foulness of his mood. Everyone was an idiot, as he was all too happy to make clear, especially the people he paid to assist him. Everyone fell short of his impossibly high standards. If he thought Natalie had lost her ability to do her job the way he liked it done, he'd fire her without a second thought. She'd never been in any doubt about that.

Which meant that really, she should have been a little more concerned about the job Valentina was almost certainly botching up right this very minute, somewhere high above the Atlantic Ocean.

But she found she couldn't work up the usual worry over that eventuality. If he fired her, he fired her. It saved her having to quit, didn't it? And when she tried to stress out about losing the position she'd worked so hard to keep all these years, all she could think of instead was the fact he hadn't known Valentina wasn't her in that bathroom. That despite spending more time with Natalie than with his last ten mistresses combined, he'd failed to recognize her. And meanwhile, Rodolfo had looked at *her*. As if he wanted to climb inside of her. As if he could never, ever get enough. And that mouth of his was sculpted and wicked, knowing and hot…

She heard her own voice asking for a message and a phone number on the other end of the line, but she didn't leave a voice mail at the beep. What would she say? Where would she start? Would she jump right into the kissing and claims that she'd sleep her way around Europe in payback for any extramarital adventures Prince Rodolfo might have? She could hardly believe she'd done either of those things, much less think of how best to tell someone else that she had. Particularly when the someone else was the woman who was expected to marry the man in question.

The fact was, she had no idea what Valentina expected from her arranged marriage. A dry tone in a bathroom to a stranger when discussing her fiancé wasn't exactly a peek into the woman's thoughts on what happily-ever-after looked like for her. Maybe she'd been fine with the expected cheating, like half of Europe seemed to be. Maybe she hadn't cared either way. Natalie had no way to tell.

But it didn't matter what Valentina's position on any of this was. It didn't make Natalie any happier with herself that she was hoping, somewhere in there, that Valentina might give her blessing. Or her forgiveness, anyway. And it wasn't as if she could blame the Prince, either. Prince Rodolfo thought she *was* Valentina. His behavior was completely acceptable. He'd had every reason to believe he was with his betrothed.

Natalie was the one who'd let another woman's fiancé kiss her. So thoroughly her breasts still ached and her lips felt vulnerable and she felt a fist of pure need clench tight between her legs at the memory. Natalie was the one who'd kissed him back.

There was no prettying that up. *That* was who she was.

Natalie put the phone aside, then jumped when it beeped at her. She snatched it back up, hoping it was Valentina so she could at least unburden her conscience— another indication that she was not really the good person she'd always imagined herself to be, she was well aware—but it was a reminder from the princess's calendar, telling her she had a dinner with the king in a few hours.

She wanted to curl back up on that chaise and cry for a while. Perhaps a week or so. She wanted to look around for the computer she was sure the princess must have secreted away somewhere and see if she could track her actual life as it occurred across the planet. She wanted to rewind to London and her decision to do this insane thing in the first place and then think better of pulling such a stunt.

But she swallowed hard as she looked down at that reminder on the mobile screen. *The king.*

All those things she didn't want to think about flooded her then.

If Erica had shortened her name… If all that moving around had been less *wanderer's soul* and more *on the run*… If there was really, truly only one reasonable explanation as to how a royal princess and a glorified secretary could pass for each other and it had nothing to do with that tired old saying that *everyone had a twin somewhere*…

If all of those things were true, then the King of Murin—with whom she was about to have a meal—wasn't simply the monarch of this tiny little island kingdom, well-known for his vast personal wealth, many rumors of secret affairs with the world's most glamorous women and the glittering, celebrity-studded life he lived as the head of a tiny, wealthy country renowned for its yacht-friendly harbors and friendly taxes.

He was also very likely her father.

And that was the lure, it turned out, that Natalie couldn't resist.

CHAPTER FIVE

A LITTLE OVER a week later, Natalie thought she might actually be getting the hang of this princess thing. Or settling into her role well enough that she no longer had to mystify the palace staff with odd requests that they lead her to places she should have been able to find on her own.

She'd survived that first dinner with the king, who might or might not have been her father. The truth was, she couldn't tell. If she'd been expecting a mystical, magical sort of reunion, complete with swelling emotions and dazed recognition on both sides, she'd been bitterly disappointed. She'd been led to what was clearly her seat at one end of a long, polished table in what looked like an excruciatingly formal dining room to her but was more likely the king's private, casual eating area given that it was located in his private wing of the palace. She'd stood there for a moment, not knowing what she was supposed to do next. Sit? Wait? Prepare to curtsy?

The doors had been tossed open and a man had strode in with great pomp and circumstance. Even if she hadn't recognized him from the pictures she'd studied online and the portraits littering the castle, Natalie would have known who he was. King Geoffrey of Murin didn't exude the sort of leashed, simmering power Rodolfo did, she couldn't help thinking. He wasn't as magnificently built, for one thing. He was a tall, elegantly slender man who would have looked a bit like an accountant if the suit he wore hadn't so obviously been a bespoke masterpiece and if he hadn't moved with a sort of bone-deep imperiousness that shouted out his identity with each step. It was as if he expected marble floors to form themselves beneath his foot in anticipation that he might place it there. And they did.

"Hello," she'd said when he approached the head of the table, with perhaps a little too much *meaning* in those two syllables. She'd swallowed. Hard.

And the king had paused. Natalie had tensed, her stomach twisting in on itself. *This is it,* she'd thought. *This is the moment you'll not only be exposed as not being Valentina, but recognized as his long-lost daughter—*

"Are you well?" That was it. That was all he'd asked, with a vaguely quizzical look aimed her way.

"Ah, yes." She cleared her throat, though it didn't need clearing. It was her head that had felt dizzy. "Quite well. Thank you. And you?"

"I hope this is not an example of the sort of witty repartee you practice upon Prince Rodolfo," was what Geoffrey had said. He'd nodded at her, which Natalie had taken as her cue to sit, and then he'd settled himself in his own chair. Only then did he lift a royal eyebrow and summon the hovering servants to attend them.

"Not at all," Natalie had managed to reply. And then some demon had taken her over, and she didn't stop there. "A future king looks for many things in a prospective bride, I imagine, from her bloodlines to whether or not she is reasonably photogenic in all the necessary pictures. But certainly not wit. That sort of thing is better saved for the peasants, who require more entertainment to make it through their dreary lives."

"Very droll, I am sure." The king's eyes were the same as hers. The same shape, the same unusual green. And showed the same banked temper she'd felt in her own too many times to count. A kind of panicked flush had rolled over her, making her want to get up and run from the room even as her legs felt too numb to hold her upright. "I trust you know better than to make such an undignified display of inappropriate humor in front of the prince? He may be deep in a regrettable phase with all those stunts he pulls, but I assure you, at the end of the day he is no different from any other man in his position. Whatever issues he may have with his father now, he will sooner or later ascend the throne of Tissely. And when he does, he will not want a comedienne at his side, Valentina. He will require a queen."

Natalie was used to Achilles Casilieris's version of slap downs. They were quicker. Louder. He blazed into a fury and then he was done. This was entirely different. This was less a slap down and more a deliberate *pressing down,* putting Natalie firmly and ruthlessly in her place.

She'd found she didn't much care for the experience. Or the place Valentina was apparently expected to occupy.

"But you have no queen," she'd blurted out. Then instantly regretted it when Geoffrey had gazed at her in amazement over his first course. "Sir."

"I do not appreciate this sort of acting out at my table, Valentina," he'd told her, with a certain quiet yet ringing tone. "You know what is expected of you. You were promised to the Tisselians when I still believed I might have more children, or you would take the throne of

Murin yourself. But we are Murinese and we do not back out of our promises. If you are finding your engagement problematic, I suggest you either find a way to solve it to your satisfaction or come to a place of peace with its realities. Those are your only choices."

"Was that your choice?" she'd asked.

Maybe her voice had sounded different then. Maybe she'd slipped and let a little emotion in. Natalie hadn't known. What she'd been entirely too clear on was that this man should have recognized her. At the very least, he should have known she wasn't the daughter he was used to seeing at his table. And surely the king knew that he'd had twins. He should have had some kind of inkling that it was *possible* he'd run into his other daughter someday.

And yet if King Geoffrey of Murin noticed that his daughter was any different than usual, he kept it to himself. In the same way that if he was racked nightly by guilt because he'd clearly misplaced a twin daughter some twenty-seven years ago, it did not mar his royal visage in any way.

"We must all make choices," he'd said coolly. "And when we are of the Royal House of Murin, each and every one of those choices must benefit the kingdom. You know this full well and always have. I suggest you resign yourself to your fate, and more gracefully."

And it was the only answer he'd given.

He'd shifted the conversation then, taking charge in what Natalie assumed was his usual way. And he'd talked about nothing much, in more than one language, which would have made Natalie terrified that she'd give herself away, but he hadn't seemed to want much in the way of answers. In Italian, French, or English.

Clearly, the princess's role was to sit quietly and listen as the king expounded on whatever topic he liked. And not to ask questions. No wonder she'd wanted a break.

I have a confession to make, Natalie had texted Valentina later that first night. She'd been back in the princess's absurdly comfortable and elegant bedroom, completely unable to sleep as her conscience was keeping her wide awake.

Confession is good for the soul, I'm reliably informed, Valentina had replied after a moment or two. Natalie had tried to imagine where she might be. In the small room in Mr. Casilieris's vast New York penthouse she thought of as hers? Trying to catch up on work in the office suite on the lower floor? *I've never had the pleasure of a life that required a confession. But you can tell me anything.*

Natalie had to order herself to stop thinking about her real life, and to start paying attention to Valentina's life, which she was messing up left and right.

Rodolfo kissed me. There. Three quick words, then the send button, and she was no longer keeping a terrible secret to herself.

That time, the pause had seemed to take years.

That sounds a bit more like a confession Rodolfo ought to be making. Though I suppose he wouldn't know one was necessary, would he?

In the spirit of total honesty, Natalie had typed resolutely, because there was nothing to be gained by lying at that point and besides, she clearly couldn't live with herself if she didn't share all of this with Valentina no matter the consequences, *I kissed him back.*

She'd been sitting up against the headboard then, staring at the phone in her hand with her knees pulled up beneath her chin. She'd expected anger, at the very least. A denunciation or two. And she'd had no idea what that would even look like, coming from a royal princess—would guards burst through the bedroom doors and haul her away? Would Valentina declare her an imposter and have her carried off in chains? Anything seemed possible. Likely, even, given how grievously Natalie had slipped up.

If she'd been a nail-biter, Natalie would have gnawed hers right off. Instead, she tried to make herself breathe.

Someone should, I suppose, Valentina had texted back, after another pause that seemed to last forever and then some. I've certainly never touched him.

Natalie had blinked at that. And had then hated herself, because the thing that wound around inside of her was not shame. It was far warmer and far more dangerous.

I never will again, she'd vowed. And she'd wanted to mean it with every fiber of her being. I swear.

You can do as you like with Rodolfo, Valentina had replied, and Natalie could almost hear the other woman's airy tone through the typed words. You have my blessing. Really. A hundred Eastern European models can't be wrong!

But it wasn't Valentina's blessing that she'd wanted, Natalie realized. Because that was a little too close to outright permission and she'd hardly been able to control herself as it was. What she wanted was outrage. Fury and consequences. Something—*anything*—to keep her from acting like a right tart.

And instead it was a little more than a week later and Rodolfo was outplaying her at the game she was very much afraid she'd put into motion that first day in her new role as the princess. By accident—or at least, without thinking about the consequences—but that hardly mattered now.

Worse, he was doing it masterfully, by not involving her at all. Why risk what might come out of her mouth when he could do an end run around her and go straight to King Geoffrey instead? On some level, Natalie admired the brilliance of the move. It made Rodolfo look like less of a libertine in the king's eyes and far more of the sort of political ally for Murin he would one day become as the King of Tissely.

She needed to stop underestimating her prince. Before she got into the kind of trouble a text couldn't solve.

"Prince Rodolfo thinks the two of you ought to build more of an accessible public profile ahead of the wedding," the king said as they'd sat at their third dinner of the week, as was apparently protocol.

It had taken Natalie a moment to realize Geoffrey was actually waiting for her response. She'd swallowed the bite of tender Murinese lamb she'd put in her mouth and smiled automatically, playing back what he'd said—because she'd gotten in the terrible habit of nodding along without really listening. She preferred to study the King's features and ask herself why, if he was her father, she didn't *feel* it. And he didn't either, clearly. Surely she should *know him* on a deep, cellular level. Or something. Wasn't blood supposed to reveal itself like that? And if it didn't, surely that meant that she and Valentina only happened to resemble each other by chance.

In every detail. Down to resembling Geoffrey, too. So much so that the King himself couldn't tell the difference when they switched.

Natalie knew on a level she didn't care to explore that it was unlikely to be chance. That it couldn't be chance.

"A public profile?" she echoed, because she had to say something, and she had an inkling that flatly refusing to do anything Rodolfo suggested simply because it had come from him wouldn't exactly fly as far as the king was concerned.

"I rather like the idea." King Geoffrey's attention had returned to his own plate. "It is a sad fact that in these modern times, a public figure is judged as much on the image he presents to the world as his contributions to it. More, perhaps."

He didn't order her to do as Rodolfo asked. But then, he didn't have to issue direct orders. And that was how Natalie found herself flying off to Rome to attend a star-studded charity gala the very next day, because Rodolfo had decided it was an excellent opportunity to "boost their profile" in the eyes of the international press corps.

If she ignored the reason she was taking the trip and the man who'd engineered it, Natalie had to admit that it was lovely to have her every need attended to, for a change. All she had to do was wake up the following morning. Everything else was sorted out by a fleet of others. Her wardrobe attendant asked if she had any particular requests and, when Natalie said she didn't, nodded decisively and returned with tidily packed luggage in less than an hour. Which footmen then whisked away. Natalie was swept off to the same private jet as before, where she was fed a lovely lunch of a complicated, savory salad and served sparkling water infused with cucumber. Things she didn't know she craved, deeply, until they were presented to her.

"Your chocolate, Your Highness," the air steward said with a smile after clearing away the salad dishes, presenting her with two rich, dark squares on a gold-embossed plate. "From the finest chocolatiers in all of the kingdom."

"I do like my chocolate," Natalie murmured.

More than that, she liked the princess's style, she thought as she let each rich, almost sweet square dissolve on her tongue, as if it had been crafted precisely to appeal to her.

Which, if she and Valentina were identical twins after all, she supposed it had.

And the pampering continued. The hotel she was delivered to in Rome, located at the top of the Spanish Steps to command the finest view possible over the ancient, vibrant city, had been arranged for and carefully screened by someone else. All she had to do was walk inside and smile as the staff all but kowtowed before her. Once in her sprawling penthouse suite, Natalie was required to do nothing but relax as her attendants bustled around, unpacking her things in one of the lavishly appointed rooms while they got to work on getting the princess ready for the gala in another. A job that required the undivided attention of a team of five stylists, apparently, when Natalie was used to tossing something on in the five minutes between crises and making the best of it.

Her fingernails were painted, her hair washed and cut and styled just so, and even her makeup was deftly applied. When they were done, Natalie was dressed like a fairy-tale princess all ready for her ball.

And her prince, something inside her murmured.

She shoved that away. Hard. There'd been no room for fairy tales in her life, only hard work and dedication. Her mother had told her stories that always ended badly, and Natalie had given up wishing for happier conclusions to such tales a long, long time ago. Even if she and Valentina really were sisters, it hardly mattered now. She was a grown woman. There was no being swept off in a pumpkin and spending the rest of her life surrounded by dancing mice. That ship had sailed.

She had no time for fairy tales. Not even if she happened to be living one.

Natalie concentrated on the fact that she looked like someone else tonight. Someone she recognized, yet didn't. Someone far more sophisticated than she'd ever been, and she'd thought her constant exposure to billionaires like Mr. Casilieris had given her a bit of polish.

You look like someone beautiful, she thought in a kind of wonder as she studied herself in the big, round mirror that graced the wall in her room. *Objectively beautiful.*

Her hair was swept up into a chignon and secured with pins that gleamed with quietly elegant jewels. Her dress was a dove-gray color that seemed to make her skin glow, cascading from a strapless bodice to a wide, gorgeous skirt that moved of its own accord when she walked and made her look very nearly celestial. Her shoes were high sandals festooned with straps, there was a clasp of impossible sapphires and diamonds at her throat that matched the ring she wore on her hand and her eyes looked fathomless.

Natalie looked like a princess. Not just Princess Valentina, but the sort of magical, fantasy princess she'd have told anyone who asked she'd never, ever imagined when she was a child, because she'd been taught better than that.

Never ever. Not once.

She nodded and smiled her thanks at her waiting attendants, but Natalie didn't dare speak. She was afraid that if she did, that faint catch in her throat would tip over into something far more embarrassing, and then worse, she'd have to explain it. And Natalie had no idea how to explain the emotions that buffeted her then.

Because the truth was, she didn't know how to be beautiful. She knew how to stick to the shadows and more, how to excel in them. She knew how to disappear in plain sight and use that to her—and her employer's—advantage. Natalie had no idea how to be the center of attention. How to be *seen*. In fact, she'd actively avoided it. Princess Valentina turned heads wherever she went, and Natalie had no idea how she was going to handle it. If she *could* handle it.

But it was more than her shocking appearance, so princessy and pretty. This was the first time in all her life that she hadn't had to be responsible for a thing. Not one thing. Not even her own sugar consumption, apparently. This was the first time in recent memory that she hadn't had to fix things for someone else or exhaust herself while making sure that others could relax and enjoy themselves.

No one had ever taken care of Natalie Monette. Not once. She'd had to become Princess Valentina for that to happen. And while she hadn't exactly expected that impersonating royalty would feel like a delightful vacation from her life, she hadn't anticipated that it would feel a bit more like an earthquake, shaking her apart from within.

It isn't real, a hard voice deep inside of her snapped, sounding a great deal like her chilly mother. *It's temporary and deeply stupid, as you should have known before you tried on that ring.*

Natalie knew that, of course. She flexed her hand at her side and watched the ring Prince Rodolfo had given another woman spill light here and there. None of this was real. Because none of this was hers. It was a short, confusing break from real life, that was all, and there was no use getting all soppy about it. There was only surviving it without blowing up the real princess's life while she was mucking around in it.

But all the bracing lectures in the world couldn't keep that glowing thing inside her chest from expanding as she gazed at the princess in the mirror, until it felt as if it was a part of every breath she took. Until she couldn't tell where the light of it ended and that shaking thing began. And she didn't need little voices inside of her to tell her how dangerous that was. She could feel it deep in her bones, knitting them into new shapes she was very much afraid she would have to break into pieces when she left.

Because whatever else this was, it was temporary. She needed to remember that above all.

"Your Highness." It was the most senior of the aides who traveled with the princess, something Natalie had known at a glance because she recognized the older woman's particular blend of sharp focus and efficient movement. "His Royal Highness Prince Rodolfo has arrived to escort you to the gala."

"Thank you," Natalie murmured, as serenely and princessy as possible.

And this was the trouble with dressing up like a beautiful princess who could be whisked off to a ball at a moment's notice. Natalie started to imagine that was exactly who she was. It was so hard to keep her head, and then she walked into the large, comfortably elegant living room of her hotel suite to find Prince Rodolfo waiting for her, decked out in evening clothes, and everything troubling became that much harder.

He stood at the great glass doors that slid open to one

of the terraces that offered up stunning views of Rome at all times, but particularly now, as the sun inched toward the horizon and the city was bathed in a dancing, liquid gold.

More to the point, so was Rodolfo.

Natalie hadn't seen him since that unfortunate kissing incident. Not in person, anyway. And once again she was struck by the vast, unconquerable distance between pictures of the man on a computer screen and the reality before her. He stood tall and strong with his hands thrust into the pockets of trousers that had clearly been lovingly crafted to his precise, athletic measurements. His attention was on the red-and-gold sunset happening there before him, fanciful and lovely, taking over the Roman sky as if it was trying to court his favor.

He wasn't even looking at her. And still he somehow stole all the air from the room.

Natalie felt herself flush as she stood in the doorway, a long, deep roll of heat that scared her, it was so intense. Her pulse was a wild fluttering, everywhere. Her temples. Her throat. Her chest.

And deep between her legs, like an invitation she had no right to offer. Not this man. Not ever this man. If he was Prince Charming after all, and she was skeptical on that point, it didn't matter. He certainly wasn't hers.

She must have made some noise through that dry, clutching thing in her throat, because he turned to face her. And that wasn't any better. In her head, she'd downgraded the situation. She'd chalked it up to excusable nerves and understandable adrenaline over switching places with Valentina. That was the only explanation that had made any sense to her. She'd been so sure that when she saw Rodolfo again, all that power and compulsion that had sparked the air around him would be gone.

He would just be another wealthy man for her to handle. Just another problem for her to solve.

But she'd been kidding herself.

If anything, tonight he was even worse, all dressed up in an Italian sunset.

Because you know, something inside her whispered. *You know, now.*

How he tasted. The feel of those lean, hard arms around her. The sensation of that marvelous mouth against hers. She had to fight back the shudder that she feared might bring her to her knees right there on the absurdly lush rug, but she had the sneaking suspicion he knew anyway. There was something about the curve of his mouth as he inclined his head.

"Princess," he murmured.

And God help her, but she felt that everywhere. *Everywhere.* As if he'd used his mouth directly against her heated skin.

"I hear you wish to build our public profile, whatever that is," she said, rather more severely than necessary. She made herself move forward, deeper into the room, when what she wanted to do was turn and run. She seated herself in an armchair because it meant he couldn't sit on either side of her, and his fascinating mouth twitched as if he knew exactly why she'd done it. "King Geoffrey—" She couldn't bring herself to say *my father,* not even if Valentina would have and not even if it was true "—was impressed. That is obviously the only reason I am here."

"Obviously." He threw himself onto the couch opposite her with the same reckless disregard for the lifespan of the average piece of furniture that he'd displayed back in Murin. She told herself that was reflective of his character. "Happily, it makes no difference to me if you are here of your own volition or not, so long as you are here."

"What a lovely sentiment. Every bride dreams of such poetry, I am certain. I am certainly aflutter."

"There is no need for sarcasm." But he sounded amused. "All that is required is that we appear in front of the paparazzi and look as if this wedding is our idea because we are a couple in love like any other, not simply a corporate merger with crowns."

Natalie eyed him, wishing the Roman sunset was not taking quite so long, nor quite so many liberties with Rodolfo's already impossible good looks. He was bathed in gold and russet now, and it made him glow, as if he was the sort of dream maidens might have had in this city thousands of years ago in feverish anticipation of their fierce gods descending from on high.

She tried to cast that fanciful nonsense out of her head, but it was impossible. Especially when he was making no particular effort to hide the hungry look in his dark gaze as he trained it on her. She could feel it shiver through her, lighting her on fire. Making it as hard to sit still as it was to breathe.

"I don't think anyone is going to believe that we were swept away by passion," she managed to say. She folded her hands in her lap the way she'd seen Valentina do in the videos she'd watched of the princess these past few nights, so worried was she that someone would be able to see right through her because she forgot to do some or other princessy thing. Though she thought she gripped her own fingers a bit more tightly than the princess had. "Seeing as how our engagement has been markedly free of any hint of it until now."

"But that's the beauty of it." Rodolfo shrugged. "The story could be that we were promised to each other and were prepared to do our duty, only to trip over the fact we were made for each other all along. Or it could be that it was never arranged at all and that we met, kept everything secret, and are now close enough to our wedding that we can let the world see what our hearts have always known."

"You sound like a tabloid."

"Thank you."

Natalie glared at him. "There is no possible way that could be construed as a compliment."

"I've starred in so many tabloid scandals I could write the headlines myself. And that is what we will do, starting tonight. We will rewrite whatever story is out there and make it into a grand romance. The Playboy Prince and His Perfect Princess, etcetera." That half smile of his deepened. "You get the idea, I'm sure."

"Why would we want to do something so silly? You are going to be a king, not a Hollywood star. Surely a restrained, distant competence is more the package you should be presenting to the world." Natalie aimed her coolest smile at him. "Though I grant you, that might well be another difficult reach."

The sun finally dripped below the city as she spoke, leaving strands of soft pink and deep gold in its wake. But it also made it a lot easier to see Prince Rodolfo's dark, measuring expression. And much too easy to feel the way it clattered through her, making her feel…jittery.

It occurred to her that the way he lounged there, so carelessly, was an optical illusion. Because there wasn't a single thing about him that wasn't hard and taut, as if he not only kept all his brooding power on a tight leash—but could explode into action at any moment. That notion was not exactly soothing.

Neither was his smile. "We will spend the rest of the

night in public, princess. Fawned over by the masses. So perhaps you will do me the favor of telling me here, in private, exactly what it is that has made you imagine I deserve a steady stream of insult. One after the next, without end, since I last saw you."

Natalie felt chastened by that, and hated herself for it in the next instant. Because her own feelings didn't matter here. She shouldn't even have feelings where this man was concerned. Valentina might have given her blessing to whatever happened between her betrothed and Natalie, but that was neither here nor there. Natalie knew better than to let a man like this beguile her. She'd been taught to see through this sort of thing at her mother's knee. It appalled her that his brand of patented princely charm was actually *working*.

"Are you not deserving?" she asked quietly. She made herself meet his dark gaze, though something inside her quailed at it. And possibly died a little bit, too. But she didn't look away. "Are you sure?"

"Am I a vicious man?" Rodolfo's voice was no louder than hers, but there was an intensity to it that made that lick of shame inside of her shimmer, then expand. It made the air in the room seem thin. It made Natalie's heart hit at her ribs, hard enough to bruise. "A brute? A monster in some fashion?"

"Only you can answer that question, I think."

"I am unaware of any instance in which I have deliberately hurt another person, but perhaps you, princess, know something I do not about my own life."

It turned out the Prince was as effective with a slap down as her boss. Natalie sat a bit straighter, but she didn't back down. "Everyone knows a little too much about your life, Your Highness. Entirely too much, one might argue."

"Tabloid fantasies are not life. They are a game. You should know that better than anyone, as we sit here discussing a new story we plan to sell ourselves."

"How would I know this, exactly?" She felt her head tilt to one side in a manner she thought was more her than Valentina. She corrected it. "I do not appear in the tabloids. Not with any frequency, and only on the society pages. Never the front-page stories." Natalie knew. She'd checked.

"You are a paragon, indeed." Rodolfo's voice was low and dark and not remotely complimentary. "But a rather judgmental one, I fear."

Natalie clasped her hands tighter together. "That word has always bothered me. There is nothing wrong with rendering judgment. It's even lauded in some circles. How did *judgmental* become an insult?"

"When rendering judgment became a blood sport," Rodolfo replied, with a soft menace that drew blood on its own.

But Natalie couldn't stop to catalog the wounds it left behind, all over her body, or she was afraid she'd simply…collapse.

"It is neither bloody nor sporting to commit yourself to a woman in the eyes of the world and then continue to date others, Your Highness," she said crisply. "It is simply unsavory. Perhaps childish. And certainly dishonorable. I think you'll find that there are very few women on the planet who will judge that behavior favorably."

Rodolfo inclined his head, though she had the sense his jaw was tighter than it had been. "Fair enough. I will say in my defense that you never seemed to care one way or the other what I did, much less with whom, before last week. We talked about it at length and you said nothing. Not one word."

Valentina had said he talked at her, defending himself—hadn't she? Natalie couldn't remember. But she also wasn't here to poke holes in Valentina's story. It didn't matter if it was true. It mattered that she'd felt it, and Natalie could do something to help fix it. Or try, anyway.

"You're right, of course," she said softly, keeping her gaze trained to his. "It's my fault for not foreseeing that your word was not your bond and your vows were meaningless. My deepest apologies. I'll be certain to keep all of that in mind on our wedding day."

He didn't appear to move, and yet suddenly Natalie couldn't, as surely as if he'd reached out and wrapped her in his tight grip. His dark gaze seemed to pin her to her chair, intent and hard.

"I've tasted you," he reminded her, as if she could forget that for an instant. As if she hadn't dreamed about exactly that, night after night, waking up with his taste on her tongue and a deep, restless ache between her legs. "I know you want me, yet you fight me. Is it necessary to you that I become the villain? Does that make it easier?"

Natalie couldn't breathe. Her heart felt as if it might rip its way out of her chest all on its own, and she still couldn't tear her gaze away from his. There was that hunger, yes, but also a kind of *certainty* that made her feel…liquid.

"Because it is not necessary to insult me to get my attention, princess," Rodolfo continued in the same intense way. "You have it. And you need not question my fidelity. I will touch no other but you, if that is what you require. Does this satisfy you? Can we step away from the bloodlust, do you think?"

What that almost offhanded promise did was make

Natalie feel as if she was nothing but a puppet and he was pulling all her strings, all without laying a single finger upon her. And what sent an arrow of shame and delight spiraling through her was that she couldn't tell if she was properly horrified by that notion, or...not.

"Don't be ridiculous," was the best she could manage.

"You only confirm my suspicions," he told her then, and she knew she wasn't imagining the satisfaction that laced his dark tone. "It is not who I might or might not have dated over the past few months that so disturbs you. I do not doubt that is a factor, but it is not the whole picture. Will you tell me what is? Or will I be forced to guess?"

And she knew, somehow, that his guesses would involve his hands on her once more and God help her, she didn't know what might happen if he touched her again. She didn't know what she might do. Or not do.

Who she might betray, or how badly.

She stood then, moving to put the chair between them, aware of the way her magnificent gown swayed and danced as if it had a mind of its own. And of the way Rodolfo watched her do it, that hard-lit amusement in his dark eyes, as if she were acting precisely as he'd expected she would.

As if he was a rather oversize cat toying with his next meal and was in absolutely no doubt as to how this would all end.

Though she didn't really care to imagine him treating her like his dinner. Or, more precisely, she refused to allow herself to imagine it, no matter how her pulse rocketed through her veins.

"My life is about order," she said, and she realized as she spoke that she wasn't playing her prescribed role. That the words were pouring out of a part of her she hadn't even known was there inside of her. "I have duties, responsibilities, and I handle them all. I *like* to handle them. I like knowing that I'm equal to any task that's put in front of me, and then proving it. Especially when no one thinks I can."

"And you are duly celebrated for your sense of duty throughout the great houses of Europe." Rodolfo inclined his head. "I salute you."

"I can't tell if you're mocking me or not, but I don't require celebration," she threw back at him. "It's not about that. It's about the accomplishment. It's about putting an order to things no matter how messy they get."

"Valentina..."

Natalie was glad he said that name. It reminded her who she was—and who she wasn't. It allowed her to focus through all the clamor and spin inside of her.

"But your life is chaos," she said, low and fierce. "As far as I can tell, it always has been. I think you must like it that way, as you have been careening from one death wish to another since your brother—"

"Careful."

He looked different then, furious and something like thrown, but she only lifted her chin and told herself to ignore it. Because the pain of an international playboy had nothing to do with her. Prince Charming was the villain in all the stories her mother had told her, never the hero. And the brother he'd lost when he was fifteen was a means to psychoanalyze this man, not humanize him. She told herself that again and again. And then she forged on.

"He died, Rodolfo. You lived." He hissed in a breath as if she'd struck him, but Natalie didn't stop. "And yet your entire adult life appears to be a calculated attempt to change that. You and I have absolutely nothing in common."

Rodolfo stood. The glittering emotion she'd seen grip him a moment ago was in his dark gaze, ferocious and focused, but he was otherwise wiped clean. She would have been impressed if she'd been able to breathe.

"My brother's death was an unfortunate tragedy." But he sounded something like hollow. As if he was reciting a speech he'd learned by rote a long time ago. His gaze remained irate and focused on her. "I never intended to fill his shoes and, in fact, make no attempt to do so. I like extreme sports, that is all. It isn't a death wish. I am neither suicidal nor reckless."

He might as well have been issuing his own press release.

"If you die while leaping out of helicopters to get to the freshest ski slope in the world, the way you famously do week after week in winter, you will not only break your neck and likely die, you will leave your country in chaos," Natalie said quietly. His gaze intensified, but she didn't look away. "It all comes back to chaos, Your Highness. And that's not me."

She expected him to rage at her. To argue. She expected that dark thing in him to take him over, and she braced herself for it. If she was honest, she was waiting for him to reach out and his put his hands on her again the way he had the last time. She was waiting for his kiss as surely as if he'd cast a spell and that was her only hope of breaking it—

It was astonishing, really, how much of a fool she was when it counted.

But Rodolfo's hard, beguiling mouth only curved as if there wasn't a world of seething darkness in his eyes, and somehow that sent heat spiraling all the way through her.

"Maybe it should be, princess," he said softly, so softly, as if he was seducing her where he stood. As if he was the spell and there was no breaking it, not when he was looking at her like that, as if no one else existed in all the world. "Maybe a little chaos is exactly what you need."

CHAPTER SIX

THE CHARITY GALA took place in a refurbished ancient villa, blazing with light and understated wealth and dripping with all manner of international celebrities like another layer of decoration. Icons from the epic films of Bollywood mingled with lauded stars of the stages of the West End and rubbed shoulders with a wide selection of Europe's magnificently blooded aristocrats, all doing what they did best. They graced the red carpet as if they found nothing more delightful, smiling into cameras and posing for photographs while giving lip service to the serious charity cause du jour.

Rodolfo escorted his mouthy, surprising princess down the gauntlet of the baying paparazzi, smiling broadly as the press went mad at the sight of them, just as he'd suspected they would.

"I told you," he murmured, leaning down to put his mouth near her ear. As much to sell the story of their great romance as to take pleasure in the way she shivered, then stiffened as if she was trying to hide it from him. Who could have imagined that his distant betrothed was so exquisitely sensitive? He couldn't wait to find out where else she was this tender. This sweet. "They want nothing more than to imagine us wildly and madly in love."

"A pity my imagination is not quite so vivid," she replied testily, though she did it through a smile that perhaps only he could tell was not entirely serene.

But the grin on Rodolfo's face as they made their way slowly through the wall of flashing cameras and shouting reporters wasn't feigned in the least.

"You didn't mention which charity this gala benefits," the princess said crisply as they followed the well-heeled crowd inside the villa, past dramatic tapestries billowing in the slight breeze and a grand pageant of colored lights in the many fountains along the way.

"Something critically important, I am sure," he replied, and his grin only deepened when she slid a reproving look at him. "Surely they are all important, princess. In the long run, does it matter which one this is?"

"Not to you, clearly," she murmured, nodding regally at yet another photographer. "I am sure your carelessness—excuse me, I mean thoughtfulness—is much appreciated by all the charities around who benefit from your random approach."

Rodolfo resolved to take her out in public every night, to every charity event he could find in Europe, whether he'd heard of its cause or not. Not only because she was stunning and he liked looking at her, though that helped. The blazing lights caught the red in her hair and made it shimmer. The gray dress she wore hugged her figure before falling in soft waves to the floor. She was a vision, and better than all of that, out here in the glare of too many spotlights she could not keep chairs between them to ward him off. He liked the heat of her arm through his. He liked her body beside his, lithe and slender as if she'd been crafted to fit him. He liked the faint scent of her, a touch of something French and something sweet besides, and below it, the simplicity of that soap she used.

There wasn't much he didn't like about this woman, if he was honest, not even her intriguing puritan streak. Or her habit of poking at him the way no one else had ever dared, not even his disapproving father, who preferred to express his endless disappointment with far less sharpness and mockery. No one else ever threw Felipe in his face and if they'd ever tried to do such a remarkably stupid thing, it certainly wouldn't have been to psychoanalyze him. Much less find him wanting.

He took care of that all on his own, no doubt. And the fact that his own father found his second son so much more lacking than his first was common knowledge and obvious to all. No need to underscore it.

Rodolfo supposed it was telling that as little as he cared to have that conversation, he hadn't minded that Valentina had tried. Or he didn't mind too much. He didn't know where his deferential, disappearing princess had gone, the one who had hidden in plain sight when there'd been no one in the room but the two of them, but he liked this one much better.

The hardest part of his body agreed. Enthusiastically. And it didn't much care that they were out in public.

But there was another gauntlet to run inside the villa. One Rodolfo should perhaps have anticipated.

"I take it that you did not make proclamations about your sudden onset of fidelity to your many admirers," Valentina said dryly after they were stopped for the fifth time in as many steps by yet another woman who barely glanced at the princess and then all but melted all over Rodolfo. Right there in front of her.

For the first time in his entire adult life, Rodolfo found he was faintly embarrassed by his own prowess with the fairer sex.

"It is not the sort of thing one typically announces,"

he pointed out, while attempting to cling to his dignity, despite the number of slinky women circling him with that same avid look in their eyes. "It has the whiff of desperation about it, does it not?

"Of course, generally speaking, becoming engaged *is* the announcement." What was wrong with him, that he found her tartness so appealing? Especially when not a bit of it showed on her lovely, serene face? How had he spent all these months failing to notice how appealing she was? He'd puzzled it over for days and still couldn't understand it. "I can see the confusion in your case, given your exploits these last months."

"Yet here I am," he pointed out, slanting a look down at her, amused despite himself. "At your side. Exuding fidelity."

"That is not precisely what you exude," she said under her breath, because naturally she couldn't let any opportunity pass to dig at him, and then they were swept into the receiving line.

It felt like a great many hours later when they finally made it into the actual gala itself. A band played on a raised dais while glittering people outshone the blazing chandeliers above them. Europe's finest and fanciest stood in these rooms, and he'd estimate that almost all of them had their eyes fixed on the spectacle of Prince Rodolfo and Princess Valentina actually out and about together for once—without a single one of their royal relatives in sight as the obvious puppeteers of what had been hailed everywhere as an entirely cold-blooded marriage of royal convenience.

But their presence here had already done exactly what Rodolfo had hoped it would. He could see it in the faces of the people around them. He'd felt it on the red carpet outside, surrounded by paparazzi nearly incandescent with joy over the pictures they'd be able to sell of the two of them. He could already read the accompanying headlines.

Do the Daredevil Prince and the Dutiful Princess Actually Like *Each Other After All?*

He could feel the entire grand ballroom of the villa seem to swell with the force of all that speculation and avid interest.

And Rodolfo made a command decision. They could do another round of the social niceties that would cement the story he wanted to sell even further, assuming he wasn't deluged by more of the sort of women who were happy to ignore his fiancée as she stood beside him. Or he could do what he really wanted to do, which was get his hands on Valentina right here in public, where she would have no choice but to allow it.

This was what he was reduced to. On some level, he felt the requisite shame. Or some small shadow of it, if he was honest.

Because it still wasn't much of a contest.

"Let's dance, shall we?" he asked, but he was already moving toward the dance floor in the vast, sparkling ballroom that seemed to swirl around him as he spoke. His proper, perfect princess would have to yank her arm out of his grip with some force, creating a scene, if she wanted to stop him.

He was sure he could see steam come off her as she realized that for herself, then didn't do it. Mutinously, if that defiant angle of her pointed chin was any clue.

"I don't dance," she informed him coolly as he stopped and turned to face her. He dropped her arm but stood a little too close to her, so the swishing skirt of her long dress brushed against his legs. It made her have to tip her head back to meet his gaze. And he was well aware it created the look of an intimacy between them. It suggested all kinds of closeness, just as he wanted it to do.

As much to tantalize the crowd as to tempt her.

"Are you certain?" he asked idly.

"Of course I'm certain."

Other guests waltzed around them, pretending not to stare as they stood still in the center of the dance floor as if they were having an intense discussion. Possibly an argument. Inviting gossip and rumor with every moment they failed to move. But Rodolfo forgot about all the eyes trained on them in the next breath. He gazed down at his princess, watching as the strangest expression moved over her face. Had she been anyone else, he would have called it panic.

"Then I fear I must remind you that you have been dancing since almost before you could walk," he replied, trying to keep his voice mild and a little bit lazy, as if that could hide the intensity of his need to touch her. As if every moment he did not was killing him. He felt as if it was.

He reached over and took her hands in his, almost losing his cool when he felt that simple touch everywhere—from his fingers to his feet and deep in his aching sex—far more potent than whole weekends he could hardly recall with women he wouldn't remember if they walked up and introduced themselves right now. What the hell was she doing to him? But he ordered himself to pull it together.

"There is that iconic portrait of you dancing with your father at some or other royal affair. It was the darling of the fawning press for years. You are standing on his shoes while the King of Murin dances for the both of you." Rodolfo made himself smile, as if the odd intensity that gripped him was nothing but a passing thing. The work of a moment, here and then gone in the swirl of the stately dance all around them. "I believe you were six."

"Six," she repeated. He thought she said it oddly, but then she seemed to recollect herself. He saw her blink, then focus on him again. "You misunderstand me. I meant that I don't dance with *you*. By which I mean, I won't."

"It pains me to tell you that, sadly, you are wrong yet again." He smiled at her, then indulged himself—and infuriated her—by reaching out to tug on one of the artful pieces of hair that had been left free of the complicated chignon she wore tonight. He tucked it behind her ear, marveling that so small a touch should echo inside of him the way it did then, sensation chasing sensation, as if all these months of not quite seeing her in front of him had been an exercise in restraint instead of an oddity he couldn't explain to his satisfaction. And this was his reward. "You will dance with me at our wedding, in front of the entire world. And no doubt at a great many affairs of state thereafter. It is unavoidable, I am afraid."

She started to frown, then caught herself. He saw the way she fought it back, and he still couldn't understand why it delighted him on a deep, visceral level. His glass princess, turned flesh and blood and brought to life right there before him. He could see the way her lips trembled, very slightly, and he knew somehow that it was the same mad fire that blazed in him, brighter by the moment.

It made him want nothing more than to taste her here and now, the crowd and royal protocol be damned.

"You should know that I make it a policy to step on the feet of all the men I dance with, as homage to that iconic photograph." Her smile was razor sharp and her eyes had gone cool again, but he could still see that soft little tremor that made her mouth too soft. Too vulnerable.

He could still see the truth she clearly wanted to hide, and no matter that he couldn't name it. "Prepare yourself."

"All you need to do is follow my lead, princess," Rodolfo said then, low and perhaps a bit too dark, and he didn't entirely mean the words to take on an added resonance as he said them. But he smiled when she pulled in a sharp little breath, as if she was imagining all the places he could lead her, just as he was. In vivid detail. "It will be easy and natural. There will be no trodding upon feet. Simply surrender—" and his voice dipped a bit at that, getting rough in direct correlation to that dark, needy thing in her gaze "—and I will take care of you. I promise."

Rodolfo wasn't talking about dancing—or he wasn't only talking about a very public waltz—but that would do. He studied Princess Valentina as she stood there before him, taut and very nearly quivering with the same dark need that made him want to behave like a caveman instead of a prince. He wanted to throw her over his shoulder and carry her off into the night. He wanted to throw her down on the floor where they stood and get his mouth on every part of her, as if he could taste what it was that had changed in her, cracking her open to let the fascinating creature inside come out and making her irresistible seemingly overnight.

He settled for extending his hand, very formally and in full view of half of Europe, even throwing in a polite bow that, as someone more or less equal in rank to her, could only be construed as a magnanimous, even romantic gesture. Then he stood still in the center of the dance floor and waited for her to take it.

Her green eyes looked a little bit too wide and still far too dark with all the same simmering need and deep hunger he knew burned bright in him. She looked more beautiful than he'd ever seen her before, but then, he was closer than he'd ever been. He couldn't count those hot, desperate moments in the palace reception room where he'd tasted her with all the finesse of an untried adolescent, because he'd been too out of control—and out of his mind—to enjoy it.

This was different. This—tonight—he had every intention of savoring.

But he wasn't sure he would ever savor anything more than when she lifted that chin of hers, faintly pointed and filled with a defiance her vulnerable mouth contradicted, and placed her hand in his.

Rodolfo felt that everywhere, as potent as if she'd knelt down before him and declared him victor of this dark and delicious little war of theirs.

He pulled her a step closer with his right hand, then slid his left around to firmly clasp the back she'd left bared in the lovely dress she wore that poured over her slender figure like rain, and he heard her hiss in a breath. He could feel the heat of her like a furnace beneath his palm. He wanted to bend close and get his mouth on her more than he could remember wanting anything.

But he refrained. Somehow, he held himself in check, when he was a man who usually did the exact opposite. For fun.

"Put your hand on my shoulder," he told her, and he didn't sound urbane or witty or anything like lazy. Not anymore. "Have you truly forgotten how to perform a simple waltz, princess? I am delighted to discover how deeply I affect you."

He felt the hard breath she took, as if she was bracing herself. And he realized with a little shock that he had no idea what she would do. It was as likely that she'd yank herself out of his arms and storm away as it was that she'd melt into him. He had no idea—and he couldn't deny he felt that like a long, slow lick against the hardest part of him.

She was as unpredictable as one of his many adventures. He had the odd thought that he could spend a lifetime trying to unravel her mysteries, one after the next, and who knew if he'd ever manage it? It astonished him that he wanted to try. That for the first time since their engagement last fall, he wanted their wedding day to hurry up and arrive. And better than that, their wedding night. And all the nights thereafter, all those adventures lined up and waiting for him, packed into her lush form and those fathomless green eyes.

He could hardly wait.

And it felt as if ten years had passed when, with her wary gaze trained on him as if he couldn't be trusted not to harm her somehow, Valentina put her hand where it belonged.

"Thank you, princess." He curled his fingers around hers a little tighter than necessary for the sheer pleasure of it and smiled when the hand she'd finally placed on his shoulder dug into him, as if in reaction. "You made that into quite a little bit of theater. When stories emerge tomorrow about the great row we had in the middle of a dance floor, you will have no one to blame but yourself."

"I never do," she replied coolly, but that wariness receded from her green gaze. Her chin tipped up higher and Rodolfo counted it as a win. "It's called taking responsibility for myself, which is another way of acknowledging that I'm an adult. You should try it sometime."

"Impossible," he said, gripping her hand tighter in his and smiling for all those watching eyes. And because her defiance made him want to smile, which was far more dangerous. And exciting. "I am far too busy leaping out of planes in a vain attempt to cheat death. Or court death. Which is it again? I can't recall which accusation you leveled at me, much less when."

And before she could enlighten him, he started to move.

She was stiff in his arms, which he assumed was another form of protest. Rodolfo ignored it, sweeping her around the room and leading her through the steps she appeared to be pretending not to know, just as he'd promised he would.

"You cannot trip me up, princess," he told her when she relaxed just slightly in his hold and gave herself over to his lead. "I was raised to believe a man can only call himself a man when he knows how to dance well, shoot with unerring accuracy and argue his position without either raising his voice or reducing himself to wild, un-justified attacks on his opponent."

"Well," she said, and she sounded breathless, which he felt in every part of his body like an ache, "you obvi-ously took that last part to heart."

"I am also an excellent shot, thank you for asking."

"Funny, the tabloids failed to report that. Unless you're speaking in innuendo? In which case, I must apol-ogize, but I don't speak twelve-year-old boy."

He let out a laugh that had the heads nearest them turning, because no one was ever so giddy when on dis-play like this, especially not him. Rodolfo was infamous because he called attention to himself in other ways, but never like this. Never in situations like these, all stuffy protocol and too many spectators. Never with anything that might be confused for *joy*.

"You must be feeling better if you're this snappish, princess."

"I wasn't feeling bad. Unless you count the usual dismay anyone might feel at being bullied onto a dance floor in the company of a rather alarming man who dances very much like he flings himself off the sides of mountains."

"With a fierce and provocative elegance? The envy of all who witness it?"

"With astonishing recklessness and a total lack of regard for anyone around you. Much in the same vein as your entire life, Your Highness, if the reports are true." She lifted one shoulder, then let it drop in as sophisticated and dismissive a shrug as he'd ever seen. "Or even just a little bit true, for that matter."

"And if you imagine that was bullying, princess, you have led a very charmed life, indeed. Even for a member of a royal house dating back to, oh, the start of recorded history or thereabouts, surrounded by wealth and ease at every turn."

"What do you want, Rodolfo?" she asked then, and that near-playful note he was sure he'd heard in her voice was gone. Her expression was grave. As if she was yet another stranger, this one different than before. "I don't believe that this marriage is anything you would have chosen, if given the opportunity. I can't imagine why you're suddenly pretending otherwise and proclaiming your commitment to fidelity in random hotel suites. What I do understand is that we're both prepared to do our duty and have been from the start. And I support that, but there's nothing wrong with maintaining a civil, respectful distance while we go about it."

"I would have agreed with you in every respect," he said, and he should have been worried about that fervent intensity in his tone. He could feel the flames of it licking through him, changing him, making him something other than the man he'd thought he was all this time.

Something that should have set off alarms in every part of him, yet didn't. "But that was before you walked into your father's reception rooms and rather than blending into the furniture the way you usually did, opted to attack me instead."

"Of course." And Rodolfo had the strangest sensation that she was studying him as if he was a museum exhibit, not her fiancé. Hardly even a man—which should have chastened him. Instead, it made him harder. "I should have realized that to a man like you, with an outsize ego far more vast and unconquerable than any of the mountain peaks you've summited in your desperate quest for meaning, any questioning of any kind is perceived as an attack."

"You are missing the point, I think," Rodolfo said, making no attempt to hide either the laughter in his voice or the hunger in his gaze, not put off by her character assassinations at all. Quite the opposite. "Attack me all you like. It doesn't shame me in the least. Surely you must be aware that *shame* is not the primary response I have to you, princess. It is not even close."

She didn't ask him what he felt instead, but he saw a betraying, bright flush move over her face. And he knew she was perfectly aware of the things that moved in him, sensation and need, hunger and that edgy passion—and more, that she felt it, too.

Perhaps that was why, when they danced past a set of huge, floor-to-ceiling glass doors that led out to a wide terrace for the third time, he led her out into the night instead of deeper into the ballroom.

"Where are we going?" she asked.

Rodolfo thought it was meant to be a demand—a rebuke, even—but her cheeks were too red. Her eyes were too bright. And most telling, she made no attempt to tug her hand from his, much less lecture him any further about chaos and order and who was on which side of that divide.

"Nothing could be less chaotic than a walk on a terrace in full view of so many people," he pointed out, not bothering to look behind him at the party they'd left in full swing. He had no doubt they were all staring after him, the way they always did, and with more intensity than ever because he was with Valentina. "Unless you'd like it to be?"

"Certainly not. Some people admire the mountain from afar, Your Highness. They are perfectly happy doing so, and feel no need whatsoever to throw themselves off it or climb up it or attempt to ski down the back of it."

"Ah, but some people do not live, princess. They merely exist."

"Risking death is not living. It's nihilistic. And in your case, abominably selfish."

"Perhaps." He held her hand tighter in his. "But I would not underestimate the power of a little bout of selfishness, if I were you. Indulge yourself, princess. Just for an evening. What's the worst that could happen?"

"I shudder to think," she retorted, but there was no heat in it.

Rodolfo pretended not to hear the catch in her throat. But he smiled. He liberated two glasses of something exquisite from a passing servant with a tray, he pulled his fascinating princess closer to his side and then he led her deeper into the dark.

CHAPTER SEVEN

MAYBE IT WAS the music. Maybe it was the whirl of so many gleaming, glorious people.

Natalie had the suspicion that really, it was Rodolfo.

But no matter what it was, no matter why—she forgot.

That she wasn't really a princess, or if she was, she was the discarded kind. The lost and never-meant-to-be-found sort that had only been located by accident in a bathroom outside London.

She forgot that the dress wasn't hers, the ball inside the pretty old building wasn't a magical spectacle put on just for her and, most of all, that the man at her side—gripping her hand as he led her into temptation—wasn't ever going to be hers, no matter what.

He'd danced with her. It was as simple and as complicated as that.

Natalie had never thought of herself as beautiful before she'd seen herself in that mirror tonight, but it was more than that. She couldn't remember the last time anyone had treated her like a *woman*. Much less a desirable one. Not a pawn in whatever game the man in question might have been playing with her employer, which had only ever led to her wearing her hair in severe ponytails and then donning those clear glasses to keep the attention off her. Not an assistant. Not the person responsible for every little detail of every little thing and therefore the first one to be upbraided when something went wrong.

Rodolfo looked at her as if she was no more and no less than a beautiful woman. He didn't see a list of all the things she could *do* when he gazed at her. He saw only her. A princessed-out, formally made-up version of her, sure. And she couldn't really gloss over the fact he called her by the wrong name because he had every reason to believe she was someone else. Even so, she was the woman he couldn't seem to stop touching, who made his eyes light up with all that too-bright need and hunger.

And it was that, Natalie found, she couldn't resist.

She'd never done a spontaneous thing in her life before she'd switched places with Valentina in that bathroom. Left to her own devices, she thought it was likely she'd never have given her notice at all, no matter how worked up she'd been. And now it seemed she couldn't stop with the spontaneity. Yet somehow Rodolfo's grip on her hand, so strong and sure, made her not mind very much at all. She let this prince, who was far more charming than she wanted to admit to herself, tug her along with him, deeper into the shadows, until they were more in the dark than the light.

He turned to face her then, and he looked something like stern in the darkness. He set the two glasses of sparkling wine down on the nearby balustrade, then straightened again. Slowly. Deliberately, even. Natalie's heart thudded hard against her ribs, but it wasn't from fear. He pulled her hand that he'd been holding high against his chest and held it there, and Natalie couldn't have said why she felt as caught. As gripped tight. Only that she was—and more concerning, had no desire to try to escape it.

If anything, she leaned closer into him, into the shelter of his big body.

"Where did you come from?" he asked, his voice a mere scrape against the night. "What the hell are you doing to me?"

Natalie opened her mouth to answer him. But whatever that dark, driving force had been inside her, urging her to poke back at him and do her best to slap down the only real Prince Charming she'd ever met in the flesh, it was gone. Had she imagined herself some kind of avenging angel here? Flying into another woman's royal fairy tale of a life to do what needed doing, the way she did with everything else? Fighting her mother's battles all these years later and with a completely different man than the one Erica had never explicitly named?

It didn't matter, because that had been before he'd taken her in his arms and guided her around a dance floor, making her feel as if she could dance forever when she'd never danced a waltz before in her life. She had a vague idea of what it entailed, but only because she'd had to locate the best ballroom dancing instructor in London when Achilles Casilieris had abruptly decided he needed a little more polish one year. She'd watched enough of those classes—before Mr. Casilieris had reduced the poor man to tears—to understand the basic principle of a waltz.

But Rodolfo had made her feel as if they were flying.

He looked down at her now, out here in the seductive dark, and it made her tremble deep inside. It made her forget who she was and what she was doing. Her head cleared of everything save him. Rodolfo. The daredevil prince who made her feel as if she was the one catapulting herself out of airplanes every time his dark, hungry gaze caught hers. And held.

He took her bare shoulders in his hands, drawing her closer to him. Making her shiver, deep and long. On some distant level she thought she should push away from him. Remind them both of her boundaries, maybe. But she couldn't seem to remember what those were. Instead she tilted her head back while she drifted closer to his big, rangy body. And then she made everything worse by sliding her hands over the steel wall of his chest, carefully packaged in that gorgeous suit that made him look almost edible. To push him away, she told herself piously.

But she didn't push at him. She didn't even try.

His dark eyes gleamed with a gold she could feel low in her belly, like a fiery caress. "The way you look at me is dangerous, princess."

"I thought you courted danger," she heard herself whisper.

"I do," he murmured. "Believe me, I do."

And then he bent his head and kissed her.

This time, the first brush of his mouth against hers was light. Easy. Electricity sparked and sizzled, and then he did it again, and it wasn't enough. Natalie pressed herself toward him, trying to get more of him. Trying to crawl inside him and throw herself into the storm that roared through her. She went up on her toes to close the remaining distance between them, and her reward was the way he smiled, that dangerous curve of his mouth against hers.

It seemed to wash over her like heat then pool in a blaze of fire, high between her legs. Natalie couldn't keep herself from letting out a moan, needy and insistent.

And obvious. So terribly, blatantly obvious it might as well have been a scream in the dark. She felt Rodolfo turn to stone beneath her palms.

Then he angled his head, took the kiss deeper and wilder and everything went mad.

Rodolfo simply…took her over. He kissed her like he was already a great king and she but one more subject to his rule. His inimitable will. He kissed her as if there had never been any doubt that she was his, in every possible way. His mouth was demanding and hot, intense and carnal, and her whole body thrilled to it. Her hands were fists, gripping his jacket as if she couldn't bear to let go of him, and he only took the kiss deeper, wilder.

She arched against him as he plundered her mouth, taking and taking and taking even more as he bent her over his arm, as if he could never get enough—

Then he stopped, abruptly, muttering a curse against her lips. It seemed to pain him to release her, but he did it, stepping back and maneuvering so he stood between Natalie and what it took her far too long to realize was another group of guests making use of the wide terrace some distance away.

But she couldn't bring herself to care about them. She raised a hand to her lips, aware that her fingers trembled. And far more aware that he was watching her too closely as she did it.

"Why do you look at me as if it is two hundred years ago and I have just stolen your virtue?" he asked softly, his dark eyes searching hers. "Or led you to your ruin with a mere kiss?"

Natalie didn't know what look she wore on her face, but she felt…altered. There was no pretending otherwise. Rodolfo was looking at her the way any man might gaze at the woman he was marrying in less than two months, after kissing her very nearly senseless on the terrace of a romantic Roman villa.

But that was the trouble. No matter what fairy tale

she'd been spinning out in her head, Natalie wasn't that woman.

She was ruined, all right. All the way through.

"I'm not looking at you like that." Her voice hardly sounded like hers. She took a step away from him, coming up against the stone railing. She glanced down at the two glasses of sparkling wine that sat there and considered tossing them back, one after the next, because that might dull the sharp thing that felt a little too much like pain, poking inside of her. Only the fact that it might dull her a little *too* much kept her from it. Things were already bad enough. "I'm not looking at you like anything, I'm sure."

Rodolfo watched her, his eyes too dark to read. "You are looking at me as if you have never been kissed before. Much as that might pander to my ego, which I believe we've agreed is egregiously large already, we both know that isn't true." His mouth curved. "And tell the truth, Valentina. It was not so bad, was it?"

That name slammed into her like a sucker punch. Natalie could hardly breathe through it. She had to grit her teeth to keep from falling over where she stood. How did she keep forgetting?

Because you want to forget, a caustic voice inside her supplied at once.

"I'm not who you think I am," she blurted out then, and surely she wasn't the only one who could hear how ragged she sounded. How distraught.

But Rodolfo only laughed. "You are exactly who I think you are."

"I assure you, I am not. At all."

"It is an odd moment for a philosophical turn, princess," he drawled, and there was something harder about him then. Something more dangerous. Natalie could feel it dance over her skin. "Are any of us who others think we are? Take me, for example. I am certain that every single person at this gala tonight would line up to tell you exactly who I am, and they would be wrong. I am not the tabloid stories they craft about me, pimped out to the highest bidder. My wildest dream is not surviving an adventure or planning a new one, it's taking my rightful place in my father's kingdom. That's all." His admission, stark and raw, hung between them like smoke. She had the strangest notion that he hadn't meant to say anything like that. But in the next instant he looked fierce. Almost forbidding. "We are none of us the roles we play, I am sure."

"Are you claiming you have a secret inner life devoted to your sense of duty? That you are merely misunderstood?" she asked, incredulous.

"Do you take everything at face value, princess?" She told herself she was imagining that almost hurt look on his face. And it was gone when he angled his head toward her. "You cannot really believe you are the only one with an internal life."

"That's not what I meant."

But, of course, she couldn't tell him what she meant. She couldn't explain that she hadn't been feeling the least bit philosophical. Or that she wasn't actually Princess Valentina at all. She certainly couldn't tell this man that she was Natalie Monette—a completely different person.

Though it occurred to her for the first time that even if she came clean right here and now, the likelihood was that he wouldn't believe her. Because who could believe something so fantastical? Would she have believed it herself if it wasn't happening to her right now—if she wasn't standing in the middle of another woman's life?

And messing it up beyond recognition, that same interior voice sniped at her. *Believe that, if nothing else.*

"Do you plan to tell me what, then, you meant?" Rodolfo asked, dark and low and maybe with a hint of asperity. Maybe with more than just a hint. "Or would you prefer it if I guessed?"

The truth hit Natalie then, with enough force that she felt it shake all the way through her. There was only one reason that she wanted to tell him the truth, and it wasn't because she'd suddenly come over all honest and upstanding. She'd switched places with another person—lying about who she was came with the territory. It allowed her to sit there at those excruciatingly proper dinners and try to read into King Geoffrey's facial expressions and his every word without him knowing it, still trying to figure out if she really thought he was her father. And what it would mean to her if he was. Something that would never happen if she'd identified herself. If he'd been on the defensive when he met her.

She didn't want to tell Rodolfo the truth because she had a burning desire for him to know who she was. Or she did want that, of course, but it wasn't first and foremost.

It made her stomach twist to admit it, but it was true: what she wanted was him. This. She wanted what was happening between them to be real and then, when it was, she wanted to keep him.

He is another woman's fiancé, she threw at herself in some kind of despair.

Natalie thought she'd never hated herself more than she did at that moment, because she simply couldn't seem to govern herself accordingly.

"I need to leave," she told him, and she didn't care if she sounded rude. Harsh and abrupt. She needed to remove herself from him—from all that temptation he wore entirely too easily, like another bespoke suit—before she made this all worse. Much, much worse. In ways she could imagine all too vividly. "Now."

"Princess, please. Do not run off into the night. I will only have to chase you." He moved toward her and Natalie didn't have the will to step away. To ward him off. To do what she should. And she compounded it by doing absolutely nothing when he fit his hand to her cheek and held it there. His dark eyes gleamed. "Tell me."

He was so big it made her heart hurt. The dark Roman night did nothing to obscure how beautiful he was, and she could taste him now. A kind of rich, addicting honey on her tongue. She thought that alone might make her shatter into pieces. This breath, or the next. She thought it might be the end of her.

"I need to go," she whispered, aware that her hands were in useless, desperate fists at her sides.

She wanted to punch him, she told herself, but Natalie knew that was a lie. The sad truth here was she was looking for any excuse to put her hands on him again. And she knew exactly what kind of person that made her.

And even so, she found herself leaning into that palm at her cheek.

"I never wanted what our parents had," Rodolfo told her then, his voice low and commanding, somehow, against the mild night air. "A dance in front of the cameras and nothing but duty and gritted teeth in private. I promised myself that I would marry for the right reasons. But then it seemed that what I would get instead was a cold shoulder and a polite smile. I told myself it was more than some people in my position could claim. I thought I had made my peace with it."

Natalie found she couldn't speak. As if there was a hand around her throat, gripping her much too tight.

Rodolfo didn't move any closer, though it was as if he shut out the rest of the world. There was nothing but that near-smile on his face, that hint of light in his gaze. There was nothing but the two of them and the lie of who she was tonight, but the longer he looked at her like that, the harder it was to remember that he wasn't really hers. That he could never be hers. That none of the things he was saying to her were truly for her at all.

"Rodolfo…" she managed to say. Confession or capitulation, she couldn't tell.

"I like my name in your mouth, princess," he told her, sending heat dancing all over her, until it pooled low and hot in her belly. "And I like this. There is no reason at all we cannot take some pleasure in our solemn duty to our countries. Think of all the dreadfully tedious affairs we will enjoy a great deal more when there is this to brighten up the monotony."

His head lowered to hers again, and she wanted nothing more than to lose herself in him. In the pleasure he spoke of. In his devastating kiss, all over again.

But somehow, Natalie managed to recollect herself in the instant before his lips touched hers. She yanked herself out of his grip and stepped away from him, the night feeling cool around her now that she wasn't so close to the heat that seemed to come off him in waves.

"I'm sorry." She couldn't seem to help herself. But she kept her gaze trained on the ground, because looking at him was fraught with peril. Natalie was terribly afraid it would end only one way. "I shouldn't have…" She trailed off, helplessly. "I need to go back to my hotel."

"And do what?" he asked, and something in his voice made her stand straighter. Some kind of foreboding, perhaps. When she looked up at him, Rodolfo's gaze had gone dark again, his mouth stern and hard. "Switch personalities yet again?"

Valentina jerked as if he'd slapped her, and if he'd been a little more in control of himself, Rodolfo might have felt guilty about that.

Maybe he already did, if he was entirely honest, but he couldn't do anything about it. He couldn't reach out and put his hands on her the way he wanted to do. He couldn't do a goddamned thing when she refused to tell him what was going on.

The princess looked genuinely distraught at the thought of kissing him again. At the thought that this marriage they'd been ordered into for the good of their kingdoms could be anything but a necessary, dutiful undertaking to be suffered through for the rest of their lives.

Rodolfo didn't understand any of this. Didn't she realize that this crazy chemistry that had blazed to life out of nowhere was a blessing? The saving grace of what was otherwise nothing more than a royal chore dressed up as a photo opportunity?

Clearly she did not, because she was staring at him with something he couldn't quite read making her green eyes dark. Her lovely cheeks looked pale. She looked shaken—though that made no sense.

"What do you mean by that?" she demanded, though her voice sounded as thrown as the rest of her looked. "I have the one personality, that's all. This might come as a shock to you, I realize, but many women actually have *layers*. Many humans, in fact."

Rodolfo wanted to be soothing. He did. He prided himself on never giving in to his temper. On maintaining his cool under any and all extreme circumstances. There was no reason he couldn't calm this maddening woman, whether he understood what was going on here or not.

"Are you unwell?" he asked instead. And not particularly nicely.

"I am feeling more unwell by the moment," she threw back at him, stiff and cool. "As I told you, I need to leave."

He reached over and hooked a hand around her elbow when she made as if to turn, holding her there where she stood. Keeping her with him. And the caveman in him didn't care whether she liked it or not.

"Let go of me," she snapped at him. But she didn't pull her elbow from his grasp.

Rodolfo smiled. It was a lazy, edgy sort of smile, and he watched the color rush back into her face.

"No."

She stiffened, but she still didn't pull away. "What do you mean, *no*?"

"I mean that I have no intention of releasing you until you tell me why you blow so hot and cold, princess. And I do not much care if it takes all night. It is almost as if you are two women—"

Her green eyes flashed. "That or I find you largely unappealing."

"Until, of course, you do not find me unappealing in the least. Then you melt all over me."

Her cheeks pinkened further. "I find it as confusing as you do. Best not to encourage it, I think."

He savored the feel of her silky skin beneath his palm. "Ah, but you see, I am not confused in the least."

"If you do not let go of me, right now, I will scream," she told him.

He only smiled at her. "Go ahead. You have my blessing." He waited, and cocked an eyebrow when she only glared at him. "I thought you were about to scream down the villa, were you not? Or was that another metaphor?"

She took what looked like a shaky breath, but she didn't say anything. And she still didn't pull her elbow away. Rodolfo moved a little closer, so he could bend and get his face near hers.

"Tell me what game this is," he murmured, close to her ear. She jumped, and he expected her to pull free of him, but she didn't. She settled where she stood. He could feel her breathe. He could feel the way her pulse pounded through her. He could smell her excitement in the heated space between them, and he could feel the tension in her, too. "I am more than adept at games, I promise you. Just tell me what we're playing."

"This is no game." But her voice sounded a little broken. Just a little, but it was enough.

"When I met you, there was none of this fire," he reminded her, as impossible as that was to imagine now. "We sat through that extraordinarily painful meal—"

She tipped her head back so she could look him dead in the eye. "I loved every moment of it."

"You did not. You sat like a statue and smiled with the deepest insincerity. And then afterward, I thought you might have nodded off during my proposal."

"I was riveted." She waved the hand that wasn't trapped between them. "Your Royal Highness is all that is charming and so on. It was the high point of my life, etcetera, etcetera."

"You thanked me in your usual efficient manner, yes. But riveted?" He slid his hand down her forearm, abandoning his grip on her elbow so he could take her hand in his. Then he played with the great stone she wore on her finger that had once belonged to his grandmother and a host of Tisselian queens before her. He tugged it this way, then that. "You were anything but that, princess. You used to look through me when I spoke to you, as if I was a ghost. I could not tell if I was or you were. I imagined that I would beget my heirs on a phantom."

Something moved through her then, some electrical current that made that vulnerable mouth of hers tremble again, and she tugged her hand from his as if she'd suddenly been scalded. And yet Rodolfo felt as if he might have been, too.

"I'm not sure what the appropriate response is when a man one has agreed to marry actually sits there and explains his commitment to ongoing infidelity, as if his daily exploits in the papers were not enough of a clue. Perhaps you should count yourself lucky that all I did was look through you."

"Imagine my surprise that you noticed what I did, when you barely appeared to notice me."

"Is that what you need, Rodolfo?" she demanded, and this time, when she stepped back and completely away from him, he let her go. It seemed to startle her, and she pulled in a sharp breath as if to steady herself. "To be noticed? It may shock you to learn that the entire world already knows that, after having witnessed all your attention-seeking theatrics and escapades. That is not actually an announcement you need to make."

Rodolfo didn't exactly thrill to the way she said that, veering a bit too close to the sorts of things his father was known to hurl at him. But he admired the spirit in her while she said it. He ordered himself to concentrate on that.

"And now you are once again *this* Valentina," he replied, his voice low. "The one who dares say things to my face others would be afraid to whisper behind my back. Bold. Alluring. Who are you and what have you done with my dutiful ghost?"

She all but flinched at that and then she let out a breath that sounded a little too much like a sob. But before he could question that, she clearly swallowed it down. She lifted her chin and glared at him with nothing but sheer challenge in her eyes, and he thought he must have imagined the vulnerability in that sound she'd made. The utter loneliness.

"This Valentina will disappear soon enough, never fear," she assured him, a strange note in her voice. "We can practice that right now. I'm leaving."

But Rodolfo had no intention of letting her go. This time when she turned on her heel and walked away from him, he followed.

CHAPTER EIGHT

RODOLFO CAUGHT UP to her quickly with his long, easily athletic stride, and then refused to leave her side. He stayed too close and put his hand at the small of her back, guiding her through the splendid, sparkling crowd whether she wanted his aid or not. Natalie told herself she most emphatically did not, but just as she hadn't pulled away from him out on the terrace despite her threats that she might scream, she didn't yank herself out of his grasp now, either. She assured herself she was only thinking about what would be best for the real princess, that she was only avoiding the barest hint of scandal—but the truth was like a brand sunk deep in her belly.

She wanted him to touch her. She liked it when he did.

You are a terrible person, she told herself severely.

Natalie wanted to hate him for that, too. She told herself that of course she did, but that slick heat between her legs and the flush that she couldn't quite seem to cool let her know exactly how much of a liar she was. With every step and each shifting bit of pressure his hand exerted against her back.

He summoned their driver with a quick call, and then walked with her all the way back down the red carpet, smiling with his usual careless charm at all the paparazzi who shrieked out his name. Very much as if he enjoyed all those flashing lights and impertinent questions.

It was Natalie who wanted to curl up into a ball and hide somewhere. Natalie who wasn't used to this kind of attention—not directed at her, anyway. She'd fended off the press for Mr. Casilieris as part of her job, but she'd never been its focus before, and she discovered she really, truly didn't like it. It felt like salt on her skin. Stinging and gritty. But she didn't have the luxury of fading off into the background to catch her breath in the shadows, because she wasn't Natalie right now. She was Princess Valentina, who'd grown up with this sort of noisy spectacle everywhere she went. Who'd danced on her doting father's shoes when she was small and had cut her teeth on spotlights of all shapes and sizes and hell, for all she knew, enjoyed every moment of it the way Rodolfo seemed to.

She was Princess Valentina tonight, and a princess should have managed to smile more easily. Natalie tried her best, but by the time Rodolfo handed her into the gleaming black SUV that waited for them at the end of the press gauntlet, she thought her teeth might crack from the effort of holding her perhaps not so serene smile in place.

"I don't need your help," she told him, but it was too late. His hand was on her arm again as she clambered inside and then he was climbing in after her, forcing her to throw herself across the passenger seat or risk having him...all over her.

She hated that she had to remind herself—sternly—why that would be a bad idea.

"Would you prefer it if I had drop-kicked you into the vehicle?" he asked, still smiling as he settled himself beside her.

There was a gleam in his dark gaze that let her know he was fully aware of the way she was clinging to the far door as if it might save her. From him. As ever, he appeared not to notice the confines or restrictions of whatever he happened to be sitting on. In this case, he sprawled out in the backseat of the SUV, taking up more than his fair share of the available room and pretty much all of the oxygen. Daring her to actually come out and comment on it, Natalie was fairly sure, rather than simply twitching her skirts away from his legs in what she hoped was obvious outrage.

"I think you are well aware that neither I nor anyone else would prefer to be drop-kicked. And also that there exists yet another option, if one without any attendant theatrics. You could let me get in the car as I have managed to do all on my own for twenty-seven years and keep your hands to yourself while I did it."

He turned slightly in his seat and studied her for a moment, as the lights of Rome gleamed behind him, streaking by in the sweet, easy dark as they drove.

"Spoken like someone who has not spent the better part of her life being helped in and out of motorcades to the roars of a besotted crowd," Rodolfo said, his dark brows high as his dark eyes took her measure. "Except you have."

Natalie could have kicked herself for making such a silly mistake, and all because she'd hoped to score a few points in their endless little battle of words. She thought she really would have given herself a pinch, at the very least, if he hadn't been watching her so closely. She sniffed instead, to cover her reaction.

"You've gone over all literal, haven't you? Back on the terrace it was all metaphor and now you're parsing what I say for any hint of exaggeration? What's next?

Will you declare war on parts of speech? Set loose the Royal Tisselian Army on any grammar you dislike?"

"I am looking for hints, Valentina, but it is not figurative language that I find mysterious. It is a woman who has already changed before my eyes, more than once, into someone else."

Natalie turned her head so she could hold that stern, probing gaze of his. Steady and long. As if she really was Valentina and had nothing at all to hide.

"No one has changed before your eyes, Your Highness. I think you might have to face the fact that you are not very observant. Unless and until someone pricks at your vanity. I might as well have been a piece of furniture to you, until I mentioned I planned to let others sit on me." She let out a merry little laugh that was meant to be a slap, and hit its mark. She saw the flare of it in his gaze. "You certainly couldn't have *that*."

"Think for a moment, please." Rodolfo's voice was too dark to be truly impatient. Too rich to sound entirely frustrated. And still, Natalie braced herself. "What is the headline if I am found to be cavorting outside the bounds of holy matrimony?"

"A long, weary sigh of boredom from all sides, I'd imagine." She aimed a cool smile his way. "With a great many exclamation points."

"I am expected to fail. I have long since come to accept it is my one true legacy." Yet that dark undercurrent in his low voice and the way he lounged there, all that ruthless power simmering beneath his seeming unconcern, told Natalie that Rodolfo wasn't resigned to any such thing. "You, on the other hand? It wouldn't be *my* feelings of betrayal you would have to worry about, however unearned you might think they were. It would be the entire world that thought less of you, forever after. Is that really what you want? After you have gone to such lengths to create your spotless reputation?"

Natalie laughed again, but there was nothing funny. There was only a kind of heaviness pressing in upon her, making her feel as if she might break apart if she didn't get away from this man before something really terrible happened. Something she couldn't explain away as a latent Cinderella fantasy, lurking around inside of her without her knowledge or permission, that had put a ball and a prince together and then thrown her headfirst into an unfortunate kiss.

"What does it matter?" she asked him, aware that her voice was ragged, giving too much away—but she couldn't seem to stop herself. "There's no way out of this, so we might as well do as we like no matter what the headlines say or do not. It will make no difference. We will marry. You will have your heirs. Our kingdoms will be linked forever. Who cares about the details when that's the only part that truly matters in the long run?"

"An argument I might have made myself a month ago," Rodolfo murmured. "But we are not the people we were a month ago, princess. You must know that."

From a distance he would likely have looked relaxed. At his ease, with his legs thrust out and his collar loosened. But Natalie was closer, and she could see that glittering, dangerous thing in his gaze. She could feel it inside her, like a lethal touch of his too-talented hands, stoking fires she should have put out a long time ago.

"What I know," she managed to say over her rocketing pulse and that quickening, clenching in her core, "is that it is not I who am apparently unwell."

But Rodolfo only smiled.

Which didn't help at all.

The rest of the drive across the city was filled with

a brooding sort of silence that in many ways was worse than anything he might have said. Because the silence grew inside of her, and Natalie filled it with…images. Unhelpful images, one after the next. What might have happened if they hadn't been interrupted on that terrace, for example. Or if they'd walked a little farther into the shadows, maybe even rounding the corner so no one could see them. Would Rodolfo's hands have found their way beneath her dress again? Would they have traveled higher than her thigh—toward the place that burned the hottest for him even now?

"Thank you for the escort but I can see myself—" Natalie began when they arrived at her hotel, but Rodolfo only stared back at her in a sort of arrogant amazement that reminded her that he would one day rule an entire kingdom, no matter what the tabloids said about him now.

She restrained the little shiver that snaked down her spine, because it had nothing to do with apprehension, and let him usher her out of the car and into the hushed hotel lobby, done in sumptuous reds and deep golds and bursting with dramatic flowers arranged in stately vases. Well. It wasn't so much that she *let* him as that there was no way to stop him without causing a scene in front of all the guests in the lobby who were pretending not to gawk at them as they arrived—especially because really, yet again, Natalie didn't much *want* to stop him. Until she'd met Rodolfo, she'd never known that she was weak straight through to her core. Now she couldn't seem to remember that everywhere but here, she was known for being tough. Strong. Unflappable.

That Natalie seemed like a distant memory.

Rodolfo nodded at her security detail as he escorted her to the private, keyed elevator that led only to the penthouse suite, and then followed her into it. The door swished shut almost silently, and then it was only the two of them in a small and shiny enclosed space. Natalie braced herself, standing there just slightly behind him, with a view of his broad, high, solidly muscled back and beyond that, the gold-trimmed elevator car. She could feel the heat of him, and all that leashed danger, coming off him like flames. He surrounded her without even looking at her. He seemed to loop around her and pull tight, crushing her in his powerful grip, without so much as laying a finger upon her. She couldn't hear herself think over the thunder of her heart, the clatter of her pulse—

But nothing happened. They were delivered directly into the grand living room of the hotel's penthouse. Rodolfo stepped off and moved into the room, shrugging out of his jacket as he went. Natalie followed after him because she had no choice—or so she assured herself. It was that or go back downstairs to the hotel lobby, where she would have to explain herself to her security, the hotel staff, the other guests still sitting around with mobile phones at the ready to record her life at will.

The elevator doors slid shut behind her, and that was it. The choice was made. And it left her notably all alone in her suite's living room with the Prince she very desperately wanted to find the antithesis of charming.

There was no Roman sunset to distract her now. There was only Rodolfo, far too beautiful and much too dangerous for anyone's good. She watched the way he moved through the living room with a kind of liquid athleticism. The light from the soft lamps scattered here and there made the sprawling space feel close. Intimate.

And it made him look like some kind of god all over

again. Not limned in red or gold, but draped in shadows and need.

Her throat was dry. Her lungs ached as if she'd been off running for untold miles. Her fingers trembled, and she realized she was as jittery as if she'd pulled one of her all-nighters before a big meeting and had rivers of coffee running through her veins in place of blood. It made her stomach clench tight to think that it wasn't caffeine that was messing with her tonight. It was this man before her who she should never have touched, much less kissed.

What was she going to do now?

The sad truth was, Natalie couldn't trust herself to make the right decision, or she wouldn't still be standing where she was, would she? She would have gone straight on back to her bedchamber and locked the door. She would have summoned her staff, who she knew had to be nearby, just waiting for the opportunity to serve her and usher Rodolfo out. She would have done *something* other than what she did.

Which was wait. Breathlessly. As if she really was a princess caught up in some or other enchantment. As if she could no more move a muscle than she could wave a magic wand and turn herself back into Natalie.

Rodolfo shrugged out of his jacket and tossed it over the back of one of the fussy chairs, and then he took his time turning to face her again. When he did, his dark eyes burned into her, the focused, searing hunger in them enough to send her back a step. In a wild panic or a kind of dizzy desire, she couldn't have said.

Both, something whispered inside of her. And not with any trace of fear. Not with anything the least bit like fear.

"Rodolfo," she managed to say then, in as measured

a tone as she could manage, because she thought she should have been far more afraid of all those things she could feel in the air between them than she was. Either way, this was all too much. It was all temptation and need, and she could hardly think through the chaos inside of her. "This has all gotten much too fraught and strange. Why don't I have some coffee made? We can sit and talk."

"I am afraid, *princesita*, that it is much too late for talk."

He moved then. His long stride ate up the floor and he was before her in an instant. Or perhaps it was that she didn't want to move out of his reach. She couldn't seem to make herself run. She couldn't seem to do anything at all. All she did was stand right where she was and watch him come for her, that simmering light in his dark eyes and that stern set to his mouth that made everything inside her quiver.

Maybe there was no use pretending this wasn't what she'd wanted all along. Since the very first moment she'd crossed the threshold of that reception room at the palace and discovered he was so much more than his pictures. She'd wanted to eviscerate him and instead she'd ended up on his lap with his tongue in her mouth. Had that really been by chance?

Something dark and guilty kicked inside of her at that, and she opened her mouth to protest—to do *something*, to say *anything* that might stop this—but he was upon her. And he didn't stop. Her breath left her in a rush, because he kept coming. She backed up when she thought he might collide into her, but there was nowhere to go. The doors to the elevator were at her back, closed up tight, and Rodolfo was there. *Right there*. He crowded into her. He laid a palm against the smooth metal on either side of her head and then he leaned in, trapping her between the doors of the elevator and his big, hard body.

And there was nothing but him, then. He was so much bigger than her that he became the whole world. She could see nothing past the wall of his chest. There was no sky but his sculpted, beautiful face. And if there was a sun in the heated little sliver of space that was all he'd left between their bodies, Natalie had no doubt it would be as hot as that look in his eyes.

"I think," she began, because she had to try.

"That is the trouble. You think too much."

And then he simply bent his head and took her mouth with his.

Just like that, Natalie was lost. The delirious taste of him exploded through her, chasing fire with more fire until all she did was burn. His kiss was masterful. Slick and hot and greedy. He left absolutely no doubt as to who was in control as he took her over and sampled her, again and again, as if he'd done it a thousand times before tonight alone. As if he planned to keep doing it forever, starting now. Here.

There was no rush. No desperation or hurry. Just that endless, erotic tasting as if he could go on and on and on.

And Natalie forgot, all over again, who she was and what she was meant to be doing here.

Because she could feel him everywhere. In her fingers, her toes. In the tips of her ears and like a breeze of sensation pouring down her spine. She pushed up on her feet, high on her toes, trying to get as close to him as she could. His arms stayed braced against the elevator doors like immovable barriers, leaving her to angle herself closer. She did it without thought, grabbing hold of his soft shirt in both fists and letting the fire that burned through her blaze out of control.

Sensation stormed through her, making and remaking her as it swept along. Telling her stark truths about herself she didn't want to know. She felt flushed and wild from her lips to the tight, hard tips of her breasts, all the way to that ravenous heat between her legs.

She would have climbed him if she could. She couldn't seem to get close enough.

And then Rodolfo slowed down. His kiss turned lazy. Deep, drugging—but he made no attempt to move any closer. He kept his hands on the wall.

After several agonies of this same stalling tactic, Natalie tore her lips from his, jittery and desperate.

"Please…" she whispered.

His mouth chased hers, tipped up in the corners as he sampled her, easy and slow. Teasing her, she understood then. As if this was some kind of game, and one he could play all night long. As if she was the only one being burned to a crisp where she stood. Over and over again.

"Please, what?" he asked against her mouth, an undercurrent of laughter making her hot and furious and decidedly needy all at once. "I think you can do better than that."

"Please…" she tried again, and then lost her train of thought when his mouth found the line of her jaw.

Natalie shivered as he dropped lower, trailing fire down the side of her neck and somehow finding his way to every sensitive spot she hadn't known she had. And then he used his tongue and his teeth to taunt her with each and every one of them.

"You will have to beg," he murmured against her flushed, overwarm skin, and she could feel the rumble of his voice deep inside of her, low in her belly where all that heat seemed to bloom into a desperate softness that made her knees feel weak. "So that later, there can be no confusion, much as you may wish there to be. Beg me, *princesita*."

Natalie told herself that she would do no such thing. Of course not. Her mother had raised a strong, tough, independent woman who did not *beg,* and especially not from a man like this. Prince Charming at his most dangerous.

But she was writhing against him. She was unsteady and wild and out of her mind, and all she wanted was his hands on her. All she wanted was *more.* And she didn't care what that made her. How could she? She hardly knew who the hell she was.

"Please, Rodolfo," she whispered, because it was the only way she could get her voice to work, that betraying little rasp. "Please, touch me."

His teeth grazed her bare shoulder, sending a wild heat dancing and spinning through her, until it shuddered into the scalding heat at her core and made everything worse.

Or better.

"I am already touching you."

"With your hands." And her voice was little more than a moan then, which ought to have embarrassed her. But she was far beyond that. "Please."

She thought he laughed then, and she felt that, too, like another caress. It wound through her, stoking the flames and making her burn brighter, hotter. So hot she worried she might simply...explode.

And then Rodolfo dropped his arms from the wall, leaning closer to her as he did. He took her jaw in his hand and guided her mouth to his. The kiss changed, deepened, losing any semblance of laziness or control. Natalie welcomed the crush of his chest against her, the contrast between all his heat and the cool metal at her back. She wound her arms around his neck and held on to all that corded strength as he claimed her mouth over and over, as if he was as starved for her as she was for him.

She hardly dared admit how very much she wanted that to be true.

With his other hand, he reached down and began pulling up the long skirt of her dress. He took his time, plundering her mouth as he drew the hem higher and higher. She felt the faintest draft against her calf. Her knee. Then her thigh, and then his hand was on her flesh again, the way it had been that day in the palace.

Except this time, he didn't leave it one place.

He continued to kiss her, again and again, as he smoothed his way up her thigh, urging her legs apart. And Natalie felt torn in two. Ripped straight down the center by the intensity of the hunger that poured through her, then. A tumult of need and hunger and the wild flame within her that Rodolfo kept burning at a fever pitch.

When his seeking fingers reached the edge of the satiny panties she wore, he lifted his head just slightly, taking his mouth away from her. It felt like a blow. Like a loss almost too extreme to survive.

It hurts to breathe, Natalie thought dimly, still lost in the mad commotion happening everywhere in her body. Still wanting him—needing him—almost more than she could bear.

"I will make it stop," Rodolfo said, and she realized with a start that she'd spoken out loud. His mouth crooked slightly in one corner. "Eventually."

And then he dipped his fingers beneath the elastic of her panties and found the heat of her.

Natalie gasped as he stroked his way through her

folds, bold and sure, directly into her softness. His other hand was at her neck, his thumb moving against her skin there the way his clever fingers played with her sex below. He traced his way around the center of her need, watching her face as she clutched at his broad wrist— but only to maintain that connection with him, not to stop him. Never that. Not now.

And then, without warning, he twisted his wrist and drove two fingers into her, that hard curve of his mouth deepening when she moaned.

"Like that, princess," he murmured approvingly. "Sing for me just like that."

And Natalie lost track of what he was doing, and how. He dropped his head to her neck again, teasing his way down to toy with the top of her bodice. He dragged his free hand over her nipples, poking hard against the fabric of the dress, and it was like lightning storming straight down the center of her body to where she was already little more than a flame. And he was stoking that fire with every thrust of his long, blunt fingers deep into her, as if he knew. As if he knew everything. Her pounding heart, that slick, impossible pleasure crashing over her, and that delicious tightening that was making her breath come too fast and too loud.

She lost herself in the slide, the heat. His wicked, talented hands and what they were doing to her. Her hips lifted of their own accord, meeting each stroke, and then the storm took her over. She let her head fall back against the elevator doors. She let herself go, delivering herself completely into his hands, as if there was nothing but this slick, insistent rhythm. As if there was nothing but the sensation he was building in her, higher and higher.

As if there was nothing left in all the world but him.

And then Rodolfo did something new, twisting his wrist and thrusting in a little bit deeper, and everything seemed to shudder to a dangerous halt. Then he did it again, and threw her straight over the edge into bliss.

Sheer, exultant bliss.

Natalie tumbled there, lost to herself and consumed by all that wondrous fire, for what seemed like a very long time.

When the world stopped spinning he was shifting her, lifting her up and into his arms. She had the vague thought that she should protest as he held her high against his chest so her head fell to his wide shoulder when she couldn't hold it up, but his gaze was dark and hungry—still so very hungry—and she couldn't seem to find her tongue to speak.

Rodolfo carried her to the long couch that stretched out before the great wall of windows with all of Rome winking and sparkling there on the other side, like some kind of dream. He laid her down carefully, as if she were infinitely precious to him, and it caught at her. It made the leftover fire still roaring inside of her bleed into…something else. Something that ached more than it should.

And that was the trouble, wasn't it?

Natalie wanted this to be real. She wanted all of this to be real. She wanted to stay Valentina forever, so it wouldn't matter what she did here because *she* would live the consequences of it. She could marry Rodolfo herself. She could—

You could lose yourself in him, a voice that sounded too much like her mother's, harsh and cold, snapped at her. It felt like a face full of cold water. *And then you could be one more thing he throws away when he gets bored. This is a man who has toys, not relationships.*

How can you be so foolish as to imagine otherwise—no matter how good he is with his hands?

"I should have done this a long time ago," he was saying, in a contemplative sort of way that suggested he was talking to himself more than her. But his gaze was so hot, so hungry. It made her shiver, deep inside, kindling the same fire she would have sworn was already burned out. "I think it would have made for a far better proposal of marriage, don't you?"

"Rodolfo..." she began, but he was coming down over her on the couch. He held himself up on his arms and gazed down at her as he settled himself between her legs, fitting his body to hers in a way that made them both breathe a little bit harder. Audibly. And there was no pretending that wasn't real. It made her foolish. "You may imagine you know who I am, but you don't. You really don't."

"Quiet, *princesita,*" he said in a low sort of growl that made everything inside her, still reeling from what he'd done with his hands alone, bloom into a new, even more demanding sort of heat. He shifted so he could take her face between his hands, and that was better. Worse. Almost too intense. "I am going to taste you again. Then I will tell you who are, though I already know. You should know it, too." He let his chest press against her, and dipped his chin so his mouth was less than a gasp away. Less than a breath. *"Mine."*

And then he set his mouth to hers and the flames devoured her.

Again.

This time, Natalie didn't need to be told to beg for him. There was no space between them, only heat and the intense pressure of the hardest part of him, flush against her scalding heat. There was no finesse, no strategy, no teasing. Only need.

And that hunger that rolled between them like so much summer thunder.

She didn't know who undressed whom and she didn't—couldn't—care. She only knew that his mouth was a torment and a gift, both at the same time. His hands were like fire. He pulled down her bodice and feasted on the nipples he'd played with before, until Natalie was nothing but a writhing mess beneath him. Begging. Pleading. Somehow his shirt was open, and she was finally able to touch all those hard muscles she'd only imagined until now. And he was so much better than the pictures she'd seen. Hot and extraordinarily male and perfect and *here,* right here, stretched out on top of her. It was her turn to use her mouth on him, tasting the heat and salt of him until his breath was as heavy as hers, and everything was part of the same shattering, impossible magic.

At some point she wondered if it was possible to survive this much pleasure. If anyone could live through it. If she would recognize herself when this was done—but that was swept away when he took her mouth again.

She loved his weight, crushing her down into the cushions. She loved it even more when he pulled her skirts out of the way and found her panties again. This time, he didn't bother sneaking beneath them. This time he simply tugged, hard and sure, until they tore away in his hand.

And somehow that was so erotic it seemed to light her up inside. She could hardly breathe.

Rodolfo reached down and tore at his trousers, and when he shifted back into place Natalie felt him, broad and hard, nudging against her entrance. His gaze traveled over her body from the place they were joined to the skirt of the dress rucked up and twisted around her hips. Then higher, to where her breasts were plumped up above the dress's bodice, her nipples still tight and swollen from his mouth. Only then did his gaze touch her face.

Suddenly, the world was nothing but that shuddering beat of her heart, so hard she thought he must surely feel it, and that stark, serious expression he wore. He dropped down to an elbow, bringing himself closer to her.

This was happening. This was real.

He was the kind of prince she'd never dared admit she dreamed about, so big and so beautiful it hurt to be this close to him. It hurt in a way dreams never did. It ached, low and deep, and everywhere else.

"Are you ready, princess?" he asked, and his voice was another caress, rough and wild.

Natalie wanted to say something arch. Witty. Something to cut through the intensity and make her feel in control again. Anything at all that might help make this less than it was. Anything that might contain or minimize all those howling, impossible things that flooded through her then.

But she couldn't seem to open her mouth. She couldn't seem to find a single word that might help her.

Her body knew what to do without her guidance or input. As if she'd been made for this, for him. She lifted her hips and pushed herself against him, impaling herself on his hardness, one slow and shuddering inch. Then another. He muttered something in what she thought was the Spanish he sometimes used, but Natalie was caught in his dark gaze, still fast on her face.

"What are you doing to me?" he murmured. He'd asked it before.

Like then, he didn't wait for an answer. He didn't give her any warning. He wrapped an arm around her hips, then hauled them high against him. And in the next instant, slammed himself in deep.

"Oh, my God," Natalie whispered as he filled her, and everything in her shuddered again and again, nudging her so close to the edge once more that she caught her breath in anticipation.

"'Your Highness' will do," Rodolfo told her, a thread of amusement beneath the stark need in his voice.

And then he began to move.

It was a slick, devastating magic. Rodolfo built the flames in her into a wildfire, then fanned the blaze ever higher. He dropped his mouth to hers, then shifted to pull a nipple into the heat of his mouth.

Natalie wrapped herself around him, and gave herself over to each glorious thrust. She dug her fingers into his back, she let her head fall back and then she let herself go. As if the woman she'd been when she'd walked into this room, or into this life, no longer existed.

There was only Rodolfo. There was only this.

Perfect, she thought, again and again, so it became a chant inside her head. *This is perfect.*

She might even have chanted it aloud.

He dropped down closer, wrapping his arms around her as his rhythm went wilder and more erratic. He tucked his face in her neck and kept his mouth there as he pounded into her, over and over, until he hurled her straight back off that cliff.

And he followed her only moments later, releasing himself into her with a roar that echoed through the room and deep inside of Natalie, too, tearing her apart in a completely different way as reality slammed back into her, harsh and cruel.

Because she'd never felt closer to a man in all her life, and Rodolfo had called out to her as if he felt the same. She was as certain as she'd ever been of anything that he felt exactly the same as she did.

But, of course, he thought she was someone else.

And he'd used the wrong name.

CHAPTER NINE

RODOLFO HAD BARELY shifted his weight from Valentina before she was rolling out from beneath him, pulling the voluminous skirt of her dress with her as she climbed to her feet. He found he couldn't help but smile. She was so unsteady on her feet that she had to reach out and grab hold of the nearby chair to keep from sagging to the ground.

He was male enough to find that markedly satisfying.

"You are even beautiful turned away from me," he told her without meaning to speak. It was not, generally, his practice to traffic in flattery. Mostly because it was never required. But it was the simple truth as far as Valentina was concerned. Not empty flattery at all.

She shivered slightly, as if in reaction to his words, but that was all. She didn't glance back at him. She was pulling her dress back into place, shaking back her hair that had long since tumbled from its once sleek chignon. And all Rodolfo wanted to do was pull her back down to him. He wanted to indulge himself and take a whole lot more time with her. He wanted to strip her completely and make sure he learned every last inch of her sweet body by heart.

He was more than a little delighted at the prospect of a long life together to do exactly that.

Rodolfo zipped himself up and rolled to a sitting position, aware that he felt lighter than he had in a long time. Years.

Since Felipe died.

Because the truth was, he'd never wanted his brother's responsibilities. He'd wanted his brother. Funny, irreverent, remarkably warm Felipe had been Rodolfo's favorite person for the whole of his life, and then he'd died. So suddenly. So needlessly. He'd locked himself in his rooms to sleep through what he'd assumed was a flu, and he'd been gone within the week. There was a part of Rodolfo that would never accept that. That never had. That would grieve his older brother forever.

But Rodolfo was the Crown Prince of Tissely now no matter how he grieved his brother, and that meant he should have had all of the attendant responsibilities whether he liked it or not. His father had felt otherwise. And every year the king failed to let Rodolfo take Felipe's place in his court and his government was like a slap in the face all over again, of course. It was a very public, very deliberate rebuke.

More than that, it confirmed what Rodolfo had always known to be true. He could not fill Felipe's shoes. He could not come anywhere close and that would never change. There was no hope.

Until now, he'd assumed that was simply how it would be. His father would die at some point, having allowed Rodolfo no chance at all to figure out his role as king. Rodolfo would have to do it on the fly, which was a terrific way to plunge a country straight into chaos. It was one of the reasons he'd dedicated himself to the sort of sports that required a man figure out how to remain calm no matter what was coming at him. Sharks. The earth, many thousands of feet below, at great speed. Assorted impossible mountain peaks that had killed many men before him. He figured it was all good practice for the little gift his father planned to leave him, since he suspected the old man was doing his level best to ensure that all his dire predictions about the kind of king Rodolfo would be would come true within days of his own death.

This engagement was a test, nothing more. Rodolfo had no doubt that his father expected him to fail, somehow, at an arranged marriage that literally required nothing of him save that he show up. And perhaps he'd played into that, by continuing to see other women and doing nothing to keep that discreet.

But everything was different now. Valentina was his. And their marriage would be the kind of real union Rodolfo had always craved. Without even meaning to, Rodolfo had beaten his father at the old man's own cynical little game.

And it was more than that. Rodolfo had to believe that if he could make the very dutiful princess his the way he had tonight, if he could take a bloodless royal arrangement and make it a wildfire of a marriage, he could do anything. Even convince his dour father to see him as more than just an unwelcome replacement for his beloved lost son.

For the first time in a long, long while, Rodolfo felt very nearly *hopeful*.

"Princess," he began, reaching out to wrap a hand around her hip and tug her toward him, because she was still showing him her back and he wanted her lovely face, "you must—"

"Stop calling me that!" she burst out, sounding raw. And something like wild.

She twisted out of his grasp. And he was so surprised by her outburst that he let her go.

Valentina didn't stop moving until she'd cleared the vast glass table set before the couch, and then she stood there on the other side, her chest heaving as if she'd run an uphill mile to get there.

His princess did not look anything like *hopeful*. If anything, she looked... Wounded. Destroyed. Rodolfo couldn't make any sense out of it. Her green eyes were dark and that sweet, soft mouth of hers trembled as if the hurt inside her was on the verge of pouring out even as she stood there before him.

"I can't believe I let this happen..." she whispered, and her eyes looked full. Almost blank with an anguish Rodolfo couldn't begin to understand.

Rodolfo wanted to stand, to go to her, to offer her what comfort he could—but something stopped him. How many times would she do this back and forth in one way or another? How many ways would she find to pull the rug out from under him—and as he thought that, it was not lost on Rodolfo that unlike every other woman he'd ever known, he cared a little too deeply about what this one was about. All this melodrama and for what? There was no stopping their wedding or the long, public, political marriage that would follow. It was like a train bearing down on them and it always had been.

From the moment Felipe had died and Rodolfo had been sat down and told that in addition to losing his best friend he now had a different life to live than the one he'd imagined he would, there had been no deviating from the path set before them. Princess Valentina had already been his—entirely his—before he'd laid a single finger on her. What had happened here only confirmed what had always been true, not that there had been any doubt. Not for him, anyway.

The only surprise was how much he wanted her.

Again, now, despite the fact he'd only just had her. She made him…thirsty in a way he'd never experienced before in his life.

But it wouldn't have mattered if she'd stayed the same pale, distant ghost he'd met at their engagement celebration. The end result—their marriage and all the politics involved—would have been the same.

He didn't like to see her upset. He didn't like it at all. It made his jaw clench tight and every muscle in his body go much too taut. But Rodolfo remained where he was.

"If you mean what happened right here—" and he nodded at the pillow beside him as if could play back the last hour in vivid color "—then I feel I must tell you that it was always going to happen. It was only a question of when. Before the wedding or after it. Or did you imagine heirs to royal kingdoms were delivered by stork?"

But it was as if she couldn't hear him. "Why didn't you let me leave the gala alone?"

He shrugged, settling back against the pillows as if he was entirely at his ease, though he was not. Not at all. "I assume that was a rhetorical question, as that was never going to happen. You can blame the unfortunate optics if you must. But there was no possibility that my fiancée was ever going to sneak out of a very public event on her own, leaving me behind. How does that suit our narrative?"

"I don't care about your narrative."

"*Our* narrative, Valentina, and you should. You will. It is a weapon against us or a tool we employ. The choice is ours."

She was frowning now, and it was aimed at him, yet Rodolfo had the distinct impression she was talking to herself. "You should never, ever have come up here tonight."

He considered her for a moment. "This was not a mistake, *princesita*. This was a beginning."

She lifted her hands to her face and Rodolfo saw that they were shaking. Again, he wanted to go to her and again, he didn't. It was something about the stiff way she was standing there, or what had looked like genuine torment on her face before she'd covered it from his view. It gripped him, somehow, and kept him right where he was.

As if, he realized in the next moment, he was waiting for the other shoe to drop. The way he had been ever since he'd discovered at too young an age that anything and anyone could be taken from him with no notice whatsoever.

But that was ridiculous. There was no "other shoe" here. This was an arranged marriage set up by their fathers when Valentina was a baby. One crown prince of Tissely and one princess of Murin, and the kingdoms would remain forever united. Two small countries who, together, could become a force to be reckoned with in these confusing modern times. The contracts had been signed for months. They were locked into this wedding no matter what, with no possibility of escape.

Rodolfo knew. He'd read every line of every document that had required his signature. And still, he didn't much like that thing that moved him, dark and grim, as he watched her. It felt far too much like foreboding.

His perfect princess, who had just given herself to him with such sweet, encompassing heat that he could still feel the burn of it all over him and through him as if he might feel it always, dropped her hands from her face. Her gaze caught his and held. Her eyes were still too dark, and filled with what looked like misery.

Sheer, unmistakable misery. It made his chest feel tight.

"I should never have let any of this happen," she said, and her voice was different. Matter-of-fact, if hollow. She swallowed, still keeping her eyes trained on his. "This is my fault. I accept that."

"Wonderful," Rodolfo murmured, aware his voice sounded much too edgy. "I do so enjoy being blameless. It is such a novelty."

She clenched her hands together in front of her, twisting her fingers together into a tangle. There was something about the gesture that bothered him, though he couldn't have said what. Perhaps it was merely that it seemed the very antithesis of the sort of thing a woman trained since birth to be effortlessly graceful would do. No matter the provocation.

"I am not Princess Valentina."

He watched her say that. Or rather, he saw her lips move and he heard the words that came out of her mouth, but they made no sense.

Her mouth, soft and scared, pressed into a line. "My name is Natalie."

"Natalie," he repeated, tonelessly.

"I ran into the princess in, ah—" She cleared her throat. "In London. We were surprised, as you might imagine, to see…" She waved her hand in that way of hers, as if what she was saying was reasonable. Or even possible. Instead of out-and-out gibberish. "And it seemed like a bit of a lark, I suppose. I got to pretend to be a princess for a bit. What could be more fun? No one was ever meant to know, of course."

"I beg your pardon." He still couldn't move. He thought perhaps he'd gone entirely numb, but he knew, somehow, that the paralytic lack of feeling was better than what lurked on the other side. Much better. "But where, precisely, is the real princess in this ludicrous scenario?"

"Geographically, do you mean? She's back in London. Or possibly Spain, depending."

"All tucked up in whatever your life is, presumably." He nodded as if that idiocy made sense. "What did you say your name was, again?"

She looked ill at ease. As well she should. "Natalie."

"And if your profession is not that of the well-known daughter of a widely renowned and ancient royal family, despite your rather remarkable likeness to Princess Valentina, dare I ask what is it that you do? Does it involve a stage, perhaps, the better to hone these acting skills?"

"I'm a personal assistant. To a very important businessman."

"A jumped-up secretary for a man in trade. Of course." He was getting less numb by the second, and that was no good for anyone—though Rodolfo found he didn't particularly care. He hadn't lost his temper in a long while, but these were extenuating circumstances, surely. She should have been grateful he wasn't breaking things. He shook his head, and even let out a laugh, though nothing was funny. "I must hand it to you. Stage or no stage, this has been quite an act."

She blinked. "Somehow, that doesn't sound like a compliment."

"It was really quite ingenious. All you had to do was walk in the room that day and actually treat me like another living, breathing human instead of a cardboard cutout. After all those months. You must have been thrilled that I fell into your trap so easily."

The words felt sour in his own mouth. But Valentina only gazed back at him with confusion written all over her, as if she didn't understand what he was talking about. He was amazed that he'd fallen for her performance. Why hadn't it occurred to him that her public persona, so saintly and retiring, was as much a constriction as his daredevil reputation? As easily turned off as on. And yet it had never crossed his mind that she was anything but the woman she'd always seemed to be, hailed in all the papers as a paragon of royal virtue. A breath of fresh air, they called her. The perfect princess in every respect.

He should have known that all of it was a lie. A carefully crafted, meticulously built lie.

"The trap?" She was shaking her head, looking lost and something like forlorn, and Rodolfo hated that even when he knew she was trying to play him, he still wanted to comfort her. Get his hands on her and hold her close. It made his temper lick at him, dark and dangerous. "What trap?"

"All of this so you could come back around tonight and drop this absurd story on me. Did you really think I would credit such an outlandish tale? You *happen* to resemble one of the wealthiest and most famous women in the world, yet no one remarked on this at any point during your other life. Until, by chance, you stumbled upon each other. How convenient. And that day in the palace, when you came back from London—am I meant to believe that you had never met me before?"

She pressed her lips together as if aware that they trembled. "I hadn't."

"What complete and utter rubbish." He stood then, smoothing his shirt down as he rose to make sure he kept his damned twitchy hands to himself, but there wasn't much he could do about the fury in his voice. "I am not entirely certain which part offends me more. That you would go to the trouble to concoct such a childish, ridiculous story in the first place, or that you imagined for one second that I would believe it."

"You said yourself that I was switching personalities. That I was two women. This is why. I think—I mean, the only possible explanation is that Valentina and I are twins." There was an odd emphasis on that last word, as if she'd never said it out loud before. She squared her shoulders. "Twin sisters."

Rodolfo fought to keep himself under control, despite the ugly things that crawled through him then, each worse than the last. The truth was, he should have known better than to be hopeful. About anything. He should have known better than to allow himself to think that anything in his life might work out. He could jump out of a thousand planes and land safely. There had never been so much as a hiccup on any of his adventures, unless he counted the odd shark bite or scar. But when it came to his actual life as a prince of Tissely? The things he was bound by blood and his birthright to do whether he wanted to or not? It was nothing but disaster, every time.

He should have known this would be, too.

"Twin sisters," he echoed when he trusted himself to speak in both English and a marginally reasonable tone. "But I think you must mean *secret* twin sisters, to give it the proper soap opera flourish. And how do you imagine such a thing could happen? Do you suppose the king happily looked the other way while Queen Frederica swanned off with a stolen baby?"

"No one talks about where she went. Much less who she went with."

"You are talking about matters of state, not idle gossip." His hands were in fists, and he forced them to open, then shoved them in his pockets. "The queen's mental state was precarious. Everyone knows this. She would hardly have been allowed to retreat so completely from public life with a perfectly healthy child who also happened to be one of the king's direct heirs."

Valentina frowned. "Precarious? What do you mean?"

"Do not play these games with me," he gritted out, aware that his heart was kicking at him. Temper or that same, frustrated hunger, he couldn't tell. "You know as well as I do that she was not assassinated, no matter how many breathless accounts are published in the dark and dingy corners of the internet by every conspiracy theorist who can type. That means, for your story to make any kind of sense, a king with no other heirs in line for his throne would have to release one of the two he did have into the care of a woman who was incapable of fulfilling a single one of her duties as his queen. Or at the very least, somehow fail to hunt the world over for the child once this same woman stole her."

"I didn't really think about that part," she said tightly. "I was more focused on the fact I was in a palace and the man with the crown was acting as if he was my father. Which it turns out, he probably is."

"Enough." He belted it out at her, with enough force that her head jerked back a little. "The only thing this astonishing conversation is doing is making me question your sanity. You must know that." He let out a small laugh at that, though it scraped at him. "Perhaps that is your endgame. A mental breakdown or two, like mother, like daughter. If you cannot get out of the marriage before the wedding, best to start working on how to exit it afterward, I suppose."

Her face was pale. "That's not what this is. I'm trying to be honest with you."

He moved toward her then, feeling his lips thin as he watched her fight to stand her ground when she so clearly wanted to put more furniture between them—if not whole rooms.

"Have I earned this, Valentina?" he demanded, all that numbness inside him burning away with the force of his rage. His sense of betrayal—which he didn't care to examine too closely. It was enough that she'd led him to hope, then kicked it out of his reach. It was more than enough. "That you should go to these lengths to be free of me?"

He stopped when he was directly in front of her, and he hated the fact that even now, all he wanted to do was pull her into his arms and kiss her until the only thing between them was that heat. Her eyes were glassy and she looked pale with distress, and he fell for it. Even knowing what she was willing to do and say, his first instinct was to believe her. What did that say about his judgment?

Maybe his father had been right about him all along.

That rang in him like a terrible bell.

"Here is the sad truth, princess," he told her, standing above her so she was forced to tilt her head back to keep her eyes on him. And his body didn't know that everything had changed, of course. It was far more straightforward. It wanted her, no matter what stories she told. "There is no escape. There is no sneaking away into some fantasy life where you will live out your days without the weight of a country or two squarely on your shoulders. There is no switching places with a convenient twin and hiding from who you are. And I am terribly afraid that part of what you must suffer is our marriage. You are stuck with me. Forever."

"Rodolfo." And her voice was scratchy, as if she had too many sobs in her throat. As if she was fighting to hold them back. "I know it all sounds insane, but you have to listen to me—"

"No," he said with quiet ferocity. "I do not."

"Rodolfo—"

And now even his name in her mouth felt like an insult. Another damned lie. He couldn't bear it.

He silenced her the only way he knew how. He reached out and hooked a hand around her neck, dragging her to him. And then he claimed her mouth with his.

Rodolfo poured all of the dark things swirling around inside of him into the way he angled his jaw to make everything bright hot and slick. Into the way he took her. Tasted her. As if she was the woman he'd imagined she was, so proper and bright. As if he could still taste that fantasy version of her now despite the games she was trying to play. He gave her his grief over Felipe, his father's endless shame and fury that the wrong son had died—all of it. If she'd taken away his hope, he could give her the rest of it. He kissed her again and again, as much a penance for him as any kind of punishment for her.

And when he was done, because it was that or he would take her again right there on the hotel floor and he wasn't certain either one of them would survive that, he set her away from him.

It should have mattered to him that she was breathing too hard. That her green eyes were wide and there were tears marking her cheeks. It should have meant something.

Somewhere, down below the tumult of that black fury that roared in him, inconsolable and much too wounded, it did. But he ignored it.

"I only wanted you to know who I am," she whispered.

And that was it, then. That was too much. He took her shoulders in his hands and dragged her before him, up on her toes and directly in his face.

"I am Rodolfo of Tissely," he growled at her. "The accidental, throwaway prince. I was called *the spare* when I was born, always expected to live in my brother's shadow and never, ever expected to take Felipe's place. Then the spare became the heir—but only in name. Because I have always been the bad seed. I have always been unworthy."

"That's not true."

He ignored her, his fingers gripping her and keeping her there before him. "Nothing I touch has ever lasted. No one I love has ever loved me back, or if they did, it was only as long as there were two sons instead of the one. Or they disappeared into the wilds of Bavaria, pretending to be ill. Or they died of bloody sepsis in the middle of a castle filled with royal doctors and every possible medication under the sun."

She whispered his name as if she loved him, and that hurt him worse than all the rest. Because more than all the rest, he wanted that to be true—and he knew exactly how much of a fool that made him.

"What is one more princess who must clearly hate the very idea of me, the same as all the rest?" And what did it matter that he'd imagined that she might be the saving of him, of the crown he'd never wanted and the future he wasn't prepared for? "None of this matters. You should have saved your energy. This will all end as it was planned. The only difference is that now, I know exactly how deceitful you are. I know the depths of the games you will play. And I promise you this, princess. You will not fool me again."

"You don't understand," she said, more tears falling from her darkened green eyes as she spoke and wetting her pale cheeks. "I wanted this to be real, Rodolfo. I lost myself in that."

He told himself to let go of her. To take his hand off her shoulders and step away. But he didn't do it. If anything, he held her tighter. Closer.

As if he'd wanted it to be real, too. As if some part of him still did.

"You have to believe me," she whispered. "I never meant it to go that far."

"It was only sex," he told her, his voice a thing of granite. He remembered what she'd called herself as she'd spun out her fantastical little tale. "But no need to worry, *Natalie*." She flinched, and he was bastard enough to like that. Because he wanted her to hurt, too—and no matter that he hated himself for that thought. Hating himself didn't change a thing. It never had. "I will be certain to make you scream while we make the requisite heirs. I am nothing if not dependable in that area, if nowhere else. Feel free to ask around for references."

He let her go then, not particularly happy with how hard it was to do, and headed for the elevator. He needed to clear his head. He needed to wash all of this away. He needed to find a very dark hole and fall into it for a while, until the self-loathing receded enough that he could function again. Assuming it ever would.

"It doesn't have to be this way," she said from behind him.

But Rodolfo turned to face her only when he'd stepped into the elevator. She stood where he'd left her, her hands tangled in front of her again and something broken in her gaze.

Eventually, she would have as little power over him as she'd had when they'd met. Eventually, he would not want to go to her when she looked at him like that, as if she was small and wounded and only he could heal her.

Eventually. All he had to do was survive long enough to get there, like anything else.

"It can only be this way," he told her then, and he hardly recognized his own voice. He sounded like a broken man—but of course, that wasn't entirely true. He had never been whole to begin with. "The sooner you resign yourself to it, the better. I am very much afraid this is who we are."

Natalie didn't move for a long, long time after Rodolfo left. If she could have turned into a pillar of stone, she would have. It would have felt better, she was sure.

The elevator doors shut and she heard the car move, taking Rodolfo away, but she still stood right where he'd left her as if her feet were nailed to the floor. Her cheeks were wet and her dress caught at her since she'd pulled it back into place in such a panicked hurry, and her fingers ached from where she'd threaded them together and held them still. Her breathing had gone funny because her throat was so tight.

And for a long while, it seemed that the only thing she could do about any of those things was stay completely still. As if the slightest movement would make it all worse—though it was hard to imagine how.

Eventually, her fingers began to cramp, and she unclasped them, then shook them out. After that it was easier to move the rest of her. She walked on stiff, protesting legs down the long penthouse hallway into her bedroom, where she stood for a moment in the shambles of her evening, blind to the luxury all around her. But that could only last so long. She went to kick off her shoes and realized she'd lost them somewhere, but she didn't want to go back out to the living room and look. She was sure Rodolfo's contempt was still clinging to every gleaming surface out there and she couldn't bring herself to face it.

She padded across the grandly appointed space to the adjoining bathroom suite and stepped in to find the bath itself was filled and waiting for her, steam rising off the top of the huge, curved, freestanding tub like an invitation. That simple kindness made her eyes fill all over again. She wiped the blurriness away, but it didn't help, and the tears were flowing freely again by the time she got herself out of her dress and threw it over a chair in the bedroom. She didn't cry. She almost never cried. But tonight she couldn't seem to stop.

Natalie returned to the bathroom to pull all the pins out of her hair. She piled the mess of it on her head and knotted it into place, ignoring all the places she felt stiff or sore. Then she walked across the marble floor and climbed into the tub at last, sinking into the warm, soothing embrace of the bath's hot water and the salts that some kind member of the staff had thought to add.

She closed her eyes and let herself drift—but then there was no more hiding from the events of the night. The dance. That kiss out on the terrace of the villa. And then what had happened right here in this hotel. His mouth against her skin. His wickedly clever hands. The bold, deep surge of his possession and how she'd fallen to pieces so easily. The smile on Rodolfo's face when he'd turned her around to face him afterward, and how quickly it had toppled from view. And that shuttered, haunted look she'd put in his eyes later, that had been there when he'd left.

As if that was all that remained of what had swelled and shimmered between them tonight. As if that was all it had ever been.

Whatever else came of these stolen days here in Valentina's life, whatever happened, Natalie knew she would never forgive herself for that. For believing in a fairy tale when she knew better and hurting Rodolfo—to say nothing of herself—in the process.

She sat in the tub until her skin was shriveled and the water had cooled. She played the night all the way through, again and again, one vivid image after the next. And when she sat up and pulled the plug to let the water swirl down the drain, she felt clean, yes. But her body didn't feel like hers. She could still feel Rodolfo's touch all over, as if he'd branded her with his passion as surely as he'd condemned her with his disbelief.

Too bad, she told herself, sounding brisk and hard like her mother would have. *This is what you get for doing what you knew full well you shouldn't have.*

Natalie climbed out of the tub then and wrapped herself in towels so light and airy they could have been clouds, but she hardly noticed. She stood in the still-fogged-up bathroom and brushed out her hair, letting the copper strands fall all around her like a curtain and then braiding the heavy mess of it to one side, so she could toss it over one shoulder and forget it.

When she walked back into the bedroom, her dress was gone from the chair where she'd thrown it and in its place was the sort of silky thing Valentina apparently liked to sleep in. Natalie had always preferred a simple T-shirt, but over the past couple of weeks she'd grown to like the sensuous feel of the fine silk against her bare skin.

Tonight, however, it felt like a rebuke.

Her body didn't want silk, it wanted Rodolfo.

She would have given anything she had to go back in time and keep herself from making that confession. To accept that of course he would call her by the wrong name and find a way to make her peace with it. Her mind spun out into one searing fantasy after another about how the night would have gone if only she'd kept her mouth shut.

But that was the trouble, wasn't it? She'd waited too long to tell him the truth, if she was going to. And she never should have allowed him to touch her while he thought she was Valentina. Not back in the palace. Certainly not tonight. She should have kept her distance from him entirely.

Because no matter what her traitorous heart insisted, even now, he wasn't hers. He could never be hers. The ring on her finger belonged to another woman and so did he. It didn't matter that Valentina had given her blessing, whatever that meant in the form of a breezy text. Natalie had never wanted to be the sort of woman who took another woman's man, no matter the circumstances. She'd spent her whole childhood watching her mother flit from one lover to the next, knowing full well that many of the men Erica juggled had been married already. Natalie always vowed that she was not going to be one of those women who pretended they didn't know when a man was already committed elsewhere. In this case, she'd known going in and she'd still ended up here.

How many more ways was she going to betray herself?

How many more lives was she going to ruin besides her own?

Natalie looked around the achingly gorgeous room, aware of every last detail that made it the perfect room for a princess, from the soaring canopy over her high, proud bed to the deep Persian rugs at her feet. The epic sweep of the drapery at each window and the stunning view of Rome on the other side of the glass. The artistry in every carved leg of each of the chairs placed *just so* at different points around the chamber. She looked down at her own body, still warm and pink from her bath and barely covered in a flowy, bright blue silk that cascaded lazily from two spaghetti straps at her shoulders. Her manicure and pedicure were perfect. Her skin was as soft as a baby's after access to Valentina's moisturizing routine with products crafted especially for her. Her hair had never looked so shiny or healthy, even braided over one shoulder. And she was wearing nothing but silk and a ring fit for a queen. Literally.

But she didn't belong here with these things that would never belong to her. She might fit into this borrowed life in the most physical sense, but none of it suited her. *None of it was hers.*

"I am Natalie Monette," she told herself fiercely, her own voice sounding loud and brash in the quiet of the room. Not cool and cultured, like a princess. "My fingernails are never painted red. My toes are usually a disaster. I live on pots of coffee and fistfuls of ibuprofen, not two squares of decadent chocolate a day and healthy little salads."

She moved over to the high bed, where Valentina's laptop and mobile phone waited for her on a polished bedside table, plugged in and charged up, because not even that was her responsibility here.

It was time to go home. It was time to wake up from this dream and take back what was hers—her career— before she lost that, too.

It was time to get back to the shadows, where she belonged.

She picked up the mobile and punched in her own number, telling herself this would all fade away fast when she was back in her own clothes and her own life. When she had too much to do for Mr. Casilieris to waste her time brooding over a prince she'd never see again. Soon this little stretch of time would be like every other fairy tale she'd ever been told as a girl, a faded old story she might recall every now and then, but no part of anything that really mattered to her.

And so what if her heart seemed to twist at that, making her whole chest ache?

It was still time—past time—to go back where she belonged.

"I am Natalie Monette," she whispered to herself as the phone on the other end rang and rang. "I am not a princess. I was never a princess and I never will be."

But it didn't matter what she told herself, because Valentina didn't answer.

Not that night.

And not for weeks.

CHAPTER TEN

RODOLFO WAS CONFLICTED.

He hadn't seen Valentina since that night in Rome. He'd had his staff contact her to announce that he thought they'd carried out their objectives beautifully and there would be no more need for their excursions into the world of the paparazzi. And that was before he'd seen their pictures in all the papers.

The one most prominently featured showed the two of them on the dance floor, in the middle of what looked like a very romantic waltz. Rodolfo was gazing down at her as if he had never seen a woman before in all his life. That was infuriating enough, given what had come afterward. It made his chest feel too tight. But it was the look on the princess's face that had rocked Rodolfo.

Because the picture showed her staring up at the man who held her in his arms in open adoration. As if she was falling in love right then and there as they danced. As if it had already happened.

And it had all been a lie. A game.

The first you've ever lost, a vicious voice inside of him whispered.

Today he stood in the grand foyer outside his father's offices in the palace in Tissely, but his attention was across Europe in Murin, where the maddening, still-more-fascinating-than-she-should-have-been woman who was meant to become his wife was going about her business as if she had not revealed herself to be decidedly unhinged.

She'd kept a low profile these last few weeks. As had Rodolfo.

But his fury hadn't abated one bit.

Secret twins. The very idea was absurd—even if she hadn't been the daughter of one of the most famous and closely watched men in the world. There was press crawling all over Murin Castle day and night and likely always had been, especially when the former queen had been pregnant with the heir to the country's throne.

"Ridiculous," he muttered under his breath.

But his trouble was, he didn't want to be bitter. He wanted to believe her, no matter how unreasonable she was. That was what had been driving him crazy these past weeks. He'd told himself he was going to throw himself right back into his old habits, but he hadn't. Instead he'd spent entirely too much time mired in his old, familiar self-pity and all it had done was make him miss her.

He had no earthly idea what to do about that.

The doors opened behind him and he was led in with the usual unnecessary ceremony to find his father standing behind his desk. Already frowning, which Rodolfo knew from experience didn't bode well for the bracing father/son chat they were about to have.

Ferdinand nodded at the chair before his desk and Rodolfo took it, for once not flinging himself down like a lanky adolescent. Not because doing so always irritated his father. But because he felt like a different man these days, scraped raw and hollow and made new in a variety of uncomfortable and largely unpleasant ways he could blame directly on his princess, and he didn't have it in him to needle his lord and king whenever possible.

His father's frown deepened as he beheld his son before him, because, of course, he always had it in him to poke at his son. It was an expression Rodolfo knew well. He had no idea why it was harder to keep his expression impassive today.

"I hope you have it in you to acquit yourself with something more like grace at your wedding," Ferdinand said darkly, as if Rodolfo had been rousted out of a den of iniquity only moments before and still reeked of excess. He'd tried. In the sense that he'd planned to go out and drown himself in all the things that had always entertained him before. But he'd never made it out. He couldn't call it fidelity to his lying, manipulative princess when the truth was, he'd lost interest in sin—could he? "The entire world will be watching."

"The entire world has been watching for some time," Rodolfo replied, keeping his tone easy. Even polite. Because there was no need to inform his father that he had no intention of marrying a woman who had tried to play him so thoroughly. How could he? But he told himself Ferdinand could find out when he didn't appear at the ceremony, like everyone else. "Has that not been the major point of contention all these years?"

His father ignored him. "It is one thing to wave at a press call. Your wedding to the Murin princess will be one of the most-watched ceremonies in modern Europe. Your behavior must, at last, be that of a prince of Tissely. Do you think you can manage this, Rodolfo?"

He glared at him as if he expected an answer. And something inside of Rodolfo simply...cracked.

It was so loud that first he thought it was the chair beneath him, but his father didn't react. And it took Rodolfo a moment to understand that it wasn't his chair. It was him.

He died, Rodolfo, his princess had said in Rome, before she'd revealed herself. *You lived.*

And he'd tried so hard to reverse that, hadn't he? He'd told himself all these years that the risks he took were what made him feel alive, but that had been a lie. What he'd been doing was punishing himself. Pushing himself because he hadn't cared what happened to him. Risking himself because he'd been without hope.

Until now.

"I am not merely *a* prince of Tissely," he said with a great calm that seemed to flood him then, the way it always did before he dropped from great heights with only a parachute or threw himself off the sides of bridges and ravines attached to only a bouncy rope. Except this time he knew the calm was not a precursor to adrenaline, but to the truth. At last. "I am the only prince of Tissely."

"I know very well who you are," his father huffed at him.

"Do you, sir? Because you have seemed to be laboring under some misconceptions as to my identity this last decade or two."

"I am your father and your king," his father thundered.

But Rodolfo was done being put into his place. He was done accepting that his place was somehow lower and shameful, for that matter.

All he'd done was live. Imperfectly and often foolishly, but he'd lived a life. He might have been lying to himself. He might have been hopeless. But he'd survived all of that.

The only thing he was guilty of was of not being Felipe.

"I am your son," Rodolfo replied, his voice like steel.

"I am your only remaining son and your only heir. It doesn't matter how desperately you cling to your throne. It doesn't matter how thoroughly you convince yourself that I am worthless and undeserving. Even if it were true, it wouldn't matter. Nothing you do will ever bring Felipe back."

His father looked stiff enough to break in half. And old, Rodolfo thought. How had he missed that his father had grown old? "How dare you!"

He was tired of this mausoleum his father had built around Felipe's memory. He was tired of the games they played, two bitter, broken men who had never recovered from the same long-ago loss and instead, still took it out on each other.

Rodolfo was done with the game. He didn't want to live like this any longer.

He wanted to feel the way he did when he was with Valentina. Maybe it had all been a lie, but he'd been *alive*. Not putting on a show. Not destined to disappoint simply by showing up.

And there was something he should have said a decade or two ago.

"I am all you have, old man." He stood then, taking his time and never shifting his gaze from his father's, so perhaps they could both take note of the fact that he towered over the old man. "Whether you like it or do not, I am still here. Only one of your sons died all those years ago. And only you can decide if you will waste the rest of your life acting as if you lost them both."

His father was not a demonstrative man. Ferdinand stood like a stone for so long that Rodolfo thought he might stand like that forever. So committed to the mausoleum he'd built that he became a part of it in fact.

But Rodolfo wanted no part of it. Not anymore. He

was done with lies. With games. With paying over and over for sins that were not his.

He inclined his head, then turned for the door. He was reaching for the knob to let himself out—to leave this place and get on with his life—when he heard a faint noise from behind him.

"It is only that I miss him," came his father's voice, low and strained. It was another man's sob.

Rodolfo didn't turn around. It would embarrass them both.

"I know, Papa," he said, using a name he hadn't thought, much less spoken aloud, since he was little more than a baby himself. But it was the only one that seemed appropriate. "I do, too."

The first week after that shattering trip to Rome, Natalie tried Valentina so many times she was slightly afraid it would have bordered on harassment—had she not been calling her own mobile number. And it didn't matter anyway, because the princess never answered, leaving Natalie to sit around parsing the differences between a ringing phone that was never picked up and a call that went straight to voice mail like an adolescent girl worrying over a boy's pallid attentions.

And in the meantime, she still had to live Valentina's life.

That meant endless rounds of charity engagements. It meant approximately nine million teas with the ladies of this or that charity and long, sad walks through hospitals filled with ill children. It was being expected to "say a few words" at the drop of a hat, and always in a way that would support the crown while offending no one. It meant dinners with King Geoffrey, night after night, that she gradually realized were his version of preparing Valentina for the role she would be expected to fill once she married and was the next Queen of Tissely. It also meant assisting in the planning of the impending royal wedding, which loomed larger with every day that passed.

Every call you don't answer is another questionable decision I'm making for YOUR wedding, she texted Valentina after a particularly long afternoon of menu selecting. *I hope you enjoy the taste of tongue and tripe. Both will feature prominently.*

But the princess didn't respond.

Which meant Natalie had no choice but to carry on playing Valentina. She supposed she could fly to London and see if she was there, but the constant stream of photographs screeching about her *fairy-tale love affair* in the papers made her think that turning up at Achilles Casilieris's property this close to Valentina's wedding would make everything worse. It would cause too much commotion.

It would make certain that when they finally did switch, Natalie wouldn't be able to seamlessly slip back into her old life.

Meanwhile, everything was as Rodolfo had predicted. The public loved them, and the papers dutifully recycled the same pictures from Rome again and again. Sometimes there were separate shots of them going about their business in their separate countries, and Natalie was more than a little embarrassed by the fact she pored over the pictures of Rodolfo like any obsessed tabloid reader. One day the papers were filled with stories about how daredevil, playboy Rodolfo encouraged Valentina to access her playful side, bringing something real and rare to her stitched-up, dutiful life. The next day the same papers were crowing about the way the proper princess had brought noted love cheat Rodolfo to heel, presumably with the sheer force of her *goodness*. It didn't matter what story the papers told; the people ate it up. They loved it.

Natalie, meanwhile, was miserable. And alone.

Everything was in ruins all around her—it was just too bad her body didn't know it.

Because it wanted him. So badly it kept her up at night. And made her hoard her vivid, searing memories of Rome and play them out again and again in her head. In her daydreams. And all night long, when she couldn't sleep and when she dreamed.

She was terribly afraid that it was all she would ever have of him.

The longer she didn't hear from Rodolfo or see him outside of the tabloids, the more Natalie was terrified that she'd destroyed Valentina's marriage. Her future. Her destiny. That come the wedding day, there would be no groom at the altar. Only a princess bride and the wreck Natalie had made of her life.

Because she was a twin that shouldn't exist. A twin that couldn't exist, if Rodolfo had been right in Rome.

Do you suppose the king happily looked the other way while Queen Frederica swanned off with a stolen baby? he'd asked, and God help her, but she could still see the contempt on his face. It still ricocheted inside of her, scarring wherever it touched.

And it was still a very good question.

One afternoon she locked herself in Valentina's bedroom, pulled out her mobile and punched in her mother's number from memory.

Natalie and her mother weren't close. They never had been, and while Natalie had periodically wondered what it might be like to have the mother/daughter bond so many people seemed to enjoy, she'd secretly believed she was better off without it. Still, she and Erica were civil. Cordial, even. They might not get together for holidays or go off on trips together or talk on the phone every Sunday, but every now and then, when they were in the same city and they were both free, they had dinner. Natalie wasn't sure if that would make pushing Erica for answers harder or easier.

"Mother," she said matter-of-factly after the perfunctory greetings—all with an undercurrent of some surprise because they'd only just seen each other a few months back in Barcelona and Natalie wasn't calling from her usual telephone number—were done. "I have to ask you a very serious question."

"Must you always be so intense, Natalie?" her mother asked with a sigh that only made her sound chillier, despite the fact she'd said she was in the Caribbean. "It's certainly not your most attractive trait."

"I want the truth," Natalie forged on, not letting her mother's complaint distract her. Since it was hardly anything new. "Not some vague story about the evils of some or other Prince Charming." Her mother didn't say anything to that, which was unusual. So unusual that it made a little trickle of unease trail down Natalie's back… but what did she have to fear? She already knew the answer. She'd just been pretending, all this time, that she didn't. "Is your real name Frederica de Burgh, Mother? And were you by chance ever married to King Geoffrey of Murin?"

She was sitting on the chaise in the princess's spacious bedroom with the laptop open in front of her, looking at pictures of a wan, very unsmiling woman, pale with copper hair and green eyes, who had once been the Queen of Murin. Relatively few pictures existed of the notorious queen, but it really only took one. The woman Natalie knew as Erica Monette was always tanned. She had dark black hair in a pixie cut, brown eyes and was almost never without her chilly smile. But how hard could it be, for a woman who didn't want to be found or connected to her old self, to cut and dye her hair, get some sun and pop in color contacts?

"Why would you ask such a thing?" her mother asked.

Which was neither an answer nor an immediate refutation of her theory, Natalie noted. Though she thought her mother sounded a little...winded.

She cleared her throat. "I am sitting in the royal palace in Murin right now."

"Well," Erica said after a moment bled out into several. She cleared her throat, and Natalie thought that was more telling than anything else, given that her mother didn't usually do emotions. "I suppose there's no use in telling you not to go turning over rocks like that. It can only lead to more trouble than it's worth."

"Explain this to me," Natalie whispered, because it was that or shout, and she wasn't sure she wanted to give in to that urge. She wasn't sure she'd stop. "Explain *my life* to me. How could you possibly have taken off and gone on to live a regular life with one of the King's children?"

"I told him you died," her mother said matter-of-factly. So matter-of-factly, it cut Natalie in half. She couldn't even gasp. She could only hold the phone to her ear and sit there, no longer the same person she'd been before this phone call. Her mother took that as a cue to keep going, once again sounding as unruffled as she always did. "My favorite maid took you and hid you until I could leave Murin. I told your father one of the twins was stillborn and he believed it. Why wouldn't he? And of course, we'd hid the fact that I was expecting twins from the press, because Geoffrey's mother was still alive then and she thought it was unseemly. It made sense to hide that there'd been a loss, too. Geoffrey never liked to show a weakness. Even if it was mine."

A thousand questions tracked through Natalie's head then. And with each one, a different emotion, each one buffeting her like its own separate hurricane. But she couldn't indulge in a storm. Not now. Not when she had a charity event to attend in a few short hours and a speech to give about its importance. Not when she had to play the princess and try her best to keep what was left of Valentina's life from imploding.

Instead, she asked the only question she could.

"Why?"

Erica sighed. And it occurred to Natalie that it wasn't just that she wasn't close to her mother, but that she had no idea who her mother was. And likely never would. "I wanted something that was mine. And you were, for a time, I suppose. But then you grew up."

Natalie rubbed a trembling hand over her face.

"Didn't it occur to you that I would find out?" she managed to ask.

"I didn't see how," Erica said after a moment. "You were such a bookish, serious child. So intense and studious. It wasn't as if you paid any attention to distant European celebrities. And of course, it never occurred to me that there was any possibility you'd run into any member of the Murinese royal family."

"And yet I did," Natalie pushed out through the constriction in her throat. "In a bathroom in London. You can imagine my surprise. Or perhaps you can't."

"Oh, Natalie." And she thought for a moment that her mother would apologize. That she would try, however inadequately, to make up for what she'd done. But this was Erica. "Always so intense."

There wasn't much to say after that. Or there was, of course—but Natalie was too stunned and Erica was too, well, *Erica* to get into it.

After the call was over, Natalie sat curled up in that chaise and stared off into space for a long time. She tried to put all the pieces together, but what she kept coming back to was that her mother was never going to change. She was never going to be the person Natalie wanted her to be, whether Natalie was a princess or a secretary. None of that mattered, because it was Erica who had trouble figuring out how to be a mother.

And in the meantime, Natalie really, truly was a princess, after all. Valentina's twin with every right to be in this castle. It was finally confirmed.

And Rodolfo still isn't yours, a small voice inside her whispered. *He never will be, even if he stops hating you tomorrow. Even if he shows up for his wedding, it won't be to marry you.*

She let out a long, hard breath. And then she sat up.

It took a swipe of her finger to bring up the string of texts Valentina still hadn't answered.

It turns out we really are sisters, she typed. Maybe you already suspected as much, but I was in denial. So I asked our mother directly. I'll tell you that story if and when I see you again.

She sent that and paused, lifting a hand to rub at the faint, stubborn headache that wouldn't go away no matter how much water she drank or how much sleep she got, which never felt at all like enough.

I don't know when that will be, because you've fallen off the face of the planet and believe me, I know how hard it is to locate Achilles Casilieris when he doesn't wish to be found. But if you don't show up soon, I'm going to marry your husband and I didn't sign up to pretend to be you for the rest of my life. I agreed to six weeks and it's nearly been that.

She waited for long moments, willing the other woman to text back. To give her some clue about…anything. To remind her that she wasn't alone in this madness despite how often and how deeply she felt she was.

If you're not careful, you'll be Natalie Monette forever. Nobody wants that.

But there was nothing.

So Natalie did the only thing she could do. She got to her feet, ignored her headache and that dragging exhaustion that had been tugging at her for over a week now, and went out to play Valentina.

Again.

CHAPTER ELEVEN

A FEW SHORT hours before the wedding, Rodolfo strode through the castle looking for his princess bride, because the things he wanted to say to her needed to be said in person.

He'd followed one servant and bribed another, and that was how he finally found his way to the princess's private rooms. He nodded briskly to the attendants who gaped at him when he entered, and then he strode deeper into her suite as if he knew where he was headed. He passed an empty media center and an office, a dining area and a cheerful salon, and then pushed his way through yet another door to find himself in her bedroom at last.

To find Valentina herself sitting on the end of the grand four-poster bed that dominated the space as if she'd been waiting for him.

She was not dressed in her wedding clothes. In fact, she was wearing the very antithesis of wedding clothes: a pair of very skinny jeans, ballet flats and a slouchy sort of T-shirt. There was an apricot-colored scarf wrapped around her neck several times, her hair was piled haphazardly on the top of her head and she'd anchored the great copper mess of it with a pair of oversize sunglasses. He stopped as the door shut behind him and could do nothing but stare at her.

This was the sort of outfit a woman wore to wander down to a café for a few hours. It was not, by any possible definition, an appropriate bridal ensemble for a woman who was due to make her way down the aisle of a cathedral to take part in a royal wedding.

"You appear to be somewhat underdressed for the wedding," he pointed out, aware he sounded more than a little gruff. Deadly, even. "Excuse me. I mean *our* wedding."

There was something deeply infuriating about the bland way she sat there and did nothing at all but stare back at him. As if she was deliberately slipping back into that old way she'd acted around him. As if he'd managed to push her too far away from him for her to ever come back and this was the only way she could think to show it.

But Rodolfo was finished feeling sorry for himself. He was finished living down to expectations, including his own. He was no ghost, in his life or anyone else's. After their conversation in Tissely, Ferdinand had appointed Rodolfo to his cabinet. He'd called it a wedding gift, but Rodolfo knew what it was: a new beginning. If he could manage it with his father after all these years and all the pain they'd doled out to each other, this had to be easier.

He'd convinced himself that it had to be.

"I am sorry, princess," he said, because that was where it needed to start, and it didn't seem to matter that he couldn't recall the last time he'd said those words. It was Valentina, so they flowed. Because he meant them with every part of himself. "You must know that above all else."

She straightened on the bed, though her gaze flicked away from his as she did. It seemed to take her a long time to look back at him.

"I beg your pardon?"

"I am sorry," he said again. There was too much in

his head, then. Felipe. His father. Even his mother, who had refused to interrupt her solitude for a wedding, and no matter that it was the only wedding a child of hers would ever have. She'd been immovable. He took another step toward Valentina, then stopped, opening up his hands at his sides. "I spent so long angrily not being my brother that I think I forgot how to be me. Until you. You challenged me. You stood up to me. You made me want to be a better man."

He heard what he assumed were her wedding attendants in the next room, but Valentina only regarded him, her green eyes almost supernaturally calm. So calm he wondered if perhaps she'd taken something to settle her nerves. But he forgot that when she smiled, serene and easy, and settled back on the bed.

"Go on," she murmured, with a regal little nod.

"In my head, you were perfect," he told her, drifting another step or so in her direction. "I thought that if I could win you, I could fix my life. I could make my father treat me with respect. I could clean up my reputation. I could make myself the Prince I always wanted to be, but couldn't, because I wasn't my brother and never could be." He shook his head. "And then at the first hint that you weren't exactly who I wanted you to be, I lost it. If you weren't perfect, then how could you save me?"

That was what it was, he understood. It had taken him too long to recognize it. Why else would he have been so furious with her? So deeply, personally wounded? He was an adult man who risked death for amusement. Who was he to judge the games other people played? Normally, he wouldn't. But then, he'd spent his whole life pretending to be normal. Pretending he wasn't looking for someone to save him. Fix him. Grant him peace.

No wonder he'd been destroyed by the idea that the

only person who'd ever seemed the least bit capable of doing that had been deliberately deceiving him.

"I don't need you to save me," he told her now. "I believe you already have. I want you to marry me."

Again, the sounds of her staff while again, she only watched him with no apparent reaction. He told himself he'd earned her distrust. He made himself keep going.

"I want to love you and enjoy you and taste you, everywhere. I do not want a grim march through our contractual responsibilities for the benefit of a fickle press. I want no *heir and spare,* I want to have babies. I want to find out what our life is like when neither one of us is pretending anything. We can do that, princess, can we not?"

She only gazed back at him, a faint smile flirting with the edge of her lips. Then she sat up, folding her hands very nicely, very neatly in her lap.

"I'm moved by all of this, of course," she said in a voice that made it sound as if she wasn't the least bit moved. It rubbed at him, making all the raw places inside him…ache. But he told himself to stand up straight and take it like a man. He'd earned it. Which wasn't to say he wouldn't fight for her, of course. No matter what she said. Even if she was who he had to fight. "But you think I'm a raving madwoman, do you not?"

And that was the crux of it. There was what he knew was possible, and there was Valentina. And if this was what Rodolfo had to do to have her, he was willing to do it. Because he didn't want their marriage to be like his parents'. The fake smiles and churning fury beneath it. The bitterness that had filled the spaces between them. The sharp silences and the barbed comments.

He didn't want any of that, so brittle and empty. He wanted to live.

After all this time being barely alive when he hadn't

felt he deserved to be, when everyone thought he should have died in Felipe's place and he'd agreed, Rodolfo wanted to *live*.

"I do not know how to trust anyone," he told her now, holding her gaze with his, "but I want to trust you. I want to be the man you see when you look at me. If that means you want me to believe that there are two of you, I will accept that." His voice was quiet, but he meant every word. "I will try."

Still, she didn't say anything, and he had to fight back the temper that kicked in him.

"Am I too late, Valentina? Is this—" He cut himself off and studied her clothes again. He stood before her in a morning coat and she was in jeans. "Are you planning to run out on this wedding? Now? The guests have already started arriving. You will have to pass them on your way out. Is that what you planned?"

"I was planning to run out on the wedding, yes," she replied, and smiled as she said it, which made no sense. Surely she could not be so *flippant* about something that would throw both of their kingdoms into disarray—and rip his heart out in the process. Surely he'd only imagined she'd said such a thing. But Valentina nodded across the room. "But the good news is that *she* looks like she's planning to stay."

And on some level he knew before he turned. But it still stole his breath.

His princess was standing in the door to what must have been her dressing room, clad in a long white dress. There was a veil pinned to a shining tiara on her head that flowed to the ground behind her. She was so lovely it made his throat tight, and *her* green eyes were dark with emotion and shone with tears. He looked back to check, to make sure he wasn't losing his own mind, but the spitting image of her was still sitting on the end of the bed, still dressed in the wrong clothes.

He'd known something was off about her the moment he'd walked in. *His* princess lit him up. She gazed at him and he wanted to fly off into the blue Mediterranean sky outside the windows. More, he believed he could.

She was looking at him that way now, and his heart soared.

He thought he could lose himself in those eyes of hers. "How long have you been standing there?"

"Since you walked in the door," she whispered.

"Natalie," he said, his voice rough, because she'd heard everything. Because he really had been talking to the right princess after all. "You told me you were Natalie."

She smiled at him, a tearful, gorgeous smile that changed the world around. "I am," she whispered. "But I would have been Valentina for you, if that was what you wanted. I tried."

Valentina was talking, but Rodolfo was no longer listening. He moved to *his princess* and took her hands in his, and there it was. Fire and need. That sense of homecoming. *Life.*

He didn't hesitate. He went down on his knees before her.

"Marry me, Natalie," he said. Or begged, really. Her hands trembled in his. "Marry me because you want to, not because our fathers decided a prince from Tissely should marry a princess from Murin almost thirty years ago. Marry me because, when you were not pretending to be Valentina and I was not being an ass, I suspect we were halfway to falling in love."

She pulled a hand from his and slid it down to stroke over his cheek, holding him. Blessing him. Making him whole.

"I suspect it's a lot more than halfway," she whispered. "When you said *mine,* you meant it." Natalie shook her head, and the cascading veil moved with her, making her look almost ethereal. But the hand at his jaw was all too real. "No one ever meant it, Rodolfo. My mother told me I grew up, you see. And everything else was a job I did, not anything real. Not anything true. Not you."

"I want to live," he told her with all the solemnity of the most sacred vow. "I want to live with you, Natalie."

"I love you," she whispered, and then she bent down or he surged up, and his mouth was on hers again. At last.

She tasted like love. Like freedom. Like falling end over end through an endless blue sky only with this woman, Rodolfo didn't care if there was a parachute. He didn't care if he touched ground. He wanted to carry on falling forever, just like this.

Only when there was the delicate sound of a throat being cleared did he remember that Valentina was still in the room.

He pulled back from Natalie, taking great satisfaction in her flushed cheeks and that hectic gleam in her green eyes. Later, he thought, he would lay her out on a wide, soft bed and learn every single inch of her delectable body. He would let her do the same when he was sated. He estimated that would take only a few years.

Outside, the church bells began to ring.

"I believe that is our cue," he said, holding fast to her hand.

Natalie's breath deserted her in a rush, and Rodolfo braced himself.

"I want to marry you," she said fiercely. "You have no idea how much. I wanted it from the moment I met you, whether I could admit it to myself or not." She shook her head. "But I can't. Not like this."

"Like what?" He lifted her fingers to his mouth. "What can be terrible enough to prevent us from marrying? I haven't felt alive in two decades, princess. Now that I do, I do not want to waste a single moment of the time I have left. Especially if I get to share that time with you."

"Rodolfo, listen to me." She took his hand between hers, frowning up at him. "Your whole life was plotted out for you since the moment you were born. Even when your brother was alive. My mother might have made some questionable choices, but because she did, I got something you didn't. I lived exactly how I wanted to live. I found out what made me happy and I did it. That's what you should do. *Truly live.* I would hate myself if I stood between you and the life you deserve."

"You love me," he reminded her, and he slid his hand around to hold the nape of her neck, smiling when she shivered. "You want to marry me. How can it be that even in this, you are defiant and impossible?"

"Oh, she's more than that," Valentina chimed in from the bed, and then smiled when they both turned to stare at her. A little too widely, Rodolfo thought. "She's pregnant."

His head whipped back to Natalie and he saw the truth in his princess's eyes, wide and green. He let go of her, letting his gaze move over what little of her body he could see in that flowing, beautiful dress, even though he knew it was ridiculous. He could count—and he knew exactly when he'd been with her on that couch in Rome. To the minute.

He'd longed for her every minute since.

But mostly, he felt a deep, supremely male and wildly possessive triumph course through him like a brand-new kind of fire.

"Bad luck, *princesita,*" he murmured, and he didn't

try very hard to keep his feelings out of his voice. "That means you're stuck with me, after all."

"That's the point," she argued. "I don't want to be stuck. I don't want *you* to be stuck!"

He smiled at her, because if she'd thought she was his before, she had no idea what was coming. He'd waited his whole life to love another this much, and now she was more than that. Now she was a family. "But I do."

And then, to make absolutely sure there would be no talking her way out of this or plotting something new and even more insane than the secret twin sister who was watching all of this from her spot on the bed, he wrenched open the door behind him and called for King Geoffrey himself.

"Make him hurry," he told the flabbergasted attendants as they raced to do his bidding. "Tell him I'm seeing double."

In the end, it all happened so fast.

King Geoffrey strode in, already frowning, only to stop dead when he saw Natalie and Valentina sitting next to each other on the chaise. Waiting for him.

Natalie braced herself as Valentina stood and launched into an explanation. She rose to her feet, too, shooting a nervous look over at Rodolfo where he lounged against one of the bed's four posters, because she expected the king to rage. To wave it all away the way Erica had. To say or do something horrible—

But instead, the King of Murin made a small, choked sound.

And then he was upon them, pulling both Natalie and Valentina into a long, hard, endless hug.

"I thought you were dead," he whispered into Natalie's neck. "She told me you were dead."

And for a long while, there was nothing but the church bells outside and the three of them, not letting go.

"I forget myself," Geoffrey said at last, wiping at his face as he stepped back from their little knot. Natalie made as if to move away, but Valentina gripped her hand and held her fast. "There is a wedding."

"My wedding," Rodolfo agreed from the end of the bed.

The king took his time looking at the man who would be his son-in-law one way or another. Natalie caught her breath.

"You were promised this marriage the moment you became the Crown Prince, of course, as your brother was before you."

"Yes." Rodolfo inclined his head. "I am to marry a princess of Murin. But it does not specify which one."

Valentina blinked. "It doesn't?"

The king smiled. "Indeed it does not."

"But everyone expects Valentina," Natalie heard herself say. Everyone turned to stare at her and she felt her cheeks heat up. "They do. It's printed in the programs."

"The programs," Rodolfo repeated as if he couldn't believe she'd said that out loud, and his dark gaze glittered as it met hers, promising a very specific kind of retribution.

She couldn't wait.

"It is of no matter," King Geoffrey said, sounding every inch the monarch he was. He straightened his exquisite formal coat with a jerk. "This is the Sovereign Kingdom of Murin and last I checked, I am its king. If I wish to marry off a daughter only recently risen from the dead, then that is exactly what I shall do." He started for the door. "Come, Valentina. There is work to be done."

"What work?" Valentina frowned at his retreating

back. But Natalie noticed she followed after him anyway. Instantly and obediently, like the proper princess she was.

"If I have two daughters, only one of them can marry into the royal house of Tissely," King Geoffrey said. "Which means you must take a different role altogether. Murin will need a queen of its own, you know."

Valentina shot Natalie a harried sort of smile over her shoulder and then followed the King out, letting the door fall shut behind her.

Leaving Natalie alone with Rodolfo at last.

It was as if all the emotions and revelations of the day spun around in the center of the room, exploding into the sudden quiet. Or maybe that was Natalie's head— especially when Rodolfo pushed himself off the bedpost and started for her, his dark gaze intent.

And extraordinarily lethal.

A wise woman would have run, Natalie was certain. But her knees were in collusion with her galloping pulse. She sank down on the chaise and watched instead, her heart pounding, as Rodolfo stalked toward her.

"Valentina arrived in the middle of the night," she told him as he came toward her, all that easy masculine grace on display in the morning coat he wore entirely too well, every inch of him a prince. And something far more dangerous than merely charming. "I never had a sister growing up, but I think I quite like the idea."

"If she appears in the dead of night in my bedchamber, princess, it will not end well." Rodolfo's hard mouth curved. "It will involve the royal guard."

He stopped when he was at the chaise and squatted down before her, running his hands up her thighs to find and gently cup her belly through the wedding gown she wore. He didn't say a word, he just held his palm there, the warmth of him penetrating the layers she wore and sinking deep into her skin. Heating her up the way he always did.

"Would you have told me?" he asked, and though he wasn't looking at her as he said it, she didn't confuse it for an idle question.

"Of course," she whispered.

"Yet you told me to go off and be free, like some dreadfully self-indulgent Kerouac novel."

"There was a secret, nine-month limit on your freedom," Natalie said, and her voice wavered a bit when he raised his head. "I was trying to be noble."

His gaze was dark and direct and filled with light.

"Marry me," he said.

She whispered his name like a prayer. "There are considerations."

"Name them."

Rodolfo inclined his head in that way she found almost too royal to be believed, and yet deeply alluring. It was easy to imagine him sitting on an actual throne somewhere, a crown on his head and a scepter in his hand. A little shiver raced down her spine at the image.

"I didn't mean to get pregnant," she told him, very seriously. "I'm not trying to trap you."

"The hormones must be affecting your brain." He shook his head, too much gold in his gaze. "You are already trapped. This is an arranged marriage."

"I wasn't even sick. Everyone knows the first sign of pregnancy is getting sick, but I didn't. I had headaches. I was tired. It was Valentina who suggested I might be pregnant. So I counted up the days and she got a test somewhere, and…"

She blew out a breath.

"And," he agreed. He smiled. "Does that truly require consideration? Because to me it sounds like something of a bonus, to marry the father of your child. But I am alarmingly traditional in some ways, it turns out."

Natalie scoffed at the famous daredevil prince who had so openly made a mockery of the very institutions he came from, saying such things. "What are you traditional about?"

His dark eyes gleamed. "You."

Her heart stuttered at that, but she pushed on. "And we've only had sex the one time. It could be a fluke. Do you want to base your whole life on a fluke?"

His gaze was intent on hers, with that hint of gold threaded through it, and his hands were warm even through layers and layers of fabric.

"Yes," he said. "I do."

It felt like a kiss, like fire and need, but Natalie kept going.

"You barely know me. And the little while you have known me, you thought I was someone else. Then when I told you I wasn't who you thought I was, you were sure I was either trying to con you, or crazy."

"All true." His mouth curved. "We can have a nice, long marriage and spend the rest of our days sorting it out."

"Why are you in such a rush to get married?" she demanded, sounding cross even to her own ears, and he laughed.

It was that rich, marvelous sound. Far better than Valentina's gold-plated chocolate. Far sweeter, far more complex and infinitely more satisfying.

Rodolfo stood then, rising with an unconscious display of that athletic grace of his that never failed to make her head spin.

"We are dressed for it, after all," he said. "It seems a pity to waste that dress."

She gazed up at him, caught by how beautiful he was. How intense. And how focused on her. It was hard to think of a single reason she wouldn't love him wildly and fiercely until the day she died. Whether with him or not.

Better to be with him.

Better, for once in her life, to stay where she belonged. Where after all this time, she finally *belonged*.

"Natalie." And her name—her real name at last—was like a gift on his tongue. "The bells are ringing. The cathedral is full. Your father has given his blessing and your secret twin sister, against all odds, has returned and given us her approval, too, in her fashion. But more important than all of that, you are pregnant with my child. And I have no intention of letting either one of you out of my sight ever again."

She pulled in a breath, then let it out slowly, as if she'd already decided. As if she'd already stayed.

"I risked death," Rodolfo said then, something tender in his gaze. "For fun, princess. Imagine what I can do now I have decided to live."

"Anything at all," she replied, tears of joy in her voice. Her eyes. Maybe her heart, as well. "I think you're the only one who doesn't believe in you, Rodolfo."

"I may or may not," he said quietly. "That could change with the tides. But it only matters to me if you do."

And she didn't know what she might have done then, because he held out his hand. The way he had on that dance floor in Rome.

Daring her. Challenging her.

She was the least spontaneous person in all the world, but Rodolfo made it all feel as if it was inevitable. As if she had been put on this earth for no other purpose but to love him and be loved by him in turn.

Starting right this minute, if she let it.

"Come." His voice was low. His gaze was clear. "Marry me. Be my love. All the rest will sort itself out, *princesita*, while we make love and babies with equal vigor, and rule my country well. It always does." And his smile then was brighter than the Mediterranean sun. "I love you, Natalie. Come with me. I promise you, whatever else happens, you will never regret it."

"I will hold you to that," she said, her heart in her voice.

And then she slipped her hand into Rodolfo's and let him lead her out into the glorious dance of the rest of their lives.

* * * * *

HIS PREGNANT
ROYAL BRIDE

AMY RUTTAN

This book is dedicated to Robin, my partner in crime for this duet. You were awesome, and I would work with you again in a heartbeat. I'm so glad we got to meet face to face finally!

For my friend Shay, who is just as giving and admirable as my heroine. You do so much and ask for nothing. So glad we're friends.

And of course Laura, my editor extraordinaire, who concocted this idea. Also for Tilda, who always helps out with my AFS and keywords and for stepping in while the rest of us were in California.

PROLOGUE

"THAT HAS TO be the most monotonous lecturer that I've ever had the displeasure to listen to," Shay teased as she took a sip of her pineapple cocktail. She glanced over shyly at Dr. Dante Affini, who was attending the same conference on trauma simulation as her in Honolulu. She felt as if she was talking too loudly, which was something she always did in the presence of a man she found utterly attractive. And Dr. Dante Affini was all that and more. Just a few days with him and she was a lost woman. Add in the tropical setting and drinks...

It was a perfect paradise.

Shay had intended to throw herself completely into her work, as she always did, but on the first day of the conference she'd bumped into Italian surgeon Dr. Dante Affini looking perplexed. He hadn't known where to go and she'd helped him.

Since she'd let him know that she was attending the same presentations as him, they'd been inseparable. She didn't mind in the least. Dante was handsome, charming, intelligent and single.

She bit her lip, blood heating her cheeks. What was she doing? She didn't get involved with doctors, but with Dante it was hard not to.

He didn't look down his nose at her for being a nurse practitioner. Usually at these kind of conferences the nurses stuck together and the physicians stuck together. Except Dante seemed to be the exception. He'd turned down golfing, dinners and drinks with the other surgeons to accompany her. They'd attended the same lectures and seemed to agree on the same approaches to medicine.

Now the conference was winding up and it had been Dante's idea to get drinks.

She knew she shouldn't have accepted his invitation. It was not something she was used to doing, but this was sort of a work vacation and for once, Shay thought, why not?

Dante was charming, sexy, and she'd been so busy with her work for the last couple of years that maybe it was the perfect time to kick back and have some fun.

"*Sì*, that was most terrible." He shuddered and took a drink of his pineapple juice, then turned around, his dark eyes flickering out over the water. "It is a beautiful night."

Shay nodded. "The breeze is nice. It was sweltering in that room."

"Yes, it was most unpleasant." He waved his hand in a sweeping arc. "This, however, is paradise."

And he wasn't wrong. The sun was setting, like molten gold against the turquoise water. Palm trees swayed gently in the breeze and the sky was darkening. Soon it would be full of stars as the hotel where the conference was being held was off the beaten track. It was on the North Shore and there wasn't much else around it. No city, no noise and no distractions. It was heavenly.

"I wish I had more time to explore," Shay said wistfully. "I never traveled much until I joined the United World Wide Health Association, but that's for work and I don't get a lot of downtime on assignments. It's all about the work."

Dante shook his head. "That is no way to live life."

"Maybe not, but I love what I do."

He smiled at her, that charming, sexy, crooked smile

she was getting used to seeing every day. She was going to miss it when the conference was over.

"Of course, who am I to talk about living life, *cara*? My main focus is also my work."

"See, then why harass me?" she teased.

"Still, when you take an assignment somewhere, you must have time off."

Shay shrugged. "A little bit, but lately my assignments have been to mainly Third World countries after they've suffered a natural disaster and it really isn't safe to wander away from base camp to take in the sights."

Dante grinned. "Did I mention how incredibly brave you are, *cara*? I admire that about you."

Warmth flooded her cheeks. She could listen to Dante talk all night. He had such a dreamy Italian accent but spoke English so fluently.

"I just do my job," Shay said, brushing off the compliment, because she was proud of the work she did. It was a way to honor her mother, who should be alive still, if it weren't for Hurricane Katrina and the aftermath. The ill-effects of a poisoned house had prematurely taken the life of her mother, in the end.

It was at that moment that Shay knew what direction she had to take her life.

She'd worked hard to get where she was.

Now her job was to train other nurses and first responders by using simulation, so that they could go into the war zones, the disaster areas, and save lives, because that was all that mattered.

Saving lives.

"You do more than that, *cara*. I see it—you care about people and that's what makes you special." That smile disappeared and he fiddled with the straw in his drink. "Not everyone cares so much about others."

She was glad that the sun was setting, so that he couldn't see the blush he was causing.

Dante affected her in a way no man had in a long time. She was nervous around him. Giddy.

If she were anywhere else, she'd distance herself from him, but because she'd never see him again she figured it was okay to engage in harmless flirtation.

In a fantasy.

Not that anything would happen between the two of them.

Says who?

"Thank you," she finally said, trying to shake out the naughty thoughts suddenly traipsing across her mind.

"So let's do something about your lack of exploring," Dante said, setting down his empty glass on the bar. "Come."

"What?" she asked, confused.

"Look, it's our last night in paradise. Let's walk down to the beach and take a walk through the waves, follow the shore. It's a beautiful night."

"I don't know…"

What're you waiting for?

She glanced up at Dante, who stood in front of her, those dark eyes twinkling in the waning sunlight, the breeze making his short mop of ebony curls stir. His white cotton shirt billowed, so she could see the outline of his hard, muscular chest. His bronzed skin glowing in the waning light and, of course, that lopsided smile.

"What about the *luau*? Aren't we supposed to go there and network? You've traveled so far to attend this, don't you want to mingle?"

He snorted. "I have done enough networking to last a lifetime. For once I've no desire to talk about medicine. Tonight is a beautiful night. Let's go."

Go.

"Okay," Shay said, not needing any more convincing. She finished her drink and set her empty glass down on the bar and took his hand. It was strong and she was surprised how easily her hand slipped into his. She hoped he didn't notice that her nails were much too short, that her palms were rough from the hard physical work. She envied well-manicured nails, perfectly coifed hair, women who had time for makeup and clothes that weren't torn, stained or scrubs.

Only Dante didn't seem to care.

She couldn't believe that he'd chosen to spend all his free time with her this week.

A surgeon and a nurse.

Don't worry about that now. Just enjoy it. Live the fantasy for one night.

They walked away from the bar, down a winding sandy path to the beach. It was tranquil and a bit deserted at the moment. It was perfect.

"Hold on," she said. She let go of Dante's hand.

"What're you doing?" he asked.

"Taking off my shoes. The sand is getting in and I hate that feeling of sand in your shoes."

He chuckled. "Good idea."

They kicked off their shoes and carried them as they headed down to the shore. The sun was almost gone, as if it were disappearing behind a curtain of water. It was picture-perfect. The water licked at their toes as they walked in silence along the shoreline.

It was the perfect end to the conference.

Tomorrow she'd be flying back to New Orleans for a short time and then off on her next assignment to the Middle East. Always moving, as she'd been doing her whole life. No stability. No roots. New Orleans was just a base for her, but it really wasn't home since her mother died and she didn't know why she kept returning to it.

"You seem sad all of a sudden, *cara*."

The way he called her *cara* made her tremble with anticipation.

"I was just thinking how wonderful this week has been." She bit her lip and sighed. "It's been amazing getting to know you, Dante."

He smiled and then ran his knuckles across her cheek. "I've enjoyed my time with you as well, *cara*."

Shay's pulse began to race and she closed her eyes, his touch making her heart skip a beat, and then, before she had a chance to say anything else, his lips claimed hers.

She dropped her shoes to the sand and sank into the kiss, wrapping her arms around him and pulling him close.

Dante's kiss deepened, his tongue pushing past her lips; it was a kiss that seared her soul.

"Shay," he whispered, his mouth still close to her, his hands cupping her face. "I'm sorry, I couldn't help myself. You're so beautiful, so wonderful…" He kissed her again.

"I don't want this to end," she whispered against his ear as he held her close, his hands drifting down her back.

"Me neither."

"Then let's not let tonight end." She took his hand. "Let's go to your room…"

"Are you sure, *cara*?" he asked.

"Positive. We can just have tonight. I'm not looking for anything long-term, Dante."

Just passion. Unforgettable passion.

That was what she craved right now.

He smiled. "I want tonight too."

Dante took her hand and they picked up their shoes and headed back to the hotel, to his room and something wonderful that she'd always remember…

Dante didn't know what he was thinking when he bent down to kiss Shay, other than that the need to connect with her was so totally overwhelming. With the tropical wind blowing wisps of her honey-blonde hair around her heart-shaped face, he couldn't resist her siren call.

He didn't know what possessed him, other than absolute desire and need, because he'd sworn when Olivia broke his heart he'd keep away from women. Love was a loss of control and he hated losing that loss of control.

Only from the moment he'd met Shay, when she'd reached out to help him, he couldn't help himself. He knew he should've stayed away, but couldn't. Her brown eyes were warm, friendly, and the more he got to know her, the more he felt completely at ease with her.

To the point where his carefully constructed walls came down.

"*Cara*, I want you so bad," he whispered against her neck.

"I want you too," she said, her breath hot against his skin. It drove him wild.

It's only for one night.

And he had to keep reminding himself of that. That it was only one night.

She only wants tonight. I can give her tonight.

His heart didn't have to get hurt.

You don't have one-night stands, a little voice reminded him, but he shook that thought away. His brother did and he fared just fine. Dante was not his father. He wasn't married, he wasn't hurting anyone, they were both consenting adults.

This was what his younger brother, Enzo, lived by; he could do that too, if only for one night.

Shay sighed as he ran his fingers through her silky hair as she wrapped her arms around him. Her long, delicate fingers tickling at the nape of his neck.

Mio Dio. It was only for tonight.

He could give himself over to one night. One night didn't mean forever.

It couldn't.

CHAPTER ONE

DANTE CLENCHED HIS fists as he jammed them into the pockets of his crisp white lab coat. Everything about him was controlled and ordered. Only today his schedule was off, and he was not in the mood for meeting the practitioner from America and running a simulation lab with him. And it wasn't just for one day; he'd then have him working under him as a surgical nurse in his operating room for twelve weeks.

Twelve weeks might not seem long in the grand scheme of things, but if Dante and this nurse practitioner didn't get along, then twelve weeks would feel like an eternity.

He remembered the last American from the United World Wide Health Association he'd worked with two years ago and that had been a nightmare. She'd been totally unorganized and needed constant guidance, which had driven him crazy.

Not all Americans are bad.

And his mood lightened as he thought of Shay and that stolen night in Oahu. She was the first woman he'd been with since Olivia had crushed his heart. Shay was one American he could get used to having around. Even now, months later, he could still feel her lips on his.

Only she was off who knew where on her latest assignment and he had to make nice with a stranger. Someone he didn't trust, and it brought back why he was in a bad mood.

His father. Someone else he absolutely didn't trust.

At dinner last night with his younger brother, Enzo, Dante had learned that their father, Prince Marco Affini, had once again sold off more of the family land. And he was eyeing the land their late mother had left in trust for Dante and Enzo until they married and produced an heir. At least their father couldn't sell it off yet. Unless they married before they turned thirty-five and produced an heir within a year of that marriage. Last night Enzo had reminded Dante once again that soon Dante would be turning thirty-five in a matter of months, without a marriage in sight.

Dante was painfully aware that his villa on Lido di Venezia was in danger of being sold as well, because that had been his maternal grandfather's home.

The villa on the sandbar, a ten-minute ferry ride from Venice proper, was part of Dante's inheritance. It would be his as long as he married and produced an heir by the time he was thirty-five, according to the stipulations of the trust fund and the marriage contract between his parents, as his mother had been a commoner and his father of royal blood.

And his thirty-fifth birthday was approaching fast, without a wife or heir in sight.

And whose fault was that?

It was his. He knew it; he just didn't have any desire to get married after what had happened with his ex, Olivia, and he didn't want to have a child out of wedlock. Even if he did, that wouldn't help him recover his inheritance, such were the archaic terms of the trust.

If he didn't get married and have a child, he would lose his home, everything that was meant for him by his late mother, including his beloved vineyard in Tuscany.

His grandfather had worked that vineyard. It was his pride and joy. Even though the family had money, his maternal grandfather always took pride in working his land. A work ethic that Dante had picked up on. He loved saving lives and he loved the life that bloomed in his vineyard in Tuscany.

Dante loved it there.

He loved working the land himself as well and the thought of someone else owning it was too much to bear.

It kept him awake most nights and he had the legal receipts to prove that he'd tried to get around the trust his mother signed on her wedding day, but it was ironclad. His father had the upper hand, until Dante and Enzo were married.

Dante downed the shot of espresso he'd grabbed before he headed to the lecture hall where he'd welcome the new United World Wide Health Association nurses and first responders who had come from all over Italy to join the organization. Here they'd learn what they needed to know, and then they would disperse over the world, providing health care.

Dante admired them and, even though he didn't want to be here and meet with his new associate from the United States, he knew he couldn't take his frustrations out on them.

He took a deep breath, ran his hand through his dark hair as he glanced in a mirror briefly, cursing inwardly for not having shaved the stubble from his face, and he hated the dark circles under his eyes, but he hadn't got much sleep last night.

Once, he'd had the chance to save all the land meant for him, but that had cost him his heart and he swore he would never fall into that trap again. He just had to get used to the fact he was going to lose it all.

He was going to let down his brother and the memory of his mother.

His father would sell it all off and Dante would have to find a new place to live in a matter of a few months. He shook his head as he tried not to think about that now. He had to be charming and affable as the head of trauma at the Ospedale San Pietro.

Bracing himself now, Dante opened the door, ready to greet the American.

"*Ciao*, I'm Dr. Dante Affini, Head of..."

The nurse turned, just slightly, and Dante couldn't believe who he was looking at. His pulse raced and a rare smile tugged at the corner of his mouth. It was Shay!

She looked stunning. She was absolutely glowing, her cheeks rosy with a bloom she didn't have before.

Her honey-blonde hair wasn't as long as he remembered. She'd cut it, shorter in a bob, but it suited her delicate heart-shaped face. Those dark brown eyes of hers were warm and welcoming as she smiled at him, her pink lips soft and inviting. He could still feel them pressed against his. A blush rose in her round, creamy cheeks, deepening the healthy glow. Her lithe frame was fuller, but the curves suited her. "Hello, Dante."

"Shay?" Dante whispered, and then he smiled, realizing it was her who was here to work with him. "What are you doing here? I thought... I thought Daniel Lucey was going to be running this program."

"He was," Shay said. "But something came up for him, so I jumped at the chance to come to Italy and take an easier job for a while."

"An easier job? You're never one to back away from a challenge, *cara*."

A pink blush deepened on her cheeks and she tucked away an errant silky strand behind her ear. "I know, but I have no choice." She bit her lip. "Dante, I took this job because...because I'm pregnant."

Pregnant. Shay was having a baby?

It hit him and for a moment he wasn't sure he'd heard her correctly. Well, that explained the glow and the newly acquired curves. And then another realization struck him...

"Is it... Is it mine?"

"Yes." She bit her lip in a way that had driven him wild before but now filled him with a sense of trepidation.

A baby.

He had put up the walls to protect himself for a reason and he'd been a fool for letting her in back in Oahu.

It had been a moment of complete weakness on his part. Dante scrubbed a hand over his face.

Why didn't she tell me? Was he really the father? Olivia had led him to believe that she carried his baby, only then he'd found out she'd tricked him. She'd already been pregnant when they'd slept together. Olivia had viewed Dante as perfect daddy material for another man's child...

He was angry. Angry at himself for thinking Shay might be different, but apparently not. He should've known better—a week and a one-night stand were no time to get to know someone. To trust someone.

A pink blush tinged her creamy cheeks. "I took this job so that I could tell you in person."

"Why didn't you tell me sooner?" he demanded. "Why didn't you contact me before you showed up here? As soon as you found out? It's been months, Shay. You can understand my trepidation. My anger, surely?"

She winced. "I know. But I've only very recently found out myself, Dante. I'm sixteen weeks."

"Four months in and you expect me to believe that you just found out?" Dante scoffed.

"Yes. I was working in a war-torn area. My periods have always been irregular and I put their absence down to stress and travel. I wasn't keeping that close an eye on dates, but something told me that it had been too long. I took a test, which came out positive, but then there was no way to contact you. Communication was spotty."

Dante saw red. "You were pregnant in a war zone?"

Her eyes narrowed. "There are lots of pregnant women in war zones."

Dante cursed under his breath and scrubbed a hand over his face. "That's not what I meant."

"Sure sounded like it." She crossed her arms and he noticed her breasts were fuller and he recalled at that moment the way his hands fit so nicely around them.

Get control of yourself.

"Fine. So you couldn't get word to me."

"No, I thought it would be news better delivered in person."

"I want a paternity test," he demanded.

Shocked and hurt, Shay glared at him. "It's your baby, Dante. I haven't been with anyone else."

"You didn't even know you were pregnant right away, so you understand my hesitancy. We used protection," he said.

"A faulty condom. They're not infallible." Shay sighed. "And I don't sleep around. I don't sleep with strangers."

"Wasn't I a stranger, *cara*?"

She shot him daggers. "I didn't come here to make you a father, Dante. I actually took the job because it paid well, so that I could take a longer maternity leave when I return to the States."

"So you considered not telling me?"

"Of course not. You have the right to know about your child, Dante. What I'm saying is that I don't expect anything from you."

Everything was sinking in and he was having a hard time processing for a moment. He wanted to believe that she was telling him the truth, but he'd been burned before. And thanks to his father's indiscretions the entire world seemed to know that he was a prince, poised to inherit a vast estate of land and money. Wasn't that what had drawn Olivia to him?

Of course, if Shay was pregnant with his child, it solved all of his problems.

He had to be married and have an heir by the time he was thirty-five. There was nothing in the will that stated he had to stay married. And while Olivia had made him very wary of marriage, he had wanted to be a father for as long as he could remember. He wanted the happy family he'd never had growing up. Plus, he knew that Shay was passionate about her job. She wouldn't want to settle down in Italy with him—hadn't she told him that she feared staying in one place for too long? What if he could get full custody of the baby? Have the child he'd always wanted without risking his heart.

"Dante, say something. Anything," Shay said. "I know this must be a terrible shock."

Before he could say anything there was a knock on his door. His assistant poked her head round it. "Dr. Affini? The trainees are gathered in the lecture theatre and are waiting for you."

Dante acknowledged the woman before he turned back to Shay. "We'll talk later. We have a job to do."

Shay smiled, relieved. "Yes. We have a job to do."

He'd let her have relief for now, but this was far from over.

Shay had wanted to tell Dante that she was pregnant from the moment she'd found out. She was frustrated when she realized she'd put their child in danger, and then when he'd insinuated that, she'd felt even guiltier. She wasn't irresponsible. Once she'd known she was expecting, she'd been flown out, leaving her free to take over this assignment from her colleague Daniel, who'd sadly just been diagnosed with stage two colon cancer. She'd dreaded telling Dante here, at work, but she respected him and he deserved to know about their child. She also wanted him to know that she didn't expect anything.

She wasn't looking for a marriage or even for him to be part of the child's life if he didn't want to be.

She knew firsthand what it was like when a man was forced into staying.

Her own father had made that painfully clear to her until the day he'd left her and her mother.

So she knew what it was like to be rejected by her father and she didn't want that for her child. And that was why she'd been terrified of telling Dante. Terrified he'd reject her and the baby, which would make the next twelve weeks working with him miserable.

Glad to be able to focus for the moment on the job at hand, Shay took the time it took them to make their way to the lecture theatre to chat about the assignment with Dante.

"I think I'm pretty much up-to-date on what Daniel was planning to do and how he was going to implement the simulation and training program," Shay said as she skimmed through the binder that she'd been given as she'd boarded the plane.

"So, what happened to Daniel?" Dante asked.

"Cancer," Shay said sadly.

"That's too bad. I wish him a speedy recovery, but I wish they had told me he wasn't coming." Dante rubbed his dimpled chin, and those butterflies that liked to dance around in the pit of her stomach months ago were starting up again. She'd forgotten how he affected her. He was still so handsome, the stubble on his chin suited him and she resisted the urge to tuck back the errant strand of his thick black hair.

"I thought you had been informed that Daniel was no longer coming," she said.

"Clearly not," he snapped.

"Dante, you're clearly not okay with this."

"I'm fine," he said, and he took the binder from her, not even looking at her.

She knew he wasn't. This was not the same man she'd spent a fairy-tale week with in Oahu. Then again, she hadn't really been herself either. Like when she'd decided to throw caution to the wind and have a one-night stand.

"Okay, you're fine, then. Shall we go and talk to the trainees? They are waiting."

"Of course." Dante didn't even look at Shay as he opened the door on the far side of the room. It was as if he was angry that she was here.

Can you blame him?

They walked out onto the stage of the small lecture theatre. The first two rows were filled with new United World Wide Health Association recruits, men and women who would be taking a crash course in first response and trauma.

Dante's job was to teach them trauma surgery and Shay was going to run them through a course of simulations. Based on situations she'd found herself in when she'd first started with the United World Wide Health Association.

She kind of envied all those hopeful faces, the thirty-odd new recruits. Her first days in the UWWHA working the field were some of her favorite times. Before she took this assignment she'd been going to take a field job in the Middle East to help vaccinate refugees.

Only that was before she'd found out she was pregnant. She couldn't go then and had been weighing up her options, and then this position had become available. The more romantically minded would probably call it fate.

This would be her last foreign assignment for a long time and she was going to make the most of it.

Her career and her unborn child mattered to her. She was going to make sure her son or daughter had a good life and this job in Venice would give her a strong foundation. Even if she had to give up on her dreams for now.

The recruits were from all over Italy and some from Switzerland and France. They could all speak English and French, which Shay understood, and she was glad when Dante started to speak French to them over Italian, which she was still trying to pick up.

If her news had shaken him before, Dante didn't show it now as he spoke highly of the United World Wide Health Association and the twelve-week training program they would be completing at the hospital under his and Shay's guidance.

A baby hadn't been in her plans either, but it had happened and she was going to be a good mother and continue with her career. Even if it was going in a slightly different direction than she'd thought. She wouldn't pine away after a man who didn't want her as her mother had done.

"Your dad'll come back, Shay. You'll see. I'm his wife. He went to Alaska to work for the crab season. He'll be back and he'll take us all up to Alaska."

Of course, he never did come back.

He was still alive, the last Shay heard, but didn't want anything to do with her.

He'd moved on and he certainly didn't care that their house had been destroyed by Katrina and that his wife had died soon after from mold poisoning.

"Shay Labadie will explain the simulation scenarios you'll be going through." Dante stepped away from the podium and Shay shook the thoughts of her father from her head.

She was here to do a job.

And she always did a good job. Always saw a position through to the end, no matter what life threw at her.

She got up and explained the simulations that she would be running them through and answered questions. When she was done, the director of the UWWHA took the podium and she went and stood beside Dante. There was tension pouring off him and he barely looked at her.

Not that she could blame him.

She had dropped the fact that he was going to be a father on his lap.

She would've been more surprised if he weren't shocked by the prospect.

Once the director finished talking, there was a mix and mingle session, so that everyone could get to know one another. Shay walked toward the stairs at the end of the stage, but Dante grabbed her arm, holding her back.

"A moment *per favore*, Shay." He pinched the bridge of his nose and sighed. "First, I was serious when I said I would like a paternity test done."

"Okay." He'd been right when he'd reminded her that they were strangers who'd slept together, much as it smarted that her word wasn't enough to convince him that she didn't sleep around. "Anything else?"

"This is hard for me to say."

"Dante, you don't have to do anything. I already told you that I'm not asking for anything."

"I know you're not," he said quickly. "I am."

"What… I… You're what?" Shay didn't know how to take that response. Now she was shocked, so she asked cautiously, "What're you asking for?"

"Not much. Just that if the paternity test proves that I'm the father—"

"Which it will," she interrupted.

"*If* it does," he said through clenched teeth, "I want you to marry me."

Of all the things she'd thought he'd say, that wasn't one of them.

She hadn't been expecting that.

CHAPTER TWO

"You want...what?" Shay was trying to process what Dante had said and she wasn't sure that she completely understood him. "Could you repeat that?"

"I said that if the paternity test proves I'm the father I want you to marry me." There was no smile on his face, no glint in his eye letting her know that he was joking, because he had to be joking, right? Men just didn't ask women they'd slept with once to marry them, did they?

"That's what I thought you said, but then I was thinking that there was no way you could be asking me that." She tried to move past him, because this was a bit crazy. This was not the Dante she remembered, the Dante she knew.

You don't know Dante, remember?

And she didn't. Usually she knew the men she slept with a bit better, but when she'd been in Oahu she'd thrown caution to the wind when she'd succumbed to Dante's kiss.

Even now, standing here in front of him, she had a hard time trying to forget the way his arms had felt around her. The way he'd whispered *cara* in her ear.

This reaction to him is why you're pregnant in the first place.

"Well, I'm not asking you," he said.

"You're crazy." She tried to leave.

He stepped in front of her to block her. "I'm not asking you, Shay. I'm telling you. If I'm the father, we will get married."

What?

"You're telling me?" She cleared her throat. "Seriously?"

Dante nodded. "Yes. You will marry me."

Shay tried not to laugh at the absurdity of it. This was not real life.

"And what about the paternity test you're so adamant I take?"

He glared at her. "I only want marriage if the test proves I'm the father."

"And if it doesn't?" Which was absurd. She hadn't been with anyone since him, and before him there'd been no one else for a long time.

"Won't it?"

She crossed her arms, glaring at him. Suddenly she was having a hard time finding him charming. Sexy, yes, but charming—heck, no. More annoying than anything.

"You're the father," she replied icily.

"Then you will marry me once we receive the results." She snorted. "How romantic."

"Nothing about this is romantic, *cara*." The endearment he used on her, his voice still deep and rich. She could hear that whisper in her ears: *cara*.

"Do you love me?" she asked point-blank, shaking those thoughts from her head.

He cocked his eyebrows. "This has nothing to do with love."

"So the answer is no," she said.

"Were you expecting me to say yes? Other than one week together, we don't know each other."

"Exactly, so why would I marry you?"

He frowned. "To give our child legitimacy. A stable home. The guarantee that it will have two parents. This is a business arrangement for the sake of the child."

The premise of giving her child a good home life was very tempting, but she knew how this played out. She'd been that child after all and she wouldn't put her child through that. Through the resentment, bitterness and heartache. To the point that her father had walked away and didn't even want to see her again.

No, she didn't want that for her baby.

She didn't want her baby to feel that pain. Only he seemed to really want this baby and her father had never wanted her.

Another parent involved, especially a stationary one, means you can pursue assignments anywhere in the world.

"I'm not going to marry you," she said. "I'm here to work." She tried to leave the room, but he stepped in front of her, grabbing her by the arm, his dark eyes blazing.

"I don't think you know what you're talking about."

"I think I do," she snapped, shrugging her arm out of his grip.

"So I'm not to have access to my child?" he demanded.

"I never said that."

"You won't marry me. So that means I won't see this child. You're only in Italy for twelve weeks. Then what happens? You won't even be here when our child is born."

"Dante, I'm not denying you access to your child. I want you to be part of his or her life. We don't have to get married to raise this child. We don't even need to live in the same country."

He opened his mouth to say more when his pager buzzed. He looked down. "Incoming trauma, *dannazione*. This conversation isn't over." He stormed out of the room, his white lab coat billowing out behind him from his long strides. He was a force of nature to be reckoned with.

Shay breathed an inward sigh of relief, because for now she was able to get a breather, but she knew that this was probably far from over.

Dante stuck his head back into the room. "Are you coming, Shay? There is incoming trauma and you're to be my nurse for the next twelve weeks. I need you by my side."

By his side.

Only she wasn't sure she was going to survive the next twelve weeks. By the way things were going she was either going to kill him or fall in love with him.

And succumbing to the passion, the desire, she felt for him was not an option. Neither was falling in love.

She had to guard her heart.

Shay was not her mother and wouldn't be easily persuaded by loving a man. This was *her* life and she was going to live by her own wit.

"Of course."

She shook her head; she had to get back in the game and focus on her work here. This was her job and, when she'd found out that she was pregnant after one night of forbidden passion, she'd sworn that she wasn't going to let the pregnancy interfere with her job performance. She was a damn good nurse practitioner and simulation trainer. And that wasn't going to change.

Even though she was starting to blossom and her center of gravity was shifting, she was able to keep up with Dante's quick pace as they navigated the hallways through the hospital. He finally slowed down when they entered the trauma ward, where there was a flurry of activity. Shay could see water ambulances outside a set of automatic doors, where they were bringing in stretchers of patients.

"What happened?" Dante asked in Italian, that much she understood. The man spoke quickly and then pointed to where Dante was needed.

"Shay, this way," Dante called, waving his hand and directing her to follow him.

They entered a private treatment bay, where a man lay seriously wounded.

"He's American. Your presence might calm him," Dante whispered.

Shay nodded. "What happened?"

"A *vaporetto* was tossed when a large cruise ship came into the lagoon. The cruise ship sent a wave into St. Mark's Square and there were some injuries there as well."

"Vaporetto?" Shay asked as she pulled on a trauma gown and gloves.

"Water taxi," Dante said as he pulled on his own gloves. "This has been happening more and more. Especially during the summer months, when the tourists flock the city. Too much traffic." He shook his head with disgust.

Shay nodded and headed over to the patient, who was conscious and had a mask on. His brown eyes were wide with fear as he looked around the room.

"I can't understand a word," he mumbled through the oxygen mask.

"Me neither," Shay said gently. "I'm learning, though."

"You're American?" he asked, a hint of relief in his voice.

"I am. I'm a nurse practitioner with the United World Wide Health Association. Can you tell me what happened?"

"I don't know, I don't remember. One moment my wife and I were taking a water taxi from Lido di Venezia to St. Mark's, and then the next thing I know we're in the water. Oh, goodness, where is my wife?"

"What is her name?" Shay asked.

"Jennifer Sanders."

"I'll find her for you in a moment," Shay said gently. "It's important we make sure you're okay first."

"I can't move. I can't feel my legs," the man said, his voice rising in panic.

Dante shot her a concerned look. "What is your name, *signor*?"

The man looked at Dante. "Are you the doctor?"

"*Sì*. Can you tell me your name?"

"James, but my friends call me Jim."

Dante smiled at him. "I'm going to examine your abdomen. Tell me if anything hurts, and then we'll get an MRI of your spine."

The man nodded. Shay lifted his shirt and there was dark bruising; his belly was distended, which was a sign there was internal bleeding. The bleeding would have to be stopped before they could worry about his back. In this case internal bleeding trumped paralysis.

The man cried out when Dante did a palpation over his spleen.

"We need to get a CT scan of his abdomen, see how bad the bleeding is," Dante whispered to Shay.

"Where do I go to order that?" she asked.

"I will. You stay with him. Prep him for the procedures." Dante left the room.

Shay calmed their patient down and got an IV started, drawing the blood work needed before surgery. She had no doubt that with extensive bruising and pain Jim would need surgery and fast.

"What's your name?" Jim asked.

"Shay Labadie," she said as she took his vitals, writing them down.

"Baton Rouge?" he asked.

"No, close, though. New Orleans proper." She smiled.

"I thought it was a Louisiana accent. I'm from Mississippi. Picayune to be exact."

"Not far, then." She smiled at him warmly, trying to reassure him as his blood pressure was rising.

He grinned faintly as his eyes rolled back into his head and the monitors went into alarm.

"I need a crash cart!" she shouted, slamming her hand

against the code blue button as the rest of the team in the room jumped into action. Some situations transcended the language barrier.

"Nurse Labadie, if you contact Dr. Prescarrie, he is the neurologist. He'll be able to determine the extent of the nerve damage in our patient." Dante wanted to keep Shay busy, keep her away from the OR table, but she didn't budge. She stood by his side, passing him the instruments he needed without him having to ask for them.

She knew exactly what he needed and when.

And she was so calm about it. That was what bothered him the most. As if nothing fazed her.

She was good at her job.

Though he shouldn't be surprised. He'd been impressed by her when they were in Oahu together at the conference. Only he hadn't got to see her actually work. Now he had that privilege, but he was also very aware of the fact that she was pregnant.

With his child.

Maybe your child.

He was still reeling over the realization Shay was here and pregnant with his child as he removed Mr. Sanders's badly damaged spleen.

"I will contact him, but does he speak English?" she asked.

"He speaks French and I know that you can speak that. I heard you speak that before."

"Okay, I'll have him paged once Mr. Sanders is stable." She handed him a cautery that he didn't ask for, but damn if he didn't need it right at that moment.

"Grazie," he said grudgingly.

"You seem tense, Dr. Affini," Shay remarked.

"Of course I'm tense. I have a man open on the table."

And you've just walked back into my life carrying my baby.

Her presence here totally threw his controlled world off balance. Thoughts of Shay were kept to the privacy of his memories. To the nights he was alone and lonely, wishing he could have more than he was allotted in life. That was when he thought of Shay and their time together.

He'd romanticized her. The one stolen moment he could treasure forever and now she was here and he wasn't sure how to handle it.

Her presence unnerved him completely.

"Is there anything I can do to ease your tension?" she asked. "I mean, if my job as a scrub nurse isn't up to scratch..."

"It's fine. There is nothing you can do. Well, there is one thing, but you refused." He quickly glanced over at her and he could see her brow furrow above that surgical mask.

"This is not the time to discuss it." There was a hint of warning in her voice.

Dante raised his eyebrows. He'd never heard Shay speak in that tone before. Even at the conference when there were idiots either hitting on her or talking over her, because she was *just a nurse*, she'd always smiled sweetly and taken them down a peg. This was something different.

A clear warning.

"Why not? I like chatting while I work." He didn't, but he liked getting under her skin the way she got under his.

She snorted. "You didn't seem very receptive to talking before."

"It depends what the subject is," he teased.

"Well, I can say in no uncertain terms the subject you want to discuss, Dr. Affini, is off-limits."

He chuckled but didn't say anything further to her as he completed the splenectomy and stabilized the patient. Once he was done, Shay walked away from him and he could see her on the operating theatre's phone, obviously paging Dr. Prescarrie about Mr. Sanders's spinal injuries.

Not only was he impressed by her skill in a surgical situation, but he admired her strength. Women in his circles usually would balk under interrogation. Of course, women in his circles, women like Olivia, wouldn't even be in an operating theatre, getting their hands dirty.

"What you do is noble, Dante. It's just that I don't want to hear about it. Can't you just keep that to yourself?"

"And what am *I supposed to talk about, Olivia? Fashion, cars?"*

"The vineyards and, yes, it wouldn't hurt you to immerse yourself in the world of privilege you were born into."

Dante snorted as he pulled off his gloves and gown, disposing of them.

Olivia had hated that he was a trauma surgeon, working in a public hospital rather than in a private clinic. And his choice of surgery. Why couldn't he do something like plastic surgery?

In her mind, a prince who was a surgeon needed to do something glamorous that dealt with the glitterati, not just anybody who stumbled in through the doors.

Only that wasn't him. That was his father's world and he loathed it.

Dante might be a prince, poised to inherit a large vineyard in Tuscany and his villa on the Lido di Venezia, as well as a hefty sum of money, but Prince was just a title. It wasn't as if he were a member of the British royal family set to inherit the throne.

Being a prince was just a status in Italy. Nothing more.

His work as a surgeon meant so much more to him.

Working with his hands, doing something important whether it was tending the vines as his grandfather so lovingly had or saving a life.

That was what mattered to him.

Just like the baby that Shay was carrying inside her.

If it's yours.

Even though there was no long-term future for Shay and him, he was determined to be a good father if she would just let him.

"Dr. Prescarrie should be down soon," Shay remarked, coming into the scrub room. "He insisted on his own scrub nurse, though."

"As well he should," Dante said as he washed his hands. "You're on my service."

Shay rolled her neck and winced.

"Are you well?" he asked, concerned, seeing the discomfort etched on her face.

"Yes, just tired. I'm still getting used to the time change. A bit jet-lagged still."

"Why don't you go home and rest?"

She frowned. "I'm fine. I can still work and my shift isn't over yet."

"Shay, you need to take care of yourself. You're possibly carrying my baby."

There was a gasp behind them and they both spun around to see another nurse standing there, her brown eyes wide with shock as she looked between them.

"Sì?" Dante asked in exasperation and frustration. He had no doubt that the nurse had overheard.

"Siamo spiacenti, il Principe, non volevo interromperla." She was apologizing for interrupting them, but Mrs. Sanders was being treated for a broken wrist and was inquiring after her husband. The patient was worried. Dante told the nurse that he would be there shortly to speak to her.

The nurse nodded and left.

Shay was standing there just as stunned. "She just called you *il Principe*. Why did she refer to you as the Prince?"

Dante sighed. This was what he'd wanted to avoid.

It was a title and a burden to him.

He was Dante and nothing more.

"Because I am," Dante said.

"You're a prince? A real prince?"

"Sì..." Dante sighed. "I am, so your child will also inherit my title if the child is mine. You may be carrying a royal baby."

"Shay!"

Shay just shook her head and kept walking. She was trying to process what Dante had said to her: that her child was going to have a royal title. Only *if* the baby was his and that annoyed her even more. He was so suspicious of her. She hadn't known that he was a prince, so he couldn't accuse her of fortune hunting.

But maybe that's why he's so suspicious of paternity?

This was all just too surreal.

Of course, it was only fitting that he drop a bombshell on her, just as she'd done to him.

"Shay!"

She stopped and sighed. She couldn't act like this. This was not professional and she'd promised herself that she would be above all professional when dealing with Dante. She was an adult and this was their child.

"I'm sorry, Dante," she said. "I guess it was a bit of a shock to find out who you are."

"It doesn't change who I am, though," he said gently.

"How would I know that? I barely know you." She shook her head. "We're strangers."

He sighed at that. "This is true. One week at a conference means nothing."

"I do realize we have to get to know each other if we're both going to be involved in this child's life."

"Sì, I agree. Which is why you will marry me if the test is positive."

Shay rolled her eyes. "Not this again. I'm not marrying you, Dante. I'm not going to marry someone I don't love."

"I'm not talking about a marriage of love," he said matter-of-factly. "I'm talking about a marriage of convenience. Just for a year. You live under my roof and we pretend to be man and wife in public."

"Dante, I'm only here for twelve weeks."

"So? You're going on maternity leave when you get back to the United States, *si*?"

"Yes, but…I have to go back to the States. My work visa is only good for twelve weeks."

"If we marry, then you won't need a visa. You say it's my child, so why not have *our* child here, in my country?"

"I…I can't—I won't—give up my life, Dante."

"After a year is over, then you can walk away. With our child, as long as I have parental rights. I will continue to financially support the child."

"What do you gain from this?" she asked, confused. It all seemed too easy.

"An heir." He dragged his hand through his dark hair. "I will support the child either way, but while you're here in Italy, under my roof, I can protect you. Care for you."

She bit her lip, mulling it over, but she didn't want to marry. Ever.

Unless it was for love. Absolute, head-over-heels, can't-get-enough-of-each-other love. She let a hand drift over her belly.

"I can't, Dante," she said.

He frowned. "You're confused. Of course you are. I can see it. You should know that the baby won't inherit any of my family land if he or she is not legitimized."

"Is that a bad thing?" Shay asked. "Perhaps it's better for our baby to be away from all of that."

His eyes narrowed. "I take my family history very seriously. Being an Affini heir is a thing of pride."

And then she felt bad because she was insulting him. His values.

Dante was not American. He came from a completely different world than she did.

How can you have family pride when you know nothing about the name you were born with?

Still, she couldn't agree to marry him. Not now. She needed time to think and she wanted to talk to her friend and colleague, Aubrey, about it. She was so confused.

"We should go and talk to Mrs. Sanders. I'm sure she's worried." She turned and kept walking toward the room where Mrs. Sanders had got her broken wrist taken care of. Dante thankfully took the hint as he fell into step beside her.

Mrs. Sanders was lying in a bed, her wrist in a cast, and Shay could see the pain and worry etched on her face. She opened her eyes when they walked into the room.

"Please tell me you have word on my husband," Mrs. Sanders said.

"I'm Dr. Affini and I did the surgery on your husband."

"Were you told why he went to surgery?" Shay asked gently.

"He had internal bleeding?" Mrs. Sanders said, a hint of uncertainty in her voice. "That's all I know."

"Your husband had major lacerations to his spleen," Dante said gently. "I had to remove it."

Shay rubbed the patient's shoulder as she began to cry.

"He came through the splenectomy well," Dante said. "Dr. Prescarrie is our neurologist. He is going to check out your husband's spine."

"Why?" Mrs. Sanders asked, her eyes tracking to Shay and then back to Dante.

"He was complaining of loss of sensation before we took him into surgery," Dante said. "Dr. Prescarrie will be able to determine if the paralysis is temporary and what damage was done to the spine. We take loss of function very seriously."

"Oh, no. This is our thirtieth anniversary. Our kids surprised us with this trip to Italy. We're on a tour, you see…"

"Were you with the tour company when it happened?" Shay asked.

Mrs. Sanders shook her head. "No, we were having some free time in Venice. We're leaving for Tuscany tomorrow."

"Give me the number of the tour operator and I'll explain what happened. She can contact your family."

"It's in my purse over there." She inclined her head. "Thankfully, I wasn't thrown into the water. Our passports are in there too if you need them."

Shay smiled and brought Mrs. Sanders her purse, holding it open so the patient could pull out the information. Shay took it.

"I'll call the tour operator and they'll take care of your belongings and everything," Shay said. "Don't you worry. Just rest."

Mrs. Sanders nodded and clutched her purse with her good arm.

"Dr. Prescarrie will update you on your husband as soon as possible, Signora Sanders. For now you'll stay in this room. Try to rest." Dante patted the patient's leg and they walked out of her room. Dante stopped at the nurses' station to give instructions to the staff about Mrs. Sanders's stay, before he headed back toward Shay.

"That was very good of you to say you'll call the tour company."

"Well, they're so far from home." Shay glanced down at the information in her hand. "Is there a place I can call from in private?"

"Sì, follow me." Dante held out his arm and led her to another part of the hospital until they were standing in front of an office. "This is my office and you may use the telephone in there to contact the tour operator."

He opened the door for her and flicked on the lights.

"Thank you, Dante."

He shrugged. "Take your time, but before you go I want to finish our conversation."

"I thought we *were* finished with that particular conversation."

A small smile twitched his lips. "No, we're not finished. Far from it. Besides, you have a test to go through, *cara*."

Dante shut the door and walked away, leaving Shay alone in his office. She breathed a sigh of relief as she took a seat in his leather office chair and punched in the number. She was connected right away to the tour operator and she explained the situation to them. Everything was worked out. Their room in Venice would be held for them for as long as they needed and the tour company would contact the emergency contacts in their file.

The tour company would also contact the insurance and everything would be taken care of.

Satisfied, Shay disconnected the call and leaned back in Dante's swivel chair. She closed her eyes and the baby fluttered around, feeling like a butterfly. Reminding her again that she was working a bit too hard.

The ob-gyn she'd seen in the United States had said she could do this work, but he had warned her to take it easy.

The only reason she had clearance to take this job was because it was less strenuous than the assignment she was originally on. Running a training and simulation program, as well as assisting a trauma surgeon in the operating theatre, should be a breeze.

The problem was, she hadn't taken a break.

Her blood sugar was dropping and she needed to eat something.

Something decent.

And she needed rest.

Dante might think their conversation wasn't over, but as far as she was concerned it was for the evening. She was going to head back to the villa she and her friend Danica were sharing, eat and get some sleep. Tomorrow was going to be a long day; she was going to run her first simulation.

She got up and found her way back to the small office she had been given on the other side of the hospital. She grabbed her purse and sweater. She headed toward the back door and from there it was a short walk to the house the United World Wide Health Association had rented for their staff.

If she had a moment, she'd talk to Dante again and tell him again that she wasn't going to marry him.

Convenience or not, she was a big girl and could take care of herself.

She didn't need his protection.

As she stepped outside she was blinded by flashing lights and a rush of people crowded her, pressing her back against the wall. She shielded her face, but she couldn't understand what they were asking her.

She caught a few words, like *prince* and *baby.*

Then there was a roar and string of loud, harsh words and strong arms came around her, pulling her close, and she realized it was Dante, shielding her. She clung to him as he shouted at the group of reporters and ushered her back inside. Once they were back inside and the shouting from the mob of reporters was drowned out, she sighed in relief.

"What in the world…?"

"The press got word that you might be carrying my heir," Dante snapped.

"*That's* what they were asking me?"

"*Sì,*" he said, his dark eyes twinkling with a dangerous light, his hands on his hips, and he began to curse in Italian again.

"I thought that Italian princes were common?" Shay said, mimicking him. "I mean, not like the British royal family..."

"Yes, but with my family there is a bit more scandal. So my brother and I are often in the spotlight. We're favorites of the paparazzi."

"And I just gave them their latest scoop." She ran a hand over her belly. "Is this going to happen all the time?"

Dante scrubbed a hand over his face. *"Sì."*

"So that's what you meant by protecting me?" she asked.

He nodded curtly. "Where are you staying?"

"At the United World Wide Health Association house. It's not far from here."

He shook his head. "Not tonight, you're not. You're coming to my place."

"I am not!" she said, getting annoyed with him.

"You're going to cause a bigger scandal if you don't agree to my marriage suggestion, especially if the child is mine," Dante snapped. "You could ruin my reputation at this hospital."

Shay bit her lip. She didn't want to ruin his career or his reputation. "You want a marriage of convenience?"

"Sì, that way I can protect you. I have a restraining order against the paparazzi and it will protect you also, if you marry me."

"So just on paper we'll be married."

"Sì, but to make it look real you will have to move into my home for a year." He rolled his neck and tugged at the collar of his shirt, as if it were suffocating him. It clearly bothered him just as much as it bothered her.

"Do you have enough room?" Shay asked.

He chuckled. "I have an entire villa to myself on the Lido di Venezia. I can give you your own wing if you desire. Just say yes. Let me protect you and our child."

Even though she should say no, she didn't want paparazzi stopping her and accosting her when she moved around Venice. Especially where there was a language barrier. Dante could keep them at bay. She ran her hand over her belly again.

This was his baby too. Even if he didn't believe it at the moment.

What choice did she have? It was just for a year. Only she couldn't do it. She couldn't agree to the marriage.

"You're coming with me," Dante said. "We'll get the paternity test done now, put this doubt to rest."

"I don't have a say in this?"

"No, you don't."

And she had a feeling this was one of many arguments she was going to have with him over the course of the next twelve weeks. He'd won this round, but she'd win the next.

CHAPTER THREE

"YOU DID WHAT?"

Dante glanced into his office, where Shay was curled up on his sofa, sleeping. She was resting after the paternity test. Now they were waiting for the results and Dr. Tucci promised to rush them. Before they left, Dante was going to make sure that they were at least on their way to being man and wife, even if Shay kept saying no. He was still having a hard time trusting her, but deep down he felt as if this child was his. So he was going to make sure she married him. Then he could protect the trust his mother left and have something for his child. His child wouldn't have to worry about the future the way his father made Enzo and him so worried. Dante wouldn't sell off his child's inheritance just because he or she wasn't married by the time they were thirty-five. He wouldn't have such a foolish restriction.

Once he brought Shay back to his villa, the press couldn't hound her. If she stayed by his side, she'd be safe as well.

There were still a few steps he had to take. Like convincing her to say yes and stay in Italy. *If* the child was his, he'd do the right thing to protect his child.

And if it's not?

He glanced at Shay sleeping so peacefully and he didn't even want to think of her betraying him the way Olivia had. His memory of Shay had been so pure and untainted.

The memory of their night together was the only thing besides the vineyard and surgery that made him happy. If she betrayed his trust like Olivia, that memory would be shattered. He'd have nothing pure to cling to when the loneliness gnawed at him.

"Dante, are you even listening to me?" Enzo asked on the other end of the phone.

"*Scusate*, it's been a trying day." He rubbed his temple where a tension headache was forming.

"I would say so," Enzo commiserated on the other end.

"I'm getting married. I just have to obtain a Nulla Osta as quickly as possible."

"She's not Italian?" Enzo asked.

"She's American."

"Why do you want to marry an American?"

"She's carrying my child."

"Are you sure?"

"*Sì*, I believe it is mine."

"You don't sound sure."

"The paternity test results will be ready soon." Dante sighed.

There was silence on the other end. "Dante, I know I have been bugging you to get married, but…did she even agree?"

"Not yet."

"Not yet?" Enzo asked.

"You don't have to say anything else," Dante said, cutting his brother off. He knew exactly where Enzo was going with this and he didn't want to be reminded about Olivia and the baby that wasn't his right now.

Shay was not Olivia.

"I don't want you to get hurt again," Enzo said gently. "It killed me to see you so hurt last time."

"I appreciate that, Enzo. However, if this is my baby, I will marry her."

"What if she's after your money? Your title? Even if the baby is yours, she could be just after the same things that Olivia was."

"She's not," Dante said. "She's already refused to marry me, remember? Several times. It's almost getting embarrassing now."

Enzo laughed. "Still…"

"No, there is no still. Shay's not after my money or anything. There will be ground rules to this marriage. It's just a marriage of convenience. Nothing more. She can continue to do her work, our baby will be protected and I will keep my inheritance. The trust Mother signed over to Father before she knew any better."

"What do you need from me?" Enzo asked.

"She's staying at our place."

"What do you mean?"

"Our childhood home, the one that was sold off before mother died and is now being rented to the United World Wide Health Association. She's staying there."

"Ah, so you want me to go collect her stuff?"

"Or at least tell someone there to collect it for her and then bring it to my place. That's where she'll be staying from now on. She was mobbed on her way out of the hospital this evening. The whole world will soon know about the Affini heir."

"I can't believe you did it, Dante. I can't believe you're going to get married and have an heir all within a year and so close to the cutoff date. You did it. You saved Grandfather's vineyard and Mamma's villa."

A smile crept across Dante's face as the reality sank in.

He had. He'd managed to keep a hold of all that was promised to him. All that money and land wouldn't pass back into their father's greedy hands. The land he loved so much, the vineyard, all of it would be saved. The relief that washed over him in that moment was almost palpable.

"Could you go and talk to her roommate as soon as possible?" Dante asked. "She's tired and I'm taking her back to my villa. She needs her rest."

"*Sì*, I'll go there as soon as I finish up at the clinic."

"*Grazie.*" Dante hung up the phone and then knelt beside Shay. She looked so peaceful sleeping, her face at ease, those long blond eyelashes brushing the tops of her round cheeks. He resisted the urge to reach out and run his thumb across those smooth, soft cheeks or to kiss her pink lips as he had back in Oahu.

The memory of which was still imprinted onto his soul. And pregnancy just made her all the more beautiful.

She glowed.

Don't. Don't get attached. The results aren't in. Don't set yourself up for hurt.

"Shay," he said gently. "Wake up."

She roused. "Is something wrong?"

"It's time to leave. The paparazzi are still waiting out back, but I have a water taxi waiting for us to take us to Lido di Venezia. They won't follow us there."

"And the results of the test?"

"They'll be ready tomorrow morning. Come, stay at my place tonight, where I can keep you safe."

She nodded drowsily. He stood and helped her to her feet.

He guided her out of his office, down a winding staircase to the canal that bordered the hospital. The water-taxi operator helped Shay down into his boat and Dante followed.

It was dark out, but the city helped light the way. The hospital wasn't too far from the lagoon, but behind him he could hear the singing of the gondoliers, tempting tourists to take a ride. Shay settled against the back of the seat.

"I'm sorry, I can barely keep my eyes open." Her head was nodding.

"Put your head on my shoulder." He rested his arm

against the back of the boat and she leaned into him. He could smell her perfume. Soft, feminine. Lilacs.

It reminded him of summers spent in Tuscany. Of the flowers blooming in his grandmother's garden, warmed by the hot sun. He couldn't help but smile. It was so right. It all seemed so right. Everything he wanted.

Be careful.

As they left the canals and headed out into the lagoon, there were stars in the sky. The city light drowned them out, but tonight the sky was clear enough you could make out a few. Ahead the Lido di Venezia was lit up with lights from restaurants and homes that littered the sandy shoal. Even farther away there were a couple of cruise ships and you could hear the music wafting from the upper decks.

It left a bad taste in his mouth.

Venice was becoming too much of a tourist trap.

Which was why he preferred Tuscany.

Sure, there were tourists, but there was more space. And there were no tourists at his grandfather's vineyard.

My vineyard.

He glanced down at the small rounded swell that Shay was instinctively cradling in her sleep. That was his child. And even though he wasn't sure, he reached out to touch it.

"Where are we?" Shay asked, waking with a start. He pulled his hand back and moved his arm.

"We're almost to my home. It's a short walk from the pier to my villa."

"I'm sorry I fell asleep. I usually have more stamina."

"You're pregnant. It's fine."

And it was more than fine.

For his family's legacy it was a lifesaver. And for his heart, his longing for a child he'd thought he'd never have, it was a dream come true.

As long as it's yours.

And that little naysaying voice slammed him back to harsh reality. He was putting his heart at risk again.

Dante climbed out of the water taxi first at the docks and then held out his hand for Shay. Which was good; she wasn't that sure-footed on boats anymore, since her center of gravity had shifted.

In some of the places she worked, boats were a way to get around, a way of life, so she was annoyed when Dante had to help her out of a modern, luxurious water taxi. It wasn't as if it were a skiff in the middle of a fast-flowing river in the South American jungle.

However, she'd forgotten how well her hand fit in his. How safe he made her feel, just like that night on the beach in Oahu. And she sighed; it slipped out unintentionally.

"What?" he asked as he helped her onto the pier.

"Nothing," she said, smiling up at him.

He smiled too and paid the water-taxi captain.

"Ciao," the captain said, waving at them as he puttered away out toward Venice. The moon was high in the sky, the dark water calm; only a few ripples from the water taxi disrupted the mirrorlike quality of the lagoon. It reminded her of nights in the French Quarter, by Jackson Square, and looking out over the Mississippi. Then there were the few scattered memories of her father taking her to Lake Pontchartrain to fish, before he left them. The moon would be so high over the large lake and New Orleans out on the delta would glow and come to life.

It was all so perfect, this moment. But that was the thing. It was just a moment. Even when the results confirmed what she was saying, she couldn't believe he'd change his tune. He was so untrusting, so guarded, and she couldn't help but wonder why. Moments didn't last. She should know. Her father had proved that, and once her father had left, those nights had no longer been so perfect.

And this situation with Dante was far from perfect.

"Come," Dante said, interrupting her thoughts. "It's only a short walk to my villa."

They walked up the ramp from the dock onto the street. Shay was surprised to see a few cars and a bus stop.

As if sensing her shock Dante chuckled. "There are no large canals here. Solid land here."

"I'm surprised you don't live in Venice."

He frowned. "I used to. I grew up there."

"Do your parents still live there?"

"No," he said tersely. "Our family home is no longer in our family."

"You sound annoyed by that."

"It's a long story," Dante said. "Besides, I prefer living here on the Lido di Venezia. It's peaceful here. There are tourists on the beach side, but I live on the lagoon side. I enjoy having a garden and trees. And most of the beaches at this end are private and owned by the hotels. Though to the south there are public beaches. The Adriatic is warm and very popular for young children. I spent many summers swimming here."

They turned down a small side street off the main street, the Gran Viale Santa Maria Elisabetta, not far from the lagoon, where residents could catch the ferries and *vaporetti*.

Shay was expecting a small home and was shocked when he opened a gate to a large, square villa that seemed to take up the entire block off the main street. At the top of the villa there looked to be a patio that would have views over the lagoon and to Venice.

"I shouldn't be surprised," she mumbled. "You are a prince, after all."

He grinned and pushed open the creaky iron gate. "This was my maternal grandparents' summer home—they were wealthy but not royalty. Unfortunately, it fell into disrepair."

"And you're putting it back together?"

He nodded quickly. "There are many rooms."

Dante unlocked the front door and led her inside. When he flicked on the light, Shay gasped at the beauty of a place so old. The stucco on the wall was painted in terra-cotta. The foyer was round like a turret, which you couldn't tell from the outside, which was square.

There were many arches leading off to various empty rooms.

"I haven't had much time," Dante said apologetically. "Just the kitchen has been renovated on this ground floor and the master suite, terrace and a couple of bathrooms on the next level."

She followed him past numerous rooms. There was a large room that looked as if it had a dining table and suspended over it was a beautiful glass chandelier, unlit as it hovered above the ghostly occupants.

"This is the kitchen. It backs onto the garden. You can't see much, but I have a couple of kiwi trees and an olive tree out there as well as a small pool." Dante flicked on another light, which illuminated a white, large and modern kitchen. "Are you hungry?"

"Yes," Shay admitted.

He smiled. "I thought as much. You need to eat."

She took a seat at the large wooden kitchen table. The garden was in darkness, but she could make out the reflection of water as it bounced off the tile of the terrace.

"It's beautiful. How old is this villa?" she asked.

"This villa was built in the mid-eighteen-hundreds to replace a crumbling home that my family had owned since the fifteen-hundreds. This land actually housed many crusaders during the Fourth Crusade." He brought her a cold glass of mineral water. "Drink it—the limes are actually mine too."

Shay took a sip. "Crusaders? How do you know?"

"Everybody knows," he said offhandedly. "Did you not learn about the Crusades in school?"

"No, it really wasn't on our curriculum."

Dante *tsked* under his breath. "The Lido was home to about ten thousand crusaders, spurred on by Pope Innocent III to sack Constantinople. They were blockaded here for a time because they could not afford to pay for the ships being built. In fact, some of my ancestors fought in the battle of Zara, but it wasn't until the fifteen-hundreds that my family gained notoriety and inherited the royal title. Of course, as this was my mother's family's home, my royal title has nothing to do with that at all. It's just a bit of interesting family history."

"I'm afraid I don't know much about my family at all."

Dante cocked an eyebrow. "Don't you?"

"No. Labadie is a French name. That much I know. My father's family came to New Orleans before it was purchased by the Americans. When it was still part of France, they, I believe, drifted down from the Maritimes in Canada during the Seven Years' War. Mostly Cajun."

"Seven Years' War?" Dante asked.

"Oh, didn't you learn about that in school?" Shay teased, and they both laughed at that.

"How does leftover risotto sound?" he asked. "Or perhaps some cheese?"

"Risotto sounds fine."

Dante went to heat the food and Shay glanced around the kitchen. She didn't do much cooking; she knew how to cook on cookstoves or an open fire. Basically anything that was propane-operated, because sometimes where she was working there might not always be electricity or even clean water.

This kitchen was opulent to her.

Even her mother's kitchen hadn't been this nice.

And then after Katrina, when the house had been condemned and her mother was dying from the effects of the mold she'd picked up in her lungs after the dikes had burst and flooded their home, the small run-down kitchen had been absolutely destroyed. Shay had had to go back into the home and try to salvage anything she could.

Only there had been nothing left to salvage, really.

A few pictures and birth certificates that had been stored in a flood-proof and fireproof box. And whatever else her mother had managed to cram into her carryall when she'd climbed out through the attic to the roof, waiting for help as the floodwaters rose.

"You look sad, *cara*."

"Do I?" she asked.

"Sì." He set the plate of risotto in front of her and then sat down next to her with his own plate. "Is something wrong?"

"No, I'm just tired." She plastered a fake smile on her face and took a bite of the risotto. "Oh, my goodness, this is so good."

He grinned. "I like to cook."

"You're not a traditional prince, then."

His brow furrowed. "What do you mean, 'traditional'?"

"You're a surgeon, you like to work with your hands and you cook. You don't have any servants."

He laughed. "I do have a lady come and clean my house, but you're right, I do most of it on my own. My maternal grandfather was a winemaker. He had a large vineyard in Tuscany and, though he was extremely wealthy, he taught me the value of hard work. I enjoy it."

"Well, you're good at it. I'm afraid my cooking would not be up to par. The only thing I can make, if I have the ingredients and the patience, is *boudin*."

"What is *boudin*?"

"A sausage stuffed with rice and green peppers."

"I would like to try that sometime."

Shay chuckled. "I'm not sure I'm up to *boudin* making at the moment."

"I can get you all the ingredients here."

"I'm sure you can, but I have a simulation course and training to run. Not to mention I'm to assist you in surgery. I'm here for work, Dante. Nothing else."

He frowned. "I'm passionate about my job too, but you have to live life as well. Work is not life."

"It is for me."

"And what happens when you have the child?" he asked. "Our child. Are you going to ignore our child for work?"

"No," she snapped. "I will balance it. A woman can work and be a mother. I think seeing me work will be a good example for our child."

Dante sighed. "I'm not saying that at all. Of course it's a good example, but you said you don't do anything *but* work. What do you do for fun?"

And the question caught her off guard, because really she didn't do much.

When she was on assignment, she put her whole heart and soul into the job.

There was no time for much else.

"You know what, I'm really tired. Is there a place I can sleep?"

"Of course, follow me."

Shay followed Dante out of the kitchen and up the winding staircase to the second floor. There were many rooms and a large open area with a couch and a desk. A living room. He led her to the back of the house and flicked on a light.

"This is the only room with a bed in it at the moment. When you move in, I'll move out of here."

"This is your room?"

"*Sì*, it is also the only bedroom with a private bathroom. I can use the one downstairs. It is no trouble."

"Where will you sleep?"

"The couch. I have some work to do. I'm not tired yet. You rest."

"I can't kick you out of your bedroom."

"You can." He smiled. "Get some rest and we'll talk about our plans for marriage tomorrow, but only if the results are positive."

"Sure. Okay." She rolled her eyes. Dante was so stubborn, so untrusting.

He nodded and shut her in his bedroom. Shay sighed and sat down on the edge of his large bed, sinking down into the soft duvet.

Tomorrow she'd tell him that it wasn't a good idea.

They weren't going to get married.

It was a foolish idea.

She lay down on the bed and thought about how she was going to tell him her reasons, but before she could get too far into her plans she drifted off into a deep, sound sleep.

CHAPTER FOUR

THE INCESSANT RINGING woke Shay up. And it took her a moment to realize where she was. She scrubbed a hand over her face and dug her phone out of her purse. It was Aubrey.

"Hello?" she said, trying not to sound too groggy.

"Are you okay?" Aubrey asked excitedly on the other end.

"Fine, just...you woke me up."

"Where did you sleep? I called last night and Danica told me that you were staying with Dr. Affini at his home and she's to send your belongings there."

"No. I'm not staying here permanently. I'll call Danica and tell her. It was just for last night. It's a long story." Shay sighed.

"Well, I told you to tell Dante about the baby, not to move in with him," Aubrey teased.

Shay laughed. "It's the pregnancy hormones that made me do it."

"I'll say."

"Where are you today?" Shay asked, hoping Aubrey was nearby. She needed to talk to her face-to-face. Aubrey had taken an assignment outside Venice but did move around a bit in Italy.

"Actually, I'm in Venice today, believe it or not."

"I'll tell you all about it at lunch, then. When is your lunch break?" Shay asked.

"Two. Do you want to meet for lunch at Braddicio's near the hospital? I heard it was good. And I know where that is."

"Sounds good," Shay said, trying to stifle a yawn. "I'll explain everything there."

"Okay, be careful."

Shay disconnected the call and then headed to the bathroom, where she quickly showered before re-dressing in yesterday's clothes.

The bathroom was white and modern like the kitchen, except for the deep, large claw tub with a shower hose placed on a rack in the middle of the room. There were long windows and the blinds were closed. There was a bit of sunlight peeking through the sides of the roman shades.

She pulled on the string and drew open the blinds, gasping when she noticed French doors that led out to a rooftop terrace. She unlatched the French doors and headed outside. From the terrace, the master suite faced the Adriatic. She could see the blue water and the sandy beaches that made the Lido di Venezia a favorite spot for tourists.

She closed her eyes and drank in the scent of fruit trees flowering in the spring, mixed with sand and surf. When she looked down, she could see the high stone walls that bordered Dante's garden. The fruit trees, the olive tree and the small pool that Dante was currently swimming laps in.

Naked.

Shay meant to look away, but couldn't. She couldn't help but watch him. His bronze form cutting through the turquoise water like a blade. It was mesmerizing. And she recalled very vividly what it was like to run her hands over that muscular body, to feel him pressed against her, his strong arms around her, holding her. His lips on her skin. Her blood heated. Drawn to him, she was so weak.

Don't look. Go downstairs and catch a ferry back to

Venice. Back to the place you're staying, so you won't be tempted.

And she was so tempted by Dante.

She tore her gaze away and collected her purse and made her way downstairs.

When she got to the stairs, she could smell coffee. It was inviting and she desperately wanted a cup, but coffee was off-limits. She made her way to the kitchen, just as Dante came walking in through the open terrace doors. He had a towel wrapped around his waist, but she got an eyeful of his broad, muscular chest.

"You're awake," he said, his deep voice making her quake with a sudden need for him.

"Yes." She tried to avert her eyes from him, because she remembered all too well that body. The touch of it, the taste of it, the way he felt in her arms, his kisses burning a path of fire across her skin. "I hope your pool is heated."

"*Sì*, it is. How did you sleep?"

"Very well. Your bed is very comfortable and I feel bad for taking it. I have a perfectly good bed where I'm staying."

"You're going to be my wife and you're carrying my child. *This* is now your place," he said matter-of-factly.

"Dante, I'm not going to be—"

"You need to eat," he said, cutting her off, which made her grind her teeth a bit. Was he this annoying in Oahu or were her hormones amplifying his annoying, arrogant habits?

"I'm trying to talk to you, Dante."

He was looking in the fridge. "How does some fresh fruit and yogurt sound?"

Great.

And her stomach growled in response.

Traitor.

"Dante, this is serious. More serious than fruit and yogurt."

He turned around then, one of those dark brows cocked. "Oh?"

"I'm not going to marry you, Dante. We can't get married."

"*Cara*, the only way I can protect you and the baby is by marrying you."

"What about the paternity test?"

"Dr. Tucci called," Dante said offhandedly. "The results came in. The child is mine."

Shay tried not to roll her eyes. "I know that, but that doesn't change the fact that I can't marry you."

"It's not permanent—the marriage, I mean. There will be rules. You will have your own room, your own space."

"You're going to give up your bed for a year?"

"I'll get another bed and I'll finish the other bedroom up on the second floor. It's not a problem. And then I'll start on the nursery."

"Dante, it's not as easy as this." She ran her hand through her hair to stop her from pulling it out.

"Why can't it be? This is a business arrangement to protect our child, and my child will have my name. A good name," he said as he scooped fresh berries into a bowl. "Now eat your breakfast and I'll shower and change before we head back to the hospital."

Dante was shutting down any further discussion to the matter and that was highly frustrating for Shay. She couldn't remember him being this stubborn before. He didn't even want to discuss the matter. Didn't he know what he was doing? He was going to blame her in a year for ruining his life.

Just as her father had done all the times when he'd been unhappy. Which had been a lot.

Sure, there had been moments when her father had been happy, but they had been few and far between. Now she couldn't even remember them.

She couldn't even remember her father's face.

All the pictures of him had been lost during Katrina, except for one that her mother had clutched to her chest when she'd taken her last breaths. And Shay had been so angry that her father had left them that way, left them in poverty, that she'd buried that picture with her mother in St. Louis Cemetery on Canal Street in New Orleans.

At least Dante wanted to give their child his name. Dante was offering their child roots, history. Permanence.

Something she couldn't give their child. Not really. He had land that was centuries old. Other than the house that Katrina had destroyed, there was no childhood home. Her mother and her always moving.

It still haunted her, the looks, the heartache of her mother, and she couldn't put her child through that. Even if it meant that she would be protected from the paparazzi. She didn't need that protection. She could take care of herself. She'd been in worse situations before and had managed.

You weren't pregnant before.

She shook that niggling thought from her head. She also couldn't help but wonder what Dante had to gain by marrying her, by supporting her. She had a hard time believing it was just for the sake of the child.

Just marry him. Take the protection. Do your work and give your child access to his or her father.

The only thing that would be different in her situation was that she would never pine over a man who didn't want her. She wouldn't waste away as her mother had. She couldn't stay in Italy and rely on a man to help her raise her child, even if that man was her baby's father.

She was stronger than that.

He'd watched her sleep. He hadn't meant to go back into the room, but when he'd been on the couch last night she'd been all he could think about.

Shay had been plaguing his thoughts since their stolen night together in Oahu and now she was under his roof. Carrying his child.

And this morning, Dr. Tucci had confirmed what he'd known, deep down. He was just too afraid to hope, too afraid of being hurt to let himself believe it.

Shay had always been beautiful, but now, pregnant with his child, she was even more so and he couldn't help but think of the night of passion they'd had together. The night that had brought about this baby and their reunion.

The first woman he'd been with since Olivia and he'd had no qualms about taking her to his bed that night months ago. He'd dated since Olivia, but never had he made love to another woman until Shay. Usually he would talk himself out of it, but with Shay the desire had been too great.

He'd wanted her.

He *still* wanted her. That had never changed. He still desired her. The urge to take her in his arms and kiss her again was too much to bear.

She was in his villa. In his bed.

He'd sneaked into his bedroom, now her bedroom, to check on how she was doing. He hadn't been able to help himself.

Shay had been sleeping, but she'd been huddled in a ball in the middle of the bed, shivering. He had forgotten that he'd left a window open. Even though it was spring and temperatures were rising, the nights were still chilly. Especially the breeze coming off the Adriatic and the lagoon.

So he'd covered her with a blanket, made sure she was comfortable.

As in the taxi, he'd wanted to touch the rounded swell of her belly, but he wasn't sure.

Dante hadn't wanted her to wake, so he'd backed away and gone back to the living room, where he'd spent the night tossing and turning on the couch.

He wasn't sure what he was doing by asking her to marry him. He'd never intended to get married after what happened with Olivia, even if that meant he was going to lose everything. The vineyards, the villa and the inheritance.

The money didn't matter to him so much, but losing his grandfather's vineyard and this villa was what was crushing him. Now Shay was pregnant with his child and all his problems were solved.

Were they?

Why did he feel so guilty about this situation? And he couldn't help but think of his own parents' loveless marriage. Well, loveless on his father's part, because even though his father insisted that he'd loved their mother, a man who loved a woman wouldn't cheat on her repeatedly as their father had.

Perhaps the guilt stemmed from the fact that it seemed too easy that his problems were solved.

Shay had made it clear that she didn't want to marry him. She didn't love him.

He didn't want to ruin her life by forcing her to marry him, but it was the best thing for the baby.

He could protect them. He was going to be a father.

Why did it have to be her to come to Venice and not Daniel? Only, if she hadn't, would he ever have known about his child? He sometimes wondered if fate had a twisted sense of humor. Nonetheless, she was here and pregnant with his child and he was going to do right by them.

Both of them.

He was going to protect them from the paparazzi and anyone else who wanted a piece of the Affini name. He quickly had a shower in the main suite's bathroom, to wash the chlorine from his skin. He noticed that the French doors leading to the terrace were open and he wondered if Shay had ended up out there and seen him in the pool.

When he went for his morning swim, he didn't even

think about putting on a bathing suit. He wasn't used to it, but if Shay was going to move in with him he'd have to remind himself of common decency.

Dante got dressed and ready to go back to the hospital for his shift in the emergency room. He had to complete rounds with students, check on his patients, including Mr. Sanders from yesterday.

When he came back downstairs, Shay was pacing, having finished her yogurt and berries. She shot him a look of frustration, but he didn't care. There was going to be no more talk about it. They were going to get married. He was going to take care of them.

By marrying her he could gain control over the vineyard and the villa, and then he could properly take care of them. His father wouldn't have any hand in it. His child's inheritance would be safe. He wouldn't sell off the estate, the land, piece by piece as his father was doing. His child would never look on him with disdain, the way he looked upon his father.

He would never hurt his child. He would be a better man than his father was.

And this was definitely his child, unlike what had happened with Olivia, when the child he'd thought was his hadn't been.

"You told me it was mine! I believed you."

She shrugged. "I wanted to marry you."

"Why? If the child wasn't mine..."

"The title. The name. Affini is respected."

"You were going to let me believe that your baby was mine, but really it's another man's? A man you were having an affair with before we even got together. Why?"

"Oh, come on, Dante. I don't love you. You don't love me. Not really. You were just excited about the prospect of family, of settling down and raising a child. I don't want

that. I thought you were different. I thought we'd go to parties and hire a nanny."

"I never wanted that. That was how I was raised. I don't want that for my child."

She glared at him with those dark, hardened eyes. "Well, it's a good thing this child isn't yours."

"Are you ready to go?" he asked, shaking away that painful memory.

"I've been more than ready. I finished my breakfast a while ago. I would've left sooner, but I didn't know my way back to catch the water taxi. I'm a bit turned around here."

"We'll take the ferry to Venice—it's running right now—or a *vaporetto* if we miss the ferry. Although the water buses are smaller than the ferry, I prefer the ferry, but they do the job."

He led her out the front door and locked up. It was a beautiful sunny day and everybody was out on the street. He put his arm through her arm.

"What're you doing?" she asked.

"Just leading you. Making sure you don't step out into the street."

"I've been all over the world in worse situations than this, in worse conditions than this. I'm not going to just step out into the street," she teased, the smile replacing the frown of worry that had been there moments ago.

"Nonetheless it is my pleasure to do so."

And it was. He liked walking with her. And he couldn't remember the last time he'd had company to work. It was nice.

They walked in silence down the Gran Viale Santa Maria Elisabetta toward the ferry landing. The ferry was there; they paid their fare and got on board just before it departed. He walked her up to the top deck to enjoy the sun and the breeze off the lagoon.

She was still slightly frustrated with him as she leaned

over the railing to look out over the water. He could tell by the way her brow was furrowed and her lips were pursed together.

"How was your breakfast? Was it adequate?" he asked.

"It was good," she said seriously. He chuckled, and then she smiled again. "It was good. Thank you."

"I'm glad to hear it. You have to remember to eat small meals all day long. It's the best for you and the baby."

"I know," she said.

"Do you have a doctor here in Venice yet?"

"No, I have to find one."

"I could send you to the clinic to talk to my brother. He's a family physician."

"Don't you think it would be odd that your brother would be my doctor in this situation?" she asked.

"Hmm, perhaps you're right. You need to go see Dr. Tucci, then. He's the ob-gyn that did the paternity test. He works in the hospital. He's quite good and he speaks English as well, as you know. He's one of the best."

"Dr. Tucci—that's good to know. I wasn't sure who to go see. I wasn't sure that he worked in the hospital. I liked him."

"I would like to go to the appointment," Dante said.

"You want to go to my appointments?" Her finely arched eyebrows rose in surprise.

"Of course. It's my baby. I'm concerned about its health too."

"Yes, of course you would be." She sighed. "When we get to the hospital, I will make an appointment on my next break, but this morning I'm swamped. I have to plan the first simulation. The trainees are with another physician this morning, so that gives me time to plan an exercise they would face in the field."

Intrigued, he asked, "What were you thinking of?"

"I was thinking of a natural disaster, like a flood or forest fire."

He nodded. "That sounds good. You should do a flood. There're lots of floods here, especially when the big cruise ships come into the lagoon and they flood San Marco's *piazza* quite often. I mean, look what happened to Mr. Sanders in the *vaporetto* that was capsized because of one of those cruise ships and the big bow waves."

"I understand that. Flooding would be a big deal here, especially since this city is basically sitting on wooden planks. I'm sure that you face that issue all the time, but this is a city. These trainees will be going out into Third World countries where the flooding is different. Where the conditions are not so sanitary."

"Have you ever been in a flood where the conditions are not so sanitary?" he asked.

Shay frowned, her gaze drifting out over the water. "Yes, yes, I have."

"Where?"

"New Orleans," she said in a faraway voice. "Katrina."

She turned and looked away from him. It looked as if there were tears in her eyes as she said it.

"I'm sorry, *cara*," he apologized. "I didn't mean to bring up something that would be hard for you. I forgot...you're from New Orleans, aren't you?"

"Yes, it was terrible. The conditions were so bad."

"It wasn't just the hurricane, though?"

"No, it was after that. I was in school, training at the hospital and helping people escape. Taking care of those who couldn't flee. First we got out the infants, and then moved down the priority list. It was pretty scary. I was one of the last people to leave as the hospital flooded."

"I bet that was scary," he said, placing his hand over hers and giving it a reassuring squeeze. There wasn't much more he could say. He'd read about the devastation.

"That was the first and worst flood I've ever been in. I've been in other floods, but Katrina was definitely the worst," she said quietly, looking off into the distance. "I don't really want to talk about it, if you don't mind."

He nodded. "I'm sorry for bringing it up, *cara*. I didn't mean to cause you pain."

"It's okay. You didn't hurt me. You're right, they could have to deal with flooding in a city like this, a city like New Orleans, during a natural disaster. They could be posted anywhere. The conditions weren't sanitary in New Orleans. There was no power, no clean water. So yeah, maybe I'll do the first simulation in a setting like this. A setting where everything you thought you had, because you're not in a Third World country and are used to having, is no longer available. You have to learn to boil water in unsanitary conditions, where your supplies can run out. Thanks for that, Dante. I think that's what I'll do today."

"I'm always here to help. I'm part of this program too. I wish I could help you more, but I have rounds in the emergency room today. And I would like to check on Mr. Sanders."

"Did you hear anything about his condition after Dr. Prescarrie saw him?" she asked.

Dante sighed. "Yes, there was some damage to his spinal cord—it's bruised and there's swelling. We're hoping his paralysis isn't permanent. He's in the ICU. The internal bleeding has stopped. That's the main thing."

"That's good," she said. "I hope his paralysis isn't permanent. That's the last thing he needs on a trip of a lifetime, all because a cruise ship taking it too fast caused a *vaporetto* to capsize."

He nodded. "Yes, it's these things that annoy us Venetians about the tourist industry. So many tourists."

"You don't like tourists?"

"We like them. I mean, it's a way of life, but then there're things like the cruise ships coming in too fast and flooding

San Marco's *piazza*, and there are issues with overcrowding. It's not the same as it was when I was young."

"I bet it's not," she said. "New Orleans gets tourists, especially during Mardi Gras. It's insane around the French Quarter. You can't walk around anywhere. It's just packed full of people."

"So you understand what I'm talking about."

"I do get it," she said. "They bleach Bourbon Street every night."

"Bleach the street?"

"Oh, yes." She grinned. "Bourbon Street is a very popular party street. There are a lot of bars and people drink a lot and sometimes they can't always find a bathroom."

He wrinkled his nose. "That's terrible."

"It is," she said. "Every night after last call and into the early morning the street cleaners go out and bleach the street with lemon and bleach. It's very citrusy if you walk down Bourbon Street just after they've sprayed it, but if you walk ahead of the cleaners, like I did one night trying to get to work, you learn to appreciate the bleach."

They laughed together at that as the ferry pulled into the docks.

It was a short walk from the ferry to the hospital. And there wasn't any press around. Dante made sure she got to her office and was settled, before he headed to his.

"Shay, if you need anything, please have me paged. I'm here for you, *cara*."

She nodded. "Thank you, but I've arranged to meet my friend today for lunch and talk to her about a few things, because I'm honestly not sure about this, Dante. I mean, a marriage of convenience... I can't agree to that."

He held up his hand, cutting her off. "It's for the best. Trust me."

"How can I trust you? We barely know each other."

He understood that. He understood about not trusting

someone. His trust had been shattered when Olivia broke his heart.

"You just have to," he said, and he walked away.

Not even sure that he could trust her either.

Dante made his rounds pretty quickly, which always gave him a bad feeling because when the emergency room was quiet it would inevitably become busy in the near future. Which meant trauma.

After he did his rounds and checked on the stability of Mr. Sanders, who was doing well in the intensive care unit, he headed back to his office. He resisted the urge to go and find Shay to see how she was coming along with the simulation planning because he wanted to give her some space. He had a feeling that he was overwhelming her and he didn't blame her one bit. He was feeling a bit overwhelmed himself.

When he walked into his office, he saw Enzo standing in front of his desk, his back to him. The expensive suits his brother always wore gave him away.

"Enzo, aren't you supposed to be at the clinic?"

Enzo turned around and flashed him that impish smile he'd had since he was a young boy. "Is that any way to talk to your brother? Not even a *ciao* and asking how I am doing, just straight to the point of why I'm here?"

"Yes, usually it is. You're a pain in my side." Dante laughed.

Enzo just shook his head. "I have some good news—"

"Did you do what I asked?" Dante said, interrupting him.

"Yes, I left a message with someone from the United World Wide Health Association who was at the house. I told her where Shay was and where she was going to be moving to. She said she would try to find time to pack Shay's personal belongings, but I don't know."

"Well, they haven't yet," Dante said.

Enzo shrugged. "I can't help that. I did what you asked me to. I wasn't about to go into some woman's room and rummage through her things. Especially if she's rooming with another woman. I really don't feel like being beaten up by a bunch of United World Wide Health Association workers. I have a practice to run and I'm going to be getting one of those United World Wide Health Association nurses in my clinic soon to deal with the tourists."

"You don't sound very happy about that," Dante said.

Enzo shrugged again. "Am I ever happy about stuff like that? It is what it is. Maybe she'll have a lighter hand with the tourists. Sometimes I don't have enough patience with them."

"So intolerant," Dante teased.

"Look, I have some news. Do you want to hear it or not?"

"Sì, I want to hear it."

"I have a friend who works for the civil court. I explained your situation and they are very aware of our situation with respect to our inheritance and the trust fund."

"Oh, yes?" Dante was now very interested.

"And instead of the four-day waiting period to get your Nulla Osta they were able to give it to me today. All you have to do is get Shay to sign it stating that there is no impediment for you two to marry, and you can marry today, provided you have two witnesses."

"I hope you'll be one of the witnesses."

"I'll try. Truly," Enzo said. "I want to make sure this is seen through. I'm still worried, Dante. I still have my misgivings about this."

"I know you do, but, trust me, Shay is pregnant with my child. The paternity result said so. I met her at that conference in Hawaii months ago. We had one night of passion. We did use protection, but you know that doesn't always work. And now she's expecting my child."

Enzo nodded. "Don't you think it's funny, though, that she came here? I mean, people know about us. The paparazzi follow us around even though we have restraining orders. Everyone knows our father is a womanizer and has sold off pieces of Affini land, just so he could pay for all his mistresses, and that he'll eventually sell off our mother's land too if he gets the chance. Affini men are cheaters, both in matters of money and women. It was the same with his father too. Affini men are a bunch of womanizers. What if she hears about that?"

"What if she does?" Dante asked, getting impatient. He knew all this. Why was Enzo so worried?

"Isn't that why Olivia went after you? She could claim that you were not being faithful to her, even though she was ultimately not faithful to you. Women like that are just looking for a handout."

"I am aware of the situation, Enzo. Because it's happened to me. It won't happen this time. This is my child. With Olivia it was different. She was pregnant before we met—that's how I knew the child wasn't mine. It was better I found out. It hurt a lot at the time, that's true, but Shay *is* pregnant with my child. I'm going to take care of them even if I have to give them a handout. I'm going to support her. I'm going to make sure my child is taken care of. That's the kind of person that I am."

Enzo shook his head. "This is why I don't want to get involved with any woman. Just give me casual relationships."

"Casual can lead to a baby too," Dante said. "Look what happened here. Shay and I were only ever going to be a onetime thing and now she's pregnant with my child. If it wasn't for the fact that I was approaching my thirty-fifth birthday, I wouldn't be pushing this marriage so hard. I would support the child, don't get me wrong," Dante said quickly. "Because, unlike you, I want to be a father."

There had been so many times when he was in that villa

that he'd felt lonely. He wouldn't admit it, but it was true. It hurt thinking about what could've been with Olivia if she hadn't betrayed his trust, if that child had been his. He wanted a family. Despite the fact that his father was a womanizer who had broken his mother's heart. He wanted what he'd never had as a child. A happy family.

Love from both parents.

What his mother had mourned, because she'd had that as a child and hadn't been able to give it to her sons.

Dante had loved his mother. She was a good mother. He loved Enzo and having a brother. He'd loved spending time with his maternal grandparents in Tuscany. Every summer they would spend their time there when they weren't in school. Then there were the times his mother would take them to the dilapidated villa that was now his home. They would spend time running on the sandy beaches at the Lido, eating olives and picking fresh fruit.

It was a happy time.

On the Lido they had been away from the hustle and bustle. From the lonely nights when their parents had gone to parties and entertained. From the fights and arguments their parents had had. From the heartbreaking cries of their mother as her heart had broken more every time their father had cheated.

He wasn't going to do that. Enzo was more afraid of becoming a womanizer than Dante was, but Olivia had crushed every little piece of trust he'd had and he wasn't sure he ever wanted to take the risk of having what he'd always wanted.

Family.

Shay showing up in Venice pregnant was scary. He was terrified, but he was going to do the right thing. Even if the marriage was for show and nothing was going to come of things between the two of them, he was going to have a child. An heir. He was going to be a part of that child's life forever. He didn't take his duty lightly.

He was going to make sure his child was happy. His child wasn't going to suffer the way he and Enzo had suffered. He wasn't going to hurt Shay, or his child.

"Come on, let's go get Shay to sign this." Dante took the forms from Enzo. "Then you can meet her and see for yourself that she's nothing like Olivia."

"I look forward to meeting her. Another time, though. I have work to take care of."

"You can come meet her here before you go."

They walked through the halls of the hospital to the other side where the simulation training was going to take place, but they found that Shay's office was locked. Dante knocked, but there was no answer.

A nurse walked by.

"She went out for lunch," the nurse said.

"Do you know where?" Dante asked.

"*Sì*, Braddicio's, which isn't far."

"Do you know when she'll be back?" Dante asked.

"I don't know," the nurse said. "The simulation is ready, but the trainees are still working with Dr. Carlo, so it's been postponed until they are done working with Dr. Carlo."

Dante cursed under his breath. *"Grazie."*

"Well, now what?" Enzo asked. "I don't have much longer before I have to get back to the clinic."

"How about we go to the restaurant? I need to talk to her privately away from here anyway. You can distract the girlfriend she's having lunch with while I talk to Shay."

"No good," said Enzo. "I'm truly sorry, but you're on your own."

Dante cursed under his breath. "You're a thorn in my side, Enzo."

And all Enzo did was grin.

CHAPTER FIVE

SHAY WALKED INTO BRADDICIO'S, which was tucked down a small canal, off the main canal near the hospital. She'd been here before. It was a nice Italian bistro, dark and romantic, and the food was good. Shay loved it here. When she went inside, Aubrey was already sitting there, waiting. She looked worried as she watched the door.

Shay headed to the booth in the corner where Aubrey was waiting for her. When Aubrey's gaze landed on her, she could see the relief wash over her face.

"Oh, thank goodness," Aubrey said. "I've been so worried about you. You didn't go into too many details on the phone this morning and I figured you couldn't speak freely. I hopped a train for you, I'll have you know."

"I was fine, Aubrey. I was with Dante—the father of my child *and* a highly respected surgeon," she teased. "I was in very good hands."

"I know, I know. I was just concerned when you weren't at the house when I called last night. I know I pushed you to take this job here and to tell Dante about his child, but I didn't expect you to run off with him."

"I didn't."

"Clearly. Still, I was picturing all these horrible things happening to you." Aubrey grinned. "I'm relieved."

"What kind of horrible things? The worst he could do is lock me up in his villa…"

"He owns a villa?" Aubrey asked with surprise. "Where?"

"The Lido di Venezia."

"He has a villa on the Lido?" Aubrey asked, impressed. "Wow, Venice is expensive."

"He's a prince."

Aubrey's mouth dropped open, her eyes wide, and she shook her head. "A what?"

"A prince. The father of my baby is a prince. Yesterday when I tried to leave the hospital after my shift ended I was accosted by the paparazzi because my baby is the Affini heir." She'd lowered her voice, not that there were many people in the restaurant while they were having their lunch break, but, still, she didn't want someone to hear.

"So that's why he wants to marry you? Because he's a prince?"

"Something like that," Shay said. "He said he could protect me. He has a restraining order against the press. Once he had me in his arms, they didn't come back again. They didn't follow us to the Lido to bother us either."

Aubrey frowned. "He wants to marry you to *protect* you? That sounds a little old-fashioned. What did you say?"

"I told him no, of course, but he's so insistent. Which is why I wanted to talk to you."

"Do you *want* to marry him? I thought you didn't want to get married."

"I don't, but he wants to give his child his name. And it would be more of a business arrangement. Dante said it need only last a year."

"You don't need to be married for him to give your child his name, you know," Aubrey said.

"I know, right? I mean, it's just that he's royalty and their name is well-known—it's a legitimizing thing apparently. And…with my work…well, I could continue to do my work if he was involved."

"You don't have to be married for him to be involved

in your child's life. Or for you to be able to continue with your career, Shay."

"I know. I'm so confused. When I woke up in his bed this morning in his villa, it felt right being with him, but… I don't know."

Aubrey's eyes widened. "You spent the night in his bed, in his villa?"

"Yes." Shay winced as Aubrey groaned. "But he was the perfect gentleman and slept downstairs on the sofa all night," she added quickly.

"Oh, Shay, are you still attracted to him?"

"Yes."

Aubrey looked even more concerned then. "And he only wants to be married for a year? That seems weird."

"I know." Shay sighed. "It sounds a little too good to be true, but there you have it. I don't know what to do."

"Well, at least he wants to be involved with his child's life."

"Yes, that much he does," Shay agreed.

"That's a good thing." Aubrey had issues with her own father, just as Shay did. Which was probably why they'd bonded so quickly when they'd met in their first years during the UWWHA. Aubrey was the one who had been so insistent that Shay find Dante and tell him about the baby. Aubrey was also the one who'd found out about this job and suggested that Shay take it when Daniel dropped out.

Shay didn't know what to do, which was why she was glad Aubrey was visiting today. She needed to talk it out. That was how she rationalized things.

"I wonder what's in it for him," Aubrey mused.

"That's exactly what I was thinking. I don't understand. Couldn't someone just offer to get the mother of their child on their restraining order without them having to marry?"

"Yeah," Aubrey said. "I'm not familiar with how that works here. I'm not too familiar with Italian laws."

"I don't know what to do," Shay said. "He promises that the marriage won't interfere with my work and that it's on paper only. Once the year is up, I'm free to go. He'll grant me a painless divorce. No fighting over custody, which we'll share. We're going to have contracts drawn up and everything."

"It just sounds *off*, Shay." Aubrey didn't look convinced. "Please promise me that you'll get a lawyer to look over everything. Especially when dealing with Italian laws as a foreigner."

"I know. I will. I just want my child to have their father in their life."

Aubrey nodded sadly. "I understand that. I get that, but you have to protect yourself too."

"There is nothing to protect myself from. I don't own any assets. It's Dante who should be worried, even though I have no interest in his money. Or his land. Or his title."

Or him? a little voice in her head asked. She shook that thought away. She did have an interest in him. A big interest, which was what had got her into this situation in the first place. Only she would never hang on to past relationships. Once it was over, it was over. With Dante, it wasn't. There was something different about him.

You're carrying his baby, that's why.

She hadn't known she was pregnant for weeks after conception, yet she'd thought of Dante every day since they'd parted. So what was it about him? Why was Dante different from her other few fleeting relationships?

You've never been this attracted to someone before.

And she *was* attracted to Dante. She still desired him. Just being around him made her pulse quicken, her blood heat, and the urge to kiss him again was strong.

"I'm not just talking legal stuff."

"Oh?"

"You're attracted to him and yet you're agreeing to this cold and loveless marriage."

Blood rushed to Shay's cheeks and she groaned. "Yes."

"Tread carefully. I don't want you to get hurt."

"Why don't we order something? I'm starving," Shay said, keen to shake away thoughts of Dante and kissing him. "I haven't had anything to eat since this morning when he made me fresh fruit and yogurt."

Aubrey chuckled. "He made you fresh fruit and yogurt?"

"He's a good cook. I tasted the risotto he made the night before. It was delicious. He says he likes to do it."

"Well, that's at least something, because you are a terrible cook."

They both laughed at that as the waiter came over to take their order. Shay ordered a glass of Italian soda, while Aubrey got to have wine.

They continued talking about their work and how Aubrey's work was going farther south in the country, and Shay talked about the simulations she was going to run the new trainees through. It was nice to chat like normal again. To not talk about babies or marriage.

"Oh, my," Aubrey said, perking up.

"What?"

Aubrey nodded at the door. "I think your husband-to-be just walked in."

Shay turned and saw Dante standing in the doorway of the restaurant.

"What is he doing here?"

Dante caught her gaze and then headed over to their table. By the firm set of his jaw and his tight gait he was on a mission.

"*Scusami*, I'm so sorry for intruding on your lunch." Dante smiled briefly, but charmingly, at Aubrey.

"What're you doing here, Dante?" Shay asked.

"I need to speak with you alone, Shay." Then he turned to Aubrey. "If you'll excuse us? This is important."

Aubrey was going to say something, because she didn't look too thrilled at having their lunch interrupted, but Dante turned his back on her. Shay sighed—this arrogant side was not what she was used to from Dante—and slid out of the booth. Dante led her away and Aubrey looked none too happy about being left alone. Her lips were thinned and her arms tightly folded across her chest.

Not a good sign. Dante didn't know what kind of trouble he was in.

"What, can't it wait until I go back to the hospital?" she asked.

"This." He held out a paper. "This is a Nulla Osta. If you sign it, we can get married this afternoon."

"Dante! This afternoon? We have to finish our shift and I haven't even agreed to marry you yet!" She rubbed her temple. "You're very persistent."

He grinned. "I know."

"Maybe I should get a lawyer."

"Shay, I promise you, you don't need a lawyer. This is just a form that states that there's nothing to stop us from getting married. You sign it and we head to the courthouse to get married now. I will provide you a contract outlining the details of our marriage within five days to a lawyer of your choosing."

"So, I have to stay married to you for a year?"

"*Sì.*"

"This is not a real marriage, though?" And warmth flooded in her cheeks as she asked that question. It was a polite way of saying that there would be no sex between them.

"Correct. You will have your own space at my villa."

"What happens after the year is up? You said I wouldn't have to fight for custody."

"*Sì*, we will have joint custody. I will take our child when you need to work. Our child will have my name and will be taken care of. You, as our child's mother, will be as well. Finally, our child will have dual citizenship."

"I don't know…" Then she thought of the schooling her child could receive with Dante's money and connections. The opportunities she'd never had as a bright child growing up in the lower ninth ward of New Orleans, moving around constantly. No roots. No family ties. No father.

She bit her lip.

Do it for your child.

"Where do I sign?" Shay asked.

Dante pulled out a pen, but before she could sign on the dotted line his pager went off. He pulled it out. "Incoming trauma. I knew it was too quiet this morning."

"We should go, then," Shay said.

"*Sì.*"

Shay turned and saw that Aubrey was frowning, her eyes narrowed as she glared at Dante.

"I have to go, Aubrey. There's incoming trauma," Shay said.

Aubrey nodded. "Don't worry. Go. I'll settle up and we'll talk later. I have a train to catch." It was as if Aubrey knew that Shay would agree to the marriage of convenience in the end.

Shay smiled and mouthed, "Thank you," as she left the restaurant with Dante. Her mind was still reeling with the fact she'd decided to marry him.

Even though she was terrified at the prospect.

Dante hated fires.

He hated when people were burned. He never did like it when people were injured, but burn victims always hit a little too close to home. His best friend had been caught in a fire and had received burns to seventy percent of his body. He'd lived for a few short days in complete agony.

And this situation was no different.

The young man was in pain and Shay was moving quickly in the chaos of a busy trauma room. He appreciated it. She knew what to do. He didn't have to tell her what to do. She just did it. She set up the IV with antibiotics and painkillers while Dante examined the extent of the burns.

"Was it a house fire?" Dante asked the paramedic who brought the patient in.

"*Sì*, it was."

Once Dante learned that, he changed his tactic. He knew that when some of the old houses caught fire, they were very enclosed and it wasn't just the burns that could kill.

It was the carbon monoxide poisoning in the blood. The patient's lungs could be scorched.

He could suffocate.

Dante immediately listened to the patient's chest. His breath was hoarse, labored. He tilted the patient's head back and examined his throat, to see black.

"We need to intubate him," Dante said to Shay. "Get me an intubation kit."

She nodded and went over to the cabinets in the bay, pulling out an intubation kit. Dante tilted the patient's head back once more and quickly intubated him. Shay bagged him once the tube was in, pumping air into the man's lungs until they could get him up into the ICU.

There wasn't much he could do for the third-degree burns in the trauma bay.

The man's blood pressure was high and he was now intubated. They had to get him stable, and then they could take him into surgery where they would clean his burns and help prevent infection.

"I want a CBC drawn. I need to see how much carboxy-hemoglobin is in his blood."

Shay nodded. "I'll do that."

"When he's stable and we have his labs back, we'll get him into the operating room."

Dante watched as Shay hooked the man up to the ventilator. The man was now in an induced coma, but it was good. This way he wasn't in pain.

Once they had the patient as stable as they could, porters came to take the patient up to the ICU. Dante and Shay removed their gloves and moved to the next bay, making their rounds through the influx of patients that had come through, but there was no one that needed immediate attention, as the burn victim had needed.

"I'd better get to my simulation training," Shay said. "I just got a page that they're ready for me now that Dr. Carlo is done with them."

"Do you need any help with that?" Dante asked.

"No, but maybe you could walk me out of the emergency room to my office? I still haven't got the lay of the land yet."

He chuckled. "Of course."

Dante led the way out of the emergency room.

"How long will the training last?" Dante asked.

"Why?"

"The courthouse closes at five."

"Oh. Right. Do we have to do it today? I signed the form. Can't we wait? I promised I would marry you. I won't run. I can't."

She was nervous and Dante found it endearing.

"*Sì*, we have to do it today because you signed the form and dated it."

"Okay, I'll make sure I'm done in time. How long will it take and who will be our witnesses?"

"It should only take a few minutes and I've asked Enzo, but he might be busy. Do you think your friend Aubrey will step in?"

"No, she's headed back to Rome, where she's working

at the moment. And my roommate is packing my belongings, since I'm apparently moving in with you tonight."

"That makes me very happy." Dante grinned that charming lopsided, dimpled smile that made her weak at the knees.

And it was true. Once she was under his roof, then he would be more at ease about this whole situation. There he could take care of her and take care of their baby.

"Does it make you happy?" she asked.

"It does. This will benefit us both, Shay."

"That's what I can't figure out. How does this benefit you?"

"By having the baby in my life, that's how it benefits me. Being a father is an honor and something I have always wanted. My name, and passing it down, is important to me." He didn't know why he couldn't tell her the real reason, why he didn't tell her about the trust fund, other than the fact that the last time he'd told someone about it, she had used him. Shay knew he was a prince, knew that he owned the villa, but she really didn't understand the scope of what was at stake.

And he just didn't trust her enough yet to tell her.

He couldn't tell her.

"So, when should I come back?" Dante asked as they stood in front of the training room.

"Two hours should suffice. The simulation is ready to go and they have to complete it in a certain time or else they don't pass."

"You're tough," Dante teased.

She grinned. "Working with the United World Wide Health Association isn't an easy ticket. It's hard work. I was put through my paces and I plan to do the same for them."

"I don't doubt it. I'll come back in two hours, then, and we'll make it official. That way you can move freely throughout Venice. The restraining order will protect you and our baby."

Shay nodded and headed into the training room.

Dante turned and walked back to the emergency room, but first he pulled out his phone and tried to call Enzo. There was no answer and it went straight to voice mail.

"Can you meet Shay and I at the city hall at half past four? She signed the papers and we're going to make it official." He disconnected the call.

His stomach twisted at the thought of Shay becoming his wife.

Having a wife was the last thing he'd wanted, but also something he'd secretly always longed for.

He was so close to having it all, but then a sense of dread sank in his stomach and he couldn't help but wonder when it would all end.

When he would lose it all.

He'd learned very young that he couldn't take life for granted. That happiness was fleeting. So when would all of this be snatched away from him?

He hated the fact he was such a pessimist. He was a surgeon. He was supposed to be an optimist.

Only he didn't feel so optimistic at the moment.

He was only feeling dread over what the future held.

CHAPTER SIX

SHAY COULDN'T FOLLOW most of the civil ceremony, but she understood when the judge pronounced them man and wife.

"You may kiss your bride," the officiant said in English.

Shay's pulse raced. She hadn't anticipated that a kiss would be part of this marriage.

Since she'd agreed to the marriage she kept trying to think of it as a business arrangement for the benefit of their child, but now as she held Dante's hand, staring up into his dark brown eyes as his wife, the prospect of kissing him made her insides quiver. Her body responded with the familiar ache, because it knew what his kisses were like.

How they enflamed her.

Dante bent down and pressed his lips against hers briefly, but in that moment a jolt of electricity raced through her, her body recalling every kiss he'd shared with her. It lit a fire in her that had never been extinguished. This marriage of convenience was going to be hard.

Dante stepped away quickly, pulling at his collar again as the officiant led them to where they were to sign the certificate.

The court had standby witnesses, who signed their names after Shay and Dante had finished signing theirs.

She accepted congratulations graciously, but there was

a little voice in the back of her head reminding her that this marriage was a sham.

That she shouldn't be here.

This wasn't real.

And it really wasn't.

She'd just entered into a marriage of convenience with the father of her baby.

This is for the baby. Dante won't leave the baby. He wants to be a father. He's not like your father.

As they stepped outside she took a deep breath to calm her erratic pulse.

"Shall we celebrate?" Dante asked as they left the courthouse.

"I'd rather have a nap," Shay teased. "I do need to collect my things if I'm moving in with you. And your lawyer will need to start looking into extending my visa."

"*Sì*, he will, and as for collecting your things—we can do that." Dante walked to the edge of the Grand Canal and flagged down a gondola.

"What're you doing?" Shay asked, bewildered.

"Flagging down a gondola. That's how we'll get to your residence. Or rather your former residence."

"A water taxi will do."

"I like this way better." He winked at her, those dark eyes of his twinkling, sending her pulse skittering.

Damn him.

"How do you know how to get to the United World Wide Health Association house?"

"Because it was my childhood home," Dante said quickly as a gondola pulled up. "Come on."

His childhood home?

He took her hand and helped her down the steps into the gondola.

"You know, we could've walked too. I don't think I've ever used the canal entrance before."

Dante smiled. "I know, but this is a celebration. We're married and the world is watching. We have to pretend that we're a happy couple out in public. You have just snagged one of Italy's most eligible bachelors."

Shay smiled ruefully as he took a seat beside her on the cushioned bench.

The gondolier used his long pole to push away from the canal ledge out into the Grand Canal. She hadn't done this before. Mostly she just walked where she needed to go. The United World Wide Health Association residence wasn't far from the hospital and Shay liked to walk, but as they slowly glided down the main canal she found herself relaxing into the ride. She could see smaller canals leading off the Grand Canal, overshadowed by old buildings and smaller bridges that connected one side to the other.

On the Grand Canal there were larger bridges, with tourists passing over them as the gondola glided underneath. She understood now why so many people loved this. Why it was popular with tourists. It was beautiful. It was calming and she was suddenly very aware that she was alone on a romantic gondola ride with Dante.

And he was so close, she could smell his masculine aftershave, feel his strong arm around her. His hand on her shoulder, his fingers making circles through the fabric of her scrubs, making her body yearn for something more.

You can't have any more. And Aubrey's warning about treading carefully went through her mind.

"So, the United World Wide Health Association residence was your childhood home?" she asked, trying to defuse the tension she was feeling and chasing the thoughts of kissing Dante away to something a little more tedious.

"*Sì*, my father sold it off a few years ago. He and my mother moved elsewhere." There was a hint of bitterness in Dante's voice.

"You sound sad about it."

"Annoyed," Dante said, and he ran his hand through his hair as he always seemed to do when he was distracted. "I didn't have as much of an attachment to that home as my younger brother did. I prefer the villa where I live and the vineyard in Tuscany."

"I would love to see the vineyard."

"You told me once that you never sightsee when you're on assignment. There is so much more to Italy than just Venice."

"Isn't that blasphemy?" she teased. "You're Venetian."

He smiled. "Perhaps, but I am Italian first."

The gondolier pulled up in front of the United World Wide Health Association house, tying up his gondola as Dante asked him to wait. Dante climbed out and helped her out of the gondola.

"Why are you asking the gondolier to wait?" Shay asked. "I didn't think they crossed the lagoon."

"No, they don't, but I thought it would be nice to take the gondola down the Grand Canal back to the hospital before we make our way to the ferry docks."

Shay didn't respond as they walked into the rental house that had once been Dante's childhood home. The moment they stepped over the threshold his demeanor changed. She could tell by the way his body stiffened. He jammed his hands in his pockets and kept looking straight ahead.

Even though he'd said that he wasn't attached to this home, it clearly brought up some painful memories for him. She knew the look, because that was the way she'd felt the day she'd walked back into her mother's house after the floodwaters had receded. After FEMA had told her it was marked condemned and that she was allowed one last look inside before it was demolished.

Yet it still stood. They hadn't demolished it yet.

It was boarded up and covered with graffiti, sitting

among the wrecks and ruin of the lower ninth ward homes. People toured the area now, which ticked Shay off no end.

It was macabre.

Don't think about it now.

"I'll just go collect my suitcase. I won't be too long."

He nodded and stood by the door. She went upstairs to her room.

She collected her few belongings and left. She was sad that she wasn't going to be living here. She'd always lived on-site wherever the United World Wide Health Association housed her.

This was a first, living off-site.

It was nerve-racking.

This is for your baby. It's only temporary. Just a year. You were going to take a year maternity leave anyways after this twelve-week assignment.

Still, a pang of homesickness washed over her.

She couldn't remember the last time she'd ever felt homesick and she wasn't sure if she ever did feel homesick.

This isn't your home.

Shay didn't have a home. And she never had, really. She and her mother were always moving and this was no different. Only it was. Dante was offering her permanence for a year and permanence for a lifetime for their child.

With a sigh she walked back downstairs. Dante met her halfway up the steps and took her suitcase from her.

"Is this it?" he asked.

She nodded. "Yes. Everything I own fits into that suitcase and my purse."

He gave her a strange look. "Strange."

"It's not strange. I travel a lot."

"Don't you have a home in New Orleans?"

"I have a place to stay, but it's not much." It was just a bed, a couple pieces of furniture. That was all. It was just a place to stay while she waited for assignments.

"Good thing you're moving in with me, then," Dante said as they went outside and he handed her suitcase to the gondolier.

"Why is that?" she asked.

"Because every child needs a place to call home."

Shay's stomach twisted in a knot and she resisted the urge to say something further. About how not every child was that lucky, but it wasn't about that. He was absolutely right. Every child deserved a home and by agreeing to marry Dante, even if on paper only, she was giving her child something she'd never had.

A home.

Which was why she'd agreed to this marriage of convenience in the first place.

And that was the most important thing.

Dante stood at the nurses' station in the emergency department filling out a newly discharged patient's chart. Soon Dr. Salzar would come and relieve him for the night shift. Dante wanted to make sure that everything was in order for the sign-off.

He glanced up to see Shay leading a group of United World Wide Health Association trainees through the emergency room. He smiled watching her. She'd been so busy since they'd got married, he rarely saw her.

It had been well over two weeks of just moving past each other like ships in the night. No more than a greeting and the odd quick meal. And then the last five mornings when he'd finished his swim she had already left, taking the first ferry across the lagoon. At night when he got home from his shift she was always fast asleep. She wasn't totally at fault. He'd been busy preparing the contract for their marriage, and when the baby was born Dante's inheritance left by his mother in trust would be his at last. At least now with the marriage his father couldn't get his hands on it.

Almost three weeks now without really talking to Shay made him realize that he missed her.

What did you expect it to be like? It's not a real marriage. You're basically roommates.

Still, he wanted to get to know the mother of his child. This marriage might be keeping her here for the sake of their baby, but he found that he liked spending time with her when he saw her. And on the occasions when they worked together with the trainees he enjoyed his time with her and he found himself wanting more.

You can't have more. She's made it clear she doesn't want more.

Besides, the press were noticing the distance between them. He'd seen the headlines. He would have to talk to Shay later about putting on a better show of marriage. At least for the year. The last thing he needed was some kind of ridiculous headline to the effect that he was buying a baby or something.

"Dr. Affini?"

Dante turned around and his intern was standing behind him.

"How can I help you, Dr. Martone?"

"I have a patient in a trauma bay. I think you need to check his EKG."

Dante took the electronic chart from Dr. Martone and frowned when he saw the chart. The patient was a sixty-five-year-old man who'd presented with dizziness, nausea, shortness of breath and severe heartburn. The ST segment of the EKG was elevated.

"What do you think?" Dante asked as he flipped through the tests. Dante had his suspicions, but he was teaching Dr. Martone, who was fresh out of medical school and a quick learner.

"STEMI."

"Which stands for?"

"Segment elevation myocardial infarction," Dr. Martone answered.

"Let's go see the patient."

Dante followed his intern into the larger trauma bay. When he walked into the room, he saw the patient already had oxygen and that an IV was started. Shay walked into the bay on the other end of the open room.

"Do you need a hand, Dr. Affini?" she asked as she came up beside him.

"I do." He handed her the chart and went up to the patient. "*Buongiorno*, I'm Dr. Affini and I'll be taking care of you."

"It's a pleasure to meet you," the patient said, his breathing labored. "I'm Giovanni Scalzo."

"Can you tell me what brought you in here tonight, Mr. Scalzo?" Dante asked as he listened to the patient's chest.

"Indigestion," Giovanni said. 'I don't know what the fuss is all about. I was hoping for a prescription antacid."

Shay handed Giovanni an aspirin. "Mr. Scalzo, can you take this, please?"

Giovanni grinned up at Shay and Dante couldn't blame him.

"Anything for you, *cara*." Giovanni grinned again and took the aspirin.

Dante chuckled. "Do you have a cardiologist, Mr. Scalzo?"

Giovanni looked confused. "No."

Shay and he exchanged looks.

"Mr. Scalzo, I'm going to page our cardiologist on duty, Dr. Fucci, to come and take a look at your labs."

"Is something wrong with my heart?" Giovanni's monitors beeped as his blood pressure rose from panic.

Shay stepped forward and placed a hand on the patient's shoulder, instantly calming the patient down with the simple reassurance of touch.

"Don't worry, Mr. Scalzo, you're in good hands here. Your EKG was a little elevated and I'd like to run it by a specialist if that's okay with you?" Dante's question also calmed down Giovanni.

"*Sì*, that's good." Mr. Scalzo lay back against the bed. Dante watched his breathing become more labored.

"Are you in pain, Mr. Scalzo?" Shay asked.

"*Sì*, the heartburn burns my throat and my arms feel heavy."

"Give him some morphine," Dante said. Then he turned to his intern. "Page Dr. Fucci and prep the cath lab for a percutaneous coronary intervention."

"*Sì*, Dr. Affini," Dr. Martone said, taking back the chart.

Dante left the trauma bay. The next ninety minutes would be crucial for Giovanni. His heart muscle was dying, as was evident from the labs drawn by Dr. Martone.

Shay fell into step beside him.

"That's quite a way to end your shift, with a STEMI."

Dante nodded. "Dr. Martone is an excellent intern and Dr. Fucci will have the block taken care of in no time. When is your shift over?"

"Now. I'm done as well."

Dante cocked an eyebrow. "I don't think we've been off at the same time since we got married three weeks ago."

"You've been working late," Shay said, and then she winced, holding her belly, instantly alarming him.

"Are you okay? Is the baby okay?"

"Yes, I'm just tired." Shay smiled. "I'm fine. I think it's just a Braxton Hicks."

"So early?"

"I'm nineteen weeks pregnant now. Almost halfway there. Braxton Hicks can start in the second trimester."

Dante was going to make her sit down, when a code blue was called from the trauma bay where Mr. Scalzo was. They turned around and walked quickly back to his room.

Mr. Scalzo was unconscious, ashen and in full-blown cardiac arrest. His heart was tachycardia, pumping too fast, and no blood was getting through. There was no blood flow to his brain or other organs. He would be dead soon. Dr. Martone was pumping on the patient's chest hard, trying to get it back into a rhythm, but only the electrical shock would reset the cells of the heart to fall back into rhythm.

"What do we do, Dr. Martone?" Dante shouted over the din as he pulled on gloves.

"Shock the heart back into rhythm and intubate."

Dante nodded and turned to Shay. "Get me an intubation kit."

A defibrillator was primed and wheeled over to the patient. The electrode path was placed on Mr. Scalzo's chest.

"Clear!" Dr. Martone shouted.

They shocked the patient's heart, his muscles twitching as the electricity moved through his body. Now all Dante could do was watch the monitors and wait for the heart, which was now flatlining, to jump back into rhythm.

Come on.

The monitor beeped as a rhythm started.

Shay handed the intubation kit to Dr. Martone while Dante took the man's pulse to confirm that the heart was back in rhythm. Then Dante guided Dr. Martone as he successfully intubated the patient. Once the ventilator was breathing for their patient, Dr. Martone wheeled the patient out of the trauma pod to go up to the cath lab, where Dr. Fucci was waiting. The room cleared and Dante finished his notes, breathing a sigh of relief that the patient wasn't lost.

"Dante…" Shay said, her voice trembling.

"Sì?" He glanced up just in time to see Shay's knees buckle as she crumpled to the floor.

He raced to catch her, his heart hammering. *"Cara,"* he whispered, but she didn't respond. So he scooped her up in his arms and got her to the table.

"Dr. Affini?" a nurse asked as he hit the call button.

"Get Dr. Tucci here now!" he shouted.

Oh, God.

He took her pulse. It was low. And he couldn't help her. He'd lost control over this moment and he hated this loss of control. Hated that he was helpless, that she brought this side out in him in this moment.

He was in danger when he was out of control. And he didn't like this one bit, but all he could do right now was cradle her.

Protect her.

Protect his child.

Later he could bury the emotions. Right now he couldn't keep them back even if he wanted to. He was only glad that Shay couldn't see him like this.

CHAPTER SEVEN

SHAY STARED UP at the ceiling tile in Dr. Tucci's office, her hands folded around her belly as she took deep calming breaths. She was still feeling a bit shaky, but she felt fine; it was the baby she was worried about now. Dante was sitting next to her, which was a relief, because a moment ago he was pacing.

"You know, Dr. Tucci wasn't even on duty. He was at home," Shay said. "This is very good of him to see me like this. We seem to keep paging him at odd hours. First the paternity test and now this."

Dante just grunted and then got up and paced again. "I thought you were going to make an appointment."

"I did," she countered. "It was for next week. I'm only nineteen weeks, Dante. It's not until I'm in my third trimester that I see an ob-gyn every week. You're a doctor, you should know this."

It was a tease, but Dante didn't take the bait. He shot her a look of frustration. He dragged a hand through his hair and glanced at the watch on his wrist. It was at that moment that Dr. Tucci walked in.

"*Scuse*, I'm sorry that I took so long," Dr. Tucci said. He saw Dante. "Dr. Affini, I'm surprised to see you here. I thought you were on duty." Dante sat down muttering under his breath.

"I'm the father. Nurse Labadie is now my wife, so I just went off duty."

Dr. Tucci's brows arched at all the answers Dante was giving him, and then he grinned. "Congratulations. I guess I should call you Principessa now."

"You don't need to," Shay said quickly. "In fact, I'd rather not be referred to as that."

Dr. Tucci chuckled and Dante rolled his eyes.

"So what happened, Shay?" Dr. Tucci asked.

"She fainted," Dante said. "Her blood pressure was low. I took it in the emergency department."

Dr. Tucci nodded. "How far along are you?"

"Nineteen weeks," Shay said. "I think I felt a Braxton Hicks."

"I think it's too early," Dante said firmly.

"No, not too early. She's nineteen weeks. They can be felt as early as sixteen weeks. Especially if the mother is tired or under stress." Dr. Tucci shot Dante a knowing look.

Shay couldn't help but laugh. "So it was Braxton Hicks?"

"Well, let's have a listen to the baby's heart." He pulled down the Doppler monitor and lifted Shay's shirt. "The gel will be cold, I'm sorry."

"It's okay. I'm used to it."

Dr. Tucci squirted the gel onto her abdomen and turned on the Doppler. He pressed into her belly and Shay held her breath, waiting to hear that familiar rapid beat of the baby's heart. Dante was frowning and she could see worry etched into his face.

He hadn't heard the baby's heartbeat yet. He hadn't even so much as touched her belly.

Then the familiar thump of the baby's heart sounded on the monitor and Dr. Tucci grinned at her. "Sounds strong, Shay."

She smiled and then glanced over at Dante. The frown of

worry was gone and now wonder was spread across his face as he listened to the heartbeat from where he was standing.

"Have you had any bleeding?" Dr. Tucci asked, wiping the gel off her belly with a towel.

"No," Shay answered. "I had some mild cramping."

Dr. Tucci frowned. "The baby's heartbeat is fine, there's no bleeding, so I just think you're overdoing it. Let's check, though."

"How?" Dante asked.

"Ultrasound," Dr. Tucci said. "Just to make sure the baby is doing well and there's no internal bleeding from the placenta. I want to make sure it's intact."

Dante leaned forward, staring intensely at the screen, and Shay couldn't help but smile. He usually was so detached, but this was different. This was nice. He was so concerned about their child in this moment.

Dr. Tucci squirted more gel onto her belly and placed the wand on her belly. The screen lit up and her breath caught in her throat at the grainy image of her child.

Their child.

Dante was beaming as he watched their child and tears stung her eyes at his reaction. Usually he was so guarded, but there was no sign of that now. Perhaps he wasn't as cold as she'd first thought. Maybe she had nothing to really fear and he'd be there for their child.

"No bleeding," Dr. Tucci said.

Dante reached out and gripped her hand, grinning at her as he squeezed it and whispering, "Good."

Dr. Tucci took some measurements and then shut off the machine, wiping her belly again. "You're a nurse with the United World Wide Health Association program, *sì*?"

"Yes," Dante grunted, his smile instantly fading. "She's running the simulation training as well as assisting me in the emergency room for the next nine weeks."

Dr. Tucci raised his eyebrows. "You're overdoing it, then."

"I eat small meals. I rest—"

Dr. Tucci shook his head, interrupting her. "You need a couple days to rest. I'm ordering it."

"Good," Dante said. "I'll take her home and make sure she rests."

"I'm on bed rest?" Shay asked, confused.

"No," Dr. Tucci said. "I want you to take three days off, and then you will go on light duty. Only half days. And that's an order."

"Grazie," Dante said. "And thank you for coming in on such short notice."

Dr. Tucci nodded. "I will see you next week and then for the scheduled ultrasound at twenty-six weeks. We'll make sure everything is still going well and take some more measurements."

"Okay," Shay said, but she wasn't exactly thrilled with the idea of going down to half days. That wasn't in her nature. Work was the only constant thing in her life, except now that it wasn't. What was she going to do with herself?

Dante shook Dr. Tucci's hand and then turned back to her when they were alone. "I'm glad the baby is well and that you're well. That it wasn't serious."

"Me too," she said. She sat up slowly. "Told you it was Braxton Hicks."

"It scared me when you fainted like that."

"I'm glad you were there to catch me." Then she blushed. "I'm okay."

He nodded and took her hand. "You will be. I'm going to take the next three days off as well and I'm going to make sure that you get rest. Proper rest. I'll cook for you and take care of you both."

Warmth spread through her chest. No one had ever taken

care of her before. The idea of Dante being there for her was nice.

You can't rely on him always taking care of you. Remember this is just for a short time.

"You don't have to do that."

"I want to do that." He grinned. "Besides, I have some business to attend to in Tuscany and we can spend a couple days at my vineyard. It's quiet there and I think you'll get more rest there than you will here in Venice."

The idea of spending a couple days in Tuscany sounded heavenly, and if she couldn't work, then she was going to do what she always wanted to do, but never found time for, and that was explore.

"That sounds great." Her stomach grumbled and Dante chuckled.

"Let's get back home and get you something to eat. It's still early. We can hit a local bistro on the Lido if you'd like. I think we've both had a long, trying day."

"Now, that's something I can really get on board with." She took his hand as he helped her to her feet.

They grabbed their coats and she had her purse. She informed the other United World Wide Health Association nurses that she was ordered by Dr. Tucci to have three days of rest. She left her simulation training in the capable hands of Danica, who could take over for her because Shay had made up copious notes and prepared the next several simulations.

She and Dante then walked to the ferry pier and caught a ferry to the Lido.

After a short ride, they disembarked.

"The bistro isn't far from here. It's right across the Gran Viale Santa Maria Elisabetta."

"Good, I'm starving."

Dante grinned and took her hand. Just as he'd done in

Oahu when they were walking along the beach at sunset. It felt so good, her hand in his large strong one.

"What're you doing?" she asked, shocked that he was holding her hand. She liked it, but she was surprised by it. He'd slung his arm through hers before, but holding her hand was more intimate. And she had to admit she liked it. It made her feel safe.

"For any press lurking around. You are my wife after all," he said, explaining it, and though it made perfect sense she was a bit disappointed in the answer.

What did you expect?

She didn't know and she didn't know why it bothered her so much.

The little bistro faced the Adriatic side and the warm breeze coming off the water was heavenly. The bistro was filled with tourists from the nearby hotels, but the maître d' found them a table out on the patio underneath lemon trees that were strewn with twinkle lights.

It was perfect and the angel-hair pasta with sun-dried tomatoes was heavenly.

It was delicious.

"You know, you make funny noises when you eat," Dante teased.

"What?"

He grinned, his eyes twinkling as he mimicked the noises she was making, noises that sounded decidedly naughty.

"Making those noises is a compliment."

"*Sì*, I know." He winked at her, grinning.

Her pulse began to race and she thought about the last time he'd looked at her like that and where it had led to.

"Have you been to this bistro a lot?" It was a foolish topic change, but she didn't want to start thinking about the last time they had shared a meal or a drink together so close to a beach.

"*Sì*, I have been here a few times, but never with a woman before if that's what you're getting at."

"No, I'm not." She looked away, knowing that she was blushing.

He winked and took a drink of his red wine, which looked so good, but she couldn't have a drop.

"Oh, I have this for you." Dante reached into his jacket pocket and slid a paper toward her. "It's in English. It's our marriage contract. It outlines our fifty-fifty custody, stipend for living and money for our child. As well as schooling."

Shay nodded as she read it over. The contract benefited her and their child. There was nothing hidden in the contract. It was straightforward.

"Also your visa, *cara*, is taken care of. My attorney arranged for it to be extended indefinitely."

"Indefinitely? I thought our marriage was only for a year."

"We're putting on a show, *cara*."

"Right. Good." She tensed. It all seemed too easy. Why was she uneasy about it?

Because you're having a hard time trusting him.

She didn't know how to trust.

Dante is not your father. He won't abandon our baby.

Shay signed the contract, although her stomach was doing flip-flops.

"Here you go," she said, sliding it back toward him. His fingers brushed hers and sent a jolt of electricity through her.

"Grazie, cara." He took the contract and placed it in his jacket. "Are you okay? Is it Braxton Hicks again?"

"No, I'm just tired." She rubbed her belly and the baby kicked. Hard, for the first time. She smiled, the kick reminding her why she was doing this.

"Is everything okay?" Dante asked again.

"Yes. I think everything is going to be okay."

Dante smiled and then paid the bill. He stood, holding out his hand. "Come, let's go."

Shay took his hand and he led her down to the beach. Her pulse began to race, thundering in her ears. She desired him. She still wanted him, even though she couldn't have him.

Dante affected her so.

They walked along the boardwalk instead of the sandy beach. It was a beautiful night. They didn't say much, but she wasn't worried about the silence between them. It was nice not talking and just enjoying the evening.

"It's a gorgeous night," Dante said.

"It is." She squeezed his hand. "Thanks for being there for me today."

"It's my job. That's our baby you're carrying, *cara*." And the way his dark eyes glowed she forgot for a moment who she was with and how this was only temporary.

She nodded. "Still, I appreciate it. I'm not used to having help."

"I understand." He stopped and tilted her chin so she was staring deep into his dark eyes. "I will be there. I'm here to help you. You can rely on me, *cara*."

And though she wanted to believe him, she was having a hard time letting her heart do just that.

They sped along the winding road that was lined with tall cypress trees. Shay enjoyed the drive in Dante's luxury car. She hadn't even known that he owned a car, until they'd got to the mainland from the ferry and he'd walked her to a car park where the red two-seater was waiting. And she had to say it was a beautiful sports car.

Dante didn't say much on the drive, but she could tell that he was visibly relaxing. He wasn't as tense as he was when he was in Venice. He was smiling to himself the closer they got to Arezzo. Dante's villa was on the outskirts of the city, lying in a valley below the city, but far enough away to enjoy the peace and quiet of the countryside.

"You know," she said, "this is a very nice sports car."

"*Grazie.*" He grinned at her briefly.

"Not very practical, though," she teased.

"What does practicality have to do with it?" he asked.

"There's no backseat—where are we going to put the baby?"

"We?" he asked.

"You." She cursed under her breath for making that assumption. This wasn't a real marriage. There would be no we at all in the near future. Just you or I.

"I can get another car for when I have the baby." He tensed, his knuckles whitening on the steering wheel.

Shay wanted to change the subject. Obviously a touchy matter for him and it annoyed her that she got so upset about it. She knew what she was getting into, but she was so sensitive lately. One moment she could be fine and then next in tears.

"Why don't you tell me a bit about the vineyard?"

"It's been in my mother's family since the seventeen-hundreds."

"Everything in your family is so ancient."

He grinned. "*Sì*, you should've met my Zia Sophia. She was very ancient."

Shay laughed. "I don't think any woman appreciates being referred to as ancient."

"She deserved the title. Enzo and I would make bets on how old she actually was when we were young, because every year she seemed to get younger. I swear her last birthday she was claiming she was younger than me and I was twenty when she passed."

"So how old *was* she?" Shay asked.

"No one knows. There were no birth certificates, but the doctors suspected that she was over a hundred."

"I take it you didn't like her?"

"I adored her. Even if she hid her age. She was young at heart."

"Was she royalty too?"

He shook his head. "No, she was part of my mother's family. I think she was my grandfather's aunt, as he referred to her as Zia Sophia too. What about you? Any elders in your family."

"No."

"No?" he asked, confused.

"Well, there probably was. I wouldn't know. My parents were quite young when they got married and…let's just say their families were extremely religious and didn't approve of a child conceived out of wedlock. My mother was disowned and my father…" She couldn't finish that sentence.

"*Sì?* Your father…?"

Abandoned me.

"My father didn't talk about his family. All I know is the name is Acadian and most of my, I guess, blood relations are in New Orleans, but they didn't want anything to do with us."

Dante frowned. "That's terrible."

She shrugged. "I'm used to it."

"Still, not to know where you come from…"

"I know where I come from. I'm from New Orleans, Louisiana. That's where I'm from." She sighed. She didn't really want to talk about the fact she knew exactly who her family was; she'd seen them. Her mother's parents and siblings. They were a family of wealth and worth in the Garden District.

And they'd let Shay's mother suffer. They'd let her live in poverty.

And when her mother had died, none of them had come to the funeral. None of them had acknowledged Shay's existence. Frankly, she was better off without them. She'd made do without the traditional family for a long time.

Her baby wouldn't have a traditional family either, but at least he or she would have two parents who cared about them. Two parents who would give him or her all they needed.

Does Dante care?

She wasn't sure. He'd seemed concerned when she'd fainted, fascinated when he'd seen the baby on-screen and relieved when the baby had been deemed well, but she didn't know if it was because of a sense of duty or because he genuinely cared about the baby. He said he wanted to be a father. She still didn't know what was in it for him. He didn't touch her belly, didn't plan for the baby or talk about her pregnancy, other than insisting she marry him.

Yet he was always concerned about her getting her rest, feeding her, making sure she took care of herself. He was taking care of her now in a way no one had before.

That meant he cared, right?

"Ah, we're almost there," Dante announced as they turned off the main road, down a small dirt road that went through a small village. "It won't be long now."

"Oh, good," Shay said. And she enjoyed the sights of the small village as Dante slowly drove through, the dirt road giving way to a cobbled stone street. They went over a narrow stone bridge suspended over a gorge, a river tripping over rocks as it wound its way down the hill the village was on.

As they rounded a small square featuring a tall bell tower on the church, the dirt road dipped again into a valley. And when they turned the corner Shay gasped at the sight of acres of vineyards, stretching as far as the eye could see.

"*Bellissimo*, isn't it?" Dante asked, the pride evident in his voice.

"*Sì,*" Shay said happily.

He turned up a long dusty drive. The name over the gate they drove under read Bellezza Addolorata.

"What does that name mean?" Shay asked.

"It's the name of the wine this vineyard produces. Sorrowful Beauty."

She cocked her eyebrows. "Ooh. Sounds wonderful."

"*Sì*, when you have the baby, we'll celebrate with a wine I've been saving for a special occasion. One my grandfather laid down."

"I look forward to that."

Dante parked in front of the house. When he opened the door to climb out, an older couple came out, smiling. Shay almost wondered if they were his grandparents, but by the looks of them they were too young. She got out of the car as Dante was embracing the couple.

He then turned, grinning, and gestured to her. "*Mia moglie*—Shay."

The woman shouted with happiness and then rushed her. Taking her in her arms and kissing her, while who Shay could only assume was her husband grinned, his hands thrust deep into his pockets.

Shay was bowled over by the woman clinging to her, saying things Shay could not understand but could only interpret as happiness.

"Who is this?" she asked, smiling back at the woman, who had finally let her go.

"This is Zia Serena and Zio Guillermo. Not relatives, but they have worked with my grandfather their entire lives. They're caretakers of the vineyard. Zia Serena took care of my grandmother after my grandfather died. They treat me a bit like a son, since they don't have children of their own."

Zia Serena nodded and then motioned to Guillermo as they marched back into the house.

"Well, the villa is big enough for them to live here."

"They don't live here. They own a house on the other

side of the property. I called them and let them know we were coming. Zia Serena made sure the house was stocked. She's made lunch." Dante grinned. "We'll get you fed, and then you can rest in our room while I go inspect the vineyards with Zio."

Shay's stomach did a flip-flop. "Our room?"

He turned around. "Of course. We're married and Zia won't understand that ours is just a marriage of convenience. She's only prepped one room. There's a couch in the room. I can sleep there."

Her pulse pounded in her ears at the thought of sharing a room with him.

Even if he was sleeping on the couch.

She was apprehensive, but honestly she had no one else to blame but herself. She'd decided to sleep with him that night five months ago and she'd agreed to the marriage of convenience.

Dante had forgotten how much he loved sitting around his late grandmother's rough-hewn wooden table in her kitchen. Even though his grandmother had died a few years ago, he could still feel her presence in the brick walls and could still see her rattling the copper pots that swung on the ceiling in the gentle breeze wafting in through the open back door to the garden.

Zia Serena had prepared a light lunch, with a *Caprese* salad and fresh-baked bread. There was *espresso* and *biscotti*. Zia Serena didn't speak a lot of English, but she knew enough to tell Shay to eat and a few stories about Dante when he was young.

Much to Dante's chagrin and Shay's delight.

Once they were done with their food, Zia Serena insisted on cleaning up. Dante made sure that Shay was settled into bed with strict instructions to nap, before he followed Zio Guillermo out the back door and down into the vineyards.

"You've been gone too long," Guillermo remarked.

"I'm a surgeon. I've been busy."

Guillermo just *harrumphed* and then stopped to examine a leaf. "It's good you got married. Your grandfather would be proud."

Dante's stomach knotted when Guillermo mentioned his grandfather.

Would his grandfather be proud of the fact he'd got married only to legitimize the child and keep the land? Essentially his marriage was a sham.

He didn't think his grandfather would be so proud about that. However, the fact Dante was thinking of his child, willing to do whatever to properly raise his child, would make his grandfather proud.

His grandparents had loved each other. When he'd spent summers here, he could see the love between the two of them. Something his parents had never had. Although Dante was sure that his mother had loved his father at some point.

"You know, there were some men here last month with your father," Guillermo said with disdain. Dante knew Serena and Guillermo didn't think much of the man who'd broken his mother's heart. The royal title and status did not impress Serena or Guillermo one bit.

"Oh, yes?" Dante inquired. "What were they here for?"

But deep down he knew.

They were eyeing up the land to sell when Dante's thirty-fifth birthday came at the end of spring and the trust slipped into his father's hands. Thankfully, the marriage put a stop to that, and once the baby was born, then it would all transfer to Dante. And Dante knew that his father was not at all pleased about the prospect.

"Your father was going to sell this vineyard, *sì*?'

Dante nodded. "They came to the Lido villa too, Zio. I sent them away."

And he had. He'd chased them off.

His father had no right to send out Realtors to his property, even if time was running out for Dante to wed and have a child.

Guillermo chuckled and then clapped Dante on the shoulder. "I would've liked to have seen you chase them away. I would've liked to have seen your father's expression."

"He wasn't with them."

His father knew better than to come near Dante.

Dante had made it clear in no uncertain terms that he wanted nothing to do with him.

His father had done enough damage over the years, lying to them, breaking promises.

Guillermo spat on the ground. "He's a coward."

"*Sì*. I couldn't agree with you more." He dragged his hand through his hair. "Show me the rest of the vines you were worried about so we can figure out what's going on."

Guillermo nodded and kept walking on.

Dante trailed behind him, taking it all in, trying to remember everything his grandfather had taught him about the delicate art of winemaking. He glanced back up at the house and saw Shay standing on the terrace in a white summer dress. His heart skipped a beat. She wasn't looking at him; her eyes were closed and her face was tilted up toward the late-afternoon sun. There was a smile on her face and the wind blew back her short blonde locks.

He could see the swell in her belly, the perfect roundness, and his heart swelled with pride. When he'd seen his baby for the first time on the ultrasound, he'd realized that this was more complicated than a simple marriage of convenience.

He liked things simple. Cut and dried, but this was more. Shay was carrying his child.

His child.

She was more than a wife on paper. Inside her was a piece of him.

It wasn't just him alone anymore.

That was his baby inside. The fact that Shay was carrying his flesh and blood made him desire her all the more.

His. Yet he was afraid to think possessively over the baby. To reach out and feel the kicks.

Olivia had made him so wary. He'd been so hurt when he'd found out the baby he'd been hoping for back then wasn't his. She'd shattered all his hopes of a family. Shay promised him an inkling of something more, but he was so afraid to reach out and take it.

She turned back toward the open doors and headed back into the bedroom.

Dante sighed and turned back to the vines.

It was better he kept his distance from Shay. She'd made it clear that she was only doing this for the child's sake. She didn't want him. It was apparent when she was horrified about the idea of staying in the same room as him tonight.

Perhaps I should sleep in the barn?

Only he didn't really ever enjoying sleeping on a bed of hay. Not that there were any animals left in the dilapidated old barn besides field mice and the occasional owl. And he couldn't sleep in the living room. Zia Serena had promised that she would be back up at the house early to cook them breakfast. She'd insisted on cooking all their meals while they were here so Dante could focus on the vines and Shay could rest.

It was dark when Dante returned from the fields with Guillermo. He washed outside with Zio and they both wandered inside, where Dante could smell something he hadn't had the pleasure of tasting in a long time.

"Braciole!" he exclaimed.

Serena grinned and nodded. "Guillermo and I will be out of your hair soon, Dante."

"You can stay for dinner, Zia."

"No, you and your bride must have alone time."

"What's going on?" Shay asked.

"I was trying to convince Zia and Zio to stay, but they refuse."

"Oh, but they must! She cooked this food for us." Shay turned to Serena. "Please stay."

Serena patted her hand but shook her head. "We'll take our dinner back to our home. Sit, Dante."

Dante took a seat next to Shay while Serena dished up the tender steak stuffed with cheese, bread crumbs and raisins that had been marinated in tomato sauce. *Braciole* was served for special occasions in his house and it was accompanied by pasta and bread so you could soak up the sauce.

"I'll be back tomorrow morning." Serena kissed the top of Dante's head and took a small covered pan with their dinner out of the house. Guillermo waved as he followed the food and his wife.

Now it was just the two of them. And an uneasy tension fell between them. Last night at the bistro and then when they had been walking along the boardwalk, all he could think about was taking her in his arms and kissing her. He could remember the taste of her sweet lips, how she'd trembled in his arms when he'd made love to her.

He had been so close to her and he wanted that closeness again.

Only she'd made it clear she didn't want that. She had been so upset when he'd said he'd extended her visa to longer than one year. As if he were trapping her or something.

"What is *braciole*?" Shay asked. "Don't get me wrong, it looks so good—and smells good too."

"It is delicious. It's steak, pounded thin and stuffed. Then it's cooked in tomato sauce."

Shay cut a piece and took a bite. "Oh, my goodness, that's so good."

"See, I told you." He took a bite and it melted on his tongue. Not as good as his grandmother's, but almost there.

"How were the vines?" Shay asked.

"Healthy. There was a bit of a problem area, but I'll get it fixed. How was your rest?"

"Peaceful." She sighed and then smiled. "I really had a good sleep. I can't remember the last time I slept so well."

"You look beautiful tonight," he said, and it was the truth. He only ever saw her in scrubs. She was still wearing that white dress, but now she was wearing a stylish wrap over her bare shoulders, because it was a bit cool in the evening. It was still spring.

A pink tinge rose in her cheeks. "Thank you."

He wanted to say that she looked as if she belonged here in Tuscany, but he didn't.

"I brought a book to read tomorrow on that terrace." Serena chuckled. "Your Zia Serena was insistent I rest. She wants to bring me my meals when you're in the fields."

Dante chuckled. "Don't try to fight her. She'll win."

"I don't have any intention of doing that." Shay sat back. "That was an amazing supper. And I thought you were a good cook. Serena is just absolutely amazing."

"I'll tell her that," Dante said. "It will make her day."

She smiled. "Well, I think I'm going to head back to bed to rest. I'm not used to eating this heavy this late."

"Farmers have to tend the land until the last drop of light is gone." He stretched. "I'll clean up. Go rest like Dr. Tucci told you to."

"I'll leave a light on." There was a nervous tinge to her voice as she left the table to head upstairs.

"Grazie," he whispered as he watched her head up the back stairs to the bedroom above him. His pulse thundered in his ears. He glanced at the couch in his grandmother's sitting room. It was old, but it was a heck of a lot more inviting than taking a chance with his self-control upstairs.

CHAPTER EIGHT

WHEN SHAY WOKE up in the middle of the night, she expected Dante to be next to her. She'd actually fallen asleep in a curled position so that he'd have lots of room and they wouldn't accidentally touch.

She made her way down the stairs quietly and found that he was sleeping on the very short couch in the sitting room. He looked very uncomfortable and his legs were propped up over the end of the couch.

Her foot creaked on the last stair and he craned his head to look at her. "Shay, what're you doing awake? You're supposed to be resting."

"I woke up and you weren't there," she said. "I thought after the big fuss you made about sharing a room in order to keep up appearances that you'd come up."

Dante sighed. "I thought better of it."

She came down the last step into the living room. She sat down on an armchair across from the couch. "You don't look very comfortable."

"I'm not," Dante groused. "I remember it being a lot more comfortable when I was younger."

She chuckled softly. "You were probably shorter."

"*Sì*, I was." He laughed and then groaned as he tried to stretch his six-foot frame out.

"I shouldn't have made such a big deal. We're grown-ups. Come upstairs. We can share a king-sized bed." Her heart skipped a bit as the words slipped past her lips.

"Are you sure?" he asked.

"Yes." And she hoped her voice didn't quiver. She stood and held out her hand, hoping it didn't shake. "Come on. If you spend another couple hours on this thing, you won't be able to move in the morning."

He took her hand, making her skin prickle at his touch, and she led him upstairs. "Yes, and if I was limping too much, Zia Serena would insist on using her homemade liniment on my back."

"Is it any good?"

"Yes, but it stings so much and smells so bad."

"I can only imagine."

"I'm not sure you can," Dante teased. "It would curl your hair."

Shay laughed, but she was unfortunately familiar with scents that could curl your toes. She'd been in enough situations where breathing through your mouth was a better solution.

"Come on," she said, changing the subject. "You can stretch out, and then you won't get attacked by Zia Serena tomorrow."

They walked into the bedroom and she crawled back into bed, adjusting the pillows so she could lie on her side, which was the only comfortable way to do it.

Dante opened up the terrace doors to let in fresh air. The moon was high in the sky and bright, casting moonlight against the white bedcover. He padded over to the bed and lay down carefully on his back, with his hands folded behind his head.

"Does the breeze bother you?"

"No," she said. "It's nice. And the moon is so bright."

"*Sì.*"

"I guess that gives credence to that old Dean Martin song."

He grinned at her—she could see his dark eyes twinkling in the moonlight. "Don't sing it."

"Why?"

"I've heard you sing."

She gasped. "When?"

"You sing when you're busy and you've tuned the world out. I've heard you singing in your office and when you're chopping fruit. You sing, but I hate to tell you that you have a terrible singing voice."

Shay hit him with a pillow. "That's not nice!"

"I am only telling the truth, *cara*."

"Oh, and you sing *so* much better?"

Dante rolled over and leaned on one elbow. He began to sing in Italian. A rich, deep baritone that made goose bumps break across her skin. As if he was wooing her in song and it was working. At the end of the song he cocked his eyebrows, as if to say *see, I told you so*, so she hit him again with her pillow.

"And what was that for?" he asked, snatching the pillow from her.

"For upstaging me."

He chuckled. "I'm sorry."

"So how long have you run this vineyard?"

"This is my first year," he said.

"I'm confused. I thought your grandfather died a while ago and left you this vineyard."

"*Sì*, but it was in the family trust until I reached a certain age." He cleared his throat and looked uncomfortable. "Now I am of age. It is mine."

"Is that why your childhood home was sold?" Shay asked.

"*Sì*," he said bitterly. He was on his back again, frowning up at the ceiling.

"Was that part of your inheritance?"

"No, that home should belong to Enzo, but father sold it off before our mother died. He's determined to get it back. All I was left was this vineyard and the villa on the Lido di Venezia. That is all I wanted and that makes me happy."

"Are you going to give up surgery for winemaking, then?"

"No, I love being a surgeon. Even more than winemaking. Zio Guillermo is perfectly capable of running the estate while I'm gone."

"Just like a prince," she teased.

"How so?"

"Vassals and serfs to attend to your every whim."

He snorted. "I'm telling you, it's just a title. Prince means nothing in my country."

"It means something to some people."

"People who live too much in the past," he said hotly. "You know, Zia Serena starts breakfast very early. I think we should try to get some sleep. I know that you need your rest."

And with that quick change in demeanor she knew that the conversation was over. There was no use trying to dig further. She'd get nowhere. He was stubborn.

That much she'd come to learn in the short time she'd been with him.

It could be a good quality some of the time, other times it was downright annoying. Just like this time.

Of course, she was no better.

She was just as stubborn too.

That was what her mother always said, but Shay's stubbornness had helped her survive. It had helped her endure her childhood, where she'd often had to parent herself. It'd helped her survive Katrina, natural disasters when working with the United World Wide Health Association and her mother's death.

She was a survivor, and if that meant being stubborn, then so be it.

She was stubborn.

The scent of pancetta frying roused Dante, but it was the thumps to his hand that caused him alarm. As he pried open one eye he saw that his hand was placed on Shay's belly and the thumping was from the resident occupant taking up space in her womb.

It was his baby.

His baby was kicking him. It wasn't very strong, but he could feel it. Like a poke of a finger under a blanket against his palm.

A smile tugged on the corners of his lips.

He wasn't sure how his hand ended up there or why he was spooning Shay, who was still sound asleep, but in that moment he didn't care either.

And he couldn't figure out why he'd been so afraid of this moment, because it was nothing to be scared of. In fact, it made him feel more connected to it all. Perhaps that was why he was always so reluctant to reach out and touch the child growing under Shay's heart: because he was too afraid.

Afraid to feel that deep connection with a child who might be taken away from him.

He snatched his hand away and rolled over.

Shay stirred. "What time is it?"

"It's seven in the morning. Don't get up," he said, sitting up and putting his feet down on the cold tile floor.

"Too late. I have to get up." She got up and padded off toward the bathroom down the hall.

He chuckled and then got ready while she was out of the room so that he was gone before she came back. If she wanted to continue to sleep, he wasn't going to stop her. She needed her rest.

Dr. Tucci had made that clear.

Dante didn't want anything bad to happen to Shay or the baby.

After freshening up in the downstairs bathroom he headed into the kitchen, where Zia Serena was laying out a large breakfast. She didn't even look at him when he entered the room.

"Guillermo is waiting in the fields for you," Serena said. "Eat and then go out and see him."

"Is something wrong, Zia?" Dante asked as she set the plate in front of him. Usually she was all smiles, especially when she was feeding people, but this morning the smile was gone and replaced with a frown of concern.

"Guillermo wasn't feeling too well this morning but still insisted on going to the fields."

"He should stay home," Dante said.

Serena threw her hands up in the air in exasperation. "That's what I told him, but he won't listen to me. Perhaps if you talk to him."

Dante nodded and took a bite of his egg. "How has his angina been?"

"He takes the medication you prescribed for him, but he doesn't always listen to the local doctor's orders."

"That smells so good," Shay said as she came into the kitchen and took a seat.

Serena lit up when she saw her and she made a plate up for Shay.

"What're you going to do today?" Dante asked Shay.

"I don't know. I thought about going for a walk."

"Do you think that's wise?" he asked, frowning.

"Dr. Tucci said to rest, he didn't say anything about complete bed rest, so why can't I go for a walk?"

Serena nodded in agreement with Shay, though she was probably only picking up the odd word. She set the plate down in front of her and went back to the stove.

"This looks so good," Shay said, eagerly eyeing the scrambled egg, pancetta and mounds of fresh fruit.

"Well, if you want to go for a walk, why don't you come down to the fields with me? I need your second opinion on something."

"I don't know much about winemaking," Shay said. "I'll gladly go for the walk, though."

Dante waited until Zia Serena had left the room and then whispered, "Guillermo has angina."

"Okay," Shay said.

"He's been experiencing some pain and I suspect he's not going to the doctor. He won't let me near him, but maybe if I had a second set of eyes…"

She nodded. "Gotcha. It's something I would often do for the doctors when we were in remote villages. Patients may not trust the doctor but could always trust me and they'd open up to me."

He grinned. "That's what I'm hoping for. Guillermo is a stubborn man."

"Are you sure he's not blood related?" There was a twinkle in her eyes and he couldn't help but laugh a bit as he finished up his breakfast and put the dirty plate in the dishwasher.

Shay finished up and he took the plate from her.

They both donned a pair of wellies because the fields were a bit muddy after a fresh round of fertilization a day before they arrived.

Guillermo wasn't too far from the main house, which was good because from a few feet away Dante could tell that Guillermo wasn't doing so well.

"He's ashen," Shay whispered. "That's not a good sign."

"I know. Serena said he was complaining of heartburn and was feeling off, but he still insisted on doing his job."

And Dante was fearful that Guillermo, standing right in

front of them now, was having a heart attack. And the nearest hospital was Arezzo, which was forty kilometers away.

"*Buongiorno*, how are you feeling this morning, Zio?"

Guillermo waved his hand but didn't answer. Also not a good sign.

Shay moved closer and Guillermo beamed at her, taking her hand. She just smiled at him and walked beside him.

"He's sweating profusely and it's not that hot out yet," Shay said over her shoulder.

"*Cosa ha detto?*" Guillermo asked. What did she say?

"Zio, did you take your angina medications this morning?"

"*Sì*, I did. I always take them, but this morning I'm having a lot of indigestion. My jaw hurts too."

Dante shot Shay a look and she nodded ever so slightly, as if in tune with his thoughts. Guillermo was having a heart attack.

"Guillermo, we need to go to Arezzo." Dante took his arm and Shay the other.

"Why?" he asked, his voice panicked.

"I want to get you looked at. I think it's more than indigestion. The hospital in Arezzo can take care of you."

Guillermo didn't try to fight, and when they got back to the main house Shay got Guillermo to sit down. Dante explained quickly to Serena what he thought was happening. And she took it in her stride, knowing that if she became overwrought it wouldn't keep Guillermo calm.

It wasn't long until an ambulance pulled up the long drive.

Dante explained what was going on with Guillermo. They got Guillermo loaded into the back of the ambulance and Serena climbed in with him to ride to Arezzo.

As the ambulance flicked on its sirens and headed away, Dante sighed. "I'm sorry."

"What for?" Shay asked.

"You were supposed to come here for rest."

"You shouldn't apologize for Zio Guillermo having a heart attack. That's not something you can control."

Dante cursed under his breath. "I should be able to control it. I like control."

"And you're a trauma surgeon?" she asked quizzically. "There's no control in that choice of profession."

He rolled his eyes and she just laughed at him.

"Well, now we have the house to ourselves." He ran his hand through his hair, because he was nervous at the prospect. At least when they were alone in Venice or at the villa on the Lido there were neighbors around. At the vineyard, they were truly alone.

And that terrified him.

Shay walked through the rows of vines, carrying an ice-cold glass of sweet tea for Dante. Dante had retreated to the vineyards after the ambulance left and she hadn't seen hide or hair of him all day. So she'd decided to make a pitcher of sweetened iced tea. Which was no easy feat.

She'd had to scour the kitchen until she'd found a few bags of black tea in the back of a cupboard.

She'd brewed it, strained it and poured it into a pitcher. Adding sugar until it was the right taste that reminded her of summer days when her mother would make sweetened tea for her. Then she'd taken one of the fresh lemons in the big bowl of fruit on the counter and sliced it thinly.

It was the best refreshing drink on a hot day and she could only imagine that Dante was out there sweltering. So she'd poured him a glass and put on her wellies under her long summer dress and headed out into the vineyard. He wasn't far from the house; he was working on the stretch Guillermo had been working on before they'd called the ambulance.

He was crouched down with pruners in his hand, staring at the leaves. His shirt had been abandoned and the late-afternoon sun made his bronzed skin glow like that of an ancient Roman god. The usually tame dark curls were haphazard and beads of sweat ran down his face and his large, muscular biceps.

She hadn't realized how muscular he was, until she saw him out here, working on the vines.

It was as if he were someone totally different, but the same.

Her heart skipped a beat and she couldn't help but admire him.

He was absolutely beautiful.

As if sensing her admiration, he glanced up. "Shay, are you okay?"

She shook her head. "Fine, I thought you might be thirsty."

"Sì." He stood and stretched and she tried not to stare at his half-naked body, because then that would remind her of that stolen night together. The way her hands felt running over his muscles as she clung to him. She handed it to him and he took a drink and then looked confused.

"What is this?" He was frowning.

"Iced tea, or, as we call it, sweet tea. True iced tea is—"

"Just cold tea." He made another face. "I don't like it. I don't like tea."

"What? Why?"

"It was kind of you, but I can't drink this." He handed the glass back to Shay.

"What's wrong with it? Is it too sweet?" She frowned at the cup in her hand, the condensation on the glass making her palm wet.

"I don't like tea."

"Why?"

"It reminds me of being sick."

She arched her brows. "Sick?"

"*Sì*, my mother would always make it for me when I was sick. I don't like tea."

Shay chuckled. "Is that why there was only a small amount in the cupboard?"

He grimaced. "Medicinal use only."

"Well, I tried. I might not be able to cook much, but I pride myself on my sweet tea."

Dante grinned. "Well, if I didn't associate tea with sickness, I'm sure I would enjoy it."

"Ha-ha."

He picked up a towel and wiped off his hands quickly. "Are you hungry, *cara*? Would you like some dinner? We can go into the village."

"That sounds nice."

"Let me just have a quick shower and we can head into the village."

They walked back in silence to the house. Dante had a quick shower and changed into jeans and a white crisp shirt that was unbuttoned at his neck and rolled up on those strong forearms. His curls were tamed once again, but he didn't shave his five-o'clock shadow off. And the bit of stubble suited him. Shay kicked off the cumbersome wellies and put on her sandals.

It was a short drive to the small sleepy village, which was built into the side of a hill and made of cobblestone. Dante found one of the few parking spaces, and then they walked together to the *piazza*, which was in the heart of the village.

A tall clock tower loomed over them and in the center of the *piazza* was a large fountain. The gentle breeze blew mist from the fountain onto them, but it felt good. It was a surprisingly warm day. Humid. Almost as warm as it was in New Orleans in the summer. Which was brutal for humidity.

Shay closed her eyes and she could almost swear she was home, except for everyone around her speaking Italian.

"This way," Dante said, and his hand touched the small of her back as he led them to a small bistro with an outdoor patio with red checkered tablecloths, which was tucked at the corner of the *piazza*.

"Ah, Principe! It's a pleasure to see you again." The maître d' turned to her and grinned. "Is this the Principessa?"

Shay plastered on a fake smile, but her stomach began to twist and turn as she thought about people knowing that she was married to him. She didn't like being in the limelight.

"Sì," Dante said graciously, but she could tell that he was annoyed by the attention too. Which just endeared him to her more.

Don't get attached. This isn't permanent.

"This way," the maître d' said, and he led them to a corner table out on the patio, so they could enjoy the twilight *al fresco* style. He left them with a menu, but Dante ordered for them.

"What did you just order?"

He grinned and winked at her. "You'll see."

"Hmm, well, I suppose I should trust your judgment. You haven't let me down yet."

"Of course, I could be getting you back for that sweet-iced-tea concoction you tried to force down me earlier today."

"I didn't force it down you." She laughed with him.

She liked laughing with him.

It was like the way it used to be. Before she got pregnant. When they didn't have to link their lives together. They'd had fun in Oahu.

Too much fun, remember?

"So tell me about your mother," Dante said softly. "You speak of her and yet you don't."

"She died as a result of Katrina. It's why I joined the

United World Wide Health Association. To help those who can't afford health care."

"I'm so sorry, Shay. How did your mother die?" he asked gently.

"The place she stayed at after the floodwaters receded was full of toxic mold, but she couldn't afford to stay anywhere else and she had to stay somewhere while she waited for FEMA to provide housing. She got really sick from the mold, and in the end the toxins overwhelmed her body."

"I'm really sorry." He reached out and placed his large hand over hers. It felt so good.

Be careful.

She cleared her throat. "Now, you tell me about your mother. You don't speak much about her either, but we're staying at her childhood home, yes?"

Dante nodded slowly. "She died a few years back. Cancer."

"I'm so sorry, Dante. That must have been hard to bear."

"Yes. She was a wonderful mother, but…" He trailed off and moved his hand off hers. "My father was difficult. She thought he was her prince and he was far from that."

I hear you.

"My father left my mother," she said. "He said he was going off to Alaska to crab fish and earn the money to bring us all up there. We never heard from him again."

"Did he die in an accident?" Dante asked.

"No, I know he's alive. I know for a fact he is. He just left us."

Dante snorted. "My father didn't leave my mother, not physically at least. That's not what marriage should be about. It shouldn't be a lie."

"I know," she said softly, but he didn't hear her or what she was implying about their own sham marriage.

The waiter brought their food.

"Panzanella," Dante announced. "I figured you wouldn't want to eat anything too heavy in this heat."

"Grazie," Shay said. The salad was filled with pieces of the traditional Tuscan bread, *fettunta*, and mixed with fresh crisp greens, tomatoes, cucumbers and onions. It was melded with olive oil and vinegar. There were also tuna and capers in this version.

It was delicious and, by the kicks she was getting, the baby approved too.

Once they were finished, Shay couldn't have dessert. She was too full. So Dante paid and they walked across the *piazza* in the dwindling light.

"I've enjoyed my time in Tuscany. It's sad that we're leaving tomorrow," she said.

"Sì, it's always hard to leave here, but I'm a surgeon and I love that just as passionately too." They stopped by the fountain to watch the water.

"It'll be good to get back to work," Shay said.

"You'll remember to take it easy," Dante warned.

She was going to respond, when she heard a screech and a crash. They both spun around in time to see two cars collide at high speed, flipping one car over and over.

When the cars finally came to a stop, Shay was running behind Dante as they rushed toward the scene.

CHAPTER NINE

SHAY SET UP a triage, as she'd done countless times in the field.

Thankfully, since the paramedics had arrived, she had more access to modern equipment. And these paramedics knew English as well. Which was heaven-sent, so she didn't have to keep getting Dante to translate for her. Though from being in Italy for almost a month now she was picking it up to the point she could be useful in emergency situations.

They had the patients laid out. Shay tagged them by priority, using the colored sticky notes that she always carried around in her purse.

The fire crew that was also on the scene was busy extracting one of the worst victims with the Jaws of Life. The crash scene was a jumble of twisted metal and fumes from the petrol.

Dante was assessing his patient through the wreckage, instructing the fire crew on how to extract him. He was up on the wreckage, aiding the occupant of the car through the broken windshield. And she couldn't help but admire him.

He was passionate about medicine. His passion and compassion just made her want him more. If she weren't pregnant, she would be doing the same thing. She'd done the same thing in the past.

Dante and she were so similar.

Only she couldn't help Dante and the driver of that

vehicle right now. Instead Shay tended to the young couple who were in the other car, while paramedics helped an elderly man who had been in a third car that was involved in the wreck.

The young man who was being extracted had been going too fast and had lost control when he'd reached down to answer his phone. That was when he'd ploughed into the young couple.

Shay knelt beside them. The young man had a few lacerations, but the paramedics had strapped the young woman down, because she couldn't feel her legs.

"I'm so sorry this happened to you," she murmured as she took her pulse rate.

"You're American?" the young woman gasped. "Oh, thank goodness."

The young man looked at her. "We're here on our honeymoon. Beatrice and Tim O'Toole."

"I'm Nurse Labadie. Shay."

Beatrice sighed with relief. "I'm so glad. I wasn't sure how I could tell these paramedics that I'm…I'm pregnant."

Shay's stomach knotted and she placed a protective hand on her belly. "How far along?"

"Just eight weeks," Tim said. "We really need to know if the baby is okay."

Shay didn't want to say anything to them. The baby was so small, it could still be alive, but if there was damage to Beatrice's spine, then the chances were slim. She didn't want to give them false hope. The only way they would know for sure was by ultrasound.

Tim turned back to the paramedic who was dressing his bandage and getting him to climb onto a gurney to be taken to Arezzo.

"Tim?" Beatrice called out frantically because she couldn't turn her head all the way to see what was happening behind her.

"He's just being put into the ambulance. He's okay."

Beatrice let out a shaky sigh. "We were just married a week ago, but we've been together for a long time."

"How long?" Shay asked as she tended to some minor scratches.

"Since we were sixteen. He's my high-school sweetheart. We've been saving a long time for this trip."

Shay smiled warmly at her. "I'm sorry that this has happened."

"As long as we're both alive and the baby is fine, we can survive anything." There was a tremble on her lips as she talked about the baby and Shay couldn't help but wonder if she was thinking the same thing that Shay was: that the baby was lost. Her hand instinctively cradled her belly. As she did that Beatrice's gaze tracked down.

"You're pregnant?" she said, grinning at her.

"I am. I'm just halfway there."

"A boy or a girl?"

"I don't know. I thought it would be nice to have a surprise!"

"Your husband must be thrilled." Beatrice smiled and then winced.

Yes. Husband.

Thrilled she had right, because Dante seemed to really want this child, but Shay still wasn't used to calling him husband because the marriage wasn't real.

Only she didn't say anything as the paramedics came and got Beatrice, loading her into the ambulance. The moment that she was loaded, Tim leaned over, bandaged up and bleeding, to take her hand. The way Beatrice looked up at him and the way he looked at her made Shay realize that she had never looked at Dante like that and he'd never looked that way at her.

Her mother had looked at her father like that, but he'd never reciprocated.

This was what true love was.

And they might lose their baby.

Shay touched her belly again as the ambulance doors closed and was reminded how life was so unfair. Dante came up behind her. He touched her shoulder. She turned around and saw his shirt was stained with oil and grease, as was his face. He was sweaty and looked tired. Almost beaten down.

"Are you okay?" he asked gently as he brushed her cheek with the backs of his knuckles. It was nice, but she didn't want the comfort. She was okay.

"I'm fine. My patient was pregnant, but only eight weeks along. I hope the baby is okay."

"Me too," Dante said gently.

She turned to see a blanket draped over the wrecked car and a sheet over a body on a gurney and her heart sank. Then she understood the weariness in his eyes.

He'd lost the battle.

"Oh, I'm sorry. You were working so hard." And then she felt bad for rejecting his comfort.

Dante sighed. "There was nothing more I could do. His body was too broken. Once he was extracted, the pressure on his internal bleeding released and he bled to death in seconds. I'm not even sure surgery would've saved him had I been able to open him up right here and now. So much damage."

"Mi scusi, Dottore..."

Shay turned and saw policemen there and she knew that they wanted a statement from him.

"I'll be back as soon as I can, then we'll get you back to the villa so you can have a peaceful sleep before we drive back to Venice tomorrow."

She nodded and he went to speak to the police about the accident. Shay wandered back over to the fountain. There were still a few curious onlookers to the accident and a few people were praying.

She sat down on the ledge of the fountain, watching Dante speak to the police officer and trying to keep her eyes off the young man whose life had been cut short due to a careless mistake, but, mistake or not, a life had been cut short. Possibly two. And if Beatrice was paralyzed, her life would be changed forever.

A twinge of pain raced across her belly. She sucked in a deep breath as it passed, assuming it must be Braxton Hicks as she had overdone it this evening. She'd spent the last couple of days relaxing and on her last night at Dante's vineyard she'd thrown herself into the fray of her work.

So she was making herself stressed again. She deep-breathed through the pain.

And soon it was gone.

She was mad at herself for not listening to Dr. Tucci and running a small triage in the middle of a *piazza*.

Because that is your true love. Work.

And what else was she supposed to do?

She couldn't leave that young couple there. Broken and in a foreign country. Pregnancy or not, she'd signed up to be a nurse. To help others.

She would continue to take it easy because that was how she could help her baby, but she had to help others too.

Her work was her love. Her reason for living.

And it was the only thing that remained true in her life.

They'd been back in Venice for a few weeks and Dante had been trying to catch up on all the work that had piled up. He knew that Shay had been as well, though most of the paperwork she did from the villa. Ever since they'd left the vineyard she'd been unusually quiet. He knew the easy workload was getting to her and now she was over halfway through her pregnancy.

He thought maybe it had to do with the accident and he thought it would cheer her up to learn that Beatrice's baby had survived and that she wouldn't be paralyzed. There was temporary paralysis, but it would abate and Beatrice would be able to walk again.

All she had said was "That's good."

Then he thought perhaps she was worried about Guillermo. She'd taken such a shine to him. When he gave her a status update on Zia and Zio, how Zio had had a mild heart attack but would recover quickly, she gave the same answer and returned to her paperwork.

He shook his head and flicked through the stack of mail his maid had left on the kitchen counter of the villa. Mail he had been ignoring because he'd been so busy.

A heavy cream envelope stood out from the rest and he opened it, groaning as soon as he saw the word *masquerade*. It was an invitation to the hospital's annual charity masquerade ball, which would raise money for funding. It was always a huge success. Everyone dressed up in their finest and hid behind Venetian masks.

It was a fancy dress gala along the lines of Venice's most infamous carnival, which was usually held in the winter months. He hated going to these affairs. Anybody who was anybody attended this event. Even heads of state, and as he was technically a head of state he had to attend. Plus he was Head of Trauma and collaborating with the United World Wide Health Association.

It was pretty much mandatory that he be there.

"What's that?" Shay asked as she came into the kitchen carrying an empty bowl.

"An invitation to a gala fund-raiser for the hospital."

"Ooh," Shay said, sounding intrigued and showing more interest than she had in the last weeks, which made him happy. "It sounds fun."

"It's not, but it's for a good cause." He stared at the envelope.

"Well, aren't you going to open it?"

"Should I?" he teased.

"Yes."

He broke open the seal and read it over. "Hmm…"

"Well, when is it?" she asked.

"It's tonight."

"Too late to RSVP?" She sounded disappointed.

"Do you want to go?"

"Not really, but you should."

"I don't want to go." He leaned across the counter. "Why, do you want me out of the house?"

"I don't…" She sighed. "I feel like I'm holding you back. You've been hovering over me like a ticking time bomb since Tuscany. I'm fine and I want you to have fun."

"Trust me, this gala isn't fun."

"Well, if you have to RSVP, then you don't have to go. You could just ignore it."

"No, it's more of a reminder. I go every year." Dante cursed under his breath. "I was hoping to catch up on some paperwork for the simulation program this evening."

"I can do that, you go." She turned her back to him, washing her dish in the sink.

"You're going to do my paperwork?"

"Sure," she said brightly. "Then you can get out instead of watching a pregnant woman sleep."

"You think you're getting off that easy?" he said as he grinned from ear to ear. "You're coming with me."

The bowl clattered in the sink and she spun around. "I'm what?"

"You're my wife." He grinned, enjoying the look of distress on her face. "And you're coming with me."

"Uh, no, I'm not."

"Of course you are. You are a princess. It's your duty." He grinned.

"Duty?" she asked, her voice rising an octave.

"*Sì*, you're coming with me." He pinned the invitation to the corkboard in the kitchen. "You seemed so excited before."

"That's when I thought you were going. I can't go." She ripped the invitation down from the corkboard and handed it back to him.

"Why not?"

"Dante, I don't have anything to wear, for starters." Then she pointed to her belly. "I don't think they make ball gowns for pregnant women."

"Of course they do. There have been pregnant women who have gone to balls before. You're coming." He slapped down the invite and walked out of the kitchen, grinning to himself because he knew full well that she was following him out of the room.

"Dante, I don't go to fancy galas." Her voice was panicked. "I've never been to one."

"Now's your chance." He was really enjoying this.

"You're teasing me."

"Well, I am a bit, but I would like you to accompany me."

"I don't want to go. I should be resting." She jutted out her chin, her pink lips pursed together in defiance.

He laughed out loud. "That's the first time you've used that as an excuse here."

"Well, a gala is… It sounds terrible. I'm not one for crowds. Can't you go by yourself?"

"You are my wife."

She crossed her arms. "I don't even know where to get a dress from. I would call Aubrey, but she's working today. How am I going to find a dress?"

"The Lido has many shops around here. You can go and find a ball gown in one of them. I'm certain."

Her mouth opened and closed a few times, as if she was going to say something, but instead she left the room, calling over her shoulder, "I'll wear what I have, but I'm not going shopping."

"The gala starts at eight. I'll be home at five to get ready, so hopefully you're ready then."

Dante picked up his keys and his briefcase. He was going to have his assistant pick out a dress for Shay and make sure it was delivered in time. She was his wife and he wanted her to feel good. She was beautiful, sexy, and he wanted the world to know it.

When he walked into the Palazzo Flangini tonight with Shay on his arm, he was confirming to the world, and to his father, that he was married. That he had it all.

That he was going to have an heir and his father's chances for getting a hold of his vineyard and the villa were gone. Dante had no doubt that his father would be there tonight with one of his mistresses and he hoped his father heeded his advice from his mother's funeral about not approaching him.

Dante had no interest in mending broken fences with that man. A father in name only. Dante would be a better father than his ever was. A better husband too, for as long as Shay would have him.

Tonight he wasn't just wearing a Venetian mask, he was wearing a different mask. One of a loving husband and father. He had to show the world that Dante Affini was happily married. And maybe then people would leave him alone.

His marriage had put an end to all that talk about the trust fund and his father's cheating. It was bad enough his mother had suffered through all those stories in the paper about his father stepping out with different women.

All Dante wanted, all he'd ever wanted, was a quiet life.

Was that too much to ask for?

* * *

The box containing the most beautiful black lace ball gown arrived at lunchtime with a note from Dante that asked her to take the ferry into Venice and then catch a *vaporetto* to the Palazzo Flangini on the Grand Canal. He also sent a Venetian mask on a handle; white, painted with black and silver filigrees.

It reminded her of Mardi Gras in New Orleans.

The only difference was that usually involved beads and bright colors such as purple and green.

This was more elegant, more sophisticated, and she was terrified. She doubted anyone would be flashing their boobs for beads tonight. She'd never done that, just as she'd never been to a gala before. She hadn't even gone to her own high-school prom. She was so worried about making a bad impression and embarrassing Dante. So she really wished that she weren't going. She was clumsy and awkward, even more so being pregnant.

However, the dress was stunning. As were the matching shoes, which were thankfully small kitten heels, and jewelry. He'd thought of everything. Except that he wouldn't be escorting her. She had to make her own way to the gala.

Dante had apologized in the note, explaining that he had to work late on a trauma case that had come in, but he promised to meet her there.

"How will I even know who he is if everyone is wearing masks?" she mumbled, looking up from the note while sitting cross-legged on his bed, and Dante's cleaning lady overheard her.

"He'll be wearing a matching mask. That's how it's done. His will be more masculine, though." Maria, the cleaning lady, patted her shoulder.

"Thanks, Maria."

Maria nodded and continued her cleaning of the en suite bathroom.

Shay stared at the gown again.

She really didn't want to go, but she didn't want to let Dante down either. And it could be good to mix and mingle with those who might donate to the United World Wide Health Association. Dante wanted this marriage of convenience. He was giving up a lot to be part of his child's life. So the least she could do was play the part.

Ever since they'd got back from Tuscany she had been a little standoffish with him because she'd thought it was for the best, but she'd been so lonely. Especially since she was on modified duties and everyone else she knew was busy with their own jobs.

She hated this feeling of helplessness she'd been experiencing lately.

She missed her work. She hated being on light duty.

She missed being in the emergency room, triaging, teaching. She missed being a nurse.

Pretending to be a wife tonight was something not very high on her list of priorities, but maybe tonight she could make connections. Tell more people about the good work that the United World Wide Health Association did.

At least that way she was doing something. She glanced at the clock. She had three hours to get ready and head over to the Palazzo Flangini.

Once Maria was done with the bathroom, Shay took over and had a shower. Her hair was a short stacked bob, so she added some curls with her curling iron, pulled on the beautiful lace dress and did her makeup. By the time she was ready, it was time to catch the ferry from the pier to Venice.

Maria walked out with her, locking up, so Shay wouldn't have to worry about wrecking her dress trying to latch an ancient iron gate.

As she walked down the main road on the Lido to the pier there were a few curious onlookers. Especially since she was carrying a Venetian mask, but she tuned them out as she boarded the ferry, just before it left. Once she disembarked at the Venice pier, she found the water taxi that could take her down the Grand Canal to the famous Palazzo Flangini, where they held the Venice Carnivale every February.

It was getting dark and the canal was lit up. There were many water taxis vying for the water entrance to the palace. Once she was at the entrance, she was helped up out of the water taxi and showed the doorman Dante's invitation. She followed the crowds inside, holding the mask up to her face as they walked into the main room, where the gala was being held. Except it wasn't one big room, but different rooms. The walls were covered with Renaissance artwork, the ceilings were gilt and there were lots of marble columns.

People in the party filtered around from room to room, chatting, and Shay didn't know how she was going to find Dante in this mess of people.

She kept to the outside of the flow of people wandering around the *palazzo*. Until a tall man in a designer tuxedo, holding a more masculine mask with the same markings, approached her. He moved through the crowd easily. They parted for him as the Red Sea parted for Moses. His presence seemed to command it so.

"Ciao, cara."

Her heart skipped a beat. She recognized his voice and he moved the mask off his face to bring her hand to his lips, kissing her knuckles, which made her stomach flutter.

This is just a show. It's all just a show.

Only it was fooling her, this show she kept reiterating she was acting through. Her heart fluttered and the baby kicked in response to her accelerated pulse rate.

She moved aside the mask. "You look very handsome."

He grinned. "You are absolutely stunning."

Warmth flooded her cheeks and she covered her face again. The mask was coming in handy for that.

"You're too kind."

"I'm not being kind. It's the truth." He leaned over and whispered in her ear. "You're glowing, *cara*, and I find it absolutely sexy."

A shiver of anticipation ran down her spine as he took her arm and led her away from the safety of the wall out into the mix.

"Thank you for the dress," she said. "It's wonderful. I don't feel like a beached whale in this."

"Since when have you looked like a beached whale?" he asked.

"Since this bump is getting bigger," she teased.

He chuckled. "You're beautiful. Radiant."

She blushed again. They moved through the social circles. Shay shook hands with a lot of people whom she couldn't speak to, but she knew that Dante was talking up their simulation program and that was all that mattered. They finally moved to a room that was full of art being auctioned off as part of the fund-raiser. The room was also thankfully mostly devoid of the crush of people, which was good because she was getting hot.

And she was exhausted by socializing with a language barrier.

"My father is supposed to be here," Dante groused. "I haven't seen him."

"And that's…?"

"Good." Dante squeezed her hand. "He likes these events. I don't. I didn't want to see him tonight, but then with you here and our baby…well, I was hoping to run into him."

"I take it my presence won't make him happy?"

"No."

"Why?" she asked, confused.

"Because he never wants me to be happy."

Her heart skipped a beat. "And you're…happy?"

"*Sì*, right now, I am."

She gasped and her pulse raced. She wanted to tell him she was happy around him too, but couldn't.

"I'm tired, Dante."

"We'll go soon, *cara*. I know you're tired."

"Thank you." She held the mask at her side and didn't look at the contemporary art that was on sale, but the Renaissance craftsmanship that was carved into the post and lintels of the *palazzo*. She ran her hand over it and she got a secret thrill of delight touching something that was so old.

"It's beautiful, isn't it?" Dante asked.

"Yes, it is. You know, Venice in some ways reminds me a bit of New Orleans."

Dante arched a brow. "How so?"

"It's close to the water. We also have canals, though not as many as you."

"Go on," he urged, smiling at her, those dark eyes twinkling. Her knees went a bit weak because the suit he was wearing fit him like a glove. It was all she could do to tear her eyes from him.

"We have Mardi Gras and you have Carnivale," she said.

"I think that's the Catholic influence," he teased.

"Perhaps, but I doubt Venice has voodoo roots."

"I don't think so."

She grinned. "So one difference."

"What else is the same?"

"I've seen plantations, on the inside, with similar architecture."

"Wasn't that the Neoclassical movement?"

"Could be," Shay said. "I wouldn't know. I didn't take history, remember?"

He shook his head. "I shall have to school you on history."

"No, thanks." And they laughed together. Her pulse was racing, they were so close, and she was fighting the urge to reach up and kiss him. "Should we make that last round?"

He sighed.

Was that disappointment?

"*Sì*, let's…" He trailed off as he stared over her shoulder. Shay turned to see what had caught his attention. It was a tall, beautiful Italian woman all dressed in red.

She was absolutely stunning.

"Do you know her?" Shay asked.

"*Sì,*" he said, through gritted teeth. If he'd been a dog, Shay would have sworn his hackles would be raised as he glared at the woman.

The woman, as if sensing she was being glared at, turned and looked at them standing at the other end of the corridor.

"Dante?" the woman asked as she glided over to them. "I thought that was you, *mi amore.*"

Mi amore? My love?

Dread knotted her stomach and for the first time in her life a flare of jealousy rose in her as the stunning woman called Dante her love and touched his arm as a lover would. She was relieved to see that Dante was none too thrilled to be in the woman's company and did not return the endearment.

"Olivia," Dante acknowledged gruffly. "I thought hospital functions were beneath you?"

"Usually, but a carnival-inspired one sounded too chic to pass up. Besides, Max wanted to come. His hotel chain is donating a vast quantity of money to the United World Wide Health Association." Olivia's cold olive-colored eyes landed on Shay. Her gaze raked her up and down, judging her and looking at her as if she were a piece of dirt. "I see you're not alone either, *mi amore*. Who is this?"

"Shay," she said awkwardly. "I'm a nurse with the organization that you donated money to."

Olivia snickered. "*I* didn't donate. My Max did."

"Well, then, remind me to thank Max," Shay snapped, instantly detesting this woman.

"Bringing a nurse to a society function, *mi amore*. How classless."

"Why? She has every right to be here, and Shay also happens to be my wife—Principessa Affini." Dante smiled down at her, with pride on his face, the way Tim had beamed down at Beatrice when they were in the back of the ambulance. Shay's heart swelled and she held on to Dante's arm.

"Your...your wife?" Olivia asked, stunned.

Dante grinned at her, but it was cold. Calculating. It made Shay shudder, and then he reached down and touched her belly, the first time he'd ever done that.

"We're having a baby." Dante took her hand and kissed it. "We're so happy. Aren't we, *cara*?"

"Yes," Shay said breathlessly. Her heart skipped a beat. Maybe he did want more. Maybe this wasn't like her parents' marriage. Maybe it was real and she was just too blind to see it. Why *couldn't* they be happy?

Olivia smiled, but it was forced. "Well, I see you got what you always wanted. A little nobody who will bear your fruit and drudge beside you in that sham of a hospital."

"Don't you dare speak about my wife like that. You have no right!" Dante growled, and a few people nearby stopped their chatter and looked. The last thing Dante would want was the press to hear about this and report on it. Shay knew how much he detested any publicity.

"Dante, it's okay." Shay tugged on his arm. "She's not worth it."

"You're right, *cara*. She's not. Good evening, Olivia." He grabbed Shay's hand and led her in the opposite direction, out of the corridor. She could barely keep up with his pace as he weaved through the crowds. Once they were at the exit, Dante waved down a water taxi. His face was like thunder as he helped her down into the boat and gave the captain strict instructions to the Lido as he climbed on board and sat next to her.

"Is everything okay?" Shay asked.

"Fine." Dante scrubbed his hand over his face. "I'm sorry Olivia said those things to you. She's mean and spiteful."

"It's okay, but I have to agree with you there."

"No, it's not okay. You're my wife. It's most definitely not okay."

"Who was she?"

"A former acquaintance." He turned to her. "She means nothing to me. You mean so much more to me, *cara*."

Tears stung her eyes and he slipped his arm around her and held her close.

Shay wanted to believe him, because he meant so much to her too.

CHAPTER TEN

THE LAST THING Dante wanted Shay to know about was his past with Olivia, but when he saw Olivia at the gala he'd become so angry. The way Olivia had looked down on Shay had angered him. No, it'd infuriated him.

His fight-or-flight instinct had kicked in and he'd wanted to fight.

And now he was angry at himself for engaging with Olivia. For not walking away and for her showing up and spoiling a magical night.

And it *was* a magical night. Shay looked so stunning in that dress. The moment he'd seen her standing off to the side, pregnant with his child, his first thought had been *She's mine.*

When he'd seen her there, he'd no longer wanted to be at that gala. He'd wanted to take her home and take that dress off her. He'd wanted to hold her in his arms and kiss her. She'd never looked so beautiful before.

He'd wanted her so badly, but he'd known they had a duty to do and he wasn't sure if she wanted him the same way that he wanted her. So he'd tamped down his ardor, but it had been so hard, and then Olivia had shown up, angering him. Directing pointed barbs at Shay, who was a thousand times a better woman than Olivia ever was, and he couldn't help but wonder what he'd seen in Olivia in the first place. They were polar opposites in personality. Shay was caring, kind and Olivia was self-centered and selfish.

The ride home in the water taxi was silent.

Shay didn't press him with any more questions.

Which was a relief. If she pressed him, he'd lose control and it wouldn't take much. His grasp on the reins of his emotions were wearing thin.

He didn't want to get into it. He didn't want Shay to know about his secret shame. The way he'd been duped by Olivia.

Once they were back at the villa, though, she made him a cup of espresso and sat down at the table with him.

"Tell me about Olivia," she said gently.

He shrugged. "There is not much to tell. She's a former acquaintance. We had a falling-out years ago."

"Obviously there's something. It was like you'd seen a ghost. You two were lovers?"

"We were. Long ago. It's not important." Dante loosened his bow tie and unbuttoned his collar.

"How long ago?"

"Long." He cursed under his breath. She deserved to know the truth, but he didn't want to talk about Olivia. "I don't want to discuss it, *cara*. It's a painful memory best left in the past."

"Okay. I'm sorry."

"You have nothing to be sorry about, *cara*. It's my fault."

"How?"

"For getting involved with a woman like her. She's a user," he said bitterly. "She wanted to be with me because I was a prince. She just wanted to be a princess."

"Ah, so that's why she seemed so ticked when you referred to me as your Princess."

"*Sì*, it was a dig." He sighed. "You see, not many people knew I was a prince until my father started selling off Affini land and real estate. Then it was outed that there were two Affini men who were bachelors, set to inherit a vast fortune. She wanted in, so she took advantage. That's why I get so angry seeing her."

Shay's eyebrows rose when he said vast and he braced himself for the fact that she would ask how much was vast, but she didn't ask him that. It was as if she didn't care about his money, but he found that hard to believe. Most women he met in his circles cared only about money and status.

Whereas Shay seemed to care most about helping those who couldn't help themselves. Even though Shay had admitted she came from the poorest of the poor in New Orleans, money wasn't what attracted her. Doing good and being passionate about saving people's lives was what mattered to Shay.

And he couldn't help but admire that; but he still wasn't sure that he could trust her.

He wasn't sure that he could ever open his heart up again.

And he hated himself for that. For being so hard-hearted.

"I'm sorry she hurt you so bad."

Dante cursed under his breath. "*Sì*, I was hurt, but I'm angry that she showed up tonight. And that she treated you so badly."

"I'm okay. She can't get to me. I've heard worse. Although it killed me that she's so beautiful and tall. Elegant."

Dante brushed his hand across her cheek. "You are more beautiful, *cara*."

She deserved so much better than him.

Shay placed her hand on his shoulder, rubbing it and trying to console him in that sweet, simple way she did.

She was an angel.

He'd forgotten.

He smiled down at her. And then he touched the swell, where their baby was, and her eyes filled with tears. "I'm happy. What I told her was true. I'm happy about the baby."

"You've never… You've never touched the baby before," she whispered as she placed her hand over his. "I liked when you did earlier at the gala and I like it now."

"I have felt the baby, but you were asleep when I did." The baby pushed back. A strong kick against his palm. Last time it was a tiny poke.

"This baby takes after its daddy, that's for sure—he kicks me enough to annoy me," she said, trying to make light, and he chuckled.

"I know," he said, and he tilted her chin to make her look up at him. Those beautiful dark eyes of hers, those soft pink lips—he'd forgotten how truly beautiful she was. He leaned in and kissed her. It was as if he were tasting ambrosia. He wanted more and he knew that if he pursued this further one kiss would never be enough.

"Dante," she whispered against his lips. "What're we doing?"

He didn't respond; instead he scooped her up in his arms and kissed her again. "I believe I'm taking you upstairs, *cara*."

Shay didn't say no, instead she kissed him back, those long slender fingers of hers brushing the hair at the nape of his neck as he carried her up the stairs to his bedroom. He'd never made love to a pregnant woman before and he wanted to be careful with her.

He didn't want to hurt her.

And most of all, he wanted to take his time.

He set her down on the floor and cupped her face to kiss her again. He couldn't get enough of her kisses. He undid the zipper in the back and helped her out of the black lace dress while she kicked off her shoes. The dress pooled at her feet as he kissed her neck, knowing how that spot had made her moan with pleasure before.

She let out a sigh, her arms wrapped around him as he trailed his hands down her bare back, undoing her strapless bra. Her hands undid the buttons to his shirt and slipped inside.

He loved the feel of her hands on his chest. Those soft, delicate hands.

Shay finished undoing the buttons of his dress shirt. Then he shrugged himself out of his jacket and let her peel off his shirt.

"I've missed you," she whispered as he held her close.

"*Sì, cara.* I've missed you too."

She led him to the bed and sat down on the edge as she guided him down with her. They sat on the bed, kissing and touching. Just as they had that night in Hawaii. Only this time it wasn't the sounds of the Pacific Ocean and palm trees swaying outside the bedroom, but the sounds of the Lido at night. Of a cruise ship blaring a horn as it came close to the lagoon.

It was the night sounds of Venice, but he drowned them all out, because all he wanted to hear tonight was Shay, moaning in pleasure and calling out his name.

Shay hadn't expected the kiss, but she didn't stop it because she wanted more than anything to be with him. She wanted that kiss. For just one brief moment she wanted to be happy.

To remember a time when she had thrown caution to the wind and experienced real passion. To that one perfect night.

Even if that one perfect night had led to an unplanned pregnancy and them being in this situation now. She'd always sworn to herself that she didn't want to have a sham marriage and she should push Dante away. Only she couldn't.

Right now, she wanted to feel.

To taste passion one more time.

His mouth opened against hers as she kissed him, his kiss deepening. His hands were hot on her bare back, holding her tight against him. And then he pushed her down on the mattress, lying beside her.

She'd never wanted someone as badly as she did Dante.

Even though they'd been apart for months, that hadn't changed. And she'd known that the moment she'd laid eyes on him that day in the hospital.

She desired Dante above all other men.

She *craved* him and that thought scared her because she knew he didn't feel the same about her. She was treading a dangerous path.

The kiss ended and she could barely catch her breath, her body quivering with desire. He trailed his hands over her body.

"Shay," he whispered. "I've missed you."

He wanted her, just as much as she wanted him. A tingle of anticipation ran through her. She remembered his touch, the way he felt inside her, the way he made her feel when she came around him.

No words were needed, because she knew they both wanted the same thing.

"So beautiful," he murmured, pressing a kiss on her shoulder. His hands skimmed over her again.

When he kissed her again, it was urgent against her lips as he drew her body tight against his. Their bodies pressed together and warmth spread through her veins, then his lips moved from her mouth down her body to her breasts.

She gasped in surprise at the sensation of his tongue on her nipple. Her body arched against his mouth and the pleasure it brought her, her body even more sensitive to his touch thanks to the pregnancy hormones.

"I want you, so much," she said, and she was surprised that she'd said the words out loud, but it was the truth.

Dante kissed her and she was lost, melting into him. "I'll be gentle, *cara*. Please tell me if I hurt you or the baby. I don't want that."

"You won't hurt me. I just want to be with you again, Dante."

He stroked her cheek and kissed her again, his hand trailing down over her abdomen and then lower. Touching her intimately. Her body thrummed with desire. She arched her body against his fingers, craving more. Wanting him.

Their gazes locked as he entered her. He was murmuring words in Italian, just as he'd done before, and that made a tear slip from her eye.

"I'm sorry," he whispered. "Did I hurt you?"

"No, I'm just remembering. Good things." She kissed him. "Don't stop. Please don't stop."

"I won't." He nipped at her neck and began to move gently. Slowly. He was taking his time. She wrapped her arms around him to hold him close as he made love to her. He kissed her again and then trailed his kisses down her neck to her collarbone. It made her body arch and she wanted more of him. She wanted him deeper and she wrapped her legs around his waist, begging him to stay close, but she couldn't get him as close as her body craved, because of her belly.

"*Cara*, let me help you," he whispered as he rolled her onto her side. He helped lift her leg and entered her from behind, her leg draped over his. His hand on her breast as he made love to her.

Her body felt alive. She had never thought a feeling like this would be possible. She had never thought that she would ever get to experience it again with him.

Even though her relationship with Dante was not real and had an expiration date, she couldn't help but care about him. Deeply.

Maybe love?

She shook that thought away. There was no room in her life for love. Just her work, just her baby.

Their baby.

And this moment.

She wanted to savor it. He quickened his pace and she came, crying out as the heady pleasure flooded through her veins. Dante soon followed and then gently eased her leg down. She rolled onto her other side to look at him.

Dante was on his back, his eyes closed. She slid close to him and laid her head against his chest. He slung his arm around her, his fingers making little circles on the bare skin of her back.

"*Cara*, that was…"

"I know," she said.

He kissed the top of her head and held her close. She didn't want to leave this bed. She didn't want to leave his side. And that thought terrified her.

She was just like her mother.

Shay was falling in love with a man who didn't love her back. A man who'd married her because there was a baby on the way.

Only she couldn't let that happen.

She wouldn't spend her life pining for a man who didn't want her.

She had to put a stop to this. To bury her emotions in her work.

Only she was so comfortable in his arms that soon she forgot about all her worries and fell into a deep, blissful slumber.

CHAPTER ELEVEN

SHAY WOKE UP in Dante's arms. As she had every day for the last week. And every day she kept telling herself this couldn't happen again.

She was weak, and he only had to whisper *cara* and she melted into his arms.

Not that it was strange to wake up beside him. She was getting used to it. During their couple of nights in Tuscany she had slept beside him and that hadn't fazed her one bit. And now, for the past seven days she'd enjoyed waking up in his arms. His breath on her neck as he slept.

It was almost natural, as if she were meant to wake up beside him.

And with that came the truth that she could no longer deny: that she was deeply in love with Dante.

Maybe always had been, and she was mad at herself for falling in love with him. She'd promised herself that she wouldn't fall in love with someone unless they reciprocated it. Sure, Dante lusted after her, but did he love her?

She didn't think so. Yet the way he'd been so protective of her last week at that gala, the way he'd told her that he was happy, the way he'd made love to her every night gave her hope. And that was scary.

She couldn't trust hope.

She slid out of bed and quietly got ready for the day.

Just as she had when she'd first moved in with Dante and headed to the hospital to run a triage simulation set in the mountains.

Today was a day that she could be at the hospital and it was the perfect place to hide. Which was why she was here setting up a triage situation.

Tarps? *Check.*

Rope? *Check.*

She went over her list on her computer pad as she laid out all the equipment. She had ten different patients in the form of mannequins who were all suffering from various ailments, but as she stared at the checklist on her computer pad she couldn't think about the various trauma that she could be facing during a volcanic eruption.

All she could think about was her own personal volcanic eruption that had happened last night. Thoughts of Dante and his lovemaking were taking over her every waking moment.

This was exactly what she didn't want to happen.

He was starting to invade every part of her. And on cue their baby kicked as if to remind her that was true.

She glanced up at the projector screen where she'd posted the levels of triage as it pertained to assessing people in the field for care. Especially when there were mass casualties involved. And a natural disaster such as a volcanic eruption or a flood, among other things, could bring in a lot of casualties.

She'd seen a volcanic eruption when she'd been working in the southern part of Mexico. A volcano had erupted and the lahar not only killed hundreds of people, but injured hundreds more. They'd had everything from broken bones, to impalement, infections from the lahar's mud getting into open wounds and dry drowning.

In cases where many were hurt, she'd learned a useful

tip from the US Army about dividing casualties into Immediate, Delayed, Minimal and Expectant.

Each of the mannequins fell into those categories, and if the trainees had been listening, they should be able to figure out what dummy fit into what category.

"Shay?"

She turned around to see Dante, dressed in his scrubs and white lab coat, standing in the door of the room where she was running the triage simulation.

"Yes, how can I help you?"

"You left very early this morning," he said as he shut the door behind him.

"Well, I was anxious to get this simulation set up." She didn't look at him; if she looked at him too long, she'd succumb to his charms again. She'd throw herself into his arms and beg to stay with him.

And that wasn't what she wanted.

Her career path was with the United World Wide Health Association. When her time was up here, she'd travel on to somewhere new, once her baby was old enough to travel with her. Of course, she would be doing training and teaching jobs in cities as opposed to dangerous fieldwork. There wasn't really any permanence to her job, a place to make roots, whereas Dante was settled here.

He had land here. He had roots.

He would never ever leave Italy. She knew that.

How could they ever even conceive of being together?

"Shay, about last night…"

"No, we don't need to talk about last night. It was wonderful, but I get it. It was one time. Of course, every time we sleep together we remind ourselves it's only one time and then fall back into bed together. We have to stop. We've breached the terms of our marriage contract. It has to stop."

It was harsh, but she had to put an end to it to protect

herself. She had to put an end to it before she got too carried away.

A strange look passed on his face briefly. "Yes. One
time."

"Is that all?" she asked, trying to ignore the fact that
he'd moved up behind her. Last night when he'd come up
behind her, he'd been buried inside her. And her blood
heated as she thought of that intimate embrace. His hand
cupping her breast, his kisses on her neck as he whispered
sweet nothings in her ear.

"I guess," he said. He sounded disappointed. "Do you
need help with setting up the triage?"

"No, I'm good." What she needed to do was get him out
of this room before the trainees came in and saw her lip-
locked with Dr. Affini.

"I can help. You're supposed to take it easy."

"I'm good," she said. Then she smiled at him. She had
such a hard time resisting him, but she had to. She couldn't
let this go any further. It was a marriage of convenience,
not a real marriage.

It wasn't permanent. Just like everything else in her life.

He liked control and she thrived on flux and change.

How could a marriage work with two individuals so
different?

No, it was better this way.

"What time is your appointment with Dr. Tucci?" Dante
asked and she could hear the frustration in his tone.

"Four o'clock. It's the ultrasound. Do you still want to
be there?"

He nodded. "*Sì*, I will be there. I will escort you up there
myself if you don't show up in time."

Shay rolled her eyes. "Well, if you would let me get to
this simulation, then the sooner it can be done and the faster
I can get up to Dr. Tucci's appointment."

"Fine. I will see you here at three fifty-five."

"Unless a trauma comes in?" she asked.

"Correct."

Shay breathed a sigh of relief that he was gone and didn't seem to be bothered by the fact that she was brushing him off. Which just firmed her belief that these feelings she had for him were one-sided.

And that nothing would come of this marriage, other than that her baby would have his surname and have his or her father in their life.

When he'd reached out for her this morning, she hadn't been there. For the past few mornings she'd been in bed beside him, but this time she wasn't, and he'd panicked.

Dante didn't know what to think about that. Only that he'd expected she would be there.

Part of him was relieved that she wasn't, but the other part of him was hurt that she'd left. *What did you expect?*

He didn't know.

Yes. You know.

Only he didn't want to admit to it, because he didn't believe in it. Sure, there were people who could find happiness, but he wasn't sure that he was one of them. He turned back to look in the room where she was teaching the nursing trainees about mass casualty triage.

A smile tugged on the corners of his lips.

They'd come from such different backgrounds. Shay was so strong. She never gave up and he admired her fortitude. It was what he was attracted to when they'd met at that conference. She didn't give a damn about what others thought of her; he wished he had an ounce of that.

Only it bothered him seeing his name and his family's name splashed over the front pages because of his father's exploits. How the world knew everything about his family and how he couldn't even go for a cup of coffee without the paparazzi lurking around the corner.

He hated it.

And that was why he tried to keep a low profile wherever he went. Why he didn't want to make a fuss, but Shay was so strong. She just jumped into the fray.

She'd been thrust into poverty as a child and he hadn't wanted for anything.

Except love.

He shook that thought away.

Love was not for him. Affini men were notoriously a bunch of womanizers.

You're not. Your mother's father wasn't.

"Dr. Affini, there's someone in a trauma pod who is insisting you attend to his stitches," Dr. Carlo, one of the interns, said as he ran up to him.

"You know how to deal with unruly patients, Dr. Carlo. I don't need to see him."

Dr. Carlo frowned. "I tried all the tactics you've been teaching us to deal with difficult patients, but this man is insistent and he's bleeding profusely."

Dante groaned. "Take me to him."

Dr. Carlo nodded and they walked to the emergency room. There was a small trauma bay that was used for lacerations that was far off from the larger trauma bays that were for patients who were in distress. Patients that needed a large team surrounding them to save a life.

Dr. Carlo handed him the electronic chart and the name that popped up caused Dante to take a pause. Marco Affini.

No.

He hadn't seen his father in years, save for pictures splashed across the headlines.

Dante had had his solicitor tell his father that he was married and a baby was on the way, because Dante couldn't stand the thought of talking to the man again.

Even when he turned in his marriage certificate to stop the process of his father having his inheritance, his father would have wanted to speak to him about the mistake he was making and Dante wouldn't have anything to do with him.

Now he was here. In Dante's emergency room. His father had his back to him, but Dante could see the arm laid out on a tray; a nurse was still cleaning the deep wound on his forearm. There were bloody towels in the trash bins. He'd had a significant blood loss.

"You can leave, Nurse. I can take care of this patient." Dante clenched his fist.

His father turned then. "Ah, look who has finally decided to come pay his respects."

The nurse peeled off her gloves and slipped out of the trauma bay, as did Dr. Carlo. Dante shut the door.

"You were giving my interns a hard time, I hear," Dante said, setting the chart down and peeling off his white lab coat, before slipping on a trauma gown and gloves.

"Is all that gear necessary?" his father asked in a snarky tone.

"Yes, this is standard protocol."

"I'm your father. The same blood runs through our veins."

Dante snorted. "That's debatable."

His father glared at him. "What is your problem?"

"My problem is that you wouldn't let my intern do his job. How else is he going to learn?" Dante snapped as he sat on the rolling stool in front of his father and began to finish cleaning the wound the nurse had started on.

"I don't want some student stitching me up. I'd rather have you," his father groused.

Dante rolled his eyes and continued to clean the laceration. He was trying to tune his father out.

"I didn't get to congratulate you personally on your marriage." His father's voice was laced with sarcasm.

Dante snorted. "As if you actually *wanted* to congratulate me. You were just angry that you couldn't get a hold of Nonno's vineyard or the Lido villa. Or my money."

"You still have to produce an heir," his father said.

"Shay's already pregnant. Congratulations, Nonno," Dante said scathingly.

His father's face paled, his mouth opening and closing like a fish out of water. "Pregnant?"

"Sì."

"Are you sure it's your child this time? Does she know about Olivia and that child that you believed was yours but wasn't?" His father was clearly relishing digging at Dante's old wounds.

Dante glared at him and then injected freezing into the cut, causing his father to curse. It took every ounce of strength not to jam the needle in hard, but he was a doctor and he would never jeopardize his career because his father was making him angry.

He got up and discarded the needle in the hazardous material receptacle. "So how did this happen? Did the current girlfriend discover you in bed with another woman?"

Marco sneered. "No, I was in a minor altercation."

Dante shook his head. "You're unbelievable. You know that? Why are you here? You didn't need to have me stitch up your wound. Are you here to torment me because I took away your opportunity to sell Nonno's vineyard off to the highest bidder?"

"What're you talking about?"

Dante leaned over him. "I know. I know that you've had investors out there poking around. I know that big company wanted Nonno's wine under their wing. I know that you've been waiting like a caged animal, waiting to sell it. And now you can't."

"You think you know me so well? You don't."

"So you've come here to make amends?" Dante asked sarcastically.

"No," Marco said. "I came here to meet your bride."

"To find out whether there was an heir on the way."

His father turned and wouldn't look at him.

Dante just shook his head and opened a stitch kit. He began to close his father's wound. Angry that he'd had to deal with his father today. Angry that his father was so unchanged.

So ignorant, so greedy.

He would never be like him. He could never be like him.

"You'll need to stay here until the effects of the pain-killers wear off. Sit back and relax and I'll send an intern to discharge you." Dante peeled off his gloves.

"You shouldn't have got married," his father said. "You're an Affini. We're not faithful."

Dante glared at him. "I may be an Affini, but I'm not like you at all."

With that, he left the room.

His father would never change. He would never accept the blame for what he did to Dante and Enzo's mother. For what he did to them.

And for that Dante would never forgive him.

And he would never forget.

Shay was lying on the bed waiting for the ultrasound.

More important, she was waiting for Dante to show up, but he was forty minutes late to her appointment. She'd had him paged, but he wasn't answering.

Which was unlike him. Even if he were tied up with a trauma, surely he'd have found a way to get a message to her?

"Are we still waiting?" Dr. Tucci asked, coming into the room.

"No, he's probably stuck with a trauma."

Dr. Tucci nodded. "Yes, it's always hard for an emergency room doctor to make appointments."

"I'm sure it's the same for an obstetrician," she teased.

Dr. Tucci grinned and tapped the side of his nose as he rolled the ultrasound machine over. "I could've tried to wait another ten minutes, but I do have a consult in about twenty minutes that will now be pushed back."

"I'm sorry about that," Shay apologized. "Usually he would get some message to me about why he was late."

Would he? Do you know him that well?

She shook that thought from her head.

"It's okay, Principessa." He grinned and lifted her shirt, tucking a paper towel just under her breasts, and Shay tucked a towel into the waist of her scrub pants, which she had pulled down. "This will be cold."

The gel squeezed out of the bottle with a little spurt of air and he turned on the monitor. She turned her head toward the screen. She closed her eyes and took a deep breath as Dr. Tucci placed pressure against her abdomen.

"Ah, there is Baby."

Shay looked at the monitor and she could see the outline of her baby, moving, the flicker of a heartbeat and the string of pearls that represented the spine.

Her heart stopped for a moment and her eyes filled with tears as she stared at her baby.

Little hands and a tiny nose and she couldn't wait to see him or her in person and hold them.

I'll take care of you.

"Do you want to know the sex?" Dr. Tucci asked as he moved the ultrasound wand over her belly.

"You know?"

"Well, I have a pretty good idea. It's not one hundred percent factual, but this baby is in pretty good position to show me." Dr. Tucci grinned. "Or shall we wait for Dr. Affini?"

"No, I'll tell him later." If he couldn't be here, then she'd tell him herself. "I'll only tell Dante if he wants to know."

Dr. Tucci nodded. "It's a girl."

A tear slipped out of her eye and rolled down her cheek; she wiped it away with the back of her hand. "A girl?"

"Sì," Dr. Tucci said happily as he continued to tap the keyboard, taking measurements.

Shay's heart overflowed with love. It was the first time since the stick had turned blue that she'd felt a real motherly connection. Probably because she was so focused on her work. So focused on keeping everything in her life the same, but nothing was the same anymore.

Nothing could be the same.

This little girl was her whole world.

"There, all done." Dr. Tucci wiped the ultrasound gel from her belly. "I'll email you the pictures of the baby. All looks good for twenty-six weeks."

"Thank you."

Dr. Tucci nodded and left the exam room.

Shay cleaned herself up. It was sad that Dante hadn't been here to see it, to share this moment, but his demeanor had changed when she'd reminded him that their marriage was a business arrangement.

I need to find him.

She left the exam room and headed down to the emergency department. She checked the updated chart and saw that Dr. Affini was in the far trauma bay. She headed down the hall and entered the room.

Only Dante wasn't there. Just an older gentleman, clad in expensive designer clothes, who had obviously been treated for a laceration to his forearm, because it was bandaged and there were blood-soaked towels in the trash.

"I'm sorry," she said. "I didn't mean to walk in on you."

He smiled and there was something familiar about the way he smiled, but his eyes were cold. He was a handsome older man, but there was no warmth about him, which gave her a bad feeling.

"You're not interrupting at all." His gaze raked her body up and down, eyeing the belly and frowning in disappointment. "Have you come to discharge me?"

"No, who is your doctor? I can check to see if they have the orders up."

"Dr. Dante Affini," the man said in a weird tone. "He's my son and I know he's anxious to get rid of me."

So that was why she'd seen the Affini name on the chart.
"You're Dante's father?"

He narrowed his eyes. "Yes. I'm Marco and you must be the blushing bride."

"Yes. I'm Shay."

"And that's my grandchild, is it?" He snorted. "Or is it someone else's?"

"The child is Dante's," Shay said, instantly detesting him. "What're you implying?"

"He didn't tell you?" There was a pleased glint to the man's eyes. "Olivia."

"What about her?"

"He was engaged to her and she was pregnant, with what he thought was his child, but of course it wasn't. What a huge blow to his ego."

"I'm not Olivia," Shay snapped. "I would never do such a thing."

"Even for wealth?"

"Money is not important to me."

"I find that hard to believe." He leaned forward. "Money is power."

"Money is not everything." She didn't like Dante's father at all and now she understood why he didn't like his father much either.

"Then why did you marry him?"

"To give my child a father."

Marco snorted. "Do you know why he married you?"

"For our child."

He shook his head. "For money."

"I don't have any money. I work for the United World Wide Health Association. I'm not in it for the money. Your son helps people as well and he doesn't get paid astronomical amounts."

Marco grinned deviously. "He didn't tell you?"

"Tell me what?" Her stomach twisted in a knot. She didn't like the way this conversation was going; she should just leave, but she couldn't move.

"He only married you to keep his trust fund. Dante and his brother have to marry by the time they're thirty-five and produce an heir from that marriage in order to keep their inheritance. If they don't, then they lose it all. It goes back to me. All their mother's dowry, which she left in trust to those boys, becomes mine again."

Her heart was crushed. She knew there was a reason why he'd been so insistent that they marry, but she didn't want to believe it.

She wanted to believe better about him.

"Shay, your father will come back. I believe in him. He's a better man than you give him credit for."

It was the douse of cold water she needed.

She fled Marco's room, tears threatening to spill.

She had to find Dante.

She had to find out if it was true, or whether his father was just being cruel.

Only deep down a little voice told her what she already knew.

And she was angry at herself for letting her guard down.

CHAPTER TWELVE

"I'VE BEEN TRYING to get a hold of you for days. Where have you been?" Dante asked as Enzo answered his phone.

"Working," Enzo said quickly, and Dante sensed there was something more going on, but he didn't have time to pry at the moment. "What do you need, Dante?"

"Father came into the emergency room with a laceration to his right forearm."

There was silence on the other end. Then Enzo cleared his throat. "Are you okay?"

"I'm fine."

"Are you sure?"

"I said the last things I needed to say to him." Dante snorted. "He's not changed one bit, has he?"

"I don't think that he'll ever change, to be honest." Enzo sighed. "How did he get the laceration?"

"I never did find out. All he said was that it was a minor altercation," Dante said. "I just stitched him up. He told me my marriage is doomed and I left. I'll have to go back and discharge him soon. Especially before Shay runs into him."

Enzo was quiet on the other end. "He said your marriage was doomed?"

"He's not wrong," Dante said. "He said all Affini men were doomed."

"Damned might be more appropriate," Enzo groused.

Dante grunted in response. "I have to find Shay. I have to tell her about the trust fund and Olivia."

"I already know," she said.

Dante spun around to see Shay standing in the doorway, her eyes moist with unshed tears and her arms crossed. "I have to go, Enzo." And he disconnected the call.

"It's true?" she asked, coming into the room and shutting the door behind her.

"What were you told?"

"Your father told me that you married me only to keep your trust fund from reverting to your father. You married me because the baby guaranteed that the money, the land would be yours. And he filled me in on your exact acquaintance with Olivia, but that doesn't bother me. I'm not like her and I'm sorry if you think that I was when I first showed up. I understand your distrust."

"You met my father?" He scrubbed a hand over his face. "I'm sorry you had to meet him."

"He wasn't exactly pleasant," Shay said. "And didn't seem too thrilled about the prospect of the baby. Of course, now I know why. You're taking money out of his pocket."

"Is that what he told you?" Dante asked.

"Are you denying it?"

"No, but we need to talk about this calmly. For the baby."

"Calmly?" she asked, tears in her eyes. It hurt his heart knowing that this was hurting her. He didn't want her to get worked up. She was too fragile.

"Shay…" He tried to hold her, but she moved away from him.

"Tell me," she said.

It's for the best. Tell her the truth.

"*Sì.* That is why I married you. It's my thirty-fifth birthday soon and our marriage put a stop to my father taking away the vineyard and the Lido villa until an heir, our baby, was born."

She shook her head. "Why did you hide this from me? Why didn't you tell me about this before?"

"Would you have married me?"

"No. Probably not." She sighed. "My parents were forced to get married and my mother loved my father. Dearly, but he didn't return those feelings. It broke her heart. She just pined for him until the day she died. I don't want that. I never want that."

"Well, why did you marry me, then?" he asked. "Did you think that this could possibly lead to something more? You reminded me yourself just this morning that this is a business arrangement."

Shay winced as if she'd been slapped and he regretted the choice of words.

"I want my baby to know their father," she said, her voice shaking. "I thought you…"

"Thought what?" Dante asked, trying to stay calm to keep her calm.

"I don't know," she said quietly.

"Then why are you angry for my reasons?"

"Because you don't want this child. Not for the reasons I thought you did."

"And for what reasons did you think I wanted this child?" he snapped. "You show up here pregnant, my one-night stand. What am I supposed to think? I've been used before, people after my money. People after my title."

"I don't want any of those things," she said. "I never have. I'm not Olivia."

"I find that hard to believe. You grew up with nothing. You've probably been dreaming of a knight in shining armor to take you away. To save you. Well, I'm not him."

Shay glared at him. "I know you're not him. I'm painfully aware of that fact."

"So now you know the truth," he said in exasperation. "The reason I wanted you to enter into a marriage of convenience with me for a year. I thought you understood the parameters to our marriage. Everything was laid out in the contract. I thought you understood that it couldn't go further than this. I thought you didn't want more, but I was wrong. You want more than I can give you."

"I wish you would have told me the reason why you wanted the marriage." Shay couldn't even look him in the eye. "This is why…marriage just doesn't work. Unless both people love each other. It just… It can't work."

"I can't give you anything more," he repeated.

"I don't want more." A tear slid down her cheek, but she held her head up high.

"Are you going to ask for an annulment?"

She shook her head. "No, I won't let you lose your property. Especially to that man. I signed a contract. I'll stay your wife. You'll give my baby a name, but when my twelve weeks' contract is up I'm leaving."

"You can't leave," he said, but he felt terrible.

"Then give me a reason to stay," she said.

Only he couldn't, because he was too afraid.

He was a horrible human being.

Why did he have to hurt her?

Because it's for the best?

Only he wasn't so sure about that.

"I'd better go," she said. "I'm going to pack and move back to the United World Wide Health Association quarters."

"What?" He stepped in front of her. "You don't have to do that."

"What's the point of staying at the Lido?"

"We have to keep up at least the pretense of being married. If you move back into the United World Wide Health Association quarters, then people will know that our marriage is a sham or on the rocks and my father will put things in motion to take back the land."

"What does it matter?" she snapped. "I'm not going to divorce you and the baby will be born. Who cares what the press thinks? Who cares what people think?"

"I do! I care. It's my family name, but you wouldn't understand about family, would you, since your own father didn't want you?"

The sting of her hand slapping him burned, but he deserved it.

She pushed past him out into the hall and he stood there, holding his face. The feel of her palm still burned into his flesh and in that moment he realized his father had been right. He was exactly like him.

It had been two weeks since their fallout and it still tormented her. He never came back to the villa. She lived there alone and, even though she was used to being alone, without him it was lonely. She missed his arms around her at night, and then she was angry at herself for shedding tears over Dante. For missing him, when he clearly didn't want her.

What did you expect? Love?

She'd thought he was different. She'd hoped he was different, but he wasn't. He was exactly the same.

The same as his father, the same as her father. So she made up her mind. Her twelve weeks were done. She was going to leave and head back to New Orleans. The place she always returned to. The only home she knew, even if it wasn't much of one.

Shay leaned against the wall, fighting the tears that were threatening to fall, and she cursed herself inwardly for letting herself fall in love with a man like her father. Something she'd always sworn she wouldn't do, but she'd done it. And she realized that she was just like her mother.

The only difference was that she wasn't going to pine away.

She was going to keep working.

She was going to make damn sure that she forgot about Dante Affini.

How can you forget about him when you carry a piece of him inside you?

Now she had to get up the courage to find him and tell him she was leaving. Contract or not, she was going back to New Orleans. Her baby wouldn't be used as a pawn for a trust fund. A sharp pain stabbed her just under her navel and she cried out. She was getting too worked up. She was supposed to be taking it easy.

Part of her wished that she'd just headed to the Lido instead of trying to find Dante. If she'd headed back to the Lido after the run-in with his father, then she wouldn't have heard from Dante's own lips the real reasons why he'd married her. Wouldn't have had it confirmed that he thought so little about her and the baby. That he'd just wanted the baby because the baby would ensure his inheritance.

Nothing more.

He didn't love the baby and she realized that she would be giving her baby the same kind of father she grew up with. It truly was all about business.

The pain hit again and she doubled over; her heart began to race. She was dizzy and she felt as if she was going to be sick.

It's stress. Just stress. You have a flight tomorrow you have to catch.

Only the pain hit once again, with a lightening of her belly, and she knew it was something more than just Braxton Hicks. She slid down the wall, crying as the pain overtook her body. She was down a hallway that wasn't busy in the evening. A hall that was filled with offices that were closed. She was alone.

Oh, God. Don't let my baby die.

"Shay? Oh, God, *cara…*"

She rolled her head to look down the hall. She could see

Dante running toward her and, even though her heart had been broken by him, she'd never been so happy to see him.

He was kneeling beside her. "What's wrong?"

"Pain" was the only word she could pant through the pain racking her body. The world was spinning and she brought her hand up from where she had been clutching her lower belly. There was bright red fresh blood on her palm.

"Oh, no," she whispered. Red fresh blood was never a good sign in a pregnant woman.

She was only twenty-eight weeks along. It was too early to have her baby.

"Oh, God, *cara*, you're bleeding." She was scooped up into his arms. He was holding her close. "We'll get you help, Shay. Please stay with me."

"It's too soon, Dante. Please help our baby. Please."

She gripped the lapel of his white jacket, holding tight to him as her body attacked her. Shay knew what was going on: she was in premature labor. She'd seen it so many times in Third World countries. And if she was bleeding, that didn't bode well for her or the baby.

Her labor was progressing so fast. Why was it happening to her? Was it punishment for entering into this sham of a marriage?

She had just seen Dr. Tucci two weeks ago.

All she wanted was for her baby to live. She couldn't care less about herself. Her baby had to survive. Her baby needed a chance at life.

Dante carried her into the trauma bay. The largest trauma bay and she buried her head in his neck while the pain coursed through her body. She was scared that he'd brought her here. The largest room was saved for the direst situations. How did she go from being normal and healthy to critical?

"Help. Me."

"I know, *cara*. I know." Dante set her down on the examination table. "Someone page Dr. Tucci to Trauma, *stat!*"

He held her hand as the trauma nurses and residents began to fill the room.

As she stared up at him she found herself slipping away from him. In more than one way.

"Shay, please stay with me."

She turned her head away as the nurses slipped on the oxygen mask. She couldn't look at him. He was concerned only because the death of the baby meant that he would lose everything. All his land, his money.

He didn't deserve to be in this room with her, but she couldn't tell him to leave either, because he was the only familiar thing in this room. She didn't like being on the other side of a trauma as she took deep breaths and tried to fight the urge to slip off.

Dr. Tucci came bursting into the room.

"I'll be back," Dante whispered in her ear. He went to speak to Dr. Tucci.

Shay tried to focus on what they were saying, but she couldn't. Instead she closed her eyes and listened to the heart-rate monitor that they had on her belly. The baby's heart rate was speeding up, but it was still there.

Her baby was still alive for the moment.

"We have to get her into an operating theatre now," Dr. Tucci shouted above the din. "Dr. Affini, you have to leave. She's your wife. You can't be in there with her."

"Husbands go into the operating theatre all the time when their wives have C-sections."

"I don't want… I don't want him in there," she managed to say from beneath the mask.

Dr. Tucci nodded at her. "Dr. Affini, please leave the bay."

Dante looked back at her, but she looked away.

If he only wanted their baby for monetary reasons, then

he had no right to be here with her while she was losing it. He had no right to share in the pain she was feeling.

"Shay, we're going to put you under general anesthesia. It's safer for you both. We have to move fast," Dr. Tucci said. "Do I have your consent?"

Shay nodded. "Yes. Please save us."

And that was the last thing she could remember before the world went black.

CHAPTER THIRTEEN

ALL DANTE COULD do was watch the clock on the wall. That was all his mind would let him do, because he couldn't let his mind wander to where it wanted to go. He couldn't let it wander to down the hall where Dr. Tucci was trying to save Shay's and his baby's lives. It crushed his heart that he had pushed her away.

That he'd hurt her. Those two weeks apart had made him regret his harsh words.

All he could think about was earning her love back again and not knowing how, but he was going to try. Without her...his world spun out of control. It was colorless. There was no light. No sun.

And the way he'd hurt her to protect his heart sickened him.

That he was like his father.

You're not your father.

He hid his face in his hands and tried to shake all the thoughts away. All those dark thoughts that were niggling away in the dark recesses of his mind.

The one that stuck out the most was that he'd failed Shay and the baby.

He'd absolutely failed them.

Don't let them die.

It was a silent plea, but one that he was hoping wouldn't fall on deaf ears.

Not today.

Lives were saved every day and he wanted to be there when Shay's life was saved, because that was all he had to cling to at this moment.

Dr. Tucci came out of the surgical hall. Still in his scrubs. The grim expression on his face made Dante want to scream; his heart sank into the soles of his feet. Further. Into the depths of absolute despair as Dr. Tucci approached him.

"Please," Dante whispered. "Please don't tell me... Don't tell me she's gone. Please."

Dr. Tucci sighed. "She survived, and so did the baby, but it's not good. Shay lost a lot of blood. A lot. We hung a lot of packed cells."

"What happened?" Dante asked.

"Placental abruption." Dr. Tucci ran a hand over his bald head. "We never know when they're going to happen. It can happen so fast. Just be thankful that it happened here in the hospital and we were able to get the baby out. Usually, by the time the women get here the baby has suffocated and the mother has bled to death."

Dante felt dizzy and he sat back down. His head in his hands, his eyes stinging from unshed tears that would not come.

Dr. Tucci sat beside him and patted his back. "The baby will be fine. She's strong."

Dante glanced up at him. "She?"

"Yes, I forgot you missed the last ultrasound. You have a little girl. She's very small, but already she's a fighter. Ideally we'd have started on steroids in utero to help mature her lungs, but obviously in this case there wasn't time. We have her hooked up to oxygen and various drips to support her while she continues to grow. Of course, you know that she'll have to stay in the NICU until she gains to what should have been close to her birth weight. We also don't let premature babies go home until they're close to their original due date."

Dante nodded. "I know. Thank you, Dr. Tucci."

"We're not out of the woods either, yet, with respect to the Principessa. The damage to her uterus was extensive. The placental abruption ripped through the wall of her uterus. It was a full uterine abruption. I had to perform an emergency hysterectomy. Shay will not carry any more children."

Dante nodded again.

Dr. Tucci left.

This is all my fault.

He was the one who'd got her pregnant and then broken her heart.

He was no better than his father. All because he was afraid of letting someone else in.

Dante left the waiting room and wandered up to the NICU. The nurse on duty pointed him in the direction of the incubator where a tiny baby weighing no more than a couple of pounds was hooked up to a bunch of machines that were helping her live.

He was scared to approach the incubator. He was afraid of what he was going to see. And he wasn't sure that he was ready for this. That he was ready for a daughter.

This is what you wanted, remember? Before Olivia crushed your hopes and dreams.

All he'd ever wanted when he was young was a family. Not that he didn't love Enzo or his mother, but he wanted some sense of normalcy. He'd wanted that family with a mother, father and child. A loving family who would celebrate holidays together.

Just as his mother had with his *nonno* and *nonna*.

They had loved each other.

All of them.

And that was what he'd always craved when he was younger.

He took a step toward the incubator and looked in to see his daughter. His beautiful daughter. She was so small and fragile. A tear slid down his face as he looked at her.

And he knew in that moment what he was.

He was a father.

This was his child.

"Can I touch her?" he asked the nurse.

"Of course," she said.

Dante put on hand sanitizer and the nurse opened one of the little portal doors to the incubator. He slid his hand in and rested it on her back. There was downy fine hair on her skin. The lanugo she'd never shed because she was born premature.

She was warm, but under the palm of his hand where she fit so well he could feel her chest going up and down. And the small flutter of her heart.

His baby.

His child.

His future.

Dante slipped his hand out of the incubator and left the NICU. He went up to the ICU, where he gowned and masked to go see Shay, who was still receiving a blood transfusion and still not awake. She was still under anesthesia, in an induced coma while they monitored her.

When he walked into the ICU room, he cried out at the sight of her. She was so pale against the crisp white hospital sheets. She was ashen.

Oh, God.

He'd been responsible for this.

The woman he loved had almost died. The realization hit him hard and it wasn't the realization that he loved her, it was the fact that he'd allowed himself to say that to himself for the first time without hesitation. Without conjecture.

He was in love with her. It was more than a marriage of convenience. It was real. She was his everything.

And it didn't matter to him about his inheritance or the trust fund. If he couldn't have her or the baby in his life, if they didn't get their chance to be a family, then life was not worth living for him. He would give up everything, his pride, his family name, everything that he'd thought he wanted, to have a chance with Shay.

To do things right. To be a real family.

"I'm sorry, *cara*. I will make things right. I promise."

Dante left the ICU room and knew exactly what he had to do. He couldn't be selfish anymore. As he left the intensive care unit floor and passed through the waiting room he saw that his father was here. Two visits in two weeks was more than he'd seen Marco Affini in the last five years and it was two too many.

Dante couldn't figure out why his father was back, but he was unwelcome.

His father turned as if sensing him there.

"What're you doing here? Why did you come back?" Dante asked.

"To see if the child survived. There was a lot of press. Word got out that Principessa Affini almost died. That she was hanging on by a thread."

"It's not any of your business and you know the press always gets things wrong."

"Were they wrong?"

"No, but it still doesn't concern you."

"I think it does," Marco said. "Well, did they live?"

"Do you care?"

Marco shrugged. "It would be a shame, but no, not really. Not for the reasons you think I should care."

"*Sì*, they both survived. So you can go now."

"I think I'll wait."

Dante clenched his fist. "Waiting around to pick at the bones?"

Marco snorted. "Hardly. I actually wanted to wish you a happy birthday. Today is your birthday, is it not?"

"I'm surprised you remembered."

"You're my son," Marco said.

"You've never remembered before now. Or was it because today happens to be my thirty-fifth birthday? Today's the day you could've had it all." It was a dig and Dante didn't care. He deserved it. "And now none of it's for you. You lost it."

"It could still be mine. I hear the baby is sick and that your wife is unable to bear any more children. If your baby dies, then that's it. Unless you leave *this* wife and find another you can breed with."

Dante resisted the urge to pummel his father in the waiting room. "I would gladly lose it all for Shay. If our baby doesn't survive, I will stay with Shay. I love her. I won't abandon her like you abandoned my mother."

"I loved your mother, Dante. It's just that Affini men aren't faithful. My father wasn't, nor his father before him…"

"I *am* faithful. I have always been faithful and I will continue to be faithful. I am an Affini and I am faithful. I am more of a man than you ever were or will be. Now, if you have nothing further to say to me, then I think this is where we part company."

Dante's pulse was thundering between his ears. He was reaching out to give his father a chance.

His father sighed and then nodded. "Good luck."

Dante shook his head as he watched his father leave.

He watched the last of a long line of Affini cheaters walk out of his life forever, because his father was going to be the last of the Affini men to be unfaithful. He wasn't going to follow in his footsteps and Enzo had no plans to settle down. Ever.

He briefly mourned the loss of his father. For the father he could've been, but Marco Affini was weak. Dante refused to be weak.

He was going to fight for what he wanted.

He was going to be strong like the person he loved and admired the most.

He was going to be strong like Shay.

His wife.

CHAPTER FOURTEEN

I'M THIRSTY.

That was Shay's first thought as she started to come out of the anesthetic. The groggy fog that compelled her to keep sleeping, but the more she struggled to stay asleep in that warm, hazy, pain-free cocoon, the more she became aware of her surroundings.

And most important, the fact that she was no longer pregnant.

She let out a small cry.

I've lost her. My baby.

And she began to weep. She wanted her mother there to console her. To ease the pain. Her whole childhood she'd been the balm to ease her mother's pain when she was sobbing over her father. Now she needed her mother's arms to wrap around her and hold her close.

To ease the heart-wrenching pain that was tearing away at her very soul.

The baby she would never get to see.

A nurse rushed in, speaking Italian to her, trying to get Shay to calm down, but she couldn't stop the sobs from racking her body, because nothing could bring back her baby.

"I'll take care of her," a deep, gentle voice said.

Shay turned her head to see Dante standing beside her

bedside. He was in his scrubs, but they were wrinkled and she noticed the cot in the corner.

He'd been sleeping here?

She glanced back over at Dante, who was issuing instructions to the nurse, who was nodding and then left the room. It was just Dante and her.

There was no baby.

There was nothing for them.

"What…?" She trailed off because she couldn't even finish the sentence. It was too painful.

"She's alive," Dante said. Then smiled. "Our daughter's alive, beautiful and in the NICU."

Tears streaked down her face. "I thought I'd lost her."

"No, *cara*. You didn't lose her. It was I who almost lost you…" He took her hand and kissed it, tears pouring down his face. "I almost lost you."

"What do you mean?"

"Your placenta abrupted, and it was so forceful it caused your uterus to do the same. It was a full uterine rupture. You almost died."

"Oh, God," she whispered.

"They had to remove your uterus to save your life. You needed several units of packed cells. You almost died. I'm so sorry, Shay. I'm devastated that you won't be able to carry another child. I'm so truly sorry, *cara*."

Tears streamed down her face.

"I'm so sorry," she whispered.

"No, never apologize," Dante said. "Never. You're alive and our daughter is alive. There is nothing to apologize for."

"What does it matter to you? You don't love me." Shay tried to take her hand away. "You have your heir. You don't need me anymore."

"You're wrong. I need you, *cara*." He kissed her hand again. "I love you more than anything. Our two weeks apart were torture. You are my world. I am nothing without you, *cara*."

"How can you love me? You only married me for the baby…" She started to weep but shrugged him away when he touched her. "You only wanted me for the baby, so you can keep your inheritance. You have that. Don't you want someone else who can give you more children? You wanted a family, to be a father."

"You're sounding like my father," he said sternly. "Besides, I am a father.

"You're being cruel."

"You're talking nonsense." He reached for her hand. "I love you, Shay. I was terrified, yes, and my heart was broken and I couldn't trust that emotion. Love was dead inside me until you came along. I don't care if I lose everything by being with you. I love you. I love you, *mi amore*. You're all that I need. You're all that I want."

"You love me?"

"*Sì*, I would give it all up for you. Only you, and if our child hadn't made it, I would still want you. Almost losing you was too much to bear. You are my heart. My soul. My everything."

"You weren't the only fool, Dante. I was a fool too." Shay sighed. "I was so afraid of falling in love and having to give up everything I knew. Giving up my career for a man. I didn't want to be my mother. I was trying so hard not to be her, when I was turning into her."

Dante chuckled. "I understand. I was trying so hard not to be my father I was doing the same. I was turning into him. The only difference in our situations is that you loved your mother. You miss your mother. My father and I, there is no love lost. All we share is a genetic link. We are not the same."

"I am very glad for that."

Dante smiled and then leaned over and kissed her. "I'm afraid I tore up that contract."

"Our marriage contract?"

He nodded. "I want you for more than just a year. I want you for a lifetime."

Shay began to cry again and he kissed her.

"Are you ready to see your daughter now?"

"Yes."

Dante called the nurse, who brought in a wheelchair. He helped Shay into the wheelchair and made sure she was comfortable. He wheeled her down to the NICU, and when they entered that room full of incubators her heart skipped a beat. Dante wheeled her over to the incubator across the room. He lifted the pink blanket and inside was a tiny baby on a ventilator.

Her little girl was so small and fragile. She was hooked up and there were many lines and leads on her tiny pink body, but Shay knew instinctively this was her baby.

"She's so small." She began to weep, not being able to hold in the emotions any longer. She'd thought she'd lost everything when she woke up. She'd thought she was waking up into some kind of nightmare, but instead she was waking up to a dream that she never wanted to end.

A dream she didn't even know she wanted until she thought it was all lost.

That it was all gone.

Dante opened the incubator and with the help of the NICU nurse they lifted the tiny baby girl from the incubator to place her on her mother's chest. Shay's heart overflowed with a love she hadn't even known was possible. A blanket was wrapped around her little girl and Shay placed her hand over the tiny round back, holding her close.

"It's okay," she whispered. "I'm here and so are you. I haven't left you."

Dante placed a hand over hers. "We're both here now, *mi amore*. And we're not leaving."

The familiar little heartbeat thrumming against her calmed Shay and the baby's vitals kicked up a notch in response to being held.

"That's a strong heartbeat," Dante said. "She's a real fighter."

"Yes. She is." Shay ran her fingers over the tiny feet that had kicked her.

Her baby was alive.

"I thought I'd lost this," Shay whispered. "I hope I never feel that way again."

"Me too," Dante said. "It was the worst feeling ever. If I lost either of you…I couldn't go on living. You are both my heart. My loves."

"I feel the same," she whispered.

"*Cara*, our little girl needs a name. I wanted you to name her."

"Me?"

"*Sì.*"

"Sophia," Shay said without hesitation. "My mother's name and your long-lived *zia*. I hope you don't mind."

"I don't. That is a good first name and how about Maria for the second? That was my mother's name."

Shay nodded. "I like that."

"Sophia Maria Affini. Or rather Principessa Sophia. It has a nice ring to it."

"It does." Shay sighed. "I guess I should tender my resignation with the United World Wide Health Association."

"Why?" Dante asked.

"It seems I'll be staying in Italy for a while."

"You don't have to resign from the United World Wide Health Association."

"Why not?"

"Because I've tendered my resignation at the hospital.

I have to give them six months' notice and finish up the work that you started."

"What?" she asked, surprised. "You resigned?"

"*Sì*, I joined the United World Wide Health Association as a trainer. I won't be doing any kind of missions that you used to do, because we have a child, but I will finish your work while you recover, and then in six months we'll head to America, where I will spend three months training trauma surgeons to head out to disaster zones. Then, who knows where we'll go? I was told that training can happen all over the world in various cities. The point is, we'll go together. The three of us. I requested that you will work alongside me. I can't work without you."

"But…but you love Italy."

"*Sì*, I do, but I love you more and your work is important to you. It's your passion and it's all you have, besides us. Anyways, Venice is our home base. We'll come back for summers on the Lido and Christmases in Tuscany. I have enough money to pick and choose when I want to work and where. Besides, time in Tuscany while you're healing will be nice. Serena and Guillermo can't wait to spoil this little girl. Italy is just a place we hang our hats. The three of us is what makes a home."

Shay smiled. Yes. Italy was a great place to live, as New Orleans had been. Just a place she'd passed through since her mother died, but her husband and her daughter were her life. Wherever they were together they were home. And for the first time in her life she had a home. Love and roots that were all her own.

* * * * *

BOUND BY THE PRINCE'S BABY

JESSICA GILMORE

For Dan and Abby, always.

PROLOGUE

Eight years ago

THE CAR PURRED to a stop and the driver got out, walking as stiffly as if he were on parade to the rear passenger side and opening the door. Amber Kireyev pulled her hated kilt down to her knees before she grabbed her rucksack and shimmied out of the car under his always watchful gaze.

'Thank you, Boris,' she said with a smile, but as usual there was no glimmer of a return smile, just a curt nod.

'Princess Vasilisa.'

'Amber,' she said, as she always did. 'Call me Amber.'

But Boris didn't acknowledge her words as he stood tall and imposing, waiting for her to walk through the entranceway; he wouldn't move until he had seen her go into the building and the doors close behind her.

Amber suppressed a sigh. She knew that most people would consider selling their soul to occupy an apartment in this grand Art Deco building overlooking Central Park, especially a penthouse in one of the two iconic towers, but to her the apartment was more prison than home. Hefting her backpack onto her shoulder, she walked, chin held high, up to the doors and pressed the button for admittance. The doors swung silently and ominously open and, without a backward glance at the sun-filled afternoon, she walked inside.

The opulent high-ceilinged marble and tile foyer was so familiar to her she barely noticed its glossy splendour, but she did notice the smiling man behind the concierge desk, dapper in his gilt and navy uniform.

'Miss Amber, Happy Birthday to you.'

'Thank you, Hector.'

'Do you have something nice planned to celebrate?'

Amber tried not to pull a frustrated face. Her fellow pupils at the exclusive girls' school she attended had all thrown extravagant parties for their eighteenth birthdays, renting out hotel ballrooms or heading off to their Hampton Beach homes for the weekend. Even if they had invited her Amber wouldn't have been allowed to attend, but they'd stopped asking her years ago. 'Grandmama said that we might go out for dinner, after my lessons, of course.' Not even on her eighteenth birthday could Amber skip her dancing or deportment or etiquette lessons.

'I have something for you,' Hector whispered conspiratorially and, after looking around, he pulled out a large brown envelope from under his desk and held it out to her.

Amber's heart began to beat faster as she took in the familiar postmark. 'Thank you for letting me have it sent to your house.' Her future lay in that envelope. A future far away from here, far away from her grandmother.

'London?' Hector asked and she nodded.

'The university prospectus. London is where my parents met and worked, although we lived just outside, in a little village. I always promised myself I would go back as soon as I was old enough. Applying to university is just the first step.' She slipped the envelope into her backpack. 'Thank you again.'

'I also have this for you.' With a flourish he produced a large cupcake, extravagantly iced in silver and white. 'There's no candle. The fire alarms, you know. But Maya told me to tell you to make a wish anyway.'

'Oh, Hector.' Amber hated crying but she could feel hot, heavy tears gathering in her eyes. 'This is so kind of you and Maya. Give her my love.'

'Come see us again soon; she has a new recipe she wants to teach you.' Hector cast an anxious look up at the huge clock which dominated the vestibule. 'Your grandmother will be calling down soon; you'd better go. And Amber? Happy Birthday.'

The lift—Amber refused to say elevator, clinging onto her English accent and vocabulary as stubbornly as she could—was waiting and she tapped in the code which would take her up to the penthouse, nibbling her cake as the doors slid shut and the lift started its journey.

The doors opened straight into the penthouse hallway. Usually Amber could barely put a toe onto the parquet floor before her grandmother querulously summoned her to quiz her about her day and criticise her appearance, her posture, her attitude, her ingratitude. Amber steeled herself, ready for the interrogation, the brown envelope, safely stored in her bag, a shield against every poisonous word. But today there was no summons and Amber, half a cake still clutched in her hand, managed to make it to her bedroom undisturbed, slipping her backpack onto the floor, taking out the envelope and concealing it, still unopened, at the back of her wardrobe. She'd look at it later tonight, when her grandmother was asleep.

Sitting back on her heels, Amber checked to make sure there was no hint of the envelope visible through her clothes and then clambered up, her feet sinking into the deep pile pink carpet. Her whole room was sumptuously decorated in bright pinks and cream which clashed horribly with her auburn hair and made her pale skin look even paler. But she had as little choice in the decor as she did about her schooling, wardrobe and pastimes.

Wriggling out of the hated blazer and kilt, she slipped on a simple blue dress, brushing out her plaits and tucking her mass of hair into a loose bundle before heading out to find her grandmother. The silence was so unusual that she couldn't help feeling a little apprehensive. For one moment she wondered if her grandmother had planned a birthday surprise, before pushing the ludicrous idea away. Her grandmother didn't do either birthdays or surprises.

Padding along the hallway, she peeped into the small sitting room her grandmother preferred, her curiosity piqued as she heard the low rumble of voices coming from the larger, formal sitting room her grandmother only used for entertaining. The room was light thanks to floor-to-ceiling windows with stunning views over Central Park but stuffed so full of the furniture that had been saved from Belravia during the revolution that it was impossible to find a spot not cluttered with ornate chairs or spindly tables, the walls filled with heavy portraits of scowling ancestors.

Amber hovered, torn. She hadn't been officially summoned, but surely her grandmother would expect her to come and greet whichever guest she was entertaining.

Just a few more months, she told herself. She'd graduate in a couple of months, and by the autumn she'd be in London. She just needed to apply to university and figure out how to pay for it first. She'd saved a couple of thousand dollars from her allowance but that wasn't going to cover much more than the plane ticket.

Okay. She would worry about all that later. Time to go in, say hello and act the Princess for as long as she needed to. It was so much easier with escape within smelling distance. And of course, now she was an actual adult, her grandmother's control over her had come to an end. At last.

Inhaling, Amber took another step forward, only to halt as her gaze fell on a masculine profile through the part-opened door. A profile she knew all too well: dark hair brushed smoothly back from a high forehead, a distinctly Roman nose flanked by sharp cheekbones hollowing into a firm chin, mouth unsmiling. Amber swallowed. She had spent too many nights dreaming of that mouth. Her heart thumped painfully, her hands damp with remembered embarrassment. What was Tristano Ragrazzi doing here, on her birthday of all days?

Tristano—or, as he was more commonly known, His Most Excellent Royal Highness Crown Prince Tristano of Elsornia—was Amber's first crush. Or, if she was being strictly honest, only crush, despite the four-year age gap and the not insignificant fact that on the few occasions they'd met he'd barely deigned to notice that she was alive. This small detail hadn't stopped a younger Amber weaving an elaborate tale around how he would one day fall in love with her and rescue her from the tower: a tale she had stopped weaving the day she had tripped over one of her grandmother's many embroidered footstools and spilt a tray of drinks and olives over him—perfect hair, exquisite suit, handsome face and all. Hard as she tried, she had never forgotten his incredulous look of horror, the scathing, contemptuous glance he'd shot her way. She hadn't seen him since—and that was more than fine with her.

Amber started to tiptoe backwards—far better to face her grandmother's wrath than His Highness—when Tristano spoke and, at the sound of her name, she froze again.

'Princess Vasilisa is still very young.'

'Yes,' her grandmother agreed in her usual icy, cut-glass tones. 'Which is in your favour. I've ensured she's been kept close; she can be moulded. And of course she has had no opportunity to meet any males. A virgin princess with no scandal attached to her name, excellent academic qualifications, educated in statesmanship and diplomacy is a rare prize and that's before we consider her dowry. She's unique and you know it, Tristano. So let's not play games.'

It was all Amber could do not to gasp. For her grandmother to be discussing her virginity with anyone was mortifying enough but with his Royal Hotness? Her cheeks felt as if they might burst into flame any moment, and not just with embarrassment, with indignation. She was *not* some prize sow to be discussed in terms of breeding! She was surprised her grandmother hadn't mentioned her excellent teeth—unless her dental records had already been discussed!

'Of course, the Belravian fortune,' a male voice she didn't recognise cut in. He had a similar accent to Tristano, only far more noticeable: a little Italian, a little Germanic. 'Is it really worth as much as it was when the country fell?'

'More, thanks to some wise investments as we waited for a Kireyev to sit on the throne once more. But empires have risen and fallen and it's clear that our country is no more, and with it our throne. So we look to another throne, another country in which to invest our money and our blood. Your throne, your country, Tristano.'

Silence fell. Was Tristano tempted, disgusted—or indignant that she was being bartered as if she were part of the fortune, not a living, breathing human? Hope for the latter filled her, only to be dashed when he finally spoke.

'But the fact remains, the Princess is still very young.'

'Let's not be hasty,' the unknown man said. 'The Princess may be too young to marry, but there's no reason not to enter into a formal betrothal. And that's what we are here to discuss. The papers are right here.'

The *what*? She had to be dreaming, surely. Amber barely breathed as she listened.

'I'm her legal guardian,' her grandmother said. 'I can sign right here, with the Duke as my witness. All you need to do is sign as well, Tristano, and then I suggest you take Vasilisa back to Elsornia with you. She can spend the next three years finishing her education to your liking and then, when she comes of Belravian age at twenty-one, she will make you a perfect bride. The perfect Queen.'

A perfect bride indeed! If Amber hadn't been so horrified she would have laughed out loud. She hadn't even been kissed yet; there was no way she was marrying a prince until she had tried a lot of frogs. Besides, she had her own plans for the next three years and they didn't include being finished off in a castle in the middle of Europe. No, she was going to live like a normal girl. She was going to laugh and learn and flirt and find those frogs and enjoy every moment.

Amber's first instinct was to burst in and tell them all in no uncertain terms that the only person who could sign that agreement was her and she did *not* consent. To remind them that now she was eighteen her grandmother was no longer her guardian—and that even if she was she had no right under US or UK law to marry her granddaughter off, that any betrothal they plotted wasn't worth the paper it was written on. But caution quickly replaced the anger. She had no doubt that her grandmother was capable of taking her forcibly to Elsornia if she chose to. No, better to be careful.

Amber backed away as silently as she could, resolution filling her. She was more than the heir to a long gone throne; she was also English on her mother's side, and it was long past time that she went home. The last sound she heard was a pen scratching over thick paper as she inched back towards her bedroom. Passport, money and she would be gone. And she wouldn't be looking back.

CHAPTER ONE

'ALEX? WHO IS THAT? Standing next to Laurent?' Amber did her best to hiss her question discreetly, aware that television cameras were pointing directly at her and her two fellow bridesmaids. A royal wedding was always An Event, even when the royal in question ruled a tiny Mediterranean kingdom. The kind of event that Amber had avoided over the last eight years—and now here she was, centre stage. But what could she do when one of the three people she loved best in the world was getting married to a Crown Prince?

'That's the best man.' Alex gave her a curious glance. 'Tristano, I think Emilia said he was called. Why the interest? He doesn't look like your type, but he is pretty gorgeous.'

'I'm not *interested* interested,' Amber protested, still in a hiss through as rigid a mouth as she could manage, the last thing she wanted was for someone to read her lips and broadcast the conversation across social media. 'I was just surprised. I thought Laurent's cousin was best man.'

'He was called into surgery.' Laurent's cousin was Head of Surgery at the local hospital and dedicated to his job. Rumour said he was openly praying for a royal heir to push him down the succession within the year. 'Tristano was on standby—he and Laurent have known each other for years apparently.'

'How convenient.' *Not.*

Amber bit her lip as she considered her options. Feigning illness would make her even more conspicuous than she already was—and, she had to face it, bridesmaid at a royal wedding televised for a global audience of millions was already a pretty conspicuous position to be in. She had thought long and hard about trying to wiggle out of the job, knowing that if she was ever going to be recognised, a room full of European royals was the time and place. But in the end she had reasoned that there were only a handful of people who had known her back then.

It was just her luck that one of those people was standing unsmilingly next to the groom, clad in a gilt-covered dress uniform that on anyone less austerely handsome would look gaudy.

She'd changed beyond all recognition, she consoled herself. Like her favourite fictional redhead, her hair had darkened from carrot to auburn and she was no longer a thin, gawky teenager. She'd grown, literally and metaphorically, during her first year of freedom, and was several inches taller and two dress sizes curvier than she had been in New York. Last time Tristano had seen her she'd been wearing a kilt and blouse, her hair in plaits, make-up free, and she'd tipped a tray of olives over him. There was no way he'd recognise that awkward teenager in the buffed and polished designer-clad bridesmaid. She was completely safe.

Besides, what was the worst that could happen if Tristano did recognise her? It wasn't as if they had ever actually *been* engaged; he had probably forgotten about that particular debacle years ago, nor could she be compelled to return to the life of a royal. It was just that she loved the anonymity of her life; not even her three close friends and business partners knew of her discarded title or those long lonely years in New York. She'd put life as an exiled royal behind her the day she'd left her grandmother's apartment and had no intention of ever reclaiming it.

The sound of the organ recalled her to her surroundings and Amber lifted her chin and squared her shoulders as the two flower girls began their sedate walk down the aisle, scattering white rose petals as they went. Alex went next, as tall and elegant as ever in the ice-blue and silver dress all three bridesmaids wore, the silk falling in perfect folds to the ancient stone floor. The choir's voices swelled, filling the medieval cathedral as Harriet, with a wink at Amber, followed Alex. Amber quickly looked back at Emilia, ethereal in white lace, her face obscured by her veil, her hand tucked in her father's arm. 'Love you,' Amber mouthed. And then it was her turn.

For the first time she could remember she was grateful for the hours and hours of deportment lessons she'd suffered in her teens as she slowly followed Harriet down the aisle, managing to block out the curious, appraising stares. Amber didn't look to the left or the right as she progressed, not until she finally reached the very front when she couldn't stop her gaze sliding right. Laurent was staring behind her, his face lit up with joy and reverence. Amber swallowed quickly, a lump forming in her throat at the sheer raw emotion the usually re-served Archduke showed so openly, only for her heart to lurch in her chest as she looked past him and met the clear grey-eyed gaze of the Crown Prince of Elsornia. A gaze directed at her, heat flickering in its depths. Had he recognised her after all?

But it wasn't recognition she saw dancing there.

It was desire.

Tris wasn't a huge fan of weddings, and he had never been attracted to redheads, so why couldn't he stop staring at the flame-haired bridesmaid as she pro-cessed with poise and ease down the aisle? Like the two bridesmaids who'd preceded her, she wore blue silk shot through with silver, the blue so faint it was like the reflection of ice, but the colour looked warmer on her creamy skin, set off by a mass of glorious hair set with crystals. She looked like the thaw, warm and welcom-ing and ever so slightly dangerous. Not that there was anything welcoming in her expression as she met his gaze squarely before turning away. But Tris could see the rosy glow spreading over her neck and shoulders and knew that she wasn't quite as impervious to his in-terest as she made out. Intriguing.

Or not. He didn't have the time or freedom to dally with bridesmaids, however enticing they were. What he needed was a wife and an heir within the next five years or he'd forfeit the throne, thanks to the crazy old-fashioned laws that still prevailed in his crazy old-fashioned country. With his reckless cousin next in line after him, failure was not an option.

The music swelled to a crescendo and as it ended Tris turned his mind back to the matter at hand. He didn't have to do much, apart from making a speech suitable for broadcasting; after all, the first rule of royal friendships was that you never spoke about royal friendships. Laurent's secrets, tame as they were, were safe with him.

The Armarian Archbishop stepped forward and the wedding ceremony began, following time-hallowed tradition with its well-worn words, repeated by millions of voices yet made unique with each new utterance. Tris couldn't help but get caught up in the spell-like moment as Laurent and Emilia made their vows, promising each other fidelity and honour, love and respect and he was aware of a momentary but sharp envy. Laurent was marrying for love. How many men or women in their position were so lucky? How many got to choose this one part of their destiny?

Not Tris. He had betrothed himself to a girl he barely knew, not for the famed Belravian fortune but because she had been available, suitable and bred for the role. No wonder she had run away at the very idea. Sometimes he envied her; other times he wondered how she could forsake her duty while he was bound to his. Princes and princesses weren't supposed to follow their hearts—although Laurent was following his right now and he had never looked happier, or more at peace.

The wedding progressed with all due pomp, tempered by the sincerity and love blazing out of the happy couple's faces as they repeated their vows. One lengthy sermon, several solemn choral songs and a demure yet smouldering kiss later, the bells rang out as the couple headed back down the aisle hand in hand, to the claps and cheers of the congregation. Tris courteously gave his arm to Laurent's mother, regal in dark blue and diamonds, but as he escorted her back up the aisle his gaze was drawn to the undulating step of the red-headed bridesmaid, the way the ice-blue silk displayed the curve of her hips, the straight line of her back.

'Her name is Amber,' Laurent's mother informed him drily. 'She works with Emilia, as do the other two bridesmaids.' She paused, eyebrows slightly arched. 'I believe she is currently single.'

'The best man and the bridesmaid?' Tris smiled. 'A bit of a cliché, is it not?'

'A cliché isn't always a bad thing; sometimes it's just that things are meant to be.'

'I didn't have you down as a matchmaker, Your Majesty.'

'I'm not planning on making a habit of it. But you're thirty, Tristano. Thirty and single. Noticing a pretty girl at a wedding is allowed, even for a Crown Prince.'

'But I'm not single. Technically, I am betrothed.'

'Technically is the right word; after all, you're betrothed to a woman you haven't seen for eight years. It's time you gave up on Princess Vasilisa. You deserve a bride who wants to be by your side.'

'We can't all be as lucky as Laurent.' Tristano slowed as they reached the end of the aisle. Photographers awaited them outside the cathedral and he automatically straightened even more, ensuring his expression was cool and bland. 'This situation is of my own making. I shouldn't have agreed to my uncle's suggestion of a betrothal, nor should I have accepted the Belravian Dowager Queen's assurances that she knew where her granddaughter was and that the marriage would go ahead as planned. I wasted too many years thinking Vasilisa was completing her education abroad, and by the time her grandmother confessed the truth the trail was cold. By Elsornian law I am engaged and cannot marry anyone else, and by that same law I must be married with an heir by thirty-five. If my cousin was a different man then it wouldn't matter so very much.'

Laurent's mother nodded. 'And, of course, Nikolai is both married and the father of a son. I do find it ridiculous in this day and age that an Elsornian Crown Prince cannot become King until he is thirty-five and must have fathered an heir to do so.'

'Agreed. The requirement that he must have led troops into battle and sacked a border town have become ceremonial only, thank goodness. I don't see my neighbouring countries taking kindly to a sacking. This law is the last remnant of our medieval customs. I plan to overturn it, and to overturn the primogeniture rule as well. But I can only do it with the agreement of my heir, and Nikolai will never agree.'

'What about Parliament? Can they not help?'

'They are reluctant to take the lead. I have lawyers trying to find a way to encourage them, but so far nothing. But this is not the occasion to discuss my troubles; it's a happy day.'

'It is. And so forget matters of state and missing brides and enjoy yourself, Tristano. Flirt with the pretty redhead, enjoy your youth, for one day at least.'

Tristano escorted the Dowager Queen out of the cathedral, posing momentarily for the horde of photographers thronging the square outside the magnificent Gothic building before handing Laurent's mother into a waiting horse-drawn carriage. She would travel alone in the ceremonial procession through the streets, Tristano was to join the three bridesmaids and two flower girls in a larger carriage. An hour with nothing to do but wave to the excited crowds and make small talk with Emilia's friends. Maybe the Dowager Queen was right, maybe today he should forget his cares and responsibilities and enjoy himself. And if enjoying himself meant exploring this unexpected attraction further then what harm would it do? A little bit of flirting hurt nobody.

Luck was with him as he approached the larger carriage. The tallest bridesmaid, Alex, sat on one side with the flower girls, the other two bridesmaids on the bench opposite, Tris's seat between them. The coach driver shook the reins as Tris sat down and the carriage jolted into movement, taking its place in the procession.

'This is so cool,' the littlest flower girl breathed as the carriage rolled out of the square. People were crowded onto both sides of the street, waving flags and holding pictures of Laurent and Emilia, cheering loudly as the carriages passed slowly.

'Wave back,' Amber encouraged them and, at first shyly but then with increasing confidence, the girls did so.

The noise of the crowds and the echo of the horses' hooves made small talk difficult and the occupants of the carriage were busy responding to the enthusiastic crowd, but Tris was preternaturally aware of every shift Amber made. She sat tall and straight, rigid, her face averted from him as if she didn't want to be seen by him, to engage with him. Tris was aware of a ridiculously oversized sense of disappointment. He didn't know this woman, had no idea of her likes or dislikes, her views, whether she had a sense of humour or not, preferred dogs or cats, savoury or sweet. Her studied indifference to him should be meaningless. And yet he had felt a sense of connection the moment he had first seen her, as if at some deep level he did know her. Clearly that sense was one-sided.

By the end of the hour even the flower girls, Saffron and Scarlett, were exhausted. 'My cheeks ache from smiling and I don't think I can wave any more,' the older one said as the carriage came to a stop. 'And I didn't know carriages were so bumpy!'

'You did really well,' Tris told her and was rewarded with a beaming smile.

The carriages pulled up back outside the cathedral, where cars waited to whisk them away to the palace just a few kilometres outside Armaria's quaint medieval capital city. Here a formal banquet awaited the five hundred wedding guests, to be followed by a much more informal and intimate party for close friends and family only. Tris exited the carriage first, aware that hundreds of cameras were trained directly on him. Now Laurent was married, Tristano was one of the few unmarried European royals left, and the only male in his early thirties. Come Monday he'd be on the front page of every gossip magazine and tabloid, a bull's-eye stamped on his face. Up to now he'd been so busy in Elsornia he'd managed to stay out of the papers, magazines and gossip sites. Being Laurent's best man meant he would be thrust straight into the spotlight, whether he liked it or not.

Ignoring the photographers' call for him to look at them, Tris handed each bridesmaid down in turn, swinging Saffron and Scarlett onto the floor before extending his hand to first Alex, then Harriet and finally Amber. She paused before taking it, her eyes averted before, with a visible breath, she tilted her head, looked him straight in the eyes and took his hand with a cool, firm grip.

Tris was unprepared for the zing that shot up his arm as she touched him, unprepared for the way his breath caught in his throat, his pulse speeded up. As soon as Amber was on steady ground, he let go of her hand. By the flush creeping up her face, he knew she had felt the connection between them too.

But it didn't matter. Laurent's mother could give him all the advice she liked but it changed nothing. He was not free to react to any woman, no matter who she was. He couldn't walk away from who he was, not even for an evening, his duty so ingrained in him that he bled Elsornia.

Tris watched Amber join her friends and head towards the nearest car and made no move to join them. It was safest alone. It always had been. He'd just never *felt* so alone before.

CHAPTER TWO

'HE HASN'T TAKEN his eyes off you all night.' Harriet nudged Amber and not too subtly nodded towards where Tristano sat, his long fingers toying with the stem of his glass in a way which made Amber's stomach clench in spite of herself. She had no idea whether the involuntary reaction was from fear that he somehow had recognised her or because of a desire she barely recognised, one that had ignited the second Tristano had taken her hand to help her from the carriage. Which was ridiculous. It was a light touch, a cursory helping hand, one that had been extended to all of them.

But Harriet was right. Amber had been aware of Tristano's hooded gaze fixed on her all afternoon and into the evening. It was like a caress, dark and dangerous, a wisp of velvet awareness across her bare skin.

'I think he just has a naturally intense, brooding thing going on,' she said with an attempt at a laugh. 'All he needs is a pair of breeches and he would be a dead ringer for Darcy at his most snooty stage.'

'And does that make you Elizabeth Bennet?' Harriet asked with a sly smile and Amber shook her head.

'I have no intention of civilising any man. I want the finished article, thank you.'

'Oh, I don't know, the civilising can be fun.' Harriet looked over at her fiancé, Deangelo, as he leaned against a wall, deep in conversation with Finn, Alex's boyfriend, and Amber groaned.

'I don't want the lurid details, thank you.'

At that moment they were interrupted by a spotlight shining on the dancefloor and an announcement that the bride and groom were about to take to the floor for their first dance. The band struck up a tune, and Laurent led Emilia out onto the floor. She'd changed into a simple long cream dress, her hair loose and Amber thought, with a lump in her throat, that she'd never looked so beautiful. More beautiful or more distant. This was it. Emilia was married, Harriet would be following her down the aisle in the summer and Alex was spending more time at Finn's country estate than she was at the Chelsea home they had all shared until this week. Her life had seemed so settled and perfect, and now it was all changing. Her friends were moving on and she just wasn't ready.

Taking a sip of the tart refreshing champagne, Amber propped her chin on her hand as she watched the pair waltz to a soft romantic tune, no showy choreography or carefully rehearsed moves, just two people holding each other, lost in each other. Slowly her wistfulness faded, replaced with happiness for her friend and she applauded enthusiastically as the dance ended and the band struck up a much jauntier tune. Other couples began to spill onto the dancefloor and Deangelo stalked over and extended a hand to Harriet, enfolding her in his arms as he led her onto the dancefloor, while Finn whirled Alex out to join them. Taking another sip of her champagne, Amber tried not to look like she minded being the bridesmaid wallflower.

'Would you like to dance?'

Amber jumped at the sound of the deep, faintly accented tones. She knew what—who—she'd see before she looked up. She took another gulp of the champagne before turning her head. Tristano stood beside her, one hand outstretched in invitation—or command.

'You don't have to ask me, you know. It's not a real rule that the best man has to dance with the bridesmaid.'

'I'm not asking you because it's my duty. I'm asking you because you are the most beautiful woman in the room and I really, really want to dance with you.'

'Oh...' Amber swallowed 'I...' She should say no. It was too dangerous to spend any time with Tristano. Besides, she had no interest in dancing with the Crown Prince of Elsornia. Even if she wasn't afraid of being recognised, she didn't actually *like* him. Sometimes she still heard his voice in her nightmares, sentencing her to a marriage she hadn't consented to, a life in a castle she didn't want to live in.

Only tonight he didn't look pompous or arrogant. He'd changed out of his glossy dress uniform into a perfectly cut dark grey suit, stubble coating his cheeks, his hair no longer neatly combed back but falling over his eyes. But it wasn't his slightly more relaxed appearance that made her pause; it was the heat in his eyes. Want. Desire. For her. Just as she had once dreamed.

'No one has ever called me beautiful before,' she

said a little shyly as she took his hand and allowed him to pull her out of her chair.

'I find that hard to believe.'

Amber tilted her chin, reminding herself that she was no longer a schoolgirl, desperate to be noticed. 'It's true. Of course, sometimes I get called hot. Often fit. Nice sometimes. Occasionally gorgeous. But never beautiful.'

Tristano's mouth curled disdainfully. 'Englishmen.'

She laughed. 'I get worse online, but that's always a useful guide—instant block. There're far too many ginger fetishists out there. One comment on my hair and that's a warning light I always heed.'

His hand tightened on hers. 'What on earth are you doing meeting men online?'

'I'm a twenty-something living in London; there's no other way to date.' She tried to sound worldly and nonchalant, not letting on how soul-destroying the apps and websites were. 'I always promised myself I'd kiss a lot of frogs before I met Mr Right. I just underestimated how un-kissable most frogs actually are.'

'Do you believe in Mr Right?' The music slowed as they reached the middle of the dancefloor and Amber tried not to tense as Tris took her into a practised hold. This was just a dance, a polite social custom, nothing more, but she could feel every imprint of his fingers burning through the silk of her dress, the places where his body touched hers igniting with a sweet, low heat.

'I believe in soulmates. My parents found each other despite leading very different lives and they were perfect together. So yes, somewhere out there is the right man for me. I just need to find him.'

Warmth flooded her cheeks as she spoke. The champagne and the candlelit ballroom must have loosened her tongue. 'What about you?' she asked, curiosity getting the better of her. 'Do you believe there's someone out there for you?'

Tristano didn't answer for a long time and when he did he sounded resigned. 'I don't believe in true love, no, although seeing Laurent so happy could make a man change his mind, tonight at least.' There was something meaningful in the way he said the last words and Amber's whole body flamed to match her cheeks, her stomach tumbling with heady excitement. She swallowed, moistening her lips with the tip of her tongue, aware of his gaze fastened on her mouth before he continued. 'But Laurent is lucky. Not every prince can follow his heart. It's easier to accept that if you never try.'

'Never try what?'

'Love. The most a man like me can hope for is mutual liking and respect.'

Mutual liking and respect. That was the fate she had been intended for, and yes, she wanted both of those in any future partner, but as part of a much larger whole, a whole that included love and desire.

'Why?' she asked, emboldened by the almost reverential yet possessive way he held her and the intensity in his eyes. 'Why settle?'

'It's complicated.' He smiled then and Amber's breath caught in her throat. The smile wiped away his rather austere, remote expression, making his good looks more boy next door rather than unobtainable gorgeous. 'I'm sorry, that's even more clichéd than the best man dancing with the bridesmaid, but it's true. To explain it I would need to bore you with one thousand years of Elsornian constitution and laws. To be honest, I'd really like to forget about it all for one evening. To just be me, Tris, lucky enough to be dancing with a beautiful woman at a beautiful occasion. You must think I'm a little mad.' His smile turned rueful and it tugged at Amber's heart.

'Not at all. I know something about expectation and tradition and wanting to just be yourself,' she confessed. For one moment, struck by the relief—and the loneliness—in his dark grey eyes, she thought about going further, thought about telling him who she was, how she maybe understood how he felt more than anyone else in the world, but the sense of self-preservation that had kept her happy and safe for the last eight years kicked in. 'So how about for tonight you forget about it? Be whoever you want to be. Who would you be if you were just Tris and not Crown Prince Tristano?'

'No one has ever asked me that before.' He looked so adorably confused for a moment that she had a crazy impulse to touch his cheek, to trace the sharp line of it round to his solemn, finely cut mouth. 'I'm a qualified lawyer...'

'By choice?'

'Not exactly; it made sense to study law as it helps me do my job. But, to be honest, constitutional and business law can be a little dry.'

'So not a lawyer, something not office based, I guess? Gardener, chef, pirate, actor, survivalist, athlete?'

'They all sound more fun than Privy Council meetings. I like looking at the stars. Maybe I'd be an astronomer?'

'Or an astronaut, living on the space station?'

'I'll imagine I'm there when the Privy Council meetings get too much. How about you? Are you living your dreams?'

Amber couldn't believe how easy it was to talk to Tris; and not just small talk either, but intimate and honest conversation. If only her teen self could hear them confiding in each other, just as she'd dreamed they would, all those years ago. 'In a way. I always wanted to go to university—my dad was an academic and he instilled this huge love of history and learning in me—but, for various reasons, I went straight to work.' Reasons that included not finishing high school, mostly because of the man holding her close and listening to every word as if she was the most interesting person he had ever met.

It was strange to think that in another universe they might be attending this wedding as husband and wife. How would her life have turned out if she had gone along with her grandmother's plans, if the betrothal had been real and followed through? Would they have danced and talked or sat in silence, with nothing to say? It was easy, nestled in his arms, desire thrumming through her in time with the music, to imagine the former, but common sense told her that the latter would have been the more likely outcome. She had been too young, too unformed to marry anyone, even if she had been in love and loved, not harbouring a one-sided crush. A crush that had never quite gone away judging by the butterflies dancing away inside her, and the way her breath caught with every one of his rare, sweet smiles. 'I would still like to take my degree one day.

But I love my job. It's different every day, always a new adventure, new things to learn, new people to meet.'

'You are very lucky,' he said softly, but Amber shook her head.

'I made my own luck,' she told him.

'Then you are beautiful and brave.' Sincerity rang in his voice, smouldered in his eyes and as the music played on and his grip tightened it was too easy for Amber to believe him, for tonight at least.

She had told herself that one dance couldn't hurt, had promised herself that she wouldn't have any more champagne, not when it loosened her tongue and made her forget who she was and who she was with. But somehow one dance turned into two and then two more, and at some point, warm from the exertion, and from Tristano's proximity, she agreed when he suggested that he collect an iced bottle of champagne and two glasses and escort her out onto the terrace. It was a crisp, cold February night, the snow still heavy on the distant mountains, the sea air sharp even on the south Mediterranean coast, and Tristano slid out of his jacket to drape it around her shoulders. Amber smiled her thanks. 'How gallant.'

'Not at all, but if you're too cold we can go in,' he said.

'Oh, no. Not when the stars are so beautiful.' What was she doing spending time in a secluded corner with Tris? Playing with fire, that was absolutely certain, because she hadn't misunderstood the heat in his gaze, the way he touched her, held her, as if they were the only people in the entire castle.

It was like all her teenage daydreams come to life, the way he had finally noticed her, seen her, wanted her... To the lonely teenager still inside her, his attention was more intoxicating than the moonlight and champagne combined. Only the reality was better than her daydreams. This older, more mature Tris had a sense of humour she had never suspected, a humanity that drew her to him.

Tris guided her to a corner of the terrace and set the bottle onto a nearby table, opening it and filling a glass before handing it to her. Amber sipped the tart fizzy liquid more quickly than she intended, suddenly shy at being alone with him, even though she could hear the music playing and the babble of voices in the ballroom just a few steps away. 'I've never seen so many stars all at once,' she said, taking another sip and realising her glass was almost empty. She held it out and, after an enquiring raised brow, Tris refilled it. 'I live in London so obviously with all the pollution the sky is never so clear, the stars are faint, but even in the countryside it never looks like this. It's like the sky is filled with crystals, each more beautiful than the last.'

Tristano was so close to her she could feel his breath. 'There's Orion.' He pointed upwards. 'Can you see his belt, and there's his bow, just there. No telescope needed on a night like tonight.'

'Yes...' She barely breathed the word, the heat of him burning into her, despite his thin shirt in the winter air and the thickness of the jacket she wore. 'I see.'

'And there...' he took her hand and moved it, so it pointed to a different spot '...those are the Pleiades, the Seven Sisters, daughters of Atlas.'

'Atlas? He holds the earth on his shoulders, right? Do you think he looks up at his daughters at night?'

'Probably.' She could feel his smile in the way he shifted, in the tenor of his voice.

'Who else can we see?'

'The twins, Castor and Pollux, just there. Twin sons of Leda and brothers of Helen, the most beautiful woman in the world, or so they said. There are some who say she was a redhead.'

She turned to face him, hand on hip mock indignantly. 'I thought I warned you about redhead comments.'

'Ah, but I didn't realise that I was susceptible until tonight.'

As soon as he said the words, Tris wanted to retract them, but how could he when he was standing so close to Amber he could feel every shift and movement, could smell the rich scent of her perfume, when his vision was transfixed by the rich red of her hair?

'Very smooth,' she said, but she was smiling as she spoke.

'Thank you. Like I said, I'm a little unpractised at this.'

'This?'

'Talking to beautiful women. Flirting.'

'Flirting? Is that what we are doing?'

'I hope so.' Tris wasn't sure what had got into him. He never forgot who he was, what he represented, his responsibilities and ties. Never allowed himself as much as a moment off, because if he did then how could he carry on shouldering the duty and the burden, the traditions and all that came with them? No, better to stay on the path he had been put on before he was even born and never look to the left or right.

Only tonight he had allowed himself to glance to the side. Tris didn't know what had caused his uncharacteristic sidestep. Was it seeing Laurent follow his heart, somehow balancing his own royal commitments with marriage to the woman he chose? Showing Tris how his life and the traditions that bound it were as archaic and pointless as he had always secretly thought they were, though so deep down he had never articulated it to himself.

But right now he actually had a choice, even if it was a temporary one-night deal. He could let the moonlight and the champagne, and the undeniable attraction lead him wherever Amber was willing to go. Or he could keep his life simple and turn back to the straight, unyielding path he trod, pick up his burden and march on, letting the last couple of hours fade away, putting them down to a temporary enchantment.

Did he always have to do the right thing? Wasn't even the Crown Prince allowed a night off? Just once?

For one long second he wavered, and then he was overwhelmed by the moment. By the cold air whistling through his thin shirt, the slender-stemmed glass in his hand, the tart champagne lingering on every taste bud, the tang at the back of his throat, the scent of winter flowers mingling with the rich scent of the woman standing before him. By her hair, long and thick, falling in waves, a deep auburn, set off by the silvery blue of her dress and the cream of her skin. By the softness of her breath and the music in her voice, the tilt of her smile and her long, long lashes, lashes half lowered as she looked up at him.

And then he could think no more. Instinct took over, the man pushing the Prince aside for the first time he could remember as he curled his hand lightly around Amber's waist and tilted her pointed chin up so that he could look her full in the face, looking for agreement, for consent, for desire.

Her mouth curved in invitation, her eyelids fluttered and she took an unmistakable step closer until their bodies were touching.

'What do you think? Have I got it wrong, or are we flirting?' He barely managed the words, the light touch of her body flaming through him.

'I think that I hope so too,' she said and with those soft words he was lost. There was no tentativeness in the kiss, no hesitancy as he pulled her to him and nothing but enthusiasm as Amber kissed him back, one of her hands sliding to fist the material at the small of his back, the other to his nape as she rose to meet him. The kiss went from nought to sixty in record time, the first touch igniting a fire and desire almost completely foreign to Tris, who had kept any previous romances as businesslike and emotion-free as he could without making the encounter an actual business transaction. Feelings were too messy for a man who wasn't free to feel. But tonight he was all feeling, every nerve alight with want, consumed by the feel, by the taste of her.

Some dim part of him was still aware of where they were, that anyone could round the corner and see them, and there was enough of the Prince in him still—and enough of the possessive lover even after such a short time—to rebel at the thought of something so intimate being witnessed. 'Come with me?' he whispered against her mouth. 'Inside.'

She pulled back to look up at him. 'Back to the reception?' He couldn't tell if she was affronted or relieved by the idea.

'If you'd like. Or we could go to the suite I am staying in.'

Something he couldn't identify flickered briefly in her eyes, so swiftly he might have imagined it, before she took his hand.

'I vote for the suite,' she said. 'Let's go.'

CHAPTER THREE

'I KNOW ALEX thinks they're worth pursuing, but seriously, is any account worth this much hassle? Amber, are you even listening to me?'

Amber blinked and tried to concentrate as Harriet paced up and down in front of her desk, but waves of tiredness rolled over her and her head was pounding. Straightening, she stretched, closing her eyes as she did so. What was wrong with her? She'd been feeling exhausted for days. At first she had put it down to the shock of seeing Tris again, but several weeks later she still felt weak, shaky and ridiculously tearful.

'Amber, are you all right?' Harriet looked at her friend with some concern. 'You are awfully pale.'

'I've been feeling a little peaky,' confessed Amber. 'I think I've picked up some kind of virus, and I just can't seem to shake it.'

Harriet perched on the edge of Amber's desk and lightly touched her forehead, her hand cool and soothing. Amber leaned against it gratefully. 'It's been a while now, hasn't it?'

Amber nodded. 'Maybe I should go and see a doctor.'

'That's not a bad idea,' said Harriet. 'How long exactly have you been feeling like this?'

Amber didn't have to think too hard; she knew exactly when she'd begun to feel ill, as soon as the guilt had hit. 'Since the wedding, I think.'

'The wedding?' Harriet raised her eyebrows. 'Since you and the luscious Prince disappeared off for the evening, you mean?'

Amber's cheeks heated. She had said very little to her friends about that night and they hadn't pressed for any details. The unwritten rule of their friendship was that they never ever pried. All four of them had come into this friendship and business partnership with secrets. Over the last year many of those secrets had been excavated, but Amber's were still intact, including her tryst with Tris. Her friends were all so happy, so in love with men who adored them, she had been ashamed to admit she'd been swept off her feet by the best man at a wedding, only to wake up with nothing more than a note, no matter how beautifully composed. She didn't want to be the single cliché in their group.

'Want to talk about it?' Harriet asked, then frowned. 'No, it's not a question; you haven't been yourself for weeks. I am going to make us both a cup of tea and then I am going to listen, just like you have listened to me and to Alex and Emilia when we needed you.'

'I didn't mind,' Amber protested. 'And really, there's nothing *to* discuss.'

Harriet crossed her arms and did her best to look fierce. 'No arguing. Leave that report and come through to the kitchen.'

Amber opened her mouth, then closed it again. Harriet was usually the easy-going one out of the four of them, but once she was set on something there was no swaying her. She pushed back her chair, closed her laptop lid and followed Harriet into the back of the Chelsea townhouse which was both their head office and their home.

Alex had inherited the Georgian terrace house a couple of years before and with her legacy came the opportunity to make the business they had planned a reality. Their skills in PR, events and administration were the perfect combination for an agency offering both temps and consultancy to private and corporate clients and a year after opening their business was booming.

There were times when Amber still couldn't believe this gorgeous space was theirs. They had decided to use most of the ground floor as both office and reception; wooden floorboards shone with a warm golden glow and the original tiled fireplaces had been renovated to shining glory. Two comfortable-looking sofas sat opposite each other at the front of the room, inviting spaces for potential clients or employees to relax in, the receptionist's desk on the wall behind. Their own desks, an eclectic mixture of vintage and modern classic, faced the reception area in two rows, paperwork neatly filed in the shelves built into the alcoves by the back fireplace. Flowers and plants softened the space, a warm floral print on the blinds and curtains, the same theme picked up in the pictures hanging on the walls.

The door at the back led to a narrow kitchen and a sunny conservatory extension they used as a sitting-cum-dining room and they each had a bedroom on the first or second floor, two to a floor, sharing a bathroom. Only Emilia now lived in Armaria, Alex spent most of her time in the country at Finn's and Harriet would move out when she and Deangelo married later in the year. Their time together had been all too brief.

Harriet directed Amber to sit on the sofa while she made tea and peered into a cupboard. 'No biscuits or cakes?' She glanced over at Amber, her forehead crinkled. 'You haven't baked this week?'

'I haven't felt like it.'

'That's it. Something is definitely up. For you not to bake? That's like, well, there's no metaphor serious enough. Amber, what's wrong? Is it to do with the wedding? With the Prince?'

Amber took the cup of tea gratefully, her eyes hot and heavy, chest tight with unexpected pain. 'Oh, Hatty, I messed up.'

Harriet curled up in the opposite corner of the huge sofa and sipped her tea. 'You don't have to tell me, but it might help. Did you and Tristano spend the night together?'

Amber stared down at her cup. 'Yes.'

'And how did you leave it?'

'We didn't. By the time I woke up he was gone.'

'And he hasn't contacted you?'

'No. But I didn't expect him to. You see, he left a note.'

'A *note*?' Harriet's tone made it very clear what she thought of that and Amber rushed to explain.

'No, no, it's fine. It was actually really lovely.' She still had it, in her bedside drawer. It was a beautifully composed note: an apology, a love letter and a farewell, all in one. He thanked her for giving him an evening where he didn't have to pretend to be someone he wasn't. He thanked her for her kindness. He apologised for leaving her with nothing but a note, but explained that he had no choice, that he couldn't offer her any more than the one night and he asked for her understanding. The part where he told her that she was the most beautiful woman he had ever met, that the memory of that night would stay with him for many, many years to come, were harder to read. For, whether she had meant to or not, Amber knew that she had deceived him…

'Hatty, do you know anything about his situation?'

Harriet frowned. 'Laurent's mother did say something. Doesn't he have to marry and have a son by the time he's thirty-five or the throne goes to his cousin? Have you ever heard anything more absurd?'

'Yes. I didn't know about it during the wedding but Laurent's mother mentioned it the next day. Apparently the cousin is a bit of a playboy and would be a disastrous king.'

'So that's why Tris snuck off, leaving you with a note? Because he needs a queen? That's even worse, no wonder you're upset. You would make a wonderful queen!'

'Harriet, I can't think of anything worse. I would hate to be a queen. But no, that's not why. There's more.' She took a deep breath. 'Eight years ago he entered into a formal betrothal with someone, but she ran away and he hasn't seen her since. But apparently the betrothal is binding in his country and he can't marry anyone else, unless she formally breaks it.'

Harriet's eyes widened. 'That's absolutely crazy! His country—Elsornia, isn't it?—sounds positively medieval. So that's why he hasn't been in touch, because he's engaged to a missing woman.'

'That's about it.' Amber could hear the blood roaring in her ears, every part of her aching with worry. How had this happened? She'd had no idea that Tris would consider the betrothal binding, that eight years after she'd left his whole life would have come to a halt because of her actions. It simply hadn't occurred to her when she had left her grandmother's house, that the freedom she had claimed came with a price. A price that Tris had to pay. Was paying.

She had to tell Tristano who she really was, now she knew the impact her actions had had on him. She could still summon up the memory of her righteous anger at his arrogance for betrothing himself to a girl who wasn't even in the same room, let alone consenting, but the bitter dislike that had fuelled that anger had dissolved, replaced with a reluctant admiration, and an even more reluctant liking. Every day she started to write to him to tell him who she was and to tell him that he was free. Every day the letter remained unwritten. Amber knew that as soon as Tris realised who she really was, his desire and admiration for her would be replaced by anger. Her friends loved her, but she was also so alone in this world that to have been seen as someone worthy of desire, to have been wanted was so intoxicating it was hard to let go. But let go she must.

'Harriet…' But she couldn't quite bring herself to say the next words. To admit that she was the missing Princess and for her world to change. She took a deep breath but before she could speak Harriet put her tea down and took Amber's hand.

'Amber,' Harriet said slowly. 'Do you think that maybe there's a reason you've been feeling so ill? I mean, you were careful, weren't you?'

'Careful?'

Harriet flushed, her cheeks staining a deep, dark red. 'Could you possibly be pregnant?'

'Of course not!' Amber's cheeks were on fire. 'That is…technically, I guess, it's possible.'

Most groups of girls in their twenties who were as close as Amber, Emilia, Alex and Harriet probably spoke about their love lives in great detail. But that kind of gossip had never been part of their friendship. Partly because of the unspoken rule not to pry, but mostly because none of them, Amber aside, had really dated before meeting their partners and as a result contraception was not something they often discussed. Especially in the practical rather than the theoretical sense.

'Possible, but really unlikely. I'm not an idiot; we used protection, obviously we did.'

'Protection?' Harriet looked steadily at her friend.

'Yes, protection.' Amber really wanted this conversation to go away now.

'Condoms?'

'Harriet! I can't believe you're asking me this. Yes, condoms. Happy?'

'You do know that those things aren't one hundred per cent, don't you? It's easy for mistakes to be made in the heat of the moment.'

Amber swallowed. 'I know that but I'm pretty sure…' She *was* pretty sure they had been careful. No, she knew they had. But they had also been a little intoxicated. Not just on the champagne, but on the night itself. With each other. And it hadn't been just once…

'Amber…' Harriet put a careful hand on her shoulder. 'Before we book that doctor's appointment, maybe we should take a pregnancy test.'

Amber managed a smile at that supportive *we*. 'I appreciate your help, but I think this is something I will definitely have to do alone.'

But Harriet was shaking her head. 'No, you are never alone. Remember that, whatever that test does or doesn't say, you are not alone.'

Amber squeezed her friend's hand gratefully, fear tumbling around inside her. Were Harriet's suspicions correct? They made perfect sense. The lethargy, the melancholy, the strangeness in her body. She'd put it down to guilt and something less definable. Not heartbreak exactly—how could she be heartbroken about a man she didn't know? More sadness for a life that wasn't hers, for the wish that she could be simply Amber Blakeley, meeting a man she liked, seeing where that liking might take her, without centuries of tradition and expectation and lies lying between them.

But if Harriet was right then Amber knew that she would be alone. Her friends couldn't support her in this. If she was pregnant with Tris's baby, then she couldn't avoid telling him who she was any longer, and not with a letter setting him free but in person. And all her work to build a life free of Belravia and her grandmother's plans would be for nothing.

But she had no choice. Honour demanded it, and she had this much honour left at least.

CHAPTER FOUR

NORMALLY AMBER WOULD be thrilled to visit Paris. The city had been her first stopping point after she had left her grandmother's apartment, when she had spent a couple of months as a chambermaid in the beautiful French capital before interrailing her way around the continent, finally ending up in London. Her initial plans to go to university had been derailed by her lack of funds and formal qualifications, but instead she had used her hotel experience to get a job as first a receptionist and then a concierge in a London hotel before Deangelo had headhunted her.

She had always meant to return to Paris; the city held such warm and happy memories—memories of freedom, of finding out who she was and what she wanted, memories of evening walks and calorie-filled dinners, of not having to watch what she ate, how she walked, what she wore, what she said and who she spoke to. She would always love the city for those precious few weeks of happiness.

But today she was sitting in the waiting room of the kind of discreet, expensive lawyers who served the royal houses of Europe, knowing that in ten minutes' time she would see Tris again. Amber pressed her hands tightly together and allowed herself a moment of weakness, a moment of wishing she had taken up her friends' offers of companionship and support. Finn, Laurent and Deangelo had all been more than willing to appoint themselves her knight in shining armour, but she had turned down both their money and attempts to accompany her here today. This was something she had to do by herself. This was an appointment only the Princess of Belravia could attend.

'Mademoiselle Blakeley?' The perfectly chic receptionist looked up unsmilingly. 'Please go in.'

Stepping through the open door, Amber looked around nervously. The lawyer's office felt more like a sumptuous library than a place of business. The glossy wooden desk was clearly antique, and the shelves were laden with leather-bound books of all types, not just dry texts. Huge windows let the sunlight bounce in, bathing the room with golden light. It reminded her of her grandmother's study, and for a moment she felt like the sullen schoolgirl she had once been, trying to wrestle her outer self into compliance, even as she raged with rebellion inside.

'Please, *mademoiselle*, sit.'

The receptionist gestured towards a brocade-covered chair by the coffee table at the far end of the room and Amber gratefully sank into it, her legs shaking with nerves and memories. This polite, ruthless, moneyed world was no longer hers, not any more. But she needed the best to guide her through the next few minutes, hours and days and, from all she had heard, Monsieur Clément was the best of the best.

'So, Mademoiselle Blakeley,' Monsieur Clément said in perfect if heavily accented English, 'it is good to finally meet you in person.' If he was at all curious about Amber and the case he was presenting on her behalf, he hid it well. She supposed that was what she was paying for. The lawyer had been suggested by Laurent, who had also offered to pay for him, but Amber had her pride; right now it seemed that was all she had.

She managed a smile. 'Will the Prince be much longer?' She hoped she hadn't betrayed her nervousness through the quiver of her voice.

'He should be here on the hour,' Monsieur Clément said reassuringly. 'I thought it best if we met first, to give you the advantage of the home ground.'

'Of course.' She stilled her trembling legs and tilted her chin. She did have an advantage here; she was the only person in the room who knew the full story. All that Tris knew was that his missing fiancée had shown up at last. He was coming here to verify her identity, and to nullify their betrothal.

And then she'd be free. If she didn't tell him, she would be free.

But how could she keep her pregnancy a secret? They had close friends in common—and she didn't doubt that his people would keep a close eye on her for some months to come. Even if telling him the truth wasn't the right thing to do, it was the only thing to do. If she was going to keep the baby...

Despite herself, her hand slipped to her stomach. As if there was really any doubt. How could a girl who had spent her life longing for someone of her own to love not jump at the opportunity of that, no matter what strings—or chains—came along with it?

She looked up at the silent clock on the wall—only five minutes until the hour. Each second lasted an eternity and yet no time at all had passed when she heard the sound of the outer door opening and the rumble of voices in the reception area. For one dizzying moment she wished she had taken up her friends' offers to accompany her, wished she had the moral support she so desperately needed. But she squared her shoulders and sat back in her chair, every single one of her grandmother's lessons echoing through her head. She was, whether she liked it or not, the Princess of Belravia. And she held all the bargaining chips. 'If you'd like to come this way, Your Royal Highness.'

This was it. There was no going back. Amber clutched the sides of her chair, her knuckles white, and waited.

She didn't recognise the first man who stalked into the room. She guessed he was in his late fifties, greying hair slicked back, dark eyes cold and keen. But the moment he greeted the lawyer she knew his voice, a chill shivering through her. This was the unknown man who had been in her grandmother's study eight years ago. The man who had bargained with her grandmother for her virginity, her hand in marriage and her substantial dowry. Her eyes narrowed even as her breath quickened. This man could be no friend of hers; she was as sure of it as she was her own name. What kind of hold or influence did he have over Tris? But the stranger was forgotten as Tris followed him into the office.

Amber had a couple of seconds to notice the shadows under his grey eyes, the faint stubble coating his sharply cut cheeks and the slight disarray of his usually meticulously combed hair. He looked as if he had barely slept for days, if not weeks. She knew the feeling. She pressed her lips together, not knowing what to say, but knowing that whatever she did say would be the wrong thing.

Tris looked around, his gaze alighting on Amber, surprise and confusion warring on his granite-like face. 'Amber?'

'Hi, Tris.' She winced. *Hi?* It was completely the most inane thing she could have said, but she had no other words.

'What are you doing here?'

'I—'

But the lawyer interjected, 'Please, Your Highness and Your Grace, be seated.'

Nothing more was said for several torturous moments as Tris and the strange man her lawyer had addressed as 'Your Grace' sat in chairs opposite Amber. The unsmiling receptionist carried in a tray stacked with cups, a jug of rich-smelling coffee that made Amber's stomach recoil in horror and tiny little dry biscuits. She set the tray on the coffee table before them and busied herself pouring drinks and handing around biscuits as if they were at a tea party. All the time Tris stared at Amber as if he could not quite believe that she was here.

It wasn't until the receptionist had left the room that Monsieur Clément spoke again. 'Your Highness, Your Grace—Her Royal Highness Princess Vasilisa of Belravia has asked me to speak on her behalf.'

But Tris was on his feet interrupting the lawyer. 'I

don't understand,' he said, looking intently at Amber.
'Amber, what are you doing here? Do you know the
Princess? Why didn't you say so at the wedding?'

Amber swallowed. She couldn't hide behind a lawyer, no matter how experienced he was, not when Tris
was looking at her with such confusion. 'Tris, I'm not
Amber... At least I was christened Amber and it's a
name I've always gone by.' She shook her head impa-
tiently. Why was she making such a mess of this? 'But
my grandmother called me a different name, ignored
the name my parents gave me and the surname my father took when he became a British citizen. She could
never accept that he had given up any claim to the long-
gone throne of a country that no longer existed, that
he wanted nothing to do with her dreams of Belravia.'

The confusion in Tris's eyes had disappeared as if it
had never been, replaced with a clear, bright anger that
hurt her to look at it. 'I am really, really sorry,' she said,
aware of how futile the words were. 'I didn't mean for
any of this to happen. I just wanted to be free.'

She just wanted to be free. *Free?* Tris could have
laughed—if he wasn't quite so angry, that was. Angry
with himself for his shock and the stab of hurt that
pierced him as her words sunk in and he realised just
who she was. Angry with her for knowing all this time
and never saying a word, even as he had bared as much
of his soul to her as he had ever bared to any other person. Angry at the whole universe for this quirk of fate,
a joke played squarely on him.

'Free?' he repeated, voice chilly with numbness.
Who did this woman think she was? No matter what

she called herself, no matter who she thought she was, she was a princess born and bred, and with that title came responsibilities not freedom. He had accepted that long ago; it was time she did too. 'So to achieve that freedom you did what? You ran away?' Scorn replaced the numbness, biting through the sunlit air.

Amber had been sitting stock-still, eyes fixed on him, a plea in them he had no intention of heeding, but at his words, his tone, her green eyes flashed. Good. She was angry too; anger he could cope with. Anger he understood. Matched.

'I'm not here to go over what happened that day. All I will say is that I don't accept any betrothal entered into on my behalf without my consent and without my knowledge was, or is, valid.'

During their brief conversation, Tris had been aware of his uncle statue-like beside him, frozen with disbelief. But as Amber finished speaking, her last hurt syllable fading away, his uncle's reserve broke at last and he jumped to his feet. 'Your grandmother had every right...'

Amber held up one slender, pale hand. 'I don't think we've been introduced.' Her voice matched his uncle's in disdain. 'Just as we had not been introduced on the occasion of my eighteenth birthday when you sat discussing my dowry, my future, my body, without *once* considering my wishes.'

Laying a calming hand on his uncle's arm, Tris pressed him back into his seat. 'This is my uncle, the Duke of Eleste. And you're right, Amber. We were wrong that day to enter into negotiations without you. I assumed your grandmother had discussed the proposal with you; I should have ensured that she had before signing anything. But I think we both know I have been punished for that presumption over the last eight years.'

Amber inclined her head, her cheeks still pale, just a spot of colour burning in the centre of them, the warm blush accentuating the cut of her fine bones, the tilt of her chin. 'Thank you.'

'But,' Tris continued; this was not a one-way blame game, no matter what she told herself, 'you were also wrong to just run away. That was the act of a naughty schoolgirl, not a princess.'

Only a faint quiver showed that his words had struck home. 'If you had ever bothered to get to know me…' Her eyes were still fixed on his, as if there was no one else in the room. Her lawyer had stopped remonstrating, his uncle silenced by Tris's gesture. 'If you had ever tried, then you would have known that I was still very much a schoolgirl at heart, even if my grandmother didn't present me as anything but the Princess-in-waiting. If you had bothered to get to know me then you would have known that my hopes and dreams didn't lie in the direction of a throne and a handsome prince.' Her voice was scathing now. 'All I wanted, just like my father before me, was a normal life. That's all I still want. What I have worked for every second since I left.'

'It's been two months.' Tris didn't have the capacity to properly consider her bitter words right now. There was too much truth in them for any quick resolution. He knew that back then uncertainty and the need to find his place in a world where his destiny was so set had made him come across as arrogant. No, not just come across as arrogant; he *had* been arrogant. Arrogant, single-minded and resolute. The last few years, with his destiny suddenly so uncertain, had chipped away at the arrogance, if not the reserve. The only time he had really lost his reserve had been at Laurent's wedding. How unspeakably ironic that it was with this woman. 'Two months since you and I spent time together. I told you I wasn't free; I thought you were aware why. I will absolve you of any deliberate malice towards me before that date. But I'm struggling to understand why, knowing what you know, it's taken you two months to come forward.'

'I was going to write. That's why I engaged a lawyer. I was hoping that you would never have to know who I really was.' Amber's gaze finally broke from his and she looked over at the window, her eyes focusing on the street outside. 'When we… I knew who you were. Of course I did. And I admit I was intrigued. How could I not be? With so much history linking us. But that's what I thought it was, I swear to you. History. I have never once considered myself engaged to you, Tris. And it didn't once occur to me that a betrothal entered into eight years ago, without my consent, thousands of miles away, was still considered valid. I didn't know the entire truth until the next day, when Laurent's mother told me everything.'

Tris briefly closed his eyes. What a mess and, unlike Amber, he knew it was a mess all of his own making.

'I take it—' the Duke finally spoke '—that you are here to revoke the betrothal agreement. That you have decided to do so in person.' Tris could see the machinations behind the smooth expressionless face. His uncle knew as well as he did that they had five years.

Five years for Tris to find a wife and father a son. No doubt his uncle had already prepared a list of suitable candidates who would be ready to wed him within the month. He should be relieved. *Was* relieved. His life could move forward at last. He wasn't going to dwell on why he suddenly felt so bereft.

For the first time, Amber faltered. Tris watched her throat move as she swallowed, reaching blindly out for the water in front of her, her gaze still fastened on the window, maybe dreaming once more of escape. 'Tris, I need to speak to you alone.'

'I don't think that's a good idea...'

'Tris, leave the details to me.'

His uncle and the lawyer spoke in unison. But their words were just background noise; all Tris was aware of was Amber. She sat fully erect, her hands folded in front of her, mouth set firm. She was every inch the Princess she was so desperate not to be.

'So be it.' He turned to his uncle. 'Thank you for accompanying me here today, but I need to do this by myself. Actually, Amber and I need to do this by ourselves. If this betrothal had started that way, maybe we wouldn't be ending it here today.'

After a quick, sharp glance at him, his uncle nodded, standing up and moving towards the door. 'I will wait for you outside.'

Amber nodded at her lawyer who, with a slightly anguished backward glance at his client, followed the Duke out of the office. The door closed firmly behind them.

Finally, they were alone. The silence echoed around them until Tris could hear every beat of his pulse, the thunder of his heartbeat as he waited for Amber to say the words severing the link between them. But after one quick glance in his direction she stayed still and silent.

Despite everything, Tris was conscious of an urge to hold her, to take her tightly folded hands in his, to touch her expressionless face and coax a smile from her bloodless lips. He still couldn't believe it, couldn't reconcile the laughing, flirtatious, fiery bridesmaid with this marble statue.

Nor could he believe he hadn't recognised her at the wedding. True, he hadn't seen her for many years, but her photograph had been on his desk for all that time—an attempt to familiarise himself with the woman who was supposed to have been sharing his life. Not that the gawky teen in the photo bore any resemblance to the woman who sat before him.

'We are alone,' he said, absurdly aware of how redundant the phrase was. 'Whatever you need to say to me, say it. We both know why we're here. Set yourself free.'

In one fluid movement Amber stood, turning to face him, her face so pale she was almost translucent. 'It's true that once I realised that you still considered yourself betrothed to me, once I realised what that meant for you, I planned to end the betrothal.'

'Planned?' Tris tried to dampen down the unwanted hope rising inside him.

'I don't want to be a princess or queen or live anywhere but London. But we don't always get what we want, do we, Tris?'

Nothing she was saying made any sense. This was the woman who had run away with barely anything but the clothes she stood in, in order not to marry him. But, of course, this was also the woman who had shared one of the most passionate nights—if he was being honest, *the* most passionate night—of his life with him.

'No, we don't. But Amber, you always had a choice. Nobody was ever going to drag you to the altar. You could have said no at any time.'

She flushed. 'I appreciate that now but, as I said before, I was very young. My grandmother is very formidable when she wants something. All she ever wanted was to see me on a throne, any throne. Saying no sounds so much easier than actually doing it.'

'Your grandmother is not here now. Say no, Amber. End it.'

'It's not that easy, Tris. You see, I'm pregnant.'

CHAPTER FIVE

AMBER SANK INTO the nearest chair, relieved that she was finally alone, and began to take in her surroundings. She'd spent her teens living in lavish if uncomfortable opulence, but she'd never seen anything like this before. Whoever had designed the suite she'd been allotted in the royal castle of Elsornia had taken luxury and mixed it with style and comfort to create something truly stunning. From the antique four-poster bed, hung with silk, to the brocade-covered walls, her allotted bedroom was perfect.

Almost perfect.

Oh, sure, it had a huge bathroom, too big to be a mere en suite, and the kind of walk-in wardrobe guaranteed to induce envy in all her friends, stairs leading down to an equally beautiful sitting room and study. Windows looked out onto views of rolling hills and green fields with snow-capped mountains rising beyond and the whole suite was tastefully and newly decorated in delicate silvery grey, blue and aqua, priceless antiques juxtaposed with expensive, handmade designer modern furniture. If she was to design an apartment for herself, money no object, then she would probably have designed something very similar to the rooms she now surveyed. But not here. Not in Elsornia, not in a castle and definitely not in rooms located in a tower.

No doubt Tris—or more likely his housekeeper—had thought it was every girl's dream to have a fairy-tale suite of rooms set on two floors in the turret of a medieval castle. But, having spent six long years staring out of the tower windows at Central Park at a world she was not allowed to be part of, Amber knew there was nothing lonelier than a tower.

'That's it!' Amber jumped up and headed to the curved staircase in the corner of her bedroom, which she had been told led up to the large terrace topping the turret. Sure enough, she emerged out onto a spectacular circular paved terrace. A glass roof covered half of the space, chairs and a sofa arranged enticingly beneath, a cosy blanket draped on the back of the sofa. She stepped out onto the exposed stone floor and inhaled the bracing spring air, the breeze refreshing on her skin.

Another deep breath of the clean air helped clear her head and she winced at the thought of how close she had come to a good bout of self-pitying tears. 'No more feeling sorry for yourself, Amber Blakeley. You are no longer a child and you're not a prisoner. You can sulk and feel sorry for yourself and spend the next few weeks feeling unhappy and resentful or you can make the best of it. After all, Tris is right. Like it or not, you were raised to cope with all this. You had eight years of freedom; now it's time to grow up.'

She wandered over to the carved stone balustrade and leaned on it, looking out over the formal palace gardens to the countryside beyond. Shivering, Amber pulled her cashmere cardigan closer around her, eyes blurring with cold as she stared out at the mountains with their promise of escape. It was insane how quickly her life had changed. Less than a week had passed since the meeting in the lawyer's office in France and, instead of interviewing new nannies for the agency as her work calendar said she should be doing, she had flown on a private jet to spend a month in a country she had sworn never to set foot in. Her friends and their partners now all knew her identity and the circumstances that had led to her leaving New York, and they all knew of her pregnancy and what that might mean for Tris and his country.

But throughout the revelations and the confessions and the arrangements she had clung onto one resolution: she wasn't here to rush into a marriage; she was here for a trial before making a decision that would irrevocably bind her life to Tris's and all that came with him. Her hand slipped down to splay over her still flat stomach. Who was she kidding? Their lives were already irrevocably bound. But that didn't have to mean marriage, didn't have to mean spending her life here. There were just too many unknowns.

At least she had ensured the betrothal agreement was nullified *before* she set foot on Elsornian soil. Any future agreement between her and Tris would be their decision to make and theirs only. She had also received a promise that her stay would be both low-key and anonymous; if she didn't marry Tris then there was no reason for anyone outside their immediate circles to know who she was.

One priority was finding out what he wanted to do

if the baby was a girl. Would he expect her to provide him with a son within the next five years? Her hands tightened on the balustrade. One child, a baby already on the way, was one thing, but planning a second...? Giving him a son would mean a full marriage in every way. And what if the hypothetical second child wasn't a boy either? She might need to give him a third, or even a fourth...

Giggling a little hysterically, she tried to ignore the heat stealing through her body at the thought. '*Making* the babies isn't the issue, is it?' she asked herself aloud, her words falling into the stillness. 'After all, if you weren't attracted to Tris then you wouldn't be in this situation, would you? Although there's a world of difference between having one baby and signing up to be a baby-making machine.'

She giggled again at the image, her smile quickly fading as the reality of what marriage to Tris would mean sank in. Attraction wasn't the problem. She'd felt its exquisite ache in Paris, despite her embarrassment and the awkwardness of the situation. But from the moment Tris had learned her identity he had been all urbane, polished politeness. Gone was the darkly desirable best man who had turned her head and in his place was the perfect Prince. But perfect princes were not the happy-ever-after she had dreamt of.

A chime rang out through the terrace, breaking into her thoughts and, turning, Amber saw a light on an intercom by the terrace door. Amber walked over, hands shaking as she pressed the button. Was it Tris? She wasn't ready for a tête-à-tête. Not yet.

'Hello?' To her relief her voice sounded steady, show-ing a confidence she certainly didn't feel.

'Hi, Amber. It's Elisabetta—Tristano's sister. Is now a good time? Tell me if not. I promise not to be of-fended!' Amber sagged against the wall, thankful that not only was her unexpected guest not Tris but by the friendliness in Elisabetta's voice.

'Now is fine. Hold on while I figure out how to buzz you in.' She pressed a green button and heard the un-mistakable sound of a door unlocking and, after giving Elisabetta a good few seconds to push the door open, released the button and made her way back down the curving stairs to meet the Elsornian Princess in the sit-ting room two floors below.

Tris's sister was standing by the window when Amber arrived, but she rushed over to greet Amber with a continental double kiss followed by a hug. An exceptionally pretty girl of around Amber's own age, the Princess had Tris's colouring, her dark hair worn long and loose, grey eyes sparking with a life and mis-chief her brother rarely displayed as far as Amber could see. Chicly and expensively dressed in a short woollen dress teamed with knee-length leather boots and a scarf knotted with elegant nonchalance, Elisabetta's smile was warm and seemed genuinely friendly and Amber returned it; it was so good to see a friendly face.

'Here you are at last! I've been dying to meet you for ever, although I quite understand why you went MIA. I am fully aware how high-handed Tris and our esteemed uncle were. Betrothal agreements indeed, the idiots. But I am very happy that you have decided to give Tris a second chance—he's not so stuffy when you get to know him. But I guess you know that, or you wouldn't be here.'

Amber had no idea how to respond. She didn't know how much Tris had told his sister about her visit here, if anyone apart from the two of them—and her friends— knew about their pregnancy.

'Hi.' It seemed an inadequate response to the voluble, friendly greeting she had received, but Elisabetta didn't seem to notice.

'So, Tris has asked me to give you a hand until you know your way around a bit more. You have your own assistant, of course—you've met Maria? Good. Maria is fantastic and will be able to help you with anything you need. She grew up here; there's nothing she doesn't know. If you need anything at any time, just ring the bell here.' Elisabetta indicated a rope pull hanging in the corner.

Amber couldn't help raising her eyebrows at the sight. 'An actual bell?'

'Oh, yes, the walls are so thick that even though Tris has tried to modernise the whole castle, it's easier to stick with the old ways. The Wi-Fi is always cutting out unless you are on the ground floor or up on the roof.'

'Maria showed me to my room; she seems very nice and her English is flawless.'

'Her mother is English and she went to London for a couple of years after school so she is pretty much a native speaker. Her grandmother was a lady-in-waiting to *my* grandmother, but in those days the poor girls were expected to be in traditional dress with hair neatly plaited at all times of the day and night. At least there's a night staff nowadays. Some of Tris's reforms are more successful than the Wi-Fi has been.'

Maria's appointment as her assistant might be a coincidence, but Amber couldn't help wondering if Tris had purposely picked a fluent English speaker to help her settle in. 'I hear that Elsornian is a mixture of French, Italian and a sprinkling of German; is that correct?'

Elisabetta nodded. 'You could say that, but it's a little bit more complicated. We have many words unknown in any other dialect or language. But don't worry, most people speak English and really appreciate anyone trying just a few words of Elsornian.'

'Hopefully, I'll pick some up. Luckily, I speak tourist-level French, Italian and German...' actually diplomatic-level, thanks to her grandmother '...and I've picked up a little Armarian over the last year, but I'm no natural linguist. Every word has been learned by repetition and more repetition.'

'Any help you need, just ask either me or Maria,' Elisabetta said. 'And when my sisters are home, I know they'll say the same. The palace can seem a little stuffy, so you'll need as many guides as possible to explain the crazy etiquette, who everyone is and, more importantly, all the secret ways we pretend don't exist. Our ancestors were robber barons, you know, so this place is a smugglers' paradise, even if the contraband is only teenagers breaking curfew nowadays!'

'Thank you.' Amber meant it wholeheartedly; it had been hard enough to wrench herself away from the life she had built for herself, but to leave her friends behind, not knowing if she would return, to consider a move to a new country had been almost more than she could bear. Elisabetta's frank, open friendliness was a balm to her soul. 'In that case, there is something you could help me with. I really want to explore the gardens, but I'm not ready to face anyone yet.' Amber was uncomfortably aware that by anyone she meant Tris. 'Do you think you could introduce me to one of those secret ways you just mentioned?'

Elisabetta's eyes lit up with glee. 'I knew I'd like you! Come on, you won't need a ball of wool when you're with me, but don't try this alone until you're a lot more confident—they say there are miles of hidden tunnels beneath the castle and it's easy to take a wrong turn, believe me. Which way do you want to go first? Wine cellars or stables? You choose. And as we walk you can tell me all about what you've been up to and how Tris persuaded you to give him a try. I promised my sisters I would ferret out all the details and I always keep my word!'

CHAPTER SIX

Tris exited the courtyard and took a moment to enjoy the late afternoon spring sunshine warming his face. He loved this time of year, when the spring flowers began to bloom in earnest and, despite the April rain and the chill that still came with the night, lighter nights and warmer days banished winter. But his moment of enjoyment was fleeting. He had given Amber several hours to settle in before offering to show her around the castle. However, when he had rapped on her door there had been no answer. A few questions had elicited the information that his sister had gone to introduce herself to his fiancée. Which meant the two women could be anywhere, inside or outside the castle.

Elisabetta knew the castle as well as he did, including every secret way out into the gardens and into the land beyond. After all, they had explored the secret passages and grounds together, along with his other sisters, their cousin Nikolai and the other palace children, before his mother and his sisters had left the castle and Tris had had to start growing up. He had never allowed himself to envy his siblings and other companions for the years of childhood they'd still enjoyed whilst he was learning about tradition, etiquette and what being King really entailed. Never allowed himself to mourn the distance that had naturally grown up between them. His father had told him that a king was always alone. It hadn't taken Tris very long to realise how true those words were. The only time he hadn't felt alone in the twenty years since his mother and sisters had left was the night he'd spent with Amber.

But that night had been a lie. Which meant that while he planned for them to marry within the next few months, live together to raise their child and do their best for the country he had been born to rule, he would still be alone, no matter that his pulse speeded up at the very sight of her, that he wanted to wipe away the forlorn look on her face and promise her that everything would be okay.

It wasn't a promise he was qualified to make; all he could do was his best. Do his best not to make Amber as lonely and unhappy as his mother had been, his best to let their child be a child and not a mini monarch in waiting.

His child. Tris stopped. What kind of father would he be? He had no concept of what a good father looked like. He set his jaw and sent out a silent promise to his unborn child; he didn't know how to let go, how to have fun, how to be anyone but the decisive and responsible King, but his child would be more. Would have a childhood full of love and laughter and fun.

The castle gardens were vast, a perfectly designed jigsaw of formal gardens, careful wildernesses, follies, lakes, mazes and woodlands. A man could wander in them for hours and not find the person he was looking for but there was one place everyone visited: the famed fountains that cascaded down the terrace leading to the lake. It was one of the most famous sites in Elsornia, pictured in a thousand books and millions of social media posts. Sure enough, as he reached the first terrace and looked down towards the lake, Amber was sitting on a bench below, the sun glinting off her red hair.

She looked up as if sensing his presence, gazing directly at him, her expression distant, as if she were only half there. Slowly but purposefully, Tris made his way down the stone steps bordering the fountains to join her.

'So, this is where you slipped off to.'

'I know it's a really obvious place to come,' she said, her welcoming smile mechanical rather than genuine. 'But I've seen this view so many times in pictures and paintings, I simply had to see it myself. It's breathtaking.'

'Which way did Betta bring you?' Tris asked. 'Through the wine cellars, or the tunnels that run behind the stables?'

Amber's smile widened, this time reaching her eyes, and Tris couldn't help responding in kind. 'So you know about those?'

'I know all the tunnels,' he said. 'I spent most of my childhood exploring them.'

Her smile dimmed. 'It's hard to imagine you as a small boy, exploring and getting dirty. I'm glad to know you did though, I'm glad to know it's possible. My grandmother always made it sound as if growing up in a place like this was all responsibility and no fun. I don't want that for my child, no matter what the future holds for him or her.'

'Nor do I, Amber.' Tris shifted round to look her

straight in the eyes, tilting her chin until her green-eyed gaze met his. 'I promise you, I promise the baby, that his or her childhood will be as full of play, magic and mayhem as any child could wish for.'

'Thank you.' Amber reached up and touched his cheek, the light caress burning through him; he could feel her touch long after her hand fell away. 'Your sister was called away, but I wanted to explore a little more. Would you like to join me?'

'Of course.' Tris stood up and extended a hand to Amber and, after a second's hesitation, she took it and allowed him to help her to her feet. 'Where would you like to go?'

'I don't mind. No, actually, I do have a request. I would like you to take me to somewhere that means something to you. Would that be possible?'

'Somewhere that means something?' Had he heard her correctly? He'd been expecting her to suggest the ornamental lake, the maze or the woodland path, or any of the other places on the tourist map.

'Yes.' She took a step away and looked back at him. 'This is where you were born, where you were brought up; I would really like to see somewhere special to you. Would that be okay?'

Tris didn't answer for a long moment. Somewhere special? The request implied an attempt at intimacy, that Amber was trying to get to know him better. Tris didn't even know where to start. His life wasn't about individual special moments or places; it was about duty.

Only, maybe there was one place...

'Are you warm enough? It's about a twenty-minute walk.'

Amber nodded and they set off. Neither spoke for the next few minutes as Tris led them down the stone steps until they reached the large pond at the bottom of the fountains. Amber turned to look at the water cascading down, a riot of froth and foam and sparkling drops, and Tris watched her, enjoying her evident awe at the famous sight, giving her plenty of time to enjoy the spectacle before resuming their walk. A small stream snaked away from the pond carrying the water towards the lake and Tris followed it, Amber by his side.

'How did you find my sister and Maria?' Tris asked at last as the silence threatened to become oppressive.

'They're both really lovely,' Amber said. 'Thank you so much for suggesting that Maria help me; it was really thoughtful to assign me someone who is both Elsornian and English. And your sister has been very kind. I think I'm going to like her a lot.'

'Betta is one of a kind; her heart is very much in the right place. Just don't believe everything she tells you; she is an incorrigible chatterbox. And I'm glad you like Maria. I hope she'll convince you that Elsornia isn't too bad a place to live.'

Tris knew a little about the life Amber had led after leaving New York, the months travelling through Europe before settling in London and painstakingly building her life there. The busy, noisy city had no parallels in his small mountainous country. If it was urban culture and living she craved, she was going to find it hard living here. His mother had struggled, had never really adjusted. He didn't want his own wife to resent his country the way his mother had.

'Oh, I'm sure she will. Even from the very little I've

seen it's clear Elsornia is extraordinarily beautiful. I love London, but I love the countryside too. But Tris, there's something I really need to make clear to you.' She paused, clearly uncomfortable.

Foreboding stole over him. Whatever Amber wanted to say, he had a feeling she didn't think he was going to like it. 'What's that?' He did his best to sound reassuring. 'It's okay, Amber. I really want you to feel that you can speak to me, however difficult it might seem. If we're going to be married we have to be able to communicate.'

'But that's it. I realised after I agreed to come here that you thought that meant I was also agreeing to marry you. But I'm not, at least not yet.'

A curious numbness crept over Tris. Of course it couldn't be this easy. Of course the girl who had looked at him with desire and light and laughter didn't want him when all the baggage that came with him was included. Of course the answer to the dilemmas he had been wrestling with for the last eight years couldn't finally be within his grasp.

'I don't understand,' he said as evenly as possible. 'In Paris, when you told me you were pregnant, you also said you knew this meant you couldn't end the betrothal. I know you are here for a month so we can get to know each other better, but I thought we would announce our engagement at the end of that month.'

'Tris, I *am* here to get to know you better—and I'm here so you can get to know me. And I am absolutely considering marriage—now I understand your situation, I know that's your preference. But Tris, if you didn't have to marry, would it even be an option for you? Honestly? Marrying someone you've met just a handful of times? Having a baby together doesn't mean we have to spend our lives together, not any more. We can easily co-parent, raise this child together; we don't have to be married to do it well. We don't have to be in a relationship at all.'

Amber's words hung in the air. Would marriage to her be his choice without the ticking clock hanging over him? He pushed the thought away—what was the point in hypotheticals?

'How exactly do you see this civilised co-parenting working? You back in London, me here, unless you're planning to settle in Elsornia?'

She shook her head. 'I don't know.'

'I thought not. So are you planning on granting me the odd weekend and a few weeks in the summer? Is that the plan?' Tris struggled to keep his voice conversational, to hide the biting anger chilling through him.

But, judging by the wary look Amber threw him, he wasn't succeeding. 'There is no plan...how can there be? This is all so new and so unexpected. There's no manual, no guidebook.'

'But there is a law and there is a deadline and I've wasted enough time, thanks to you...'

'That agreement had nothing to do with me.' Her green eyes flashed and his own blood stirred in response to her passion. 'I did you the courtesy of nullifying it, but my lawyer agreed the only court it would ever stand up in was here in Elsornia—and even then there were no guarantees.'

'Maybe. But the fact remains you are carrying my child.'

'And you think that means I have to marry you? Like some medieval maiden, compromised and helpless?'

'Amber, you came to my bed willingly. You came to my bed willingly and in full knowledge of who I was and what our relationship was. Knowledge you didn't share with me. If anyone was compromised by the events of that night, it was me.'

'You? You've got exactly what you wanted. An heir on the way and if I marry you a substantial dowry, along with the Princess your family chose for you. It's all worked out for you, hasn't it?'

Tris bit back an angry retort. He knew how she felt, the lack of control, the realisation that life would never be the same—it was the feeling that had forced her to flee eight years ago. He couldn't let her leave again, but he had to allow her to feel she had a say. More, he had to actually give her a say—and ensure, however difficult, that her answer was the one he needed.

'What exactly are you proposing?'

Amber turned to him, eyes bright with hope. 'I'm proposing that you convince me that Elsornia is right for me and, more importantly, right for this child. If we don't marry, he or she can still grow up with two loving parents, can grow up wanted and cherished and happy, free from all the obligations that you and I know come with a royal title. That's all my father wanted for me; of course I want the same for my child. But it's your baby too. So I need you to show me that if I marry you Elsornia is worth all the sacrifices we both know this baby will make. That it's worth the sacrifices I'll make. That I can be happy here and with you. Are you willing to show me that, Tris?'

Tris had been so intent on the conversation that he hadn't noticed how far they had walked and, with a jolt of surprise, realised they had entered the woods and were close to their destination: the large hollow tree where he had played countless games pretending to be one of the fearless folk heroes he had idolised as a child stood right next to them. And as he put a hand onto the rough bark, realisation hit him hard. He wanted his child to play in this tree, in these woods, to grow up with Elsornia in his or her veins and blood, just as it was in his. All he had to do was convince Amber that it was the right place for her, the right place for their child. Convince her to marry him. How hard could it be?

'How long do I have?'

'I agreed to a month and I'll keep my word,' Amber said. 'At the end of the month I'll be fourteen weeks along, and I'll have had the first scan so hopefully we'll know the baby is healthy. You have until then. Show me your Elsornia, show me why you love it and if you can convince me then we'll talk next steps. I know how important marriage is to you, and why. But you have to understand that I always wanted a very different kind of marriage, a very different life. I am willing to put that aside if you convince me that staying here and marrying you is the right thing for me, for the baby and for you. Fair?'

Was it fair? Tris had less than five years to marry and father an heir. The solution to all his problems was tantalisingly in reach and yet frustratingly far away. But he couldn't deny that Amber had a point. She had to come to this marriage willingly. And if he couldn't convince her, what kind of king was he anyway?

He extended a hand and she took it cautiously. 'Okay. You have a deal.'

He wasn't usually a gambling man, certainly not with stakes this high, but he had no choice. He had to win.

CHAPTER SEVEN

'You're a real natural with children,' Tris said. He sat beside Amber in the car as tall, straight-backed and formal as ever, expression neutral and eyes unreadable. But he was trying; she had to give him credit for that. True to his word, Tris was showing her Elsornia. Over the last week Amber had accompanied Tris and Elisabetta on a tour of a chocolate factory and stood unobtrusively in the background on visits to a hospital and schools. They'd taken her to a production at the Theatre Royale, an impressive baroque building in the capital city, and to several fancy restaurants as well as a trip to a glacier.

But she still hadn't seen beneath the tourist-friendly sites and gloss. She hadn't visited small neighbourhood restaurants or strolled along cobbled streets or shopped in little local stores. The only people she spoke to for more than five minutes were Tris, Maria and Elisabetta, who weren't exactly representative of the normal population. She had yet to use public transport, to order her own drink, to ask directions or sit with a coffee and watch the world go by. How could she decide if this was a place where she could live when she was sheltered from the real world?

It had been an entertaining week, but it felt more as if she was on a whirlwind tour—*The Highlights of Elsornia*—rather than beginning to know and understand Tris more. At no point in the last week had she seen any sign of the man who had made her head spin, for whom she had thrown caution to the wind. They were rarely alone, barely even made eye contact and never touched. She'd asked for time and space and she'd got it, but instead of it helping her resolve her feelings she just felt more and more confused with every busy and courteous day.

'I'm really fond of children; I've worked with a lot, especially since working for Deangelo and starting the agency.' Amber looked out of the window at the gorgeous mountain scenery, so different to the Chelsea streets she usually trod, and her chest ached with homesickness—for the city, for her friends, for her work. For the life she had worked so hard for.

She made herself carry on, cringing at the artificial brightness in her voice. 'It's strange to think that we've only really been open for a year. Things have changed so much, not just our personal lives, but for the agency too. When we started I was busy with small concierge jobs, sourcing babysitters, doing a bit of nannying and arranging domestic chores. Alex was pleased to be doing the PR for a couple of local restaurants and Emilia's first event was the opening of the café down the road. Opening a new agency was tough without contacts and a reputation. That's why Harriet went back to work for Deangelo for what was supposed to be a short contract.' She smiled a little wistfully. 'Looking back, I think we all knew that she was in love with him but hadn't admitted it to ourselves. They're so perfect for each other.'

Amber stopped, painfully aware that yet again she was babbling to fill a silence Tris seemed far more comfortable with than she was. At least talking about her friends was a small step up from this morning's small talk attempt, which had incorporated everything from the cuteness of the local Alpine cattle to the excellence of the palace food to that old staple, the weather. It was a lot easier on the days when Elisabetta accompanied them—or when Tris had to work and the two girls went out alone.

They'd decided to tell people that Amber was a friend of Elisabetta, which meant that she would attract minimal attention, although her presence at Laurent and Emilia's wedding alongside Tris had started some low-level speculation. Luckily, any rumours were still confined to Elsornia and hadn't yet reached the royal-gossip-hungry European magazines. Amber hoped it would stay that way; if she and Tris decided against marriage she didn't want anyone to know who she was or guess at the parentage of her child. Tris's involvement meant secrecy wouldn't be easy but, luckily, she was an old hand at staying under the radar.

Another silence fell and Amber resumed her study of the landscape, searching for a new topic of conversation, one that actually would help her understand Tris better. 'The nursery school was so cute; I loved the song they did. Do you spend a lot of time on visits like this?' Amber hadn't imagined him being quite so visible day to day. Her grandmother's preparation for Amber's future royal life, hopefully on the miraculously restored

Belravian throne, had concentrated more on entertaining diplomats and neighbouring royals and less on visiting schools.

'Not a lot, no.' Tris looked regretful. 'Which is a shame because I actually quite enjoy them now. When I was younger I found it a chore to have to try and connect with every single person I met, to shake all those hands and keep smiling so people didn't think I was standoffish. To find things to say that didn't seem stuffy or dull.'

Amber blinked in astonishment. This was probably the most insightful thing Tris had said to her since she had arrived in Elsornia. 'My grandmother insisted I learn how to make small talk; she said it was one of the most invaluable tools in a royal's arsenal. Although, as she spent most of her time interrogating people rather than talking to them, I'm not sure how she knew.'

'My father was more of an interrogator too, which is probably why I found small talk so excruciating. But now my time is so taken up with diplomatic business, politics and negotiation that a day out actually talking to people is a relief. Sometimes visits and openings seem like an indulgence, especially with three sisters who are so popular with the people and who all find it a lot easier than I do, but it's really important that I remember why I do what I do. When I'm in a school, a hospital or retirement home or at a village fair, I can see exactly why it's so important that we have the right deals in place, why I have to spend hours in meetings that seem to have no point. I don't do it for me but for the children who need a solid economy to pay for their schools.'

'I'd never thought about it like that,' Amber confessed. 'My grandmother never really made me see the point of being a princess; it felt like unnecessary rules and restrictions, etiquette for etiquette's sake.'

'There's an element of that, and for a long time I would have put public appearances and visits in that category. Like I said, it was a chore. Something I had to do because, rightly or wrongly, it makes people feel special when someone from my family visits their place of work or their home town or village. Also, it brings attention. If any of my sisters are photographed at a museum, gallery or a nature reserve then the footfall for that place instantly doubles. We know that our attention has an economic benefit. We can't ignore that, just because we might want to stay home and relax.'

'What? You never get to chill out? In that case I'm definitely not staying.'

'Never officially.' For the first time Tris's smile looked both easy and genuine and Amber's heart gave a small traitorous leap. She mentally scolded it and kept her attention on the conversation at hand.

'Okay. It's time to confess—what do you do when you relax? What's your comfort watch of choice? It's been a long day, it's raining outside, you've put on...' Amber had been about to say PJs but thought better of it; this conversation might be flowing easier than usual and she and Tris might have managed to achieve a truce over the last week, but she wasn't ready to talk nightwear with him yet, especially when even the word PJs made her remember in such vivid detail the night when he hadn't bothered with any nightwear at all '...casual clothing,' she managed lamely. 'You're curled up on the sofa, phone set to silent, the remote in your hand. What do you watch? And what do you eat while watching it?'

'I…' Tris looked genuinely discomfited. 'My phone is switched off?'

'On silent,' she corrected him. 'My imagination isn't strong enough to imagine you without a phone or two.' Tris seemed to carry at least three phones at all times, all switched on, all checked regularly and all needing constant attention.

'Usually one of my sisters would choose,' he prevaricated, and Amber shook her head mock sternly.

'That's cheating and you know it. Go on, are you a sci-fi movie franchise man? Must-see dramas? Or do you prefer an epic fantasy series, complete with battles for the throne and dragons? Or is it a little bit too close to home?'

'Honestly? No drama or fantasy series has anything on my ancestors,' he said. 'Remind me to take you to the portrait gallery soon; there's more betrayal, treason, adultery and murder in one room than all of Shakespeare's plays.'

'From what I can tell, my ancestors were pretty bloodthirsty too,' she confessed. 'I don't think my many times great-grandfather got to be King because of his diplomatic skills; I think he hacked his way to the throne. Not that I know much; my grandmother wasn't interested in any of the really fascinating history. She was more concerned with the wrongs done to us during the revolution. But, to be honest, I don't think I blame the populace for getting rid of us. Sounds to me like we were a fairly shady lot, looting half the country's wealth as we left, for instance.'

'Your dowry?'

'My dowry.' She sighed. 'You know, when I left New York I felt completely free for the first time in so many years. I didn't feel guilty about not letting my grandmother know where I was because I never felt like she ever cared for me, just what I represented. I was always flawed, a disappointment. I still don't feel guilty. But I've never felt comfortable about that money. It doesn't really belong to us, does it? I'd like to give it back, only my grandmother still has it and will have until I marry, I guess.' She managed to refrain from adding *If I marry*, but the words hung there.

'You're of age now; it belongs to you and you can do anything you like with it, including giving it back. The only problem is, Belravia doesn't exist any more. It's been carved up and absorbed into at least three countries.'

It belonged to her? It had never occurred to Amber that once she'd turned twenty-one she would legally have charge of the famed Belravian fortune. 'So I just keep it? I couldn't—it doesn't seem right.'

'I'm not saying keep it, but how you'd go about restoring it when Belravia no longer exists I'm not sure. If you'd like, I can do some investigating. There might be some charities or hospitals in the old Belravian towns and cities where the money could be distributed. Or you could set up a charitable foundation; a lot of your people dispersed during the revolution and people continue to be dispersed from their countries today and need a lot of financial aid; that might be a fitting use for it.' He paused then turned to look at her, sincerity in his face and voice. 'Amber, it's important that you know that your dowry was never part of my motivation back then. Although I am sure my uncle thought differently.'

Amber stared at Tris in some confusion, her thoughts in tumult. She'd been so used to thinking of her dowry and the betrothal as one, it was odd to have to disentangle them—and to absolve Tris of being only interested in her money. Plus the insight he showed in thinking of ways she could use her fortune was illuminating, his insightful solutions for a problem that occasionally kept her awake at night. Whether she married him or not, she knew it was finally time to face her grandmother, reclaim the money and do something good with it.

'Thank you. I'd really appreciate your help and advice. It's too important a job to get wrong and I don't really know where to start.'

'You're not even slightly tempted to keep it, to keep any of it?'

Amber shook her head. She might be confused about many things at the moment, but she'd always known that the fabled fortune wasn't hers morally, even if the law said differently. 'No, I know my dad always intended to return it somehow, but his father was still alive then—he didn't die until a few months after my parents' accident—and so he hadn't figured out what to do with it yet.' She stopped, remembering the austere, autocratic old man who'd barely spoken to her in those long, lonely first few months in New York. Maybe he'd been grieving his son; she'd never know. She did know that neither he nor his wife had treated her own grief with any consideration or empathy.

She pushed the memories away and tried to lighten the mood. 'However, I am tempted to see what it's like when you relax. You still haven't answered my question. Is it shameful? You don't have to worry. I'm not going to judge you.'

'Okay then.' Tris's expression was as unreadable as ever. 'Why don't you come over tonight to my rooms for dinner and a movie?'

Go over to his rooms? Amber hadn't been invited into Tris's quarters since she'd been at the castle, nor had she attempted to go there. The invitation was a definite step in the right direction. Nerves fluttered in her stomach. Every small step brought her closer to a decision, closer to deciding the course her life would take.

'Okay, then.' Amber tried her best to look as inscrutable as Tris. 'You choose the movie and I'll bring popcorn.'

She sat back and stared out of the windows again. This was her chance to find out something real about Tris. To discover who he was when he wasn't the perfect prince, the consummate host or the seductive dance partner. It was a lot to ask of dinner and a movie, but right now she would take whatever insight into Tris she could get. Time was ticking away and she was as far from a decision as she had been the day she arrived. Something had to change and maybe, just maybe, tonight was the night.

CHAPTER EIGHT

'THIS SHIRT? OR this one?' Tris held up first a blue and then a grey shirt and looked hopefully at his sister.

'I thought this was supposed to be a relaxing evening.' Elisabetta raised a knowing eyebrow. 'Box sets and chill? We all know what *that* means. About time, big brother, about time.'

'I barely know her,' Tris protested, trying not to think about how in some ways he knew Amber very well indeed. He knew how silky her skin was beneath his fingertips, he knew the taste of her, the way she gasped, the way her eyes fluttered half shut and she lost herself in sensation. He knew all that and yet in many ways he didn't know her at all.

'Those shirts make you look a little...' Elisabetta put her head to one side and studied him '... stuffy.'

'Stuffy?' Tris regarded the shirts in consternation. They were handmade linen shirts. 'What on earth is wrong with them?'

'You're supposed to be sitting on the sofa, sharing pizza and watching a film. Don't you think you should be in something a little more casual?'

'More casual?' These were casual. They were open-necked and short-sleeved; he'd never wear them in public. 'Like silk pyjamas and some kind of smoking jacket?'

'I was thinking about jeans and a T-shirt,' Elisabetta said. 'But if you want to scare the girl off then go with silk pyjamas.' She studied him, eyes narrowed. 'This means a lot to you, doesn't it? Do you like her?'

Tris refused to meet her gaze. 'She's very pleasant.'

'It's okay; you're allowed to like her, you know. Don't take our parents' marriage as a template; most people *want* to be with the person they marry.' She wandered over to the window and said with studied nonchalance, 'I was talking to Mama earlier; she sends her love. I didn't mention Amber, but I know how relieved she would be to know she was here and that you might be marrying soon. Why don't you take Amber to visit her? Mama would like that.'

'If she wants to know anything about me then she is always welcome here,' he said gruffly. His mother hadn't set foot in Elsornia since the day after his father's funeral and Tris had neither time nor inclination to assuage her conscience by visiting her. He knew the distance between them upset his sisters, but it wasn't of his making, His mother's rooms were always ready if she should change her mind.

Elisabetta didn't answer but he could feel her disappointment as she sighed and looked out of the window.

'What film shall I choose?' The question was a way of changing the subject and it worked as she turned immediately, rolling her eyes in exasperation.

'How can you be so bad at this?'

'Because I've been engaged for eight years with no actual fiancée to spend time with?'

'And because, between Father and our uncle, you've been brought up to be a cross between a monk and a robot? But I know you dated before the betrothal and I know you've had a few *friendships* in the last four years. It's not as if you've never spent time alone with a woman before.'

Tris compressed his mouth grimly. There were many things he and his sisters never discussed—their parents' separation and their mother's decision to leave Tris with his father; the countdown to Tris's thirty-fifth birthday; their father's autocratic ways—and they certainly never discussed the few relationships Tris had had after they'd learned that Amber wasn't studying but had disappeared without a trace.

His partners had been carefully chosen for their discretion: an old friend hopelessly in love with another man, a widow who had no intention of remarrying, a friend of Elisabetta's who was training to be a doctor and had no time for a serious relationship. Trustworthy women who didn't want a long-term love affair, didn't mind secrecy and who would never go to the press. Each affair had lasted for just a few months, ending by mutual agreement when the secrecy became too oppressive. Tris wasn't proud of these relationships, but neither was he ashamed. They'd been necessary, brief interludes of humanity in his duty filled life. If at some level he'd felt that something was missing, he'd pushed that feeling away. He knew that in his world it was all too rare to find true understanding in friendship or relationships. Far better to keep expectations simple than hope for too much and be disappointed.

'I'm sorry,' Elisabetta said, walking over to give him a hug. 'I know being yourself isn't easy for you. But that's all you need to do. I promise, just let Amber get to know you, Tris, let her see the man we see.'

Tris hugged her back, but it was already too late. He had shown Amber his true self and it had made him vulnerable. He had no intention of being vulnerable in front of her again. He needed her and she knew it. He wanted marriage and to be a father to their child all the time, not just on weekends and the occasional holiday. But that was it; he didn't need her to understand him or to see inside his soul.

It was far safer if she didn't.

An hour and two changes of clothes later, Tris was beginning to wish he'd never *heard* the word relax. He'd ordered two pizzas and a salad from the palace kitchen and they sat in a small kitchenette he barely used, ready to be heated up. Elderflower *pressé* cooled in the fridge alongside non-alcoholic beer and sparkling water.

'Get hold of yourself, Tris,' he told himself aloud, pacing over to the open French windows that led out onto his terrace. 'It's just dinner and a film—how hard can it be?'

He turned at the sound of a gentle rap at his door. Opening it, he saw Amber standing there, wearing light blue trousers in some kind of silky material teamed with a creamy-coloured T-shirt and a large white cardigan which she held wrapped about her as if it was armour.

'Hi,' she said.

'Come in.'

She stepped inside, her posture wary, and looked around. 'This is lovely,' she said but her voice sounded carefully neutral. Tris looked at his rooms and tried to see the familiar furniture and decor through her eyes.

His suite of rooms were on the first floor, looking out over the front of the castle, and the large sitting room doubled as an informal receiving room. White walls topped with intricate gilt coving and lined with valuable landscapes of the Elsornian countryside were matched by a polished wooden floor and a selection of antique furniture. Everything in the room was made in Elsornia, the only personal touch a photo of his three sisters on one of the bookshelves. His study was furnished in a similar fashion; his bedroom likewise. His sisters were always trying to persuade him to redecorate, but Tris didn't see the point. He was the Crown Prince, and no amount of wallpaper, photos or cushions would change that.

'Make yourself comfortable,' he said and, with a slightly doubtful look, Amber perched on the nearest brocade sofa.

'This is very…erm…firm.' She wriggled as if trying to get comfortable. True, the sofa wasn't very comfortable. None of the furniture was, but Tris had got used to it. It wasn't as if he spent much time relaxing anyway. In fact, he spent very little time in his rooms, apart from his study, at all.

'Would you like a drink?'

'Thank you, that would be lovely.'

Tris busied himself with getting them both drinks and checked that Amber was happy with the pizzas he had selected before giving her a quick guided tour of his rooms. She seemed interested and asked several questions, but her gaze was a little puzzled and she glanced at Tris several times as if considering saying something. It wasn't until he showed her out to the terrace that ran the full length of his rooms that her smile seemed to become more genuine. She walked from one end to the other, pausing to admire the plants and potted trees that turned the austere stone space into a green paradise, stopping by the telescope set up at the far corner. Reaching out one hand, she touched the telescope lightly and Tris wondered if she, like him, was thinking about the evening he'd shown her the stars. 'So, this is where you spend most of your time when you're alone?'

'I suppose it is.' Tris had never really thought about it before, but she was right. 'How can you tell?'

She shrugged. 'It just seems a little bit more like you, I suppose. Your rooms are lovely, but they're a little impersonal. I could be walking through any show room in any stately home. But out here? This doesn't look like it's been put together out of the Palaces-R-Us catalogue. It looks like someone has curated it with love and care.'

For a moment Tris was so taken aback he didn't know how to respond, and Amber covered her mouth, eyes huge with embarrassment. 'I am so sorry...' she began but Tris interrupted her.

'I moved into these rooms when I was sixteen,' he said. 'My uncle arranged for them to be prepared for me in what he deemed to be the most appropriate style, and I've never got around to changing them; there doesn't seem to be much point. I don't spend much time here anyway. But the terrace is different, I designed it myself and this is where I come when I need to think, to remind myself that the world is bigger than this castle and my responsibilities.' He stopped, a little embarrassed by how much he'd given away.

Amber nodded. 'That makes sense. I couldn't quite believe it when I stepped in…the difference between your rooms and the ones I've been given…mine are so beautiful and so individual.'

'You can thank Elisabetta for that. I asked her to make them as welcoming as she could. I tried to tell her a little bit about you so that you felt at home; I hope I got it right.'

'They're perfect,' she said softly. Amber looked up at him, confusion, doubt and something that looked a little like hope mingling in her eyes. Tris wanted to reach out and touch, to run his finger down her cheek, to bend his head to hers to taste her once again. He wanted to pull her into his arms, to run his hands through her glorious mass of hair, to slide his hands down to her waist, to touch her silky skin, as he had dreamt of every night over the last few weeks. If he did, he was almost sure that she wouldn't push him away; he could almost taste the anticipation in the air.

For all the awkward silences, for all the ways they danced around each other, trying to work out just how much they would need to give and take in any future relationship, for all they avoided any conversation about the night they'd spent together, barely even mentioning her pregnancy even though it was the reason she was here, attraction still hummed in the air between them. Almost visible, tangible, audible it surrounded him every time she was near. And by the way she was so careful not to touch him, the way she sometimes slid a glance his way, Tris knew she felt it, saw it, heard it too.

Kissing Amber, reminding her of that physical attraction, reminding her of how good they were together in one way at least, would give him a shortcut to the marriage he needed. But he'd never been a man for shortcuts; he needed Amber to agree to stay because she wanted to, not because she had to. That ill-judged betrothal needed to be wiped out of history. Seducing her into a decision would be almost as bad as coercing her through a legal document she had had no say in. It almost physically hurt to step back, to keep his polite mask in place, but Tris was used to doing things the hard way.

'I don't know about you,' he said as smoothly and unemotionally as possible, doing his best to pretend the moment that had flared up between them had never happened, 'but I'm hungry. Let's go in and I'll heat up the pizzas. There is a selection of films lined up; you choose.' Tris didn't know if the disappointed glance she sent his way was because Amber had thought he had been about to kiss her or because he was ducking out of their agreement by giving her the choice of film but, either way, this choice was right, safe. And Tris always did the right thing, no matter the personal cost.

CHAPTER NINE

FEELING SLIGHTLY RIDICULOUS, Amber tiptoed along the corridor, unable to stop herself glancing over her shoulder—although whether she was checking for flesh and blood or ghostly watchers, she wasn't sure. What she was sure of was that there was nothing quite as eerie as a seemingly deserted castle at night.

The dimly lit, thickly carpeted corridor which led from her turret into the main part of the castle eventually gave straight onto the grand main staircase which descended majestically into the huge receiving hall at the front of the castle. But somewhere before there was a discreet door which opened into the passages and stairs the servants used to move around the castle relatively unseen. She had had a full tour the day after she'd arrived but there were so many twists, turns, rooms leading into each other, hidden doors and staircases that she wasn't entirely sure which piece of panelling was the door she needed, and which was a secret way into a bedroom or receiving room; the castle was riddled with secret connecting doors and passages, most of them used either for smugglers or affairs. Tris was right; his ancestors were a scandalous lot.

Pausing beside an engraved panel, Amber could see the tell-tale break in the carving that indicated a door. But was it the right door? More by luck than judgement she selected the right door first time and found herself descending the back stairs leading to the kitchen areas. She'd only had a whistle-stop tour of the palace kitchens, which were ruled over by the kind of temperamental French chef she'd thought only existed in films and who even confident, vivacious Elisabetta regarded with wary respect.

Once down in the airy basement that housed the service apartments and rooms, Amber found she remembered the way to the kitchen easily. Pushing the heavy door a little nervously, she peeped into the simply lit room, her heart jolting with relief when she saw it was both empty and tidied up and cleaned ready for the next day. She stepped in, closing the door softly behind her, and looked around the huge room, with its stainless steel worktops, saucepans hanging from racks and range ovens. It was almost impossible to believe that next door there was an even bigger kitchen used for state occasions and this gleaming, gadget-filled professional room was used just for day-to-day catering.

Tiptoeing over to the light switches, Amber put on the spotlights which illuminated the side benches, holding her breath in case she triggered some kind of alarm, but the only sound was that of her own wildly beating heart roaring in her ears. The night staff had an office at the other end of the basement with another small kitchen for late night orders. She should be able to use this kitchen completely undisturbed.

Fifteen minutes later Amber had filled the worktop

in front of her with a selection of eggs, flour, sugar, flavourings and a whole host of bowls, baking tins and wooden spoons. The terrifyingly technical oven nearest her was finally switched on after several false starts, and she had started to mix ingredients together for a simple sponge cake, propping her tablet in front of her and logging into her video chat, hoping that one of her friends might also be finding it hard to sleep.

Amber preferred to cream the butter and sugar by hand, the repetitive exercise giving her the brain space she needed. As she started to turn two separate substances into one she recapped the evening she'd just spent with Tris in excruciating detail. There was so much to unpick she didn't quite know where to start. The shock of his impersonal rooms followed by the relief when she'd stepped onto the terrace and seen the beautiful outside space he'd created. The moment by the telescope when he'd looked at her in exactly the same way he'd looked at her at the wedding, all heat and want. With that one look turning her bones molten, her body limp with need. Only for him to turn away as if it had never happened.

She mixed harder, mind ruthlessly marching on to the disappointment flooding her when he'd left it to her to select the film as if he couldn't share even his cultural taste with her. Choosing a three-hour Jane Austen adaptation was maybe cheap revenge, but he deserved it.

Was it too soon to give up? He was trying, she knew that, probably as much as he was able, but she could not live the rest of her life in bland companionship, no matter how luxurious the surroundings. Her unhappiest years had been spent in the lap of luxury.

The sugar and butter were creamed at last, so smooth a paste it was almost impossible to imagine that just ten minutes ago they had been separate substances. Picking up the first egg, Amber amused herself by cracking it on the side of the bowl and letting the contents slide into the bowl one-handed. She picked up the second egg and at that moment an alert from her tablet showed her Harriet was trying to call. For one moment she considered not answering, despite her earlier need to speak to her friends, unsure what to say and how much to give away. But her need for companionship was greater than her desire for secrecy and she accepted the call.

'Harriet! How lovely to hear from you.' Amber hoped her cheery smile and tone would be enough to fool her friend that all was fine. She should have known better. Harriet narrowed her eyes.

'You're baking?' Harriet said it in the same way that she might have said *You're drinking* or *You're weeping on a sofa watching a sad film*. 'What time is it there?'

'Not yet midnight,' Amber said airily, mixing in the eggs as if making a cake in a castle kitchen at midnight was a completely normal thing to do. 'Why, what time is it where you are? Actually, where are you?' Since Harriet had got engaged to Deangelo she spent a lot of time travelling around the world with him.

'I'm in New York,' Harriet said. 'I've been catching up with the company Alex worked with at Christmas and my report will be with you all at the end of the week, but right now I'm sitting in a hotel room waiting for my fiancé to finish *his* business and to take me out for dinner. Amber, what's going on? You only midnight bake when you're stressed.'

'I'm not stressed,' protested Amber, sieving in the flour and folding it a little more vigorously than usual. Harriet didn't reply, her silence all too effective, and Amber rolled her eyes in the direction of the tablet. 'Okay, okay, maybe I'm a little stressed. Did I tell you that Tris put me in a freaking tower? Like I'm some helpless princess and now he's impregnated me he's ready to save me.'

'To be fair, it's not as if he knew you were a princess when he impregnated you,' Harriet said, a smile twitching her mouth. 'None of us did.'

'I was talking about a metaphorical princess,' Amber said with as much dignity as she could as the flour flew into the air under her less than tender care and coated her nose and top. 'Dammit, look at the mess I'm making. Besides, I'm not here because I'm a princess, and I'm definitely not here to be saved. I'm here because I'm pregnant and I promised myself to give Tris a chance to show me I could be happy here. Happy with him.'

'And how is that going for you? Or does the large amount of flour currently decorating your face tell me everything I need to know?'

'The pregnancy? I feel surprisingly well, not so tired and I haven't been sick once. It's easy to forget I'm pregnant at all and then I wonder what on earth I'm doing here. I guess that will change next week; I'm flying home for the first scan. Harriet, will you be around? I really don't want to go on my own. Part of me wonders if I'm going to get there and the doctor is going to tell me I'm crazy and there's no baby; I'd like someone else to prove it's real.'

Amber paused. Despite all the problems the pregnancy was causing her, the question marks over her future, she couldn't help but be thrilled at the thought of a baby. Her baby. Her own family for the first time in more years than she cared to remember. No, she reminded herself as she looked at Harriet. She did have a family, one born of love and respect and friendship. Their marriages would inevitably change that, especially as they would no longer live together, but they wouldn't change those bonds. No matter what happened, the baby had three readymade aunts and godmothers ready to love him or her.

'Of course I'll be there if you want me. But Amber, shouldn't Tris be with you?'

Shaking her head, Amber dislodged flour, sending even more to the floor. 'We're still keeping the pregnancy and, more importantly, Tris's involvement, a secret for now. To be honest, if we don't get married, I'd really like to keep it a secret for as long as possible, until the baby is an adult at least. Growing up with that kind of interest and publicity is not ideal, to put it mildly. Nor is growing up with a meaningless title healthy either. I should know; I crossed an ocean to escape mine.'

'I thought it was your grandmother you wanted to leave behind, not the title. After all, if you know it's meaningless, then what does it matter?'

'It matters because I'm here. Do you think if I was just some random bridesmaid Tris had got pregnant I'd be living in the castle being prepped for Queen? No way—they'd be paying me off quicker than you could say *royal emergency.*'

'Do you really think that?' Harriet shook her head, her eyes warm with understanding. 'I think you're there because Tris wants you there, because he wants to be part of the baby's life and part of your life.'

'Harriet, he barely speaks to me. There is no trace of the man I met at the wedding, at least barely any trace. I can't see beneath the surface; he won't let me in.'

'Why is that, do you think?'

Amber huffed a little as she started to prepare the ingredients for shortbread biscuits. She couldn't just stand here and chat while her cakes cooked; she had to stay busy. Maybe pastry after this, puff or filo—something tricky which needed a lot of physical work. 'He thinks I lied to him that night.'

'And did you?'

'No! I mean, he didn't ask me, did he? At no point did he say, *Excuse me, are you the long-lost Belravian Princess who I managed to get engaged to without once asking her if it was what she wanted?*' Amber could hear the bitterness in her voice and concentrated on beating the butter as hard as she could.

'Be careful with that butter, Amber, or it will have you up for assault. Okay, he didn't ask you and he didn't recognise you, so why does he think you lied?'

'He thinks I lied by omission.' Amber put the bowl down and faced the screen—and her friend. 'In some ways, I guess I did. Obviously, I knew who he was, but I had no idea he still considered himself betrothed to me. If I had, I wouldn't have danced with him, I wouldn't have slept with him. I wouldn't have complicated things so badly.'

Harriet's nod was full of understanding. After all, she and Deangelo had had to find their way from desire towards love. 'Amber, tell me to mind my own business, but *why* did you sleep with him? Knowing who he was, knowing he is the reason you left your grandmother's house before graduating. I'm not judging,' she added hastily as Amber picked the bowl back up.

The heat in Amber's face had nothing to do with the vigorous beating of butter and the newly added sugar and everything to do with embarrassment. Harriet had just said what they were all thinking, herself too, no doubt Tris as well. What *had* she been thinking?

'At first I was terrified he would recognise me and, although there's no way anyone could make me go back to my grandmother or force me into marriage, for a few moments I was a terrified schoolgirl again, hearing her future planned out for her with no say and no way out except to run. When I realised he had no idea who I was, I was curious I suppose, curious how my life might have turned out if I hadn't had the strength to disappear. And—' the heat of her face intensified '—the truth is, when I was a teenager I had a huge crush on him, although he looked at me as if I was nothing more exciting than a cockroach. When it became clear he was attracted to me it went to my head. I felt powerful after all those years of feeling powerless. It was more intoxicating than the champagne. He wanted me not because I was a princess and a means to a throne and a fortune, but me, Amber Blakeley, and that night it seemed like I could see into his soul.'

She stopped, unable to believe the words that had just spilled out of her, unable to believe their truth, but when she finally got the courage to look at Harriet she didn't see surprise or condemnation, but understanding—and confirmation—as if Harriet had suspected how Amber felt all along. But how could she when Amber herself hadn't known?

'I came here because I thought there was a connection,' she said quietly. 'But I was wrong. I didn't see into his soul. I just fancied him, that was all. I made a huge mistake, and now I don't know what to do for the best. Apart from bake.'

Tris paused at the closed kitchen door, unsure whether to open it or not. When he'd received the call telling him that Amber had been in the kitchen for almost an hour he had immediately got dressed and left his apartments to come and find her. It wasn't that he was worried she was hurt but he had noticed a curiously blank look in her eyes when she had left earlier. He had failed her. He was fully aware of that.

Tapping lightly on the door, he waited for an answer and, when none was forthcoming, he carefully turned the handle and pushed the door open just a fraction. His immediate attention was caught by the mass of bowls, cutlery and baking paraphernalia on the worktop opposite, only for the whole scene to fade as he heard Amber speak.

'I just fancied him, that was all. I made a huge mistake, and now I don't know what to do for the best.'

Something brittle, something in the region of his heart, twisted and cracked. She had made a mistake, of course she had. One of the things he respected about Amber was her refreshing honesty when it came to his title and position. The knowledge that she'd chosen him not because of what he was but because of who he was. But she'd chosen him for one night only, not for a lifetime, and now she realised that the night they had shared was a mistake. Carefully, silently he closed the door and took a step back.

He should turn around, go back to his apartments, the soulless, lifeless apartments Amber had been so un-impressed by earlier, go back to bed and forget he had overheard anything. Tomorrow they could resume their slow, stately, courteous courtship and he could rely on Amber's upbringing and sense of fairness to make up for his inability to woo her. To let her in. That was the safest option, the option that gave him the best chance at his desired outcome.

He inhaled slowly.

His desired outcome, the right outcome, was a sensible marriage where both parties knew exactly what they wanted from the union. A marriage giving him the son he needed and a consort willing and capable to put Elsornia first. Even if Amber hadn't been his betrothed, wasn't raised for a situation such as this, she would still be suitable. She was warm, approachable, hard-working with an innate sense of responsibility. And she was carrying his child. What else did he need? He certainly didn't need to remember the night when her smile was full of promise, her eyes full of stars, and she made him feel like a man, not a prince. And that was an outcome best achieved by pretending he had seen and heard nothing.

But the desolate ring in her voice echoed through him. He had let her down tonight, withheld himself, just as he withheld himself from everyone, even his sisters. It was safer that way. A king was always alone; his father had taught him well. But he wasn't King yet, just a prince, and without Amber and the child she carried maybe he never would be.

Without stopping to think, Tris reached for the door handle again and this time made a show of fumbling as he turned it, making plenty of noise as he pushed the door open. Amber turned, surprise mingling with guilt on her face as she closed her tablet. Dressed in pyjama bottoms, a soft cashmere hoodie, with her hair scraped off her face, no make-up and a liberal dusting of flour over her hair, cheeks and front she looked more like the teenager he had first met than the desirable bridesmaid or the elegant companion of the last week. The girl he owed a duty of care to, a girl he had let down.

'Tris! What are you doing here?'

Tris thought quickly. He didn't want Amber to feel that she was under surveillance or that she couldn't wander wherever she wished. 'I wanted a snack.'

'A snack?' One arched eyebrow indicated her disbelief. 'Isn't there an army of night staff ready to bring you whatever you need?'

'A snack and a stroll,' he amended, his urbane smile daring her to question his word. 'I thought it might help me sleep. But the real question is, what are you doing?'

'What do you think I'm doing?' Her words and tone were sassy, but her expression was anxious and still a little guilty. 'I'm baking. Can't you tell?'

Even without the flour and all the ingredients and bowls scattered around, the enticing aroma wafting from the oven would have been a gigantic clue. 'Something gave me that impression, I'm more interested in why. You often bake at midnight?'

'I wouldn't go so far as to say often, but it's not unusual. I bake when I need to think. Like you and astronomy, I suppose.'

With an effort, Tris didn't react to her words. He shouldn't be surprised at her deduction. After all, not only had she seen the telescope on his balcony, but he had used the stars to seduce her. He just hadn't realised that she'd understood that astronomy wasn't just a hobby but a way of centring himself. A way of reminding himself that the universe was bigger than one almost-king and his small, beloved and all-consuming country.

'What are you making?'

'Nothing at all complicated, just a plain sponge and some shortbread. But I was thinking of making pastry or something with dough. My mind is still not settled; I need something more absorbing.'

'A cake seems pretty complicated to me,' Tris said and was rewarded with a genuine if pitying smile.

'It's just mixing things together in the right quantities in the right order, nothing complicated about that. It's no different to making little cakes or tarts as a child.'

'Is that what you did? Is that how you learned to bake?'

Amber looked surprised. 'Of course, didn't you?'

Tris picked up an egg. 'Baking isn't really part of a king's curriculum.'

'No, but you must have at least made little fairy cakes, rubbery and almost inedible but your parents had to eat them anyway?'

Tris tried to imagine his austere, remote father sampling any cooking his children brought him, but his imagination failed him. 'The girls may have, but I doubt it. I don't remember my mother ever setting foot in the kitchen. Of course they spent most of their time with her when she moved out of the castle and into the lakeside villa. It's possible they baked then, but not here. We were never encouraged to hang around the kitchens here.'

'It's never too late to learn.' Amber handed him a bowl and Tris automatically took it, placing the egg carefully inside. 'What do you want to bake? I'll show you.'

'What, now? It's after midnight.'

'Why not? Have you got anything better to do?'

Tris automatically opened his mouth to say of course he had something better to do, but then he looked over at Amber, her hair beginning to fall out of its messy bun, tendrils framing her heart-shaped face, hope in her large green eyes. He'd been unable to let her in earlier, hadn't known how to do anything but keep her at arm's length, but maybe he could—maybe he should—try harder.

'I guess not. Okay, I'm all yours.'

CHAPTER TEN

AMBER STARED AT TRIS, her mouth dry. She hadn't really expected him to agree. The thought of the usually immaculate Tris in an apron, hands covered in flour, was so incongruous her mind couldn't conjure up an image.

'Great.' Incongruous or not, this was an opportunity she couldn't throw away. Wasn't she down here, baking furiously and complaining to Harriet, because Tris was resolutely keeping her at arm's length?

'Great,' Tris repeated. 'What do I do first?'

Amber eyed Tris assessingly. He was still wearing the beautiful grey shirt and well cut tailored trousers he'd been wearing earlier. For a prince the outfit might count as casual but in an already flour-filled kitchen he was dangerously overdressed.

'An apron might be a good start. There're a couple hanging up over there.'

The beep of the timer interrupted her, and Amber busied herself with taking the cakes out of the oven and replacing them with the shortbread before turning to Tris.

'Where shall we start? Cake, cookies, pies, bread— or would you like to go straight for the jugular and have a go at a soufflé?'

'Tempting as a soufflé sounds, I think I'll stick with something simple for now.'

'That sounds like a good plan.' Amber tried to ignore noticing just how close Tris was standing, tried to ignore his distinctly masculine scent, the way his proximity made the hairs on her wrists rise and her pulse beat just a little faster. 'A simple loaf cake. There are some lemons over there; how do you feel about lemon drizzle?'

'I'm not sure I've ever tried lemon drizzle, but I'm willing to give it a go.'

'You've never tried lemon drizzle? How is that even possible? It's a good thing I came along.' She paused. 'But if I'm going to teach you to bake, I need something in return.'

'That seems fair. Name your price.'

'Have you never read a fairy tale? You should never just invite anyone to name their price. What if I asked for your soul, or your firstborn child...?' Her voice trailed off, aware that his firstborn child was indeed in her possession. She rallied. 'Don't worry, I'm not going to ask for anything lasting. But in return for the lesson I'm going to ask you a question and you are going to promise to tell me the truth as best you can.'

Tris didn't respond for a long moment, his smile still in place but his expression the shuttered one she was beginning to know all too well.

'I did tell you to name your price, didn't I? Okay, ask away.'

Amber fumbled for a glass of water, her throat suddenly dry. This was it, this was what she'd been wanting. The opportunity to get to know the real Tris, not the public persona he presented.

'First things first, you need to get your ingredients together. Right, I hope you've got a good memory. You want two hundred and twenty-five grams of butter...' She reeled off a long list of ingredients and first steps. 'Got all that? I'm going to put my favourite recipe on the tablet for you to follow, but yell with any questions. Okay?'

'Yes, chef.' Tris gave a cheeky grin and half salute as he started to gather all the ingredients she'd specified together on the workbench next to hers and she couldn't help but return his smile, warmed by his informality— and the ridiculousness of the starched white apron covering his shirt and trousers.

Humming to herself, Amber started to tidy up and prepare the things she needed to sandwich the cake she'd already made while supervising Tris and thinking about what to ask him. She felt like a princess in a fairy tale with only three chances to get her questions right before he disappeared in a wisp of smoke, leaving her no further forward than she was right now.

'My mother was a doctor.' Amber hadn't meant to say that; she hadn't meant to talk about herself at all. But now she'd started it felt easier than simply interrogating Tris. She needed to learn about him, but maybe he needed to learn about her as well. 'That's how she met my dad. He fell off his bike and she was the surgeon who operated on his knee. I don't think marriage or kids were really on her radar at all. I remember her telling me that as a scientist she absolutely didn't believe in love at first sight, but when she did her rounds to check on Dad after his operation she could barely concentrate on her notes. Of course, ethically, she couldn't do anything about it, but luckily Dad felt the same way and once he was discharged he came back with a thank you card and asked her out. They got married a year later and I showed up a year after that.'

She stared down at her hands, her eyes blurring as she remembered her sweet, slightly eccentric parents. 'Dad was in his forties, Mum almost there. I think it was a shock to both of them, becoming parents. They were both so dedicated to their jobs, but I always felt loved and wanted. That made it easier later, after they died. Anyway, my mum loved to bake. It was how she de-stressed. One of my earliest memories is being given pastry to play with at the table while she made pies. As you can imagine, my grandmother did *not* encourage the habit; baking is very much something that servants did. But her cook used to teach me secretly, as did my favourite doorman's wife on the rare occasions I could sneak away. I'm not sure I could have survived that penthouse if I couldn't bake.'

Amber couldn't believe she had just blurted out so much. But when she looked up at Tris she saw his gaze fastened on hers, empathy warming his grey eyes. 'Your parents sound lovely,' he said softly, and she nodded, her heart and throat too full to speak. 'It must have been really tough for you when they died.'

'It was.' Amber laid the back of her hand onto one of the sponges, relieved that it was cool enough for her to start whipping the cream. She couldn't just stand here blethering on about a past she never really spoke to anyone about. But she also wanted honesty from Tris, and that meant being honest in return. 'I was devastated. Even if my grandparents had been different, I would still have found the whole situation inconceivably difficult. Maybe, in a way, the sheer surrealism of what happened next shielded me from the worst of my grief. My life changed so absolutely that I think I was numb for many, many months. Moving from a small village where I was just Amber Blakeley, normal middle-class girl living a normal middle-class life, to New York, where I was Vasilisa Kireyev, Crown Princess of Belravia and heir to a vast fortune, would have been the most discombobulating thing ever, even if I hadn't been dealing with my parents' deaths.'

Amber swallowed and concentrated on the cream so she didn't have to look at the pity on Tris's face. She'd never really talked about the car accident that had stolen her parents from her. Her grandparents must have grieved in their own way, but Amber had never been encouraged to discuss her feelings or offered counselling. One of the hardest things about opening the Pandora's box that contained her past was realising how much she still had to come to terms with the loss.

'My grandfather died just a few months after I moved to New York and so it was just my grandmother and me. It was hard. She was hard. Leaving the house my parents bought when I was a baby, all my memories, was bad enough, but the sheltered existence she insisted on... I felt like I was imprisoned in that tower. My grandmother would never let me out unaccompanied, wouldn't allow me to select my friends or my hobbies. I used to stand at the window and stare out at Central Park, at the joggers and the dog walkers and the kids and wish that someone would rescue me.'

Amber could feel her cheeks heating; there was no

way she was letting Tris know that the first time she'd seen him she'd cast him in the role of knight in shining armour. She'd spent way too many long, lonely evenings conjuring up tales of rescue, some actually including Tris on a white horse. She busied herself ladling cream into a bowl and fetching the jam. Anything not to look at him.

'Did you know your grandmother well? Before you went to live with her?'

Amber shook her head. 'I'd met her twice, I think. She never came to the house and we never visited her in New York but once or twice she came to London and we met her for dinner in whichever fancy hotel she was gracing with her royal presence. My grandfather never accompanied her. Truth is, my dad barely ever mentioned the whole royal thing. He changed his name when he went to boarding school in his teens as a security measure, but liked being plain Stephen Blakeley so much he just stayed as him; he said he was really proud of his doctor title because he'd earned it with his PhD, but a royal title just meant his ancestor had been more of a thug than the next man.' She managed a smile. 'Anyway, I didn't mean to bore you with the life and times of Amber Blakeley; I was clumsily trying to tell you why baking is important to me. It's not just the creative part of it or the fact that I really, really like cake, but it's tied into the happiest memories of my childhood.'

While Amber spoke, Tris had been busy following the instructions she had brought up for him on her tablet. It was oddly soothing combining the ingredients, seeing all the disparate parts turn into a creamy whole.

Meanwhile, with practised ease, Amber was whipping cream, smoothing jam onto a cake and removing tantalisingly aromatic biscuits from the oven, her every move graceful as if she were in a well-known dance, one whose steps he could barely comprehend. He was glad of something to do with his hands and something to focus on completely as she completely un-self-pityingly laid bare the reality of her childhood. It must have been much harder for her, those long lonely teenage years, after knowing such warmth and happiness, than it had been for him, raised solely for duty and responsibility.

'Okay, let me take a look,' Amber said, coming to stand next to him. She smelt of vanilla and sugar and warmth. How did she have so much light and optimism after so much darkness? 'That's not bad at all. Now, pour it into the tin and smooth out the top and then you can pop it into the oven. A loaf cake takes about forty minutes to bake, so we'll have to think of something else to make while we are waiting. Something quick or we'll be here all night and I want to tidy up and hide all evidence long before the kitchen staff turn up.'

'Or we could eat some of that amazing-looking cake instead,' Tris suggested.

'We could. Of course, for that I need a cup of tea. You can take the girl out of England, but you can't stop her craving her daily cuppa.'

Five minutes later Amber had managed to find a brand of tea she was happy with and made herself a large cup, Tris opting for a glass of wine instead. Two generous slices of the cake she'd made lay on plates before them as they perched on stools side by side. He couldn't remember when he'd last had such an informal meal, even when it was a simple snack. Even the pizza he had painstakingly heated up earlier had been served on a table, already laid with silverware and linen.

Amber took a sip of her tea and then took an audible breath, as if trying to find the courage to speak. 'Thank you for listening just now. I've never actually said any of that to anybody before. Not even to myself really. At the time it was all too much and afterwards I was just so relieved to be away. In a funny way, I should thank you for that as well. I mean I always meant to leave as soon as I'd graduated from high school, but you gave me the impetus to start living my own life the way I wanted to.'

'And was it? The life you wanted?'

Amber forked a portion of cake, looking thoughtful as she did so. 'It wasn't the life I planned,' she said at last. 'I had wanted to study history like my dad. Maybe even become an academic like him. But actually I loved being a concierge, I loved working for Deangelo and setting up the agency was just so exciting and empowering; it felt like I was in the right place at the right time doing the right thing for me.'

Tris laid down his fork. All that had changed thanks to him. Amber was no longer in the right place for her, even if she was exactly where he needed her to be. Victory tasted bitter, no matter how delicious the cake.

But Amber didn't look bitter; instead she leaned back on her stool and pointed her fork at him. 'You know, this whole baking experience was meant to be a chance for me to ask you some questions and instead all I've done is talk about myself. That's partly my fault, but don't think I haven't noticed you encouraging me to carry on. You don't get away with it that easily, Your Royal Highness.'

Tris sipped his wine and tried to look as nonchalant as Amber did. 'I was just showing an interest in everything you said,' he protested. 'Ask away. I've got nothing to hide.'

Her snort was frankly disbelieving. 'In that case, tell me your favourite film.'

Tris took another sip of his wine and another mouth of cake, barely tasting it. Of course she wasn't going to let that one lie and why should she? He knew she'd noticed his earlier evasion. 'I don't really have a favourite film,' he confessed and watched her eyebrows shoot up in surprise.

'Everybody has a favourite film. Or at least several films they'd find it really hard to decide between; is that what you mean?'

'Not really.' Tris broke off a piece of cake and crumbled it with his fork. 'I just haven't seen a lot of films. I attend premieres on the rare occasion Elsornia hosts them but settling down and watching one isn't something I do for fun.'

'More of a box set guy? We always have a box set or two on the go at the house. Usually some kind of reality guilty pleasure for when we're all exhausted and a dark, twisty detective series for the rare occasions when we are alert.'

'Actually, I don't really watch much TV at all. I don't read fiction either or listen to much music.' He might as well pre-empt the inevitable next questions before Amber asked him to name his favourite song or book.

'Not into culture?' Amber's eagerness had faded,

her body language on high alert as she imperceptibly leaned away from him. 'Not everyone is, I suppose.' But her voice was full of doubt.

'It's not so much that I'm not into it; it's more that I don't really know what I like. Taking time out to read, to listen to music or to watch TV wasn't really encouraged. My father thought activities should be improving. Obviously, a good history documentary or non-fiction book would be tolerated, a visit to the royal box to watch opera or ballet or even live theatre was work and therefore acceptable, but that was it.'

'But your sisters... I was talking to Elisabetta about a show we both liked just yesterday.'

'It was different for my sisters; they lived with my mother, whereas I was brought up here with my father and tutor. My father took my training very seriously; that's why he didn't send me to school and wanted to make sure I used every hour wisely.' Tris deliberately took a large gulp of wine and pushed his plate away. Amber had been so candid with him earlier, had even confessed that she had told him things she'd never told anyone else before, and her trust in him was the greatest gift he'd ever been given. But he didn't know how to return it, didn't know how to put into words how it had been, growing up here on his own with the weight of expectation crushing him, feeling guilty for missing his mother and sisters, guilty for resenting his father and the regime imposed on him.

He started as Amber laid a warm hand on his, her touch shooting through him. 'Tris, you've been an adult for a long time now; your father died a decade ago. Haven't you ever been tempted to do things another way? To veg out and binge on a box set or a really good book?'

'Tempted? Of course, all the time. But my father was right; there's always too much to do to relax. Duty comes first. Besides—' honesty compelled him to continue '—like I said earlier, I don't know where to start. Even if I had the time, I wouldn't know what to choose.' Tris stopped, embarrassed. Not knowing was weakness and weakness was intolerable in a king. He didn't want to look at Amber and see pity in her face.

Amber jumped to her feet and gathered up the plates and her cup. 'I can see I'm going to have my work cut out,' she said. 'Not only am I going to have to teach you to bake, but I'm going to have to teach you to relax as well. I'm going to need to up my rates. My agency is very expensive, you know, and right now you're getting a lot of hours.'

'Oh, I know how to relax,' Tris said, and Amber laughed.

'You're going to have to prove that to me, I'm afraid.' She smiled over at him and their eyes held. Despite, or maybe because of, the lateness of the hour, the confidences shared, Tris could feel his pulse begin to race, the blood rushing around his body heightening every nerve, every sinew, every muscle. He couldn't take his gaze off Amber as her smile wavered and disappeared as she visibly swallowed. He'd desired the elegant bridesmaid in her silk and jewels, but he wanted this tousled, flour-spattered baking goddess so much more. She wasn't an illusion, a dream, a siren ready to seduce and be seduced, but so real she made his heart and body ache, thrilling and terrifying in equal measure.

Slowly, purposefully, Tris got to his feet, the invisible thread connecting their gazes, their bodies, tightening. 'I can absolutely prove it to you. Any time.' He took a step closer and then another as Amber stood still, as if paralysed. There was no champagne to fuel him, no violins serenading them, no stars to witness, just two of them in the dimly lit kitchen, the scent of vanilla and lemon and sugar permeating the air.

All Tris knew was that he had mishandled the situation from the moment he'd set foot in the lawyer's office in Paris. He'd allowed hurt and anger to guide him, keeping Amber at a dignified arm's length, too proud to woo her. He'd blamed her for deceiving him without ever considering her reasons. He shouldn't have had to listen to her starkly told tale of loneliness to trust her. He'd been in the wrong all those years ago and he was in the wrong now. Elisabetta was right; if he wasn't careful, he was going to give Amber every reason to walk away, taking their child with her.

It wasn't just anger and wounded dignity that had made him keep Amber at a distance. The Tris who danced and flirted and seduced wasn't the Tris who worked so tirelessly and endlessly to keep Elsornia healthy and profitable. He barely recognised the man he'd been that night—and that was the man Amber had chosen. Not the workaholic prince who never even took time out to watch a film and couldn't name his favourite song. How could he compete with the fairy tale he'd pretended to be? But how could he not? Not just because he needed Amber to want to stay, but because he needed her. All of her.

Tris pushed away the warning voice reminding him

just how badly this could go, pushed away the memories of his mother's unhappiness as his father put duty before their marriage and her needs time and time again. His father had done his best to make him in his image and mostly he'd succeeded, but couldn't Tris do better here? With Amber staring at him, eyes wide, full mouth parted, sweet, beguiling and so beautiful she took his breath away, he had no choice but to try.

Slowly, slowly he sauntered across the floor towards her. Amber made no move to meet him but neither did she retreat. She simply stood stock-still, luminous green eyes fixed on him, her full mouth half parted, her chest rising and falling. Tris stopped still a pace away and held out his hand. There could be no seduction, no coercion, no expectation. No champagne or stars or beguiling words, but a meeting of equals.

Amber didn't move for several long, long seconds and then finally, just as Tris was beginning to wonder if he had imagined the whole connection between them, she took his hand and half stepped a little closer. Neither spoke, fingers entwined as Tris reached out and drew a finger down her cheek, lingering slightly on her lips before skimming down the long column of her neck, finally resting on her shoulder. She barely moved as he touched her, just an almost imperceptible tremble, her eyes half closing. One more step and she was snug against him, her breasts soft against his chest, long firm legs pressed to his, the warmth of her hair on his cheek.

'I've been thinking about kissing you again ever since I woke up the morning after the wedding,' Tris said hoarsely.

'In that case you should go ahead.' Amber smiled

up at him as she spoke, her shy yet teasing smile full of promise and anticipation. Heat flooded him. She wanted him, physically at least, and that was far more than he deserved. But only a fool would turn down such an invitation. Slowly, savouring every millisecond, Tris ran his hand along her shoulder, cupping the glorious weight of her hair as he reached the tender skin at the nape of her neck before dipping his head to cover her mouth with his.

Last time they had both been too impatient. The moment they'd kissed had been incendiary, sending them both into a dizzying spiral straight into his bed. Despite the insistent demands of his body, Tris had no intention of taking Amber back to his room tonight. Nor, tempting as it was, was he planning to seduce her in the palace kitchens. This kiss wasn't about seduction but about wooing and so he started slow, nibbling her lower lip, holding her gently as if she were made of porcelain. It was almost more than he could bear, the slow, sweet kiss, harder than anything he'd ever done before as he gently but firmly stopped Amber from speeding things up, holding her lightly, not allowing himself to explore her curves even as she pressed against him. He was playing a long game here, not looking for the easy victory, and so he allowed himself to savour every moment of the kiss, to take in every detail, the fresh floral scent of her hair, her sweet vanilla taste, part-cake part-her, the warmth of her touch, the way her fingers entwined in his, caressing and holding, the softness of her mouth, a mouth made for kissing and being kissed. He needed to savour and remember, imprinting every touch and sensation in his memory.

It was a long time since Tris had believed that his future held anything but duty and responsibility. But standing here, the most beautiful and beguiling woman he'd ever met in his arms, he knew that he had a chance at something more. His future was in her hands. As, he suspected, was his heart.

CHAPTER ELEVEN

AMBER COULD TELL that it was late when she woke the next morning, the angle of the sun slanting into her bedroom a tell-tale clue. She stretched, savouring the sweetness that came from a good night's sleep. It had been late, very late, when she'd finally got to bed. She and Tris had done their best to return the kitchen to the spotless state she'd found it in, hiding every trace of their night-time antics. Baking always made her feel better but for once it wasn't the soothing action of creating that had enabled her to fall into the deep sleep she needed, but those minutes, those wonderful, frustrating, unforgettable moments she'd spent in Tris's arms.

What on earth had happened? One moment she'd been telling Harriet that she had made a terrible mistake, allowing a teenage crush and a night's illusion to give her false hope that she might forge a lasting relationship with Tris, the next she'd found herself confiding in him in a way she'd confided in nobody, not even her friends. Not only that, but he had started to let her in, not all the way, but she understood him a lot more than she had this time yesterday.

And then there were the kisses. Just as intoxicating

as she remembered, turning her body limp with desire, her brain to a single-minded entity wanting nothing more than him. She'd yearned for far more than sweet, chaste kisses but this morning she was grateful for Tris's restraint. Their situation was complicated enough without adding sex into it. Of course, some might point out that that particular horse had already bolted but it wasn't the physical consequences of lovemaking that concerned her; it was the emotional ones. Not that she'd been thinking so clearly last night. If the timer hadn't gone off when it had, Amber wasn't sure Tris would have managed to stay so restrained either...

But a proper conversation and a few kisses didn't solve anything. Yes, she felt a little closer to Tris, but whether that closeness would still exist in the morning light she had yet to find out. One thing she knew: she couldn't leave her future in either Tris's or fate's hands; it was time to take some control of her destiny. No more waiting around for Tris to talk to her or let her in; she was ready to start battering down the drawbridge if that was what she had to do.

Reluctantly, Amber pushed back the sheets and swung her feet to the floor. She wasn't going to solve anything or change anything lying in bed, nor was she going to get where she needed to be living in a luxurious apartment two staircases and three corridors away from Tris, surrounded by servants and aides and soldiers.

Pulling on her robe, she padded upstairs to her turret-top terrace, texting Tris as she did so, rewarded five minutes later when he walked in carrying a tray heaped with fresh fruit, coffee and still warm pastries.

'Good morning,' he said and then looked at the sun. 'Or should I say good afternoon?'

Amber was acutely aware that she was still in her pyjamas and robe, her hair barely brushed, her face make-up-free, although she had managed to clean her teeth. But she wanted intimacy and there was nothing as intimate as breakfast. 'Don't tell me you've been up for hours?'

'Since six,' he said and laughed as she pulled a horrified face.

'That's less than four hours sleep; you'd better sit down and have a pastry. As you may have realised last night, I'm a firm believer that food solves everything, even if you don't make it yourself.'

'Yes, last night was very informative.'

Amber felt her cheeks heat at the unexpectedly teasing tone in Tris's voice. 'I'm glad you thought so.' She managed to keep her own tone light. 'I'm planning a repeat as soon as possible. You made a very creditable cake; more lessons are definitely in order.'

'With a teacher like you, how can I fail to improve?'

Amber was fully aware that Tris wasn't really talking about baking. 'I don't know; it seems to me that you weren't quite as inexperienced as I thought.'

This was definite progress, sitting here in the late spring sunshine enjoying brunch together, the conversation easy yet intimate with a subtext only they understood, but there was still a long way to go. Tris hadn't touched her since he'd arrived, let alone kissed her; there was still a distance between them, physically and mentally. Amber's parents had touched all the time, little caresses and pats, careless kisses dropped on cheeks and foreheads, hands reaching for each other automatically. She hadn't realised as a child how rare that casual intimacy was between married couples; it was something she'd always expected to experience herself one day. Now, even though she knew it was rare, she still yearned for a marriage as complete as her parents' had been.

Maybe it was unfair to expect that kind of relationship from a man who had had a very different kind of childhood. But last night there had been glimpses of another Tris, of the man she had danced and laughed and made love with just a few weeks ago.

She sipped her coffee and summoned up her courage. 'I have a request.'

'Anything.'

'I thought we discussed the folly of making unlimited promises last night. What if I asked for half the kingdom or insisted you only served pink food? Although you might find either of those requests a little easier to agree to.'

'Intriguing.' But Tris looked more wary than intrigued.

'I'd like you to take a vacation. A fortnight somewhere here in Elsornia that you really love. Not the castle, not surrounded by servants and guards and bureaucrats and people needing you every second of the day, but somewhere where we can just be ourselves. Somewhere I don't have to sneak into the kitchen to bake if I don't want to be surrounded by sous chefs trying to anticipate my every need.'

Tris put down his coffee, his forehead creased. 'Amber, I understand, I really do, but it's not that easy for me to just take time off.'

She held up her hand to forestall the inevitable reasons why. 'I don't mean today. This time next week I'm flying to London for a couple of days to have my twelve-week scan. I don't expect you to come with me; in fact it's easier if you don't, not until we have a better idea of our future. All it needs is one picture leaked to the press of you and me near a maternity unit and our secret is out.'

'That makes sense,' Tris agreed, but he was wearing the shuttered look that frustrated her so much, hiding his real thoughts and emotions from her.

With a deep breath, Amber continued. 'Normally, if this scan is okay, which, fingers crossed it is, I wouldn't need to have another one until about twenty weeks. But if you want I could book a private scan for sixteen weeks. That's a good time to find out the sex of the baby with some accuracy. I do understand how important having a son is to you. If the baby is a girl...'

'If the baby is a girl I still want to marry you.' Tris's jaw was set, his grey eyes dark with an emotion she couldn't identify. She tightened her hold on her cup, wishing the coffee had the kick of caffeine she needed to help sharpen her mind. Did he mean that? Or was he saying what he thought she wanted to hear? But through the doubt there was a tinge of relief—she would rather wait to find out the sex of the baby. She'd always imagined having a family of her own and, so far, none of this pregnancy had borne any resemblance to those dreams. It would be lovely to keep an element of surprise and anticipation, no matter what happened.

Choosing her words carefully, she looked over at him. 'I appreciate you saying that, I really do, but surely if we know the baby's a girl it would simplify things somewhat? I know co-parenting without marriage will be tricky for you, with the eyes of the world on you the way they are. And I'm fully aware of how difficult life will be for the illegitimate daughter of the King, if her parentage was known. But it would be just as difficult if she was brought up with parents who marry for the wrong reasons. I'm not willing to sacrifice all our happiness for a throne, Tris. I know your parents weren't happy; surely you don't want to repeat that history with your own children?'

'I promise to do all that is in my power to make you happy,' Tris said stiffly and Amber raised her hand and laid it upon his cheek.

'I know, and I also know that I can't rely on you or anyone for my happiness, that I have to take responsibility for myself. But marriage does need two people's focus to make it work, even ones with a much more auspicious start than ours, and my worry is how much of that focus will be actually in your power and how much you will sacrifice to duty. How much *we* will have to sacrifice to duty. So please, when I get back from London, let's spend time alone, just the two of us, and decide if this is something that we can both not just live with, but *want* to live with.'

Tris reached up and covered her hand with his. 'Let me see what I can do; maybe two weeks isn't impossible if I move some things around.'

Amber squeezed his hand in relief. 'Thank you, Tris. I know I'm not the only one trying to work out the right thing to do here. I do appreciate everything you're trying to do, I really do.' She turned her hand and threaded her fingers through his, his clasp warm and strong and comforting.

Amber had no doubt that Tris would try his hardest to be supportive and to make her feel that she belonged in his world. She also suspected that he was beginning to care for her, Amber Blakeley, not just the mother of his unborn baby. But was that enough? Once they were safely married, once the baby was here, would duty dominate his life as it had done in the past, leaving her just a few scraps of his attention? Amber didn't need a man to dance attendance on her all the time, but neither did she want the kind of marriage where she felt she'd be better off alone. She'd seen what was possible in a partnership of equals; could she really settle for less? But sitting here, her hand in Tris's, the sun warm upon her face, she had hope for the first time in months that things might just work out the way she hoped.

Tris stood in the small private courtyard and watched the car containing Amber, and with her all his hopes, disappear out of the discreet side entrance. In less than an hour she would be on a private flight back to London, not returning for a couple of days. If at all. There was nothing compelling her to come back, just her promise.

'You should have gone with her,' Elisabetta said softly, coming to stand beside him. 'That's your baby too. Or she could have had the scan here.' Tris had finally, with Amber's permission, told his sister about the pregnancy the day before, upon the promise of the utmost secrecy. She'd been delighted, if more than a little confused. No wonder when she'd seen the awkwardness

between them, the constrained silences as they sought
to understand the other better, although the week since
his bakery lesson—and the kisses they had shared—had
been different. There had been no repeat of the kisses
or of the lesson, but there had been an ease which was
as welcome as it was new.

'There's no way we could keep the pregnancy private if she had the scan here, you know that. And she
wanted to be in London, with her friends. They mean
a lot to her, they're her family.' Tris completely understood Amber's reasoning, the common sense part of
him agreed with her, but there was another part of him
that wished she wanted him there; he couldn't imagine
how it would feel to see a glimpse of the baby for the
first time, for them to experience that moment together.

Elisabetta shot him a quick glance. 'You're her family too. No matter what happens next, being parents
will bind you.'

'Like it bound our parents?' Tris said more bitterly
than he meant to, and his sister looped her arm through
his.

'No, because you are better than that. Our father
failed when he tried to turn you into a carbon copy of
him, thank goodness, and Amber has more optimism,
more independence than Mama ever did. She'll find
her path no matter what—her life so far is proof of that.
Leaving New York with less than a thousand dollars in
her pocket at just eighteen to start a new life in a new
country? That takes a lot of grit, Tris.'

'She should never have had to leave like that. I should
never have agreed to our uncle's proposal. But I knew
it was what Father would have wanted. Pathetic, isn't

it, trying to make a dead man happy? Especially as I never really managed it when he was alive.'

'He was proud of you, Tris, I genuinely believe that; he just had no idea how to show it. You were a good son, just like you are a good brother and I know you will be a wonderful father.'

Tris didn't answer, his eyes still fixed on the spot where the car had disappeared. *A father.* It was strange, but he hadn't really thought about what that meant before. Oh, he had thought about the throne and cementing his position as King, thought about marriage to the woman who had eluded him for so long, but not about the reality of what being a father meant. Not about an actual baby who would need to be cared for, held and rocked and changed and fed. A small child who would need to be played with and taught right from wrong. An older child with opinions and likes different to his own. A combination of Amber and him, maybe with her hair and his eyes, her smile and exuberant sweetness or his diffidence and reserve. Excitement and panic filled him in equal measure. There was so much at stake, so much scope to get things wrong. How did anyone feel fit to embark on parenthood, with all its mishaps and pitfalls?

'How do you know that?' He turned to face his sister. 'What if I get it wrong? I'm too strict? Always too busy? Expect too much? Show my disappointment?'

What if he or she doesn't love me?

He couldn't say the last words but Elisabetta must have sensed them because she wrapped her arms around him in a brief hug before stepping back with a warm smile.

'The very fact you are asking these questions shows

what a wonderful father you'll be. I bet our father never once doubted himself, never once wondered if he was making a mistake. Keep wondering, Tris, keep questioning, keep listening—and, most importantly, keep loving and you will do just fine.'

Keep loving.

It sounded so easy, but Tris knew how hard that could be—and knew how dark the consequences of a loveless childhood could be. Things would be different, he vowed. Whatever Amber decided, he would love their baby, make sure it knew how much it was wanted, how special it was. No matter what.

CHAPTER TWELVE

Tris's hands tightened on the steering wheel as he navigated his car around a tight bend. On one side a sheer wall of rock rose dizzyingly into the heights above them, on the other an even more sheer drop fell straight into the valley below. This drive was not for the faint-hearted, but Amber didn't seem afraid; she'd wound the window down and the wind ruffled her hair as she looked out at the countryside spread before her.

This was the wilder, more remote side of Elsornia, an area where few foreign tourists ventured, where villages were few and far between and sheep and goats outnumbered people. Down in the valley the forests spread as far as the eye could see, although Tris knew that another bend in the road would reveal the lake that was their destination.

It was years since he'd last driven along this road, years since he'd been to the villa his mother had retreated to as her marriage broke down, to raise his sisters. He knew the price of that separation was leaving him behind; knowing he'd have chosen to stay didn't make the pain of that choice any easier to forget.

His grip tightened further. Not for the first time, he

questioned his decision to bring Amber to the place which provoked such conflicting feelings in him. But he'd prevaricated enough. Amber needed to know more of him, and the villa by the lake was the only place he had ever allowed himself to feel free. As soon as she'd asked him to take her somewhere special, he'd known this was the only possible destination.

Tris glanced quickly at Amber as she leaned into the breeze, her gaze still fixed on the distant horizon. 'You're sure you're not queasy?'

Despite his attempt to remain nonchalant, a thrill ran through him as he awaited her answer. She looked exactly the same, not an ounce heavier yet, but everything had changed nonetheless. She'd barely greeted him at the private airfield before she handed him a small, fuzzy black and white photo of something that looked like a cross between an alien and a tadpole. Their baby. Staring down at the indistinct image, Tris had experienced emotion like he'd never felt before, pure, overwhelming and all-encompassing, a knowledge that he'd do anything, sacrifice everything to keep this tiny, vulnerable hope and the woman who bore it safe.

'I'm fine,' Amber said, leaning back in her seat. 'I'm officially past the first three months now so hopefully I've avoided all queasiness. Apparently this is when I get lots of energy.'

Tris couldn't stop the wry smile curling his mouth. 'So the last few weeks you've been lacking in energy? Was that when you insisted on learning that country dance at the school, or was it when you walked up to the glacier and refused the lift back down? You *did* look weary when we finally finished washing up after your mammoth baking session, but you are the one who thought eleven p.m. was a good time to start making cakes.'

'Any time is a good time for baking,' Amber said with dignity. 'Have I taught you nothing?'

Tris didn't reply, the next hairpin bend needing all his concentration, but despite the difficult roads he was aware that for the first time in a really long time he was actually relaxed. More than that, he was happy. Waiting at the airfield, he'd been fully prepared for the news that Amber had changed her mind, that she'd decided to stay in London and continue her pregnancy there. But it hadn't just been relief he'd felt when he saw her disembark from the plane; it had been joy. Not because of the child she carried, but because she'd returned. Returned to give him a second chance. He couldn't— mustn't—blow it.

He'd missed her while she'd been away. Missed the way she hummed as she busied herself, her bright, cheery conversation. Missed the way she drew him out, until he found himself opening up, surprising himself. Somehow, over the last two weeks, she'd got under his skin. Tris had no idea what that meant for their future, but he knew he had to do his utmost to make sure the next two weeks were everything she needed to make a decision to stay.

'Do you mind if I put some music on?' Without waiting for his assent, Amber pulled out her phone and connected it to the car's Bluetooth. 'I'd ask you what you wanted, but after the other night I realised that you need a little bit of educating. A lot of educating if I want to be brutally honest rather than diplomatic. Baking obviously, films absolutely, books without a doubt and, most importantly of all, music. Music is good for the soul whether it's classical, pop, reggae or R&B, so I put together a playlist. It's a little eclectic, but I wanted to cover as many bases as possible. Okay, your education starts here...'

The sound of a piano filled the car, soon joined by a soaring soprano voice, followed by a thumping dance track and then an upbeat musical number. Amber hadn't been kidding when she said her playlist was eclectic, but Tris didn't care what the music was. He was just absurdly touched that in the short time she'd been away she'd spent thought and effort putting together a playlist just for him.

In no time at all they started the descent down the mountain to the huge lake which made this part of Elsornia a popular holiday destination. One or two villages turned into fashionable resorts during the summer months, with swimming areas and plentiful berths for boats along the shoreline, but most of it remained unspoilt.

When Tris was small, the lake had been the royal family's favourite summer vacation spot, but after his mother moved permanently to their holiday home his father stayed away, allowing Tris just a month there every summer. He'd worked hard not to envy his sisters growing up in the relative freedom of the countryside, away from castle politics and the prying eyes of the media, spending their term times at boarding school and the holidays with their mother, but there had been times when the contrast between their carefree childhood and his own was too stark and he hadn't returned here since his mother had left, ten years before.

'This is absolutely gorgeous.' Amber stared out of the window like a child looking for the sea. 'The lake is so blue. I don't think I've ever seen water that colour before.'

'Legend says it's so blue because when Hera found out about Zeus's affair with Europa she flew off in anger until she reached this valley. The trees sheltered her from the other gods' view and so she allowed her tears of humiliation and rage and sadness to flow. Of course, Zeus was known for his affairs and there were a lot of tears when she started to shed them. So many that she flooded half the valley with her melancholy.'

'I can't decide if that's a beautiful tale or just a really sad one,' Amber said. 'I suppose creating a lake was a better thing to do than torturing some poor girl who had no choice once Zeus had decided to turn into a ball or a swan or shower of gold, whatever shenanigans he decided upon that time. I always thought it really unfair that the goddesses went around punishing the poor women when it was the gods who did the preying.'

'You know your mythology.'

'I can thank my dad for that; he loved Greek myths. He used to read them to me every night. The children's version at first, then his favourite translations of Ovid, the *Iliad*, the *Odyssey*. We were about to move on to the *Aeneid* when he died. I've still never read it; I didn't have the heart somehow. Maybe one day I'll read it to our baby.' Her voice was wistful, and she blinked a couple of times before turning back to look out of the window.

Tris wanted to say something comforting, something

wise, but couldn't find the words so he drove instead, after a while humming along a little to the music until Amber laughed at his attempts to follow the tune. In no time at all they were on the lakeside road leading to the villa. It was all so achingly familiar. Trees lined the road on one side, the lake glinted in the late spring sun on the other. A few boats bobbed up and down on the water, birds circling overhead, occasionally diving into the blue depths and emerging triumphantly, something silver glittering in their beaks.

Amber was transfixed. 'Can you swim in the lake?'

'You can, but it's fed from the mountains so only the hardiest souls venture in before the summer. And it's never exactly warm even then, but the outside temperature can get so hot that no one cares.'

'I love to wild swim,' Amber said dreamily. 'Sometimes in London I go to the pond on Hampstead Heath or the Serpentine Lido but it's not the same as really wild swimming. I'd like to come back here when it's warm enough.' Her words warmed him. In spite of the memories the lake held, maybe because of them, Tris had known it was the right place to bring her. The right place to see if the liking and understanding so slowly growing between them could become something more permanent.

They drove on through several villages, the first two full of second homes owned by wealthy Elsornian families, filled with fashionable restaurants and bistros and plenty of expensive shops. The next village along was less well-to-do but a great deal more charming with its neighbourhood cafés and small *tavernas*. Amber exclaimed in delight as they passed through it, proclaiming her intention to return and sample cakes from the bakery on the high street. As they drove out, the road began to snake away from the lakeside, skirting round a tall metal fence. A few hundred yards later Tris turned in at a pair of huge iron gates which swung open at his approach.

'I know you asked for us to spend time alone,' he said as he eased the car along the driveway. 'I can't quite give you that, but I can promise you no officials or secretaries or aides. We employ several local people here—gardeners, maids, people to look after the villa—but they live out. There will always be a handful of bodyguards around, I couldn't lose those if I tried, but they're trained to be discreet. You shouldn't even notice they are here.'

'Thank you,' Amber said. She touched his arm, the ease of the gesture warming him through. 'I really appreciate all the effort you've gone to.'

Just a few moments later they were inside the pretty white villa. It was a complete contrast to the thick-walled stone medieval castle where Tris had been brought up and now lived. Built on graceful Italianate lines, the rooms were light-filled and airy, tiled floors and high ceilings offering respite from the hot summers, whilst large stoves in every room ensured warmth in the brief but cold winter months. Elegantly furnished in shades of blue, it was an inviting space, enhanced by breathtaking views from the floor-to-ceiling windows which ran along the whole back wall of the house, looking out onto the lake.

'Privacy glass and bullet-proof,' Tris informed Amber as she exclaimed in delight. 'The royal guard had a fit when we first started coming here; they said that anyone could just zoom in from the lake.'

'They have a point, I suppose.' Amber stared out at the lake. 'Is it likely?'

'I doubt it. A large area of the lake is a no-go zone and anyone who enters it is immediately accosted. Guards are stationed at checkpoints whenever the family is resident and there's a panic room in the basement, so don't worry. The truth is Elsornia has always been fairly stable; even at the end of the nineteenth century when most small kingdoms were hotbeds of revolutionaries, we only had a few half-hearted attempts. From what I can tell, our firebrands were more interested in cryptic passwords and hosting meetings than actually overthrowing the government. We managed to ride out the period between the Wars and post-war turbulence with nothing more than some fiery speeches and the odd badly attended parade.'

'I don't know much about when my family left Belravia,' Amber said, turning away from the window and walking over to look at a landscape on the wall, 'but it must have been terrifying. My grandfather was only a tiny baby and he had to be smuggled out—they would have shot him if they'd found him. I've never understood why he was so keen to go back after that experience.'

'If he hadn't left then he would have had to go when the Soviets moved in. All that area became part of the Soviet Union. I think your father was very sensible, moving on the way he did.'

'Wise and more than a little relieved. He hated bureaucracy and meetings. I think he'd have been a terrible king, found it all too tedious.' She looked at him curiously. 'Are you ever bored?'

The obvious automatic reply was a quick negative.

Of course he wasn't bored. How could he be? After all, it was a huge privilege to serve his country; his father had impressed that on him every day. But sometimes, sitting in yet another long meeting or budget discussion or on yet another formal visit, Tris had been aware that something was missing. Over the last few weeks he had started to realise just what that something might be: companionship, laughter, maybe even love. 'It's not something I let myself think about,' he said honestly.

'Everyone should be bored sometimes; Dad always said that learning to cope with it builds character. But I promise there will be no character-building in that way this holiday; I have too much educating to do. I hope you got the shopping list I sent you?'

'Kitchen fully stocked, ma'am.' He saluted her and his heart lifted as Amber let out a peal of laughter. It couldn't be this easy, this simple, spending time together. Could it?

'Come on then, show me around,' she said, taking his arm. 'I want every detail of every scrape you got into when you were young. No matter how embarrassing.'

'I'll do my best but, I warn you, my childhood was about as exciting as my adult life so don't expect too much.'

Amber raised her eyebrows. 'I don't know; you managed to get a stranger pregnant from a one-night stand and then found out you were engaged to her all along. That doesn't sound boring to me.'

'No,' he agreed. 'Things have definitely livened up recently.'

Amber kept her hand tucked into his arm as Tris showed her around the villa. Imposing as it was, it was still a family home, not a political seat like the castle, and the tour didn't take too long, even with Amber stopping to admire the view from every single room.

'I've put you in what used to be my mother's room,' Tris said, opening the door into a charming suite of rooms overlooking the lake, a balcony leading from the dressing room.

Amber stopped and looked at him anxiously. 'Won't she mind?'

'Oh, no. She lives in Switzerland now, with her second husband; she never comes back here.'

'That seems so sad when she lived here for such a long time. Why doesn't she come back?'

Tris stepped over to the window. How many times had his mother looked out at the lake and the mountains beyond, feeling trapped and helpless? 'She feels that she was exiled here.'

'Oh?'

Tris had known that visiting the villa again meant laying some ghosts, even if not all the spirits were dead. He tried to keep his voice neutral. 'What do you know about my parents?'

Amber glanced at him quickly. 'Not much. I mean I know your father died when you were about twenty, but I don't think my grandmother ever really mentioned your mother. Nor have you. There're no pictures of her anywhere.'

'No, my father gradually removed them all. He was an unforgiving man and she hurt his pride, if not his heart.'

'I'm sorry, I didn't mean to pry. You don't have to tell me anything else if you don't want to.'

Amber might have meant every word, but Tris knew

that this holiday was crucial in her decision whether to stay in Elsornia with him or return home, and that his inability to open up was weighing against him. 'Do you want some air?' he asked and, without waiting for an answer, unlocked the door to the balcony and stepped outside. How many times had he found his mother out here, a forbidden cigarette in one hand, a black coffee in the other as she stared bleakly at the mountains which cut her off from the parties and company she craved. Only in the summer, when the villages were filled with visitors, did she come alive. He knew without looking that Amber had joined him, leaning on the wooden balcony by his side.

'My mother, like you, came from a dispossessed royal house, which is why my father considered her a suitable bride. Also, like you, a life full of pomp and duty wasn't really what she wanted. Oh, she tried, but my father was a very austere and conscientious man. Elsornia always came first and she really struggled with that, with him. When I was ten, she and my sisters moved here. They told everyone it was temporary, for her health, but the reality was she left my father, and she left me with him.'

'Oh, Tris, that must have been so hard for you.'

His throat dried; the sympathy in her voice was almost more than he could bear.

'My father refused to grant her a divorce. Instead he gave her an ultimatum: live here with her daughters, stay at the castle with us all or leave alone. She chose the girls. She left the villa the week after my father's funeral; less than a year later she remarried.'

'Did you see much of her? Of your sisters?'

'A few weeks in the summer, that was all. My father didn't have much time for my sisters. Girls were no use to him; they couldn't inherit and marrying them off wasn't really an option in the twenty-first century. His loss. My sisters are lovely, warm women and they are also scarily brilliant. As you know, Elisabetta works with me, she speaks four languages fluently and has a PhD in International Relations. Giuliana is a trained pilot and is a shining light in the Air Force and Talia is still at university, doing something with physics I quite frankly don't understand.'

'They sound most formidable; if I didn't already know Elisabetta I'd be terrified of them.' Amber moved closer, placing a soft hand on his shoulder. 'It sounds like your mother had to make some very difficult choices. I'm sure she loves you.'

'It was a long time ago. I don't really think about it any more.' The lie hung there as he turned away and the pressure increased on his shoulder, her other arm sliding around his waist as she pressed herself against his back, all softness and warmth and understanding. It was almost more than he could bear.

'You don't have to pretend with me, Tris. You never have to pretend with me.'

Tris wanted to tell her that he wasn't pretending, that he'd been fine then and he was definitely fine now. That his father had been right, Tris had needed to grow up and start being responsible, not spend his days larking around on the lake and wasting his time playing with his sisters and cousins. But the words wouldn't come. Instead he turned, gathering her into his arms, burying his head into her hair, holding her close.

Her understanding, her comfort was dangerous, but he couldn't step away. He didn't want to need her; he didn't want to need anyone. Need led to betrayal and disappointment; he'd learned that lesson young and never forgotten it. The formal agreement he'd signed with Amber's grandmother, the formal arrangement he'd assumed they'd come to in the lawyer's office in Paris had suited him fine: a wife, an heir, his life neatly tied up with no emotional mess. How could he have believed that future possible when he knew how she felt, how she tasted, how her warmth enveloped him until the chill deep in his bones disappeared? There was nothing neat or tidy about Amber and the way she made him feel. And that made him so, so vulnerable.

Right now Tris couldn't help but accept the comfort she offered, tilting her chin, searching her gaze with his for consent before taking her mouth in a deep claiming kiss that branded her on his heart. This was no seduction, no tease, no sweet playfulness but deep and raw and almost painful.

Amber didn't pull back. Instead she pressed closer, entwining her arms around him, kissing him back fiercely as if trying to prove that he was worth something after all. How he wished he could believe it, could believe in himself as much as he believed in her.

Amber stretched out on the sofa and waved her book at Tris. 'Look what Harriet gave me. Us,' she corrected herself.

'What is it?'

'Baby names. You don't have one of those lists that royal children have to be named from, do you? As someone saddled with Vasilisa as my middle name, I have strong feelings about names.'

'No, no lists.' Tris perched on the arm next to her and Amber leaned her head against his leg, enjoying the intimacy. They'd been at the villa for a couple of days now and every moment felt easier and easier, as if they were together by choice, not circumstance. Tris seemed younger, lighter, away from the castle and the all-consuming summons of his phones and aides, and in return Amber felt herself drawn more and more to him.

Theirs was a slow courtship, a contrast to the way they'd met, when they'd rushed into intimacy with such life-changing consequences. Instead they held hands as Tris showed her his favourite lakeside walk and in-dulged in long, sweet, slow kissing sessions that left Amber breathless with desire. If this was being wooed then she liked it, this anticipation of touch, this easy communication. It was everything she had always hoped for in a relationship. She couldn't believe this was Tris, the uptight, upright, closed-off prince, jeans-clad and relaxed beside her.

'In that case, do you have any favourites?' Amber was aware she held all the cards in this pregnancy; it was her decision whether they married, whether she stayed in Elsornia, whether Tris was a full-time father or an occasional parent. She wanted the name to mean something to him. As long as he didn't saddle the baby with something as hard to live with as Vasilisa, that was.

Tris took the book from her and leafed through the pages. 'You've been busy underlining,' he said, one hand resting casually on her hair. 'Artemis, Athene, Hector? I sense a theme.'

'My dad really wanted to call me Athene, but my mother said no way—but if the baby has your eyes then it would be fitting, don't you think? Grey-eyed Athene?'

'I don't know; naming a baby after a goddess seems to give it an awful lot to live up to. What was your mother's name?'

'Rosemary. My dad was Svetoslav, but he changed it to Stephen when he moved to the UK.'

'Okay then, Rosa or Stefano. How does that sound?'

Amber sat up, turning to Tris in surprise. 'Really?'

'If it would make you happy.'

She blinked, her throat tight. 'If it would make me happy? I can't think of anything that would make me happier. I've been missing them so much recently. I don't know if it's talking about them with you, or realising I'm going to have this baby without my mother to help me.' She tried to summon a smile but could feel it wobbling. 'I know it's silly, I've had to do so much without her, but I really wish she was here. She would have been such a great grandmother.'

'She'll be with you,' Tris said, cupping her cheek softly. 'Every time you bake with our daughter or son your mother will be there, every myth you read our child your dad will be reading along with you.'

For a moment all she could do was stare wordlessly at him as his words sunk in, each one warming her soul. 'You're right. As long as I keep our traditions alive, as long as they're in my heart they're here. Thank you, Tris.' She leaned in and kissed him, a brief, sweet caress. 'And thank you for the names. It's the most beautiful gesture; I'll never forget it. Never forget that you brought me here to this beautiful place...'

'Amber. It's the least I can do. You're not just giving me a baby; you're giving me a chance to prove myself to you. I know what it's cost you. I just want you to know that I appreciate it.'

'Right now, you're making it very easy...' She didn't know who kissed who this time, the kiss lengthening as she lost herself in him, Tris shifting until Amber was pressed close, her arms entwined around his neck, his hand on her back, warming her through as her body trembled with want, needing him closer, not wanting any barriers between them.

'Tris?' She pulled back, looking him full in the face, letting him see her desire and need, letting everything she felt show in her eyes, in her parted mouth, her ragged breath. 'I want you, all of you. Make love to me, Tris, please.'

He was almost preternaturally still, only his eyes alive, scorching as he stared at her, his gaze moving slowly to her mouth, to the exposed skin at her neck where her pulse beat frantically, to her chest. Slowly, oh, so slowly, he moved it back up to meet her gaze. 'Are you sure?'

'I've never been surer of anything in my life.' And she hadn't. This wasn't the combined magic of moonlight, champagne and a long dormant crush; this was the knowledge that the man beside her would never intentionally hurt her, was beginning to know her heart, and that was far more intoxicating than any romantic evening. 'I want you, Tris.'

Finally, his mouth curved into a wolfish smile and she shivered at the heat in his eyes. 'In that case, my lady, how can I refuse?'

CHAPTER THIRTEEN

'WHAT DO YOU want to do today?' Amber leaned back against the pillows and watched Tris dress with unashamed appreciation. He had far too good a body for a prince who claimed to spend most of his time in meetings; those lean muscles didn't come from a gym but from a man who loved the outdoors and knew how to handle himself in it. She wriggled with contentment as she shifted. It wasn't the only thing he knew how to handle...

They'd been at the villa for nearly two weeks now and Tris had spent every night, since the afternoon they'd started to pick baby names and ended up making love, in her bed. She loved waking up with his arm wrapped around her waist, the warmth and heaviness of him next to her. He made her feel safe. Wanted. Needed—and not just because of the baby she carried. And it wasn't all one-sided. She valued his opinions, his thoughtfulness and good sense, just as she enjoyed watching him relax more and more each day. Amber wasn't entirely sure what she'd expected from their holiday, but it certainly wasn't this contented ease and intimacy.

Sliding her hand down to caress the slight curve of

her belly, she sat up a little more, all the better to watch him dress. 'We made good progress on the films yesterday, although how you fell asleep during my favourite dance movie I do not know. Definitely several marks lost there.'

'No films today.' Tris pulled a T-shirt over his head.

Amber approved of this more casual Tris. His hair was a little messy and he had even allowed a hint of stubble to appear, giving him an edgy sexiness. She especially liked knowing that this relaxed part of him was kept secret from nearly everybody, that it was hers alone.

'Not even one film?'

They'd quickly fallen into a pattern. If the weather was good they went out for a walk or a sail on the lake, coming back mid-afternoon to either watch one of the films from the list Amber had put together or to read in companionable silence. Whilst in London she'd bought an e-reader and filled it with a selection of her favourite books for him.

'You have to start at the beginning,' she'd explained to Tris, so she'd included some of her own coming-of-age favourites and if they weren't exactly Tris's preferred reading he hadn't said so. Like the playlists of songs and the list of movies, she'd tried to put together a real mix to allow him to discover his own preferences—although if that preference didn't include *Dirty Dancing* she had a lot more educating to do.

On cooler or wet days they either explored the charming villages and towns along the lakeside or carried on with baking lessons. The quiet, tranquil days suited her perfectly. The pregnancy and its ramifications had rocked her more than she'd realised; it wasn't until she had her scan that she really understood just how much her life was going to change. She also knew she really didn't want to raise a baby alone if she didn't have to, that she was going to do everything in her power to make a relationship with Tris work.

She just hadn't expected spending time with him to be so easy, to make the thought of extending her stay, even making a life here actually enticing not just bearable. Gone was the austere, closed-off Prince from the castle; instead Tris was proving to be a really entertaining companion. An entertaining companion and a good lover. More, she was beginning to see beneath the surface, beginning to understand how his father's demands and his mother's desertion had shaped him. Every time he let her in she felt herself fall a little more.

If only this holiday could go on for ever, but all too soon they would return to real life and then she'd discover if this was just a holiday romance and all the steps they'd made would be wiped away by the tide of reality.

It was scary how much she hoped for the former, even as she prepared herself for the latter.

Tris crossed the room and sat down beside her, taking her hand in his, his grip firm and tender. 'I hope you don't mind, but when my sisters heard we were here they went on a big nostalgia trip. To be fair, it was their home for a decade; Talia was only four when she moved here. Somehow they seem to have invited themselves for the weekend. I only realised they actually meant it and are on their way this morning when I checked the family group chat. I know you wanted to be alone…'

'I did, but your sisters are different. Of course I'd like

to spend some more time with Elisabetta and meet your other sisters. What do they know about me? About us?'

'Elisabetta knows everything, of course, but the other two know nothing more than when you came: that we met at the wedding and I somehow persuaded you to spend some time here before making up your mind whether to cancel the betrothal agreement or not. I have to warn you that Talia thinks it's all very romantic. In her head the betrothal and your disappearance has made you into some kind of fairy tale heroine. Giuliana, on the other hand, thinks you did exactly the right thing to run away and can't understand what on earth made you come back.'

Interesting—that was pretty much how she'd felt, torn between knowing that life wasn't so easy and neat, that a happy-ever-after was more of a dream than a reality, and the romantic fantasies of her lonely teens. Fantasies that felt more and more real with Tris next to her, lean and strong and still absurdly handsome. But now there was a third way, not so all or nothing, a way of compromise and learning and understanding and, yes, affection and liking at the very least. Maybe even more one day, if the happiness of the last couple of weeks didn't evaporate when they returned to the castle. And guests, even welcome ones, signalled the start of that reality seeping into their idyll.

'Your other sisters don't know about the baby?'

'No. I didn't want to tell them until I knew what your decision was. Although, Amber, even if you decide not to stay, they have a right to know...'

'Of course they do!' Amber interrupted him. 'Both my parents were only children and I'm an only child too. I can give this baby the best three honorary aunts in the world, but how amazing for it to have three actual aunts as well.'

She pushed back the covers, optimism filling her. Staying in Elsornia and marrying Tris wouldn't be easy, she knew that. She'd have to give up her job, live far away from her friends and her life would be under the kind of scrutiny she'd always avoided. But hadn't she been bemoaning the fact that the agency was changing? Weren't her friends moving on to start lives of their own away from the Chelsea townhouse? And although she would have to endure some media scrutiny, Elsornia was a small country with little international influence. Her position would be very similar to Emilia's, and so far she and Laurent seemed to be avoiding too much press speculation. Maybe this would, could, work out after all.

She smiled over at Tris. 'What time are they getting here?'

'About lunchtime. I thought we might pop into the village to stock up. Talia loves the little cakes from the bakery there and Giuliana has been emailing me demanding a specific kind of bread she claims only they make. What do you think about barbecuing tonight? The evenings have been so warm, and I think the girls would enjoy it.'

The optimism deepened. A life with Tris wouldn't be all pomp and circumstance; their child's life needn't be too unconventional. There was still space to live like this, with no servants, to discuss casually popping into the village to buy food for weekend visitors.

'After lunch?' Amber sauntered over to him and entwined her arms around his neck. 'In that case, there's no need to rush. Why don't you come back to bed for a while…?'

Several hours later, she was a little more nervous. After they'd eventually got up, they'd wandered along the lakeside path into the village to stock up on enough food for an entire week of guests, not just a twenty-four-hour visit. Amber loved how little notice the villagers took of Tris and her. They were treated just like any other citizens, with a disinterested friendliness that disarmed her. Afterwards she'd rushed around tidying the villa and making sure that Tris's sisters' bedrooms, still decorated for the teenagers they had been when they'd left, were aired and made up. Tris had suggested asking one of the live out maids who cleaned the villa to come and help, but Amber had wanted to hold on to the sweet normality a little longer. There was something endearing about Tris's complete lack of household skill and he was more of a hindrance than a help as she made up the beds and arranged the flowers she'd bought in the village in each of the rooms. She was aware that this was their home not hers and it was a fine line between making their rooms welcoming and stamping her mark on their childhood home.

'Don't worry, they're going to love you,' Tris reassured her, and Amber leaned into him gratefully.

'I always wanted sisters,' she told him wistfully. 'Maybe it's the books I read. *Little Women, Ballet Shoes*—all those school stories my mother passed on to me, but it always seemed that even when you weren't getting on, sisters were a team. Maybe that's the rose-coloured view of an only child, but I do want to make a good impression on yours.'

She was still patting the last cushion into place when the buzzer indicated that a car was approaching the gate. The invisible guards responded and by the time Tris had opened the front door Amber could see two cars proceeding down the driveway.

'That's odd,' Tris said. 'I wonder why they brought two cars.'

'Maybe they want to leave at different times?' Amber suggested, taking a step closer to Tris, relieved as he clasped her hand in his.

'Maybe. But both Elisabetta and Talia hate the mountain roads; Giuliana is designated driver.' His grip tightened and apprehension crept over her as a cloud covered the warm spring sun. The first car drew up by the side of the house, the second parking next to it and within ten seconds Amber was enveloped in hugs and kisses as Elisabetta and her sisters swooped upon her.

'It's so lovely to see you again—you look really well; the lake air suits you.'

'At last! I've been so excited to meet you. I hope Tris is looking after you properly; he is not half as stuffy as he seems, you know.'

'I can't believe my brother has actually persuaded you to give him a chance; you'll have to tell me how he did it. Tris has many redeeming qualities, but charm is not one of them!'

It was almost overwhelming, but the friendly greetings were a balm to Amber's soul. To be able to give her baby a warm, loving family like this was more than she had ever hoped for, but alongside the relief her heart ached for Tris, raised so differently to his sisters. How different would he have been if his mother had been able to raise him too? But she knew it wasn't too late for him; the last weeks had shown that.

Amber looked around for him, hoping that he'd see how happy this visit was making her, only to realise that he stood stock-still, staring at the occupants of the second car. A tall man, holding the hand of a little girl aged around three, stood next to it, making no move to join their group.

'Nikolai? I didn't know we were going to have the pleasure of your company as well.' It was as if they were back in Paris, Tris's voice was so cold and emotionless.

'Tris.' Nikolai nodded in greeting. 'I bumped into Giuliana yesterday and when she said she was coming here I invited myself along. I hope you don't mind, but I was intrigued to meet your mystery guest.'

'Of course, we are delighted to have you. Amber, this is my cousin Nikolai, and his daughter Isabella. Nikolai, I would like to introduce you to Her Royal Highness Princess Vasilisa of Belravia.'

A chill stole over her, just as much at the formality in his voice as the use of her hated name and title. Somehow Amber summoned up a welcoming smile and held out a hand to Tris's cousin as he sauntered slowly over to them, his daughter still holding his hand tightly. 'It's a pleasure to meet you, and I'm very excited to meet you, Isabella. I know for a fact that we have some delicious cakes in the house; would you like to come and see?'

At the small girl's delighted acceptance, Amber took the proffered hand and, along with Tris's sisters, took Isabella into the house, leaving the two men standing staring at each other. It was no secret that Nikolai's position as next in line to the throne was behind Tris's need to marry and consolidate his role as not just Crown Prince but King, and as far as she knew the antipathy Tris so clearly felt for his cousin was reciprocated, but she had no idea why Nikolai had decided to visit them today.

But what she did know was that their idyllic escape was over and real life had resumed once again. Was the new, fragile tenderness she and Tris had discovered here at the villa strong enough to weather a return to real life or had it all been an illusion? And what did she want? A life here or to return to London? She still had no idea, but she did know that time was running out. She had to make a decision, and soon.

CHAPTER FOURTEEN

'WHY ARE YOU HERE?' With Nikolai's daughter out of earshot, Tris no longer needed to be civil.

His cousin raised an eyebrow. 'Marcel has a cold and my wife has been kept busy caring for him. My poor Isabella is bored with being confined indoors; I thought she might enjoy a trip to the lake.'

'Quit playing games, Nikolai.' Why did it always have to be this way? It would have been easier in the olden days when a duel was a respectable way to solve conflict.

'What do you think I'm going to do, Tris? Break into the villa and kidnap your beautiful Princess? You think I'm that desperate for the throne?'

Tris's jaw tightened. 'This is how it's going to be: go into the villa, make your excuses, collect your daughter and leave. There are plenty of places you can entertain her, places where I am not.'

For a moment Tris saw something flicker across Nikolai's face, something that looked a little like hurt, before the expression was wiped away as if it had never been.

'I came here because I have something to say to you,

and it's in your best interest to listen. Take a boat out with me, Tris? Like old times?'

The request struck a chord. He and Nikolai had been at odds for so long, it was easy to forget the time when they had been close friends, boy adventurers escaping from the castle through the tunnels whenever they could. When did that change? When had his childhood companion become his enemy?

'Half an hour,' he said curtly.

Neither spoke as they made their way to the small dinghy moored on the villa's jetty. Nikolai started the engine as Tris cast off and his cousin expertly steered the boat away from the shore, just like they had all those years ago, both falling back into half remembered roles. Nostalgia and something like regret bit hard as Nikolai coiled the rope: regret for the closeness and companionship he had lost and never replaced.

After they'd travelled a few hundred metres Nikolai slowed down, killing the engine as he turned to face his cousin. 'Remember that time we went fishing at midnight? Your father was furious when they caught us. But then it didn't take much to make him furious, did it?'

'That's what you came here for? To talk about our childhood?'

'I was just wondering where it all went wrong.' Nikolai looked out over the lake. 'It used to be you and me, remember? Betta tagging along, Giuliana furious when we said she was too young, Maria and the other castle kids following our lead. Days and days outside, escaping the confines of our castle, your tutor, our uncle and his lectures. Your mother aiding us with picnics and hidden treasure. It was idyllic, especially when your father was away and the Duke was too busy to worry about us. Idyllic, until one day you stopped playing and suddenly I was the enemy. I admit I hated you for it, partly because I lost my best friend and partly because you were so damn smug all the time. It was amusing shocking you, shocking my uncles, gaining and living up to a reputation. But when I spoke to Giuliana, I realised it was time to put a stop to all this.'

'Put a stop to what?' Tris could hardly believe what his cousin was saying. Was that how he saw it, their growing apart, growing up into such different men? One a playboy prince, partying in every continent, always in the tabloids and the gossip websites, the other dedicating himself to their country. He could hear their uncle, the Duke, reading out yet another headline in the cutting tone he reserved for Nikolai, impressing on Tris his duty to keep his cousin from the throne no matter what. And Tris had agreed. Nikolai was a womaniser, a spendthrift and a drunk and he had started early, embroiled in scandal long before he became an adult.

He looked over at his cousin, ready with a retort, but the words disappeared unsaid. Nikolai had been married for five years now and Tris had heard no hint of infidelity. He was clearly a loving father and even if he hadn't settled to a job or role within the castle, he was no longer living in nightclubs and casinos.

Their uncle was convinced that Nikolai's marriage was a ploy simply to father a son and strengthen his own claim to the throne. Seeing the way he had held his daughter, Tris doubted it. Besides, Nikolai hadn't simply married; he had disappeared from the headlines. If his marriage was merely part of his game-playing, then wouldn't he have continued as before? Their laws demanded a wife and son but not fidelity. There was barely a king in their ancestral line who hadn't had a string of lovers throughout their reign.

Nikolai trailed a hand in the water; he suddenly looked very young and tired. 'I should have said something a long time ago but, I have to admit, it was too amusing being cast in the role of ne'er-do-well villain. But the truth is, Tris, I don't want to be the heir. I certainly don't want to be King.'

There was nothing but sincerity in his cousin's face. Tris folded his arms. 'Why now? What game are you playing, Nikolai?'

'Come on, Tris. I have the perfect life. I love my wife and my children, I have money, can travel anywhere I wish, have all the benefits of being a Ragrazzi and none of the negatives. Why would I want to change that to spend my life wrestling with Parliament and dealing with politics? Why would I want to have to put the country before my own desires? And, more importantly, having seen what being the heir did to you, why would I want to inflict that on my own son?'

They were all good points but, more importantly, sincerity rang in every word.

Nikolai straightened. 'I'd have told you this years ago, but you and the Duke were so convinced I was dying to step into your shoes, I thought I'd string you along for a little longer. But the truth is I am very happy to help you break the covenant. Make women equal in the line of succession, get rid of the ridiculous married-with-a-son-by-thirty-five rule, bring this beautiful and ridiculous country of ours up-to-date. We can ensure that me and mine move far away from the line of succession—let Elisabetta be your heir; she is probably the most qualified out of all of us.'

Tris stared out at the mountains across the lake, barely able to focus on the snow-topped peaks. Nikolai was offering him all he had ever wanted: an update to the succession laws, respite from a hasty marriage. But the freedom weighed heavily upon him.

'Why now?'

Nikolai didn't answer straight away, starting the engine up again and sending the boat flying through the lake. Looking back, Tris could see the villa receding, the guards' towers, hidden from the villa's view, clearly visible from here. They would have binoculars trained on them, their every move tracked. His freedom was, as ever, merely illusory.

Finally, Nikolai slowed the boat down again, running a hand through his hair, his expression thoughtful, his grey eyes sadder than Tris had ever seen them. 'I don't know why my father turned out so differently to his brothers,' Nikolai said. 'The Duke is as joyless and obsessed with tradition as your father was. If only my father had still been alive to be joint guardian after your father died, maybe he could have tempered the Duke's influence. But maybe it was already too late.' Nikolai's father had died in a plane crash when his son had been just fourteen. The tragedy should have brought the cousins closer together, but instead they had been pushed further apart. It was around that time that Nikolai had started to drink and party. Older and wiser now, Tris could see that grief had played its part in his cousin's rebellion. Back then he had merely censured him. No wonder Nikolai had called him smug. He deserved a far more stinging reproof than that.

'I couldn't believe it when I heard that he'd arranged a marriage for you, and that you simply went along with it,' Nikolai continued. 'When the rumours of your intended's disappearance started, I have to admit I was pleased. Not because that left you in an awkward situation, but because it gave you a chance of avoiding your father's mistake, marrying for prestige and position not for love. Marriage is a gift, Tris. My wife makes me a better man every day; you may not believe that but it's true. To marry because of a contract, to marry because of a ridiculous law put in place hundreds of years ago is wrong. If I really hated you, if I really was envious of you, maybe I'd let you carry on. But we were good friends once, practically brothers, and I can't help hoping that a good marriage, to someone who truly loves you, might help you remember the boy you used to be, not the man your father forced you to be.'

Nikolai stopped abruptly, red colouring his haughty high cheekbones. 'I can't believe I just said all that; blame my wife. She believes in talking about feelings. And she wanted me to come here today to tell you this. To set you free. Maybe it's too late for us to be friends again, Tristano, but we are family. It would be good to remember that more often.'

Tris didn't, couldn't, speak as Nikolai picked up speed once again, steering the boat round in a wide arc before heading back towards the jetty. Nikolai was going to help him change the inheritance laws, update them so his sister could be his heir, so that he could become King without a wife and a son beside him. Everything he had planned was now possible—without Amber. He didn't need her, not any more.

The thought echoed around and around in his mind. He no longer needed her, nor did he need the baby she carried. She was free. She could carry on with the life she had built for herself, the life she loved, surrounded by people who cared for her. She had chosen her own path, walked away from her title, fortune and royal destiny without so much as a backward glance. Now she could resume that path guilt-free. It was within his gift to give it to her.

His heart clenched, the pain so fierce, so all-encompassing he almost gasped aloud. It might be within his gift but he didn't *want* to set her free. He didn't want to wake up alone, didn't want to spend the rest of his life in his soulless, impersonal apartments, no time to work out who he was and what he wanted. He liked the way she teased him, enjoyed watching the way she put so much energy into educating him and the pleasure she got when he reported back that he liked a book or a film or a song she had chosen, how she tried to argue with him when he didn't.

He liked the way she was so wholehearted in everything she did, whether that was baking enough food for an entire children's party, filling an e-reader with a library's worth of books or explaining to him in vivid detail just why the original movie was the only one worth watching. Everything she did she did in luminous colour, such a contrast to his own grey life, and she lit up his soul.

His thoughts continued to whirl relentlessly on, examining his feelings in painful forensic detail. He liked the way she drew him out, was interested not just in what he was but in who he was, his title the least meaningful thing about him. The way she embraced everything they did, no matter how dull, how interested she was to meet new people, to discover new things. How she'd sat next to him on the balcony last night as once again he'd named the stars and she'd related the myth behind every constellation, making them laugh as she attempted to make sense of the shapes each constellation was meant to represent. She had an insatiable appetite for life and all it offered, those lonely years in her grandmother's penthouse watching rather than doing making nothing too small to interest her.

There were lots of things he liked about her. Most of all he liked how real he felt with her, but marriage was a two-way deal. What did he have to bring to the table except a title she didn't want and to be a hands-on father for her child? Their child.

Tris knew all too well that Amber's own sense of responsibility and a longing for family weighed heavily in his favour. But was that enough? He loved her, appreciated her efforts to make the relationship work, but he wasn't kidding himself. Amber was working hard because that was what she did. She made the best out of every situation.

Hang on…he *what*? His mind skidded back. He *loved* her?

Tris almost laughed aloud with the inevitability of the discovery. Of course he did. He'd been drawn to her the moment he first saw her, the dazzling bridesmaid with a glorious mane of hair and the wide smile. But he'd fallen in love with the gallant, open-hearted girl who still believed in love and kindness and hope even after her sad and difficult teenage years. Amber might admit to dreaming of rescue, but she'd buckled up and rescued herself. She had a courage and spirit that made her beautiful within as well as without. But he wasn't kidding himself; she was trying to forge a relationship with him because that was what she did, but she didn't love him. And she dreamed of love; she'd been frank about that from the beginning.

With a start, Tris realised the boat had slowed and they were back at the jetty, Nikolai looking at him quizzically, waiting for him to throw the rope around the mooring pole. Hurriedly, Tris gathered it in his hands and with practised ease looped it around the pole. He pulled the rope until the boat was tight against the jetty and the two men clambered out.

With a deep breath, Tris turned to his cousin. 'Thank you.' It was all he could manage, his head filled with too many thoughts and scenarios and feelings.

'I'm sorry things got to this stage,' Nikolai said. 'I'm fully aware how much I'm to blame, that I never reached out even after your father died. I hope it isn't too late.'

'Me too.' With a jolt of surprise, Tris realised he meant the words. 'It couldn't have been easy coming here today.'

'It wasn't. I had to bring my small daughter to give me courage; there was no way she'd allow me to turn back, not when I'd promised her that she'd see her cousins and she could paddle in the lake. But I had to come. My father used to say how vivid and alive your mother was when he first met her, but after several years married to your father she became just a shadow of herself.

That all the expectation and your father's autocratic ways nearly crushed her. How he wished he had said or done something earlier. I didn't want to stand by and see history repeat itself. Maybe I'm wrong, maybe you and the Princess are meant to be, but either way I want you to go into marriage for the right reasons.'

'Come to the villa, Nikolai. Stay for dinner, you and Isabella. My sisters would like that, I'd like that.'

'Thank you.' Nikolai smiled, looking so like the carefree youth Tris remembered it was impossible not to smile back, despite the tumult of emotions tumbling around his brain. 'That would be good.'

The two men walked back to the villa side by side in a surprisingly companionable silence as Tris came to a resolution, as painful as it was necessary. Tonight he would play the host and enjoy the evening with his family and the woman he loved.

Tomorrow he would set her free.

CHAPTER FIFTEEN

'IT'S BEEN SO lovely to see you again.' Amber embraced Elisabetta with a warm hug. 'And absolutely gorgeous to meet you both.' She hugged first Talia and then Giuliana before stepping back, oddly bereft as the girls headed towards the car.

How ridiculous! Talk about an overreaction. She barely knew them for a start, and it wasn't as if they were going far. Elisabetta was returning to the castle, where she both lived and worked, Talia to the University of Elsornia which was based in the country's charming capital city just a few miles from the castle, whilst Giuliana needed to report back at the airbase just outside the city. She and Tris would be returning themselves in just a couple of days; she could renew her acquaintance with his sisters at any time. So why did this feel more like a *goodbye* than a *see you soon*?

As Tris walked his sisters back to their car, Amber tried to shake off the foreboding that had plagued her ever since Nikolai's unexpected arrival. She knew she was just being silly yet somehow her usual pep talks weren't helping and every hour her feeling that things weren't right deepened. She couldn't put her finger on why exactly. After all, Nikolai and Tris had returned from their boat trip if not the best of friends, cordial and with an understanding that evidently astonished Tris's sisters. Nikolai had even stayed until late the previous evening, before scooping up his adorable small daughter to drive her home, laughing that they would both be in trouble with his wife for staying out so late.

Sure, Tris had slept in his own room last night but that had been to allay any suspicions his sisters might have had about their relationship while it was still so fragile and undecided. But Amber had still half expected him to tiptoe down the corridors to her room after she had gone to bed and lain awake far too late waiting for him. She knew he was probably just being careful and had decided not to risk sneaking in, but it had been hard to sleep with his absence somehow filling the bed far more than his actual presence did.

She had also expected him to make an announcement about the baby, or maybe mention it casually while they were out walking, but nothing had been said. Elisabetta was obviously expecting him to say something too, judging by the quizzical glances she had sent Tris's way throughout the evening and today. Amber wanted to believe that Tris had decided to give her more time to decide, to ensure she wasn't ambushed by his excited sisters, but the explanation didn't quite ring true. His distance seemed emotional as well as physical, all the closeness and intimacy gone, as if he were now acting her suitor instead of becoming her lover.

Amber watched him as he closed the car door, standing back as Giuliana reversed the car and he waved his sisters goodbye. There was no discernible difference in him that she could articulate; he was still lighter and warmer than he had been back at the castle, but she *felt* a difference. The lightness seemed forced, his good humour put on, and she would look up to find him gazing at her with such a deep sadness in his eyes that her stomach twisted and her chest ached to see it.

She waved to the Princesses until the car disappeared behind the closing gates before turning to Tris as he made his way slowly towards her. They were alone once more. She should be looking forward to another comfortable evening together, enjoying the still so new intimacy whilst anticipating the night after their separation the night before; instead the silence was weighted with expectation and an air of something momentous left unsaid.

'Should we go inside?' Amber asked with as breezy a smile as she could manage Other words trembled on the tip of her tongue: what had Nikolai said? What was wrong? But the words stayed unsaid; she wasn't sure she wanted to hear the answer. Folding her hands into fists, she tried again but still couldn't speak. She wasn't usually a coward, preferring to make the most out of any situation, no matter how bleak it might seem. Her Pollyanna attitude had got her through tighter spots than this, and yet her usual courage ebbed away. Looking at Tris's set face, it was hard to feel anything but apprehensive.

'Go in? Yes, that seems best. Amber, there is something I need to say to you. Could you spare me five minutes?'

'Of course.' Her apprehension heightened, the cool civility in his voice chilling her. The politeness of his request was so at odds with the companionship they'd shared. Something had happened, something linked to Nikolai's unexpected arrival and their long trip out on the lake. Amber swallowed. She had thought she was used to being alone but not since her teens had she felt as isolated and friendless as she did right now.

Following Tris into the sitting room, Amber perched on a sofa, folding her hands neatly, feeling a little like she had as a teenager sitting in her grandmother's formal, overstuffed room, waiting to be told how to live her life. Sometimes she thought she'd never get rid of her grandmother's critical voice in her head, telling her she was too loud, too exuberant, too impulsive, too untidy. Not regal enough, not poised enough, not good enough.

Elisabetta had warned her that news of her reappearance was beginning to leak out. Amber knew that she couldn't avoid facing her past any longer; she needed to visit her grandmother, not to berate her or blame her but to lay all her ghosts to rest before the baby came.

The irony didn't escape her; if she took Tris with her she would merely be confirming to her grandmother that the harsh treatment and isolation had been right and had led to the desired outcome. Conversely, turning up as a single mother would probably have the same effect, proving that she couldn't be trusted to behave in an appropriate fashion on her own. But she no longer yearned for her grandmother's approval, no longer considered her family. Her opinion didn't matter. Any future relationship would be on Amber's terms, if they had one at all.

She also needed to take control of her own fortune and look at how she could redistribute it, right the wrongs of her great-grandfather when he'd extracted the money from their small country. Tris was right; the best way would be through some kind of charitable foundation. It was that kind of forward thinking that made him such a good king. A good king and a good man.

She pushed the thoughts from her head and tried instead to concentrate on the scene unfolding before her, feeling more like a spectator than a participant. Tris hadn't joined her on the sofa; he stood in front of the window, his expression becoming bleaker and bleaker as he seemed to search for the right thing to say.

The silence stretched on until she could take it no longer. 'Tris, what's happened? Something's changed between yesterday and today; is it to do with Nikolai?'

Tris inhaled. 'Nikolai came here to tell me that he will support my bid to change the constitution.'

Okay. But that was good news, wasn't it? 'In what way? To make it possible for you to be King now, without a son? That's brilliant! It must be such a relief for you.' Numbness crept over her as she saw Tris wince at her hearty tone. But hiding behind good humour and positivity had been her defence for far too long; she couldn't drop it now.

'Exactly that. More, we have decided to legislate to ensure that the current generation will benefit from the change in the law. This means that the oldest child will inherit whenever the existing monarch dies or abdicates, regardless of age, marital status or offspring. By doing so, he has effectively removed himself from the succession as all three of my sisters now come before him. If Parliament ratifies these changes, and there is no reason for them not to with the current existing heirs both sponsoring the bill, I can be officially crowned within the year, with Elisabetta taking on the role as the formal heir to the throne. She will be eminently suited to the role.'

'Oh, yes, Elisabetta will be perfect,' Amber agreed, her hand creeping to her stomach. Surely Elisabetta would only be heir for a short while? If she and Tris were to marry then, no matter whether she was expecting a boy or girl, their baby would inherit the throne one day. Wasn't that what these changes meant?

Only…if Tris didn't have to get married, didn't have to have a son, then their marriage was no longer such a burning issue. In fact, it wasn't even necessary. Her chest tightened, the air closing in around her. No wonder he had withdrawn from her; she was no longer of any use to him.

Here was proof; the intimacy of the last week or so was merely an illusion. He'd tried hard, she had to give him that, but it had all been an act. Numbness began to steal over her as she tried to digest the implications. Had her instincts been so wrong? Was she so desperate after all for a happy-ever-after that she had fallen for a façade?

It had seemed so real. 'I see.'

Tris tried to smile, but there was no happiness or warmth in it. 'The good news for you is that there is no longer any need for you to make a life here. You can go back to your normal life, your agency and your friends. I know how much you hate the idea of living in a castle, being a queen, living the life I must lead. Now you don't have to.'

'No. I suppose I don't.'

'I've ordered you a car; it will be here shortly to take you to the airport. You can go home, Amber. Your kindness in coming in the first place will never be forgotten. I can't tell you how much I appreciate it. But there's no need for you to sacrifice your happiness any longer. You're free.'

Amber tried to find the right words, but for once she, who could usually chatter on to anyone about anything, was lost. What was wrong with her? She should be happy. Tris was right; this was exactly what she wanted made easy and guilt-free.

She had done the right thing in giving both him and Elsornia a chance but they both knew that living in the confined box of royalty wasn't what she really wanted. Yes, she was pregnant, and he was the father, but this was the twenty-first century; she had a home, a job she loved and friends who, even if they were far apart, would always support her. She could and would love and raise their baby alone. Far better to do so than to raise it in a loveless marriage where hope and willingness to try would be bound to end in disappointment and bitterness.

She lifted her head and met his gaze. 'That sounds very sensible. I'll go and pack now. Tris, I'm glad that everything has worked out for you. But I hope you know that I still would like you to be part of our baby's life. Every child needs a father if at all possible, and I think you are going to make a pretty remarkable one. I know your position makes it a little more complicated and I would rather not be the subject of any kind of media circus, but I'm sure if we're careful we can find a way for you to be as hands-on as possible. If that's what you want.'

Tris blinked and for a second Amber could have sworn she saw sorrow and disappointment cross his face. 'Thank you. I would very much like to be involved. I don't intend to marry, not now I don't have to. I'm not sure it would be fair on any woman to always be second best to my role. But I would like to be a father, to be involved.'

Somehow, Amber managed a smile, even though her chest was ever tighter and her heart pulsing with a pain she couldn't identify. 'You're only thirty, Tris. And you have such a huge capacity for love; don't close yourself off from all that, please. I'd better go and pack. I am happy for you, really I am. You've got what you wanted; that must be amazing.'

She got up from the sofa, walked over to him and kissed his cool cheek, feeling him tremble under her touch. For one wild moment she wanted him to seize her, to hold her, to pull her to him and kiss her properly and tell her he couldn't live without her. But instead he stood stock-still as she walked from the room, blinking hot, heavy tears from her eyes.

An hour later, Amber stood outside the villa, the car and driver waiting for her and her small amount of baggage, Tris next to her, still so remote and unreachable. This was what he wanted; surely he should be happy? Surely *she* should be happy instead of feeling utterly bereft. Sick with disbelief and unexpected loss.

'Text when you're safely home,' Tris said, his words so ordinary they seemed utterly incongruous in the charged, unhappy atmosphere.

'Of course.' Amber took a step towards the car then stopped. 'I'll let you know the date of the next scan.

Maybe there's a way you can come, if you have time? I'll have been home for almost two months by then so no one will be watching us; we might make it work. I'll send you the date.' She couldn't help thinking that if he wasn't involved now, then he would just get more and more remote until he was barely part of their lives at all. The thought of a future without him in it was too bleak to contemplate.

'If you'd like me to be there then of course I will be. I don't intend to just abandon you, Amber. I hope you know that.'

'I do.' But her words were more hope than an affirmation. Tris didn't know what unconditional love, what family was, didn't know he could be integral to someone's happiness. He was so likely to assume that she and the baby would be better off without him, to think he offered nothing of substance. By leaving, was she just proving that assumption true?

But he wanted her to leave. Had ordered the car before he had even told her of the change in his fortunes.

The driver put her few bags in the car and Amber didn't move, still not quite ready to say goodbye. Tris stood framed by the villa, the white paint gleaming gold and pink thanks to the setting sun. Her eyes burned. The time she'd spent here had been the happiest of her adult life. Somehow, the villa felt like home.

'Okay then.' Tris leaned forward and dropped a single chaste kiss on her cheek. 'Thank you again. For everything.'

'Read the books, okay? And finish the playlist and watch the films; let me know what you think. And keep baking! You're not too terrible.' She took a reluctant step towards the car, still hoping, but she didn't know for what. This was what she wanted. Why on earth did she feel as if she was being wrenched from all she held dear?

'I will.' He stepped away, face shuttered, mouth set firm.

'Goodbye, Tris. Look after yourself.' Amber took another few steps to the waiting car, where the driver held a door open for her. Suddenly, impulsively, she turned around. 'Tris? Why did you agree to marry me all those years ago?'

She didn't know why, but somehow the question had been niggling away for weeks now, and suddenly it felt imperative to have an answer. Amber knew she was a fool but the teenager staring out of the turret window at the park below, hoping for someone to rescue her, who had spent far too many bored hours weaving elaborate daydreams about the man standing opposite her, still yearned to hear him say that she was worth something. That she had been more than a title and a convenience.

Tris looked away, but not before she saw the bleakness in his eyes. 'You looked lonely,' he said. 'And I understood loneliness. I guess I thought that together we could forge some kind of companionship. That what I could offer you here was better than what you had there. But that was then; you're not that girl any more. You have a career you love, friends who are more like a family, you're confident and beautiful and you bring sunshine everywhere you go. You are going to be an amazing mother. And you deserve more than what I can give you. So go, shine, raise our baby to see life the way you do. I'll take care of you both financially, I hope you know that, but you're free, Amber. Enjoy that freedom for both of us.'

She held his gaze and saw his grey eyes darken and for one long breathless moment Amber thought he might change his mind. Even though she missed her life and the dreams she'd had before Emilia's wedding, she had new dreams now, dreams she had barely known before today and certainly never articulated, but dreams centred around the man in front of her.

'Tris?' The hope swelling in her chest was almost unbearable as their gazes locked and she allowed all the emotion inside her to show in her expression, in her eyes, in the hand she held out towards him. But all he did was lean over to place one light kiss on her cheek before walking away. He didn't look back once.

CHAPTER SIXTEEN

'*Signorina?*' The driver indicated the open door with a smile. 'I am ready to go if you are?'

Amber stood, torn, her old life beckoning, the life she'd been contemplating receding into the distance. All she had to do was get into the car, let the driver take her to the airport and she could be home, tucked up in her own bed before midnight. Things would never be exactly the same; she knew that even with the money Tris could give her, a secure home in Chelsea and the agency ensuring she would always have a job, raising a child mostly alone would be difficult, but she never shied away from hard work and a family of her own was all she'd ever dreamed of. This wasn't the picture book two point four children and big golden dog and house in the country of her dreams, but it was real and it was hers. All she had to do was get in the car…

And yet she stood, anchored to the spot, replaying Tris's every word in her mind. He'd never said that he *didn't* want her, but he had said more than once that he was setting her free. Obviously, he thought he was doing the right thing. Hadn't she told him herself how much she loved her life, how little she wanted to change it?

So why was she still standing here, unable to get in the car and return to it, guilt-free?

Amber looked around, at the villa, warmed by the setting sun, the lake tranquil behind, the mountains purple in the distance. Did she really want to leave this land of mountains and lakes and valleys? Did she really want to throw away the chance of calling Tris's sisters her family? And, most importantly of all, did she really want a life without Tris in it? She closed her eyes and saw him, gazing up at the stars, expression intent as he explained the constellations to her. Saw him poised, camera in hand, finding beauty in a commonplace scene and helping her to see the beauty as well. She saw him covered in flour, doing his best to follow her instructions, making her laugh as he did so. She saw him sprawled on the sofa with a careless grace, watching a film for the first time, showing every emotion like a small child rather than a jaded adult. She saw him that first night, the way he moved, the way he watched her, the way he touched her... And she remembered the nights here in the villa, sensual and tender and, yes, loving.

Amber swallowed, every nerve reacting to the memory of his sweet, skilled lovemaking. Sure, at times he could be closed off, but she of all people understood the reasons for that. Underneath the dignity he wore like armour, there was a man capable of more love and passion than she'd ever believed possible, eliciting love and passion in response.

Love. The word slammed into her and she gasped at the impact. Of course she loved him, this proud man who bore his responsibilities with dignity, this seductive man who had whirled her away in a dance and changed her life, this thoughtful man who listened to her and made her want to be a better person. She'd expected to recognise love straight away, to be floored by it, but she'd confused love with desire. If love was easy to recognise then there would be no need to kiss frogs…this bone-deep need and certainty was nothing she'd ever felt or even comprehended before.

Was she really going to get in the car and drive away from the one man she had ever loved? He wasn't the Prince she'd daydreamed about in her lonely teens, no perfect knight in shining armour riding to her rescue. That was okay; she didn't need to be rescued.

But maybe he did.

Tris strode towards the lake, needing something physical and hard and exhausting to do. Chopping down a tree maybe, or sawing logs. Anything to stop him thinking, to stop him turning back to the house to beg Amber not to go. He was doing the right thing, the noble thing, so where was the comforting sense of righteousness, of peace? Instead the pain inside was almost overwhelming as he kept replaying the confused expression in Amber's eyes, kept hearing her call his name.

Hang on, that wasn't his imagination. Tris stopped and looked back, incredulous, as he saw Amber making her way towards him, hair tumbling around her face as she hurried along the path.

'Is something wrong?' Panic warred with hope.

She stopped and folded her arms. 'Yes, there is something wrong.'

Panic won out. 'Amber? Do you feel ill? The baby?'

'Not physically, but with this whole situation. You don't get to decide for me, Tris.'

'Amber…'

'When I was twelve my grandmother took me away from everything I knew and told me my entire life was flawed. She told me she knew how I should dress, what I should eat. Who I should be friends with, what I should do with my own time, and she was wrong. The only thing she might have been right about was who I should marry, but not for the right reasons.'

The air stilled around him, as if time had stopped and only the two of them existed. 'It's okay, Amber, there's no need for you to be here. Honestly.' No need but his own almost overwhelming need to hold her. Tris stood very still, watching her as she threw her hands up in frustration.

'You told me you are setting me free as if I'm some kind of bird you caged, but I'm not. I have my own mind, Tris, and I get to make it up. I am *always* free, no matter where I am, no matter what's happening because I don't let anybody cage me, not any more. If I decide to marry you it's because that's what I want, not because I've been coerced into some kind of sacrifice in order to do the right thing. Do you understand that?'

'I… What are you saying, Amber?'

'I'm saying you don't get to push me away before I get to tell you that I love you. You don't get to decide on your own that I don't need you. Because I do. I need you and I want you and I love you, Tris. I don't want you to hop in and out of this baby's life, but to be there all the time.'

Was this a dream? Was he hallucinating here on the

lake shore while Amber was really on her way to the airport? She looked and sounded real, but the things she was saying made no sense. She couldn't really love him; this had to be her sacrificing herself, just the way he was trying to sacrifice his own happiness for her. It was almost funny in a twisted kind of way.

'I appreciate what you're saying, Amber, but...'

'You're not listening to me, Tris. I'm not making some kind of grand gesture, not being some kind of self-less martyr. I am, in fact, being very selfish indeed and claiming exactly what I want. I don't want to have to live without you, Tris, I don't want to go back to Chelsea alone. I want to stay here, marry you and raise a child together. Only...if that's what you want too. If you don't then please just say...' Her voice petered out and the fire in her eyes dimmed. Dimmed because of him, because he was just standing there like an utter fool.

'You really want to stay? With me?' He still couldn't believe it, even though sincerity rang true in every word, in every line of her body.

She smiled then, her whole face lit from within. 'You were my first crush, Tris, even though I pretty much made up your personality. To be honest, I wasn't really sure what I wanted, and my imaginings were a little dull. Lots of holding car doors open for me, bowing over my hand and staring in awe as I descended grand staircases in gorgeous ball gowns.'

'All the above could be arranged; just give me the word. We have plenty of grand staircases at the castle,' he promised, and she laughed.

'Maybe sometimes for old times' sake. Back then I fell in love with an ideal, a face I saw occasionally, and it was that ideal I wanted to sleep with at the wedding. A way of finally putting the past behind me. But you're not that fantasy figure; you're so much better than that. So much more. I know you hide it, even from yourself, but you've shown yourself to me and what I see is pretty damn special. I see a man who is kind and considerate and clever, who can describe the stars to me and makes me want to listen all night. A man who is far too sexy for his own good, a man who will do anything for the people he loves. A man I trust with my heart because I know he'll always look after it. Tris, you are right, this isn't the life I wanted, but if it's a life I share with you, then it's the life I choose. If you will have me.' Doubt crept into her voice and tore at Tris's heart.

He tilted her chin and smiled into her eyes. 'If I'll have you? Amber Blakeley, there is nothing I want more. I can't claim to have fallen in love with you back in New York; you were just a child. But I did see you then, I noticed you and I wanted to help you. I didn't fall in love with the bridesmaid either, although I thought she was one of the most special, most beautiful people I'd ever met. I fell in love with you, the you right here with all your enthusiasms and optimism and dreams. I want your light in my life.'

'Always,' she whispered, her green eyes filled with tears and he wiped them away tenderly.

'I love you, Amber, not because you carry our child and not because I need a queen, but because of everything that you are. Will you marry me, despite all that comes with me? I know we haven't known each other that long, and if things were different then I would have loved to have courted you properly...'

Amber reached up to lay a hand on his cheek. 'But things are the way they are. Fun as courting sounds, I know it's easier if we marry before the baby is born, but there's no reason you can't court me after we're married.'

'Every day,' he vowed, and she smiled softly into his eyes.

'I want to marry you sooner rather than later and embrace all that comes with you, because that's what makes you who you are. I love you, Tris, and I can't wait for the baby to be here and for us to be a family, just like I always dreamed. Here, in the castle or anywhere as long as we are together that's all that matters. Life has taught me that.'

'I love you too, and I promise to do everything in my power to make you happy every day,' Tris vowed as he finally kissed her the way he'd always wanted to, with all the love and hope and passion bursting within him, her own kiss warm and sweet and passionate. As he held her, Tris promised himself that she would never be lonely again; like all the best fairy tales he might have rescued her, but she'd turned around and rescued him right back. And that was how all the best happy-ever-afters were supposed to be.

EPILOGUE

'OH, EMILIA, HE is *gorgeous*.' Harriet picked up the three-week-old heir to the Armarian throne and cradled him tenderly. 'You clever, clever girl.' She looked over at Amber and grinned. 'Wouldn't it be amazing if your Rosa and Emilia's Max made a match of it?'

'No royal matchmaking betrothals in our households, thank you very much,' Amber retorted as she adjusted the frills on Rosa's christening gown—Tris had made several inroads in updating some of Elsornia's more antiquated laws over the last year, but even he couldn't save their daughter from being baptised in the traditional Elsornian royal christening gown, a delicate Victorian confection comprising of several long layers of silk and lace and more buttons than any baby should have to endure. 'Just because mine worked out in the end doesn't mean we're reviving that particular custom. But if I was a matchmaking mama, then obviously I would choose Max to be my son-in-law. Em, he is beautiful. And you look amazing, Thank you for coming so soon after the birth.'

'I wouldn't miss my goddaughter's christening for the world.' Emilia reached out to stroke three-month-old Rosa's cheek. 'I'm so excited to celebrate with you, little one.'

'How are you feeling, Amber?' Alex asked from the sofa she was sharing with her two soon-to-be nieces, a beautiful vintage diamond ring glinting on her left hand. 'It was so brave of you to invite your grandmother. Brave and very forgiving. I'm not sure I could have been so generous.'

Amber looked round at her friends, her heart so full of love and happiness she could hardly believe it. Although they still owned the Happy Ever After Agency, both Emilia and she had had to take a step back, thanks to their royal duties, and since her marriage Harriet spent more and more time in Brazil with Deangelo. The Chelsea house was still the agency's headquarters, but paid staff occupied the vintage desks, the bedrooms turned into more offices for the increasing number of employees whilst Alex ran the agency from the countryside home she shared with Finn and his nieces. Amber spoke to at least one of her friends every day, but they hadn't all been in the same room since Harriet's wedding eight months before. To have the four of them here, in her charming sitting room overlooking the palace gardens, celebrating her daughter's birth, was very special indeed. Even her grandmother's presence in the castle couldn't disrupt her happiness.

Gently shifting her sleeping daughter to her other arm, Amber smiled at Alex, who was as elegant as ever in a green silk shift dress. 'When I visited my grandmother in New York she wasn't the fierce autocrat I remembered; she was just a lonely woman. All she had were her dreams of a throne in a country that doesn't exist any more, acquaintances instead of real friends, no hobbies, no one or anything to love. It made me feel so sorry for her. I have so much and she so little—inviting her to the wedding and the christening was the least I can do. We'll never have the kind of relationship I used to yearn for, but that's okay. I have Tris, Rosa and his sisters, and I have you three, my sisters in every way that counts.'

'You'll always have us,' Emilia said softly, her words echoed by Harriet and Alex.

'And you me. Our lives have changed so much in the last two years, but we're still the same girls who dreamed of our own business and made it happen, the same girls who met one Christmas Eve and realised we weren't alone. Marriage and babies don't change that; it just enhances it, makes our family even bigger. Rosa is so lucky to have you three as her godmothers and aunts, just as I am lucky to have you as friends and sisters.'

She blinked, emotional tears threatening to spill down her cheeks, relieved when the door opened to reveal Tris, smart in his dress uniform, flanked by Deangelo, Finn and Laurent, who immediately made a beeline for his son, pride etched on his features.

'The cars are here,' Tris said, carefully lifting Rosa off Amber's knee and then extending a hand to help her rise. Amber curled her fingers around his, grateful for his strength and solicitude. 'Ready to get this young lady christened?'

'Absolutely.' Amber watched her friends file from the room: Deangelo and Harriet, hand in hand, Finn and Alex, shepherding his nieces in front of them, sharing an intimate smile as they did so, Laurent and Emilia, his arm around her as she carried their newborn son. She turned to press a kiss on Tris's cheek. 'I love you,' she whispered. 'Thank you for making me so very happy.'

'I should be the one thanking you,' Tris said, his eyes soft as he smiled down at their daughter. 'For everything you do and everything you are.' He squeezed her hand. 'Come on, let's celebrate our daughter with our friends and family. She's done the impossible; my mother is considering getting a house in the city so she can see Rosa regularly and your grandmother is both here and behaving. She's a miracle child.'

'She is.' Amber allowed Tris to escort them from the room, knowing she would be able to face the pomp and ceremony of a royal christening with him by her side, flanked by her friends. They'd named the agency well all those months ago. Life was bound to have bumps in the road, its trials and tribulations, but as long as they kept loving each other then she knew they would live happily ever after, just as she'd always dreamed.

* * * * *

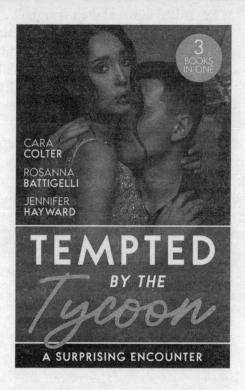

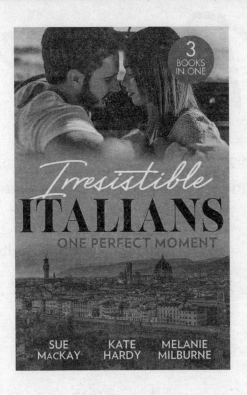

MILLS & BOON

THE HEART OF ROMANCE

A ROMANCE FOR EVERY READER

MODERN

Prepare to be swept off your feet by sophisticated, sexy and seductive heroes, in some of the world's most glamourous and romantic locations, where power and passion collide.

HISTORICAL

Escape with historical heroes from time gone by. Whether your passion is for wicked Regency Rakes, muscled Vikings or rugged Highlanders, awaken the romance of the past.

MEDICAL

Set your pulse racing with dedicated, delectable doctors in the high-pressure world of medicine, where emotions run high and passion, comfort and love are the best medicine.

True Love

Celebrate true love with tender stories of heartfelt romance, from the rush of falling in love to the joy a new baby can bring, and a focus on the emotional heart of a relationship.

Desire

Indulge in secrets and scandal, intense drama and sizzling hot action with heroes who have it all: wealth, status, good looks…everything but the right woman.

HEROES

The excitement of a gripping thriller, with intense romance at its heart. Resourceful, true-to-life women and strong, fearless men face danger and desire - a killer combination!

To see which titles are coming soon, please visit

millsandboon.co.uk/nextmonth

JOIN US ON SOCIAL MEDIA!

Stay up to date with our latest releases, author news and gossip, special offers and discounts, and all the behind-the-scenes action from Mills & Boon...

 @millsandboon

 @millsandboonuk

 facebook.com/millsandboon

 @millsandboonuk

It might just be true love...

GET YOUR ROMANCE FIX!

Get the latest romance news, exclusive author interviews, story extracts and much more!